THE

llareggub
Lagoon

Graham Tottle

Cover design by www.spiffingcovers.com

Snippet

The lovely trainee journalist, Nadine, returned with her work a week later. BLZ, the editor, scanned it.

"Hmm. Maybe we should get together about this this evening? I'm out all day at the Treasury – 'fraid you can't come. Not allowed to take fledglings!"

"Er, well, I've unfortunately…"

"Early working dinner perhaps? That little place called 'á l'Écu de France'. Off St James's Square." His eyes glinted. "Six thirty prompt; I've got to get away by eight. And we've got to meet the weekend edition."

"Er, well. Er, right. Thank you very much, BL." She smiled warmly at him. He seemed bemused, then dismissed her peremptorily.

Later, she dressed for the evening and left for the "á l'Écu de France". She wore a dark blue swirling skirt, a hip length jacket, a lovely, deep red, sort of raspberry colour, and a wispy floating silk scarf. BL's "little place" turned out to be large, spacious and beautifully decorated in cream, jade and midnight blue, with much seemingly genuine Regency furniture. Known only to the cognoscenti. Rather reminiscent of the Mayfair in Washington, where her father had once given her a splendid American working breakfast, including hot waffles and maple syrup. It lay just between the bustle of the Strand and the quiet roller-girt mega affluence of St James's Square.

She went in diffidently, left her coat, and decided to go right through to the ante-room, since BL would no doubt be in a hurry. A waiter came up questioningly.

"Yes, madame?"

"I'm meeting a Mr Bubb."

"Ah, *bonsoir*, madame. Monsieur Bubb, of course. It is Mme Humphrys Jones, *n'est ce pas*? He leaves a message, maybe perhaps a little late at the Treasury. Some wine, perhaps?"

Nadine ordered a Bloody Mary. Not her usual, but she felt like it. Later, another. Then he arrived.

Two agents sitting nearby tried to listen intensely and unobtrusively. Never get a finer meal again, and, all on expenses. And just look at the popsey. Out with the directional mike. Caught a bit of the argument as voices rose. Would report it back to their infuriating boss in MI6.

"So sorry, my dear. We'll have to rush, I'm afraid."

* * *

Later she left, furious.

"Buggeration," said BL under his breath.

The head waiter came up with a slight commiserating smile.

"The hunting tonight," he murmured, "not so good, Monsieur Bubb, *n'est ce pas*?"

"*Vous avez raison, mon vieux. Mais je ne la laisserai pas la. Il y a encore de methodes.*"

"*Pas avec celle-la. Elle me semblait sauvage comme une lynxe.*"

"And all the better for it," muttered BL to himself. And in due course, his chance might come.

The Arctic

Below the towering heights of the mountains, well inside the Arctic Circle, sprawled a fascinatingly complex lake, crystal clear, dotted with rocky glacier-spawned islets and merging at its western outlet with swamp, tussocks and marshland. The eastern end was dominated by two brutal rectangular blocks of undressed concrete, 150 feet high, linked halfway up by a long open-sided girdered bridge. A notice at the high security entrance said, *"электростанция"*.[1] Clearly a nuclear power station. The station's centre was a globe, the pressure vessel, a twenty-metre sphere of four-inch thick steel. Graphite cum boron/steel rods were lowered as needed for immediate power consumption. The remainder would drop in an emergency to stop the reaction and cool down.

A 100-metre long pool was later to prove important. It was under the bridge between the two blocks, out in the open air to disperse the exhaust heat at the back end of the process – raising the water temperature about five degrees centigrade. From there the warm water went into the lake. A tall, bold shoreside notice, scarlet on white, said:

опасность

Опасные минеральные породы

купаться запрещено.[2]

---

[1] *Gorsaf Drydan*, Nuclear power station. Embrittlement described in Appendix 4.
[2] *Puy sy'na! Stopia!* You there stop!

There was a tunnel from the railway to the turbine housing.

A westerly gale which had been building up through the morning was in full chat, the panoramic window showing white spray creamed off the wave tops, driving across the lake. A little, blond man, pointed nose, stood apparently spaced out and bemused near the middle of the empty main hall. He was wearing an expensively tailored formal dinner jacket, hand tied bow tie, and all the trimmings. His hands were held out sideways, palms downwards, as if resting on the tops of two posts. There were in fact two posts of the same height standing five feet away.

"Oh, Susanna, won't you come to me?" drifted into his mind. But no, never ever. Just a spasm of aching sorrow.

After a bit, he seemed to realise where he was. He scanned around, then slipped quickly through a passage and up some stairs into a long, echoing square vault. There was a door at the far side. He opened it to look through. A vast empty cavern of a hall, brightly lit. Square, wide and squat old-fashioned control consoles were bunched together just off-centre – the station control point. From an office on the left he heard sounds of two people conversing. An unfamiliar language. Russian. Suddenly there was a shout behind him:

"*Кто и?! Стоп!*»[1]

He ran across to the far side, down an alleyway and onto the turbine decks. More people. They turned, saw him, and one shouted:

"*Стоп!* Safa!»[2]

They joined the chase. He heard a clicking and a fizzing, then a voice over a booming intercom.

"Hold hard," it was saying in high-pitched tightly metallic Russian. "Hold hard. Intruder on control, intruder on control. Security alert five. I say again, security alert five."

He nipped up a steel stair and over the bridge. Then down again. He saw the cooling pool forty feet below. The chasers and some odd looking mechanical boxes were coming from either direction. Back onto the bridge. Trapped. He climbed onto the rail, steadying himself against a strut, and dived down. Boyhood memories of similar dives, competing with his mates off the cliffs in Llanbedrog, had come back. Who can dive in from highest? Flatten your wrists, they'd found, flatten your wrists, clasp your hands and bend your forearms, and you'll be able to dive safely into only three feet of water. You can turn on a ten pence piece. He flattened his wrist and bent his forearms, and hit the water with an almighty thump. The top of his skull felt as if it had at once been violently hammered, lacerated and stung. An adult presents un-boyish parameters to the unforgiving water. But turn he did, and just grazed the bottom. There was a tunnel ahead. The water pulled him along into it. He clawed at the sides, but it was slimy; a no go.

Then, astonishingly, he passed through and out into the lake. The pumps had worked from the pool's far end, pushing the water rather than sucking it, so that the water flowed straight through unimpeded. There were significant waves on the lake. He swam steadily across westwards, and rolled and clambered flat on his side, low profile like they'd taught in the cadet force, over the jagged rocky coffer dam separating the cooling water enclave from the main lake. A rattle of heavy machine gun fire. Then on, into rough, rolling, chilly water.

A high-powered outboard run-about buzzed and whined and skipped into view. But by hanging still in the water and ducking beneath the passing crests like the Porthmadog Fairway buoy, he kept unseen as it patrolled around searching. Another burst of gun fire, and he threw himself up in the air as if hit. Eventually the run-about disappeared and he continued the mile swim, breathing in the troughs, to the far shore. Uninjured but for a gashed wrist where he had grazed the bottom in diving. He bound it with his handkerchief. A handkerchief to remember. Large, white silk with a scarlet monogram:

Rundle J

That evening he staggered, gradually drying, into a little village, down off the mountains, near a river estuary. It was completely deserted. He threw himself painfully against a house door. Then round into the backyard. There was his Triumph Thunderbird.

He recalled previous trips, dropping down from Lusaka to the Zambezi, entering shade like a sudden breath of delicious chill rolling from the jungle across the road, and then back again into the dry heat. Or throttle open, climbing away from some cliffs, the exhaust crackling away, echoed and re-echoed, thrown from one krans[3] to another. Then dropping down again. Winding down through happiness. He was a man for whom the past, and past fantasies, could come suddenly to vivid life in the present.

---

[3] Krans – Afrikaans for cliff. From one of the two South African national anthems, the other being the Ndebele song *Shokoloza*. Chosen by Nelson Mandela for his newly created Rainbow Nation.

Back in the present, he climbed up some darkened stairs, rolled into the first bed he could find, and crashed out.

At nautical twilight the next morning, he rolled the bike out. He kicked it over and set off. Dirt track tyres, not slicks, on the rims. A short way up the road, and then he turned off onto a reindeer track. Dropping the back wheel down on the sharp turns, just like Split Waterman at the Croydon Stadium when his dad took him there. But spurting out moss and lichen, not the stadium cinders. Open the throttle to bring her up.

The reindeer knew their way well and he wriggled around the lakes, across the Finnish frontier and on to a friend and his sauna near Kilpisjarvi. Crouched on the top shelf in the sauna hut. Sloshing water onto the stove. Hissing clouds of steam. Slapping his body with birch twigs. Out to plunge into the freezing lake. Tremendous.

On the floor lay his fine white cotton shirt. Made from Ugandan cotton. One and a quarter inch staple, better than the American or Sudanese best. Across the inside of the collar:

"Rundle J"
"Tailored by Stevens, Great Jermyn St."

"mischief thou art afoot
take thou what course thou will"

Marc Antony,
William Shakspur 1588

"Show the reader what it's like to be me"
Been there, done that
got the T-shirt

And this is how our village stands
Not with a whimper but with a snarl[3]

4 July 2031

PROLOG.DWEEB

All this stuff is from 2031.

This guy Rundle is a nerd and a geek. He is also peak and lik, and an FBCS[4] no less. He is from MI6 and MI5. The UK's Special Intelligence Services.

Like I said, he's on a Triumph Thunderbird. 1952 revolutionary twin.

How did he come by his Thunderbird? Let's fastback some years to 2017 and we'll see.

This is a complicated report, so I've put the contents list at the back.

Much better there – I always enjoy reading as an exploration and ignore the blurb. And remember Scottish Independence.

---

[4] Fellow British Computer Society… peak, lik contemporary teenager slang

Introduction

It's June 2039.

An aged historian sits penning a document, one jagged leg crossed unbelievably over the other, right ankle on left knee. Revealing white, aged stick-like legs below long woollen combs and black trousers. A well-known high-hurdler sixty years ago. Snap the leading leg down immediately after you cross the bar. A fire blazes in the grate. It's a warm summer's day. Sometimes his cackles of laughter at his unfortunate students' solecisms resound around the courtyard. For some, a route to a double first. For others, anger, humiliation and another discipline, maybe Social Anthropology.

I write this, he writes, *in Old Court in my old college, Emma. Emmanuel College, in the British University of Cambridge. British, be it noted. Not Welsh, not Scottish, not English, not Irish. It was not these little countries that helped to transform our world in three centuries. It was UKEIRE, the Brits.*

As a genuine historian, I will avoid the tens and twenties historians' practice of writing all history in the present continuous tense. To give, they said, a sense of immediacy.

When writing about the past, I will use the past tense. When writing about the future, I will use the future tense. When writing about the present, I will use the present tense. Unlike our colleagues from Oxford, I will use the present continuous tense for things that are actually happening now.

I should explain that we are concerned with the lagoon in Llanbedr village in Southern Snowdonia, Wales, UK. This book is titled "Llareggub" as a gesture towards the greatest poet of the twentieth century, Dylan Thomas.

And describes how this parochial debate came to figure in the global battle against hard drugs.

How the village, really named "Llanbedr", fought against the Westminster and Welsh Assembly "Llanbedr Spaceport Plan" which would emasculate this, the loveliest village in Snowdonia. Just as the governments had done to other villages nearby. How this parish battle became intertwined with another battle by the international organisation dedicated to the elimination of a notorious hard drug-supplier chain.

And how the development of Llanbedr's massive, empty airfield, wartime host even to Lancaster bombers, came to the forefront among the revolutionary technological events of that decade.

To hold the readers' interest, I have sometimes condensed the timelines.

And for the sake of an interesting account, I have taken liberties with the times of the events. As with Eric Morecambe's performance of Grieg's Piano Concerto, they all happened, but they are not necessarily all in the right order.[5]

Most of the text and graphics are from original documents or sources.

Where I need to explain the documents, etc., I have added linking pieces that are underlined and in italics.

---

[5] The performance of Grieg's Piano Concerto by Eric Morecambe and the world famous orchestral conductor, Mr Andrew Preview, actually Andre Previn, chief conductor of the Chicago Symphony Orchestra. Morecambe ordered Previn to jump up and down to get the timing right.
Previn: "You're playing the wrong notes."
Morecambe grabbed him by the lapels and hoisted him up to his face.
Morecambe: "Listen, sonny, I play all the right notes. All the right notes. But not necessarily… not necessarily… in the right order."

For place names in Wales, I have used standard Welsh rather than international Welsh. Llanbedr, for example, not Hlun Bedder, Penrhyndeudreath, not Pen rin Daydreth. I have strung together excerpts from the various documents, official and unofficial narratives (though the thirty-year rule may eventually reveal more) and also hearsay about this attack on Llanbedr village. And the byways worldwide, which this attack opened up.

Notable are Dr Majid Dujaily of the UN Drugs Enforcement Agency, and a Jock Rundle. Plus a notorious rogue.

H. B. Goulding-Williams, Emmanuel College, Cambridge 11 June 2039.

Chapter 1

The VEM and the Dronebots

On a Tuesday in March, Mike Johnson of ICL (International Computers Limited; International leaders until sold to Japanese Fujitsu, who knew when they were on to a bargain) walked down the street from Victoria tube station, London, Britain, towards DIFID, the Ministry for International Development, in Eland Place. A blustery wind, sky studded with white clouds on the blue, daffodils a-flower in Grosvenor Gardens. With a lifting heart, he recalled the serendipitous concert yesterday evening, chancing on the final celebratory concert of this year's graduands from the Royal College of Music in the Queen Elizabeth Hall. The Thames's flood tide flowing past the South Bank terraces, rippling into wavelets against a vigorous north-wester. In front of the National Theatre, a rough-hewn statue of St Clair, standing beaming enigmatically, like the Roman God Janus. Sinclair, innovative genius. Inventor of the C9. And in the hall, Prokofiev's Classical Symphony, a splendidly light, exuberant vehicle for the feelings of the occasion. Admiring parents and friends. Themes thrown with a passing smile from flute to bassoon to clarinet, classmates in three years' musical journeyings, celebrating with joy their friendship and intense application. A snatch of civilisation unsurpassed.

Meanwhile, he ran over in his mind the key points in the coming meeting. How far could the VEM project be held to fit the ministry's guidelines for Third World development?

He passed the entrance to Force Four Chandlers and into Eland Place, and his mind trundled off down a siding familiar to boat owners in the springtime – more varnish and anti-fouling needed? What about the echo sounder and those funny random numbers which suddenly appeared and suggested alarming shallows in the middle of the Irish Sea? No, no time to go into it now.

He pushed through the glass doors into Eland House and declared his business.

"I'm with Professor Stag and Dr Colin Leakey. I'll wait here if you don't mind, until they come."

"All right, dear. But don't lose the pass, mind, or we won't be able to let you out."

This description of Leakey is from his close friend and colleague, Graham Tottle.

They worked together for over twenty years, mostly in developing countries in the tropics.

"Colin was the first son of the great anthropologist Louis Leakey, who established, when he found a heel print in the Olduvai Gorge, Kenya, that the human species was three million years old, considerably more than the biblical quota. Among a host of other achievements, Louis Leakey persuaded two young women to work as anthropologists. Karen Blixen who studied the mountain gorilla and was killed by poachers whom she terrified at night when trying to safeguard the gorilla in the high mountains and volcanoes of south-west Uganda. What do you mean by saving the species? You are supposed to be studying them. And Jane Goodall who achieved astonishing results in her study of the chimpanzee in Tanzania.

Colin tended to wear light grey tropical safari suits, usually short-sleeved, but in one case long-sleeved. The long-sleeved suit had been tailored for him overnight in Thailand when the king's tailor had to prepare him suddenly for an interview with the monarch. Colin was far from being an Imperialist, but Rudyard Kipling's poem "If" has a fine quote:

"If you can mingle with princes, nor lose the common touch, if you can deal with triumph and disaster

And treat those two imposters just the same...

And what is more, you'll be a man my son."

To illustrate the common touch, he was assigned by the UN's Food and Agriculture Organisation to study possible crops in the high Andes of South America. He reached a village, and there in the market was an old lady with two piles of beans.

Why did one pile cost twice as much as the other?

The old lady drew a shawl across part of her face and whispered, blushing, to the interpreter:

"The expensive beans do not make you fart."

The expensive beans Colin replicated for FAO and developed further in the UK, rivalling the Heinz beans from the US mid-west.

Seeing as I often did from the side, Colin had a visage akin to those on Roman coins. Prominent nose and chin, slightly receding cheeks, a broad forehead and fine blond hair. He was tall, athletic and totally committed. As a result of a bee sting (he was a beekeeper), he was slightly deaf. This sometimes led to misunderstandings, often fruitful.

He was a fellow of King's College, Cambridge where, as a student, he had organised and run the students' project in Ethiopia. He studied agricultural plant pathology and after some years was appointed to Makekere University in Uganda, where he taught students who frequently became the heads of their national departments in eastern African countries.

I remember the director of agriculture in Tanzania greeting him:

"For you, Colin, anything!"

Often impetuous and unpredictable. I remember him stopping a cavalcade of cars in Malaysia to allow him to climb a tree and look at a pigeon orchid. He was testing a theory that the orchid knew of coming rain fall in advance. If true, very valuable.

Back in DIFID:

Colin arrived. As usual, before key meetings, he was sharp and alert; a restless and demanding companion.

No sign of Professor Stag. Colin was uneasy:

"Hope Peter's not up to one of his devices. If he doesn't show up, perhaps you'd like me to introduce the project?"

Mike felt robust. It was going to be a good day. His project after all, wasn't it? These two had contributed a lot, but ICL's stamp on the whole thing should be maintained.

"No, that's okay," he said confidently. "You come in when we get to questions."

"Well, if you're sure."

They talked over the White Paper issues until interrupted.

"Mr Bosley will see you now."

They reached room H54. A. Bosley. Chief Natural Resources Advisor.

The view from outside his tenth-floor room was stunning. A complete traverse across the Thames from Chelsea Bridge in the west via the Festival Hall, the Tate Modern and east right round to St Paul's.

To quote Wordsworth:

Dull would he be of soul who could pass by
A sight so touching in its majesty.
This city now doth like a garment, wear the
beauty of the morning; Silent, bare,
Ships towers domes theatres and temples lie
All open to the fields and to the sky.

They knocked and entered Bosley's office. It indicated his concerns, particularly the desk which appeared to be from Ugandan muvule. A fine, rare, deeply grained hardwood which appeared to have a slight transparency in the texture if you looked at it diagonally. Probably from the Budongo forest in Bunyoro.

Bosley greeted them with his colossal Battle of Britain RAF moustache. He introduced two colleagues whose names they missed. One, the dark-haired one, looked smooth and urbane, the administrator perhaps. The other, red-haired, kept in the background. All had the courteous, slightly withdrawn watchfulness of senior civil servants when in contact with industry.

Bosley kicked off:

"My role is that of so-called expert." He glanced at them quizzically. Both Colin and Mike knew the "so-called" was uncalled for. In their background research, Bosley's name had cropped up several times as the incisive author of monographs or whatever on this or that aspect of rural development. No doubt Bosley knew that they knew that, but nevertheless he took evident pleasure in enlarging on his role, his deep concern to verify the theoretical content and quality of the project, and his total inability, as one who was strictly an advisor, to do anything or decide anything whatsoever.

He would place his views on record for those who decide in these matters to take a decision at the stage at which it was appropriate for a decision to be taken. The decision would be taken by the all-powerful committee, **ESCOR.**

Mike felt anchored to his seat as if by a puddle of brown sticky porridge. The contrast with the sharp action-focused development review meetings in ICL was total. Thirty or so key managers at the weekly review, each with a few short seconds to defend his people and patch.

"You committed to deliver issue 3.1.5 of the microcode for the SCU at the start of week 17. Is it delivered?"

"No, because…"

"I'm not interested in excuses. That project's a can of worms. Did you raise an Orange Alert? What recovery action have you taken? Be at a meeting on my lawn by the Thames on Sunday morning." Even if you lived in Manchester.

The culture is familiar as we later saw with US President Trump in action. Tweets from the top, totally undemocratic and unexplained, can move mountains. For example, in ICL, a brilliant designer protested against a fundamentally wrong decision:

Here in ICL, Mister Mack, we are used to reason being given for key decisions.

You want a reason? I'll give you a reason…" Pause. "… I'll give you a reason… **Do it or you're fired."**

Here in the ministry, Mike was out of his depth, feeling he was among people who were stringing together familiar words, but producing language whose real meaning was elusive, and yet immensely important and well-understood, moreover, by everyone else present.

Better start by explaining about the technology. Any questions, gentlemen? No. They obviously understood.

Then he moved on to give a greatly simplified outline of artificial intelligence.

"This all reached a climax," he went on, "in Sidney Coleman's seminal paper, 'Why There is Nothing Rather than Something."

"'Why There is Nothing Rather than Something," he repeated with emphasis. "Coleman's paper proved, or nearly proved, I should say, that the cosmological constant is zero, with the obvious implications for AI."

He paused meaningfully.

"The cosmological constant is zero."

"Coleman," said the dark one suspiciously. "Isn't he an American? Harvard, I think I remember."

Mike fumbled his way onwards into AI theory. Theory propounded by Steven Giddings. And ICL's machine, the VEM, was designed to do just this. He paused excitedly.

"Giddings. Yet another American. Also from Harvard, I think," said the dark guy severely.

"Yes," said Bosley uneasily, "I think you're right. Not that…"

"No, of course. But you know ESCOR, Arthur. What would ESCOR say for God's sake? Still," he said kindly, "do carry on, Mr, er… Jimson."

Mike felt his audience slipping, their eyes glazing, their watch arms twitching. He went on to introduce the artificial intelligence project briefly; why ICL had taken it up; how the two universities came into it; why they merited funding, despite the fact that the proposals were high-tech and did not come from typical sources for new DIFID proposals for overseas development and countering global warming. For example, Oxford, Reading, Norwich and Sussex.

"Yes," said the second guy. "We've read the papers carefully, haven't we, Arthur? But our feeling really, given the absence, and this is crucial of course, of a request from a Third World country, and bearing in mind the weight of deserving and immediately appropriate…"

Colin Leakey chipped in quickly:

"If I may just interject. I think it might be helpful to you, gentlemen, since Mike comes from a discipline with which you and I are unfamiliar, if I amplify a little on how these suggestions strike me as a simple, practical man. Like me, you are perhaps strangers to the particularities of these arcane avenues of recent AI and mathematical research."

He smiled warmly, persuasively at each. Bosley glanced with raised eyebrows at the dark-haired guy. He nodded.

Colin then entered a light-hearted but exciting justification for the proposal. Like many whose brains work over-fast, he had the unconscious habit of repeating phrases with swift paraphrases in a tumbling rhythm which was elusive and invigorating. People had to listen hard just to keep up.

"Those among us," Colin continued, "whose arteries are not yet hardened" – a beaming, reassuring smile made it clear that the present company were numbered among those whose arteries were indubitably youthful – "see the vitally important and constructive role this sort of initiative can play at the leading edge of technology against global warming."

The civil servants relaxed. Bosley began to probe with a few questions.

At this stage, there was an urgent knock at the door.

"Professor Stag, Mr Bosley." Bosley's PA appeared, but was suddenly and startlingly replaced by the tall burly figure of Professor Stag.

"Mu my dear chuch-chap."

Stag came in, his right hand eagerly and warmly out-thrust at Bosley, his coat, hat and briefcase hugged precariously under his left arm.

"Suho nice to meet you at last. I'm mu-most awfully ssu-s-s-horry. Those Manchester tut-trains. The 7.53 as usual, you know." Stag stammered out his apologies.

"No, no, professor, delighted…"

The civil servants seemed bemused, sympathetic and immensely deferential.

"H engine bub bub."

"We're delighted to have you here."

They mustered to help the professor sort himself, his coat, his hat and his papers, out. They sat anxiously alert while he painfully expressed his views. A most praiseworthy Bub Bub Bu British initiative. The stammering was sometimes quite harrowing. Stag's tongue would twist and lollop distressingly in and out of his mouth like a purple epileptic serpent.

Outside, distant drums and fifes approached, increasingly loud.

"We cuc cuc cu hant be left behind."

"The Scots Guards," explained Bosley quietly; the civil servants were clearly accustomed to the din. The band came closer. The guards' boots crunched and echoed dramatically below, the insistent rattle of the kettle drums drawing Colin's pencil to tap in time. Stag entered into a long description of how he had, as a budding researcher in the late fifties, publicly declared his own field, computing, to be a specialists' backwater. Massive number crunching, weather forecasting, nuclear physics, artillery range tables. Not much else. World demand for computers by 2024 in the region of seventeen machines.

"How wrong cu cu cu han you be?" he concluded with rueful humility. "How r r r hong can you be?"

The civil servants looked warmly respectful. Takes a big man to recount his blunders.

Might it not be so, suggested Stag, with this current proposal? So easy to reject the far-sighted in favour of the conventional. To select with tunnel vision the meticulously presented conformant pap, and let the seeds of the future float by. Bosley smiled sympathetically. The Scots Guards gradually receded towards the Sinclair memorial. The fresh leaves on the plain trees shone green and translucent in the sunshine. Mike relaxed, delight suffusing his veins.

"We've done it," he thought. "We've done it. We're going to win after all."

Bosley stressed again the informative and advisory nature of his role. But sometimes there was a need for pump-priming. He might prime the pump.

They discussed the plan – budget, allowances, insurance. The dark-haired civil servant suddenly chipped in quite eagerly:

"It occurs to me, taking a global view, that we really need a crisp means of defining the project."

"Interesting," said Stag. "How do you mu mu mu hean?"

"Well, we could call the project VEM – Vehicle for Environmental Management."

"Excellent. An extraordinarily succinct way of pu pu hutting it. What du du yu hoo think, Ccol?"

"I think perhaps that is a central contribution to the project. Slices through a forest of technical jargon to the core idea. Proactive communication at equivalent levels is of course absolutely crucial."

They talked further over the ministry's protocols and procedures.

"But what about ESCOR?" asked Colin Leakey. He was worried about this all-powerful committee.

"ESCOR?" said Bosley, puzzled. "Oh, Humphrey will take care of ESCOR."

His dark-haired colleague smiled with easy, lofty, enigmatic confidence.

The three later surrendered their passes and came out of the ministry doors.

"Dr hink and a bu bite?" suggested Stag.

"Good idea."

Colin looked carefully around and behind them as they strode cheerfully to the pub.

"Peter," he said to Stag, "that was magnificent. Confess now, the Mu-Mu-Mu-Mu Hanchester train was spot on time, wasn't it now?"

Stag's face reddened and swole into a massive schoolboy grin, uncontainably pleased with himself, unable to squeeze his pleasure into the habitual gravitas, the sober cast of academic propriety. They all hugged themselves with laughter.

They ordered pints and ploughmans all round and settled down to savour the meeting. Then in came the third civil servant. Lightly bronzed, freckled, curly red hair.

"Du do j hoin us," said Stag courteously.

It turned out that he was called McMichael, Robert McMichael. They chatted for a little.

McMichael turned to Stag:

"You know, Professor, I'm a Mancunian also. Came down on the 7.53. Thought it got in on time. Could have sworn it did if I'd not heard you say differently. But I find this project worthwhile and fascinating," he added hastily, "and I believe I can help."

"Ah," said Stag.

"Well, come on then, tell us all about it," he added.

As described later, in 2023, Professor Stag was to play a key role with the two Prime Ministers at the control of Scottish Independence in Dalkeith.

After lengthy debates, it was agreed that implementation of the VEM would be under Prof Wargrils at Macclesfield. Close enough to Llanbedr and Manchester, and Prof Stag, but not so close as to have him visiting and issuing streams of "enhancements". Destructive enhancements were a byword in the industry.

Manufacture of any kit would be in Shrewsbury (Amwythig), to help keep the Welsh on side. The Anglo-Welsh city and its culture were tremendous, particularly the Italian restaurant "Carluccio's" with its massive dark blue paper bags, and the Prince Rupert Hotel.

Besides, the CEO was an old-boy of Shrewsbury school.

Chapter 2

Beelzebub BLZ

A slender dark-haired woman, a young graduate trainee, stood outside the office of BL, legendary Chief Executive. Awesome. The guy who'd had the bottle to throw over a brilliant career as a physicist for the swirling maelstrom of journalism. PLUS, PLUS many obscure side interests. Not short of the odd million or two. Or more.

On the door was a simple plaque:

B. L. Z. Bubb – Deputy Reporter-in-Chief

BL in his serious guise presented a long box-shaped face, beaky nose with a bulbous tip and level thin lips, a monument to committed and rather critical observation; ugly, friendly, yet alarming to his colleagues and subordinates.

But this could dissolve in an instant to the broadest and most infectious of smiles, lips lifting way up at the corners and eyes crinkled warmly with mirth. Occasionally, glimpsed in profile, this same image could momentarily take on a fearsomely different shape. The smiling mouth seemed tautened upwards and opened as if poised to cackle, the jaws becoming shark-like and voracious, the nose probing predatorily forward. Truth will out.

Turned on a rival or enemy, the mirth resolved sometimes into searing derision, accompanied by loud guffaws and coarse observations. Reminiscent of a vitriolically hostile Renaissance gargoyle, tucked way up in the ancient heights of a cathedral, spurting venom with inexplicable savagery at a chosen human target.

With a boss, for example, Sir Stan Barker, this image melted into one of concerned and committed support – understand me, Barks? You're with me, Barks? These fuckers; we've got to grasp them by the goolies and squeeze till they squeak. Believe me, Barks, they're after you.

Women were a different target; treated with warmth, consideration and friendly sexual innuendo. He'd call out to a cleaning lady as she stood near the car:

"Hallo, my love. Treating you well, isn't he then? Well I certainly would."

And then a loud, harsh aside as he pulled away in the car, audible not to her but to his male passengers:

"Wouldn't root you, my dear? Pay me fifty grand and I still wouldn't."

He had, people now say, one redeeming feature, a love for the sea. He was heard occasionally singing softly, sometimes humming:
"I must go down to the seas again, to the vagrant gypsy life.
To the gull's way and the whale's way where the wind's like a whetted knife." (from John Masefield)

The trainee raised her hand and knocked hesitantly. Why did he want to see a cub reporter? She recalled his powerful, moving presentation of the journalist's place in society, the gentle, un-intrusive, caring manner with which his eyes had slowly scanned their ranks at the start of their training.

"Come!"

She entered.

"Ah yes. Nadine. Nadine Humphrys Jones, isn't it?

"I was most interested in your piece on North Korea. Perceptive, orthogonal. A nice piece of lateral thinking.

"Take a pew. I have decided this year to take a personal hand for one or two of our brighter prospects. A bit of accelerated development to see if we can get you on stream without the usual lag while trainees learn from experience. Do we have to accept the hoary old dictum that you can only learn from your own mistakes? What's wrong with other peoples'?"

Nadine smiled. The subdued light emphasised the gold sparkled grey in her eyes. He caught his breath, slightly shaken. Then he went on.

"I think not," he said easily. "*Si la jeunesse savait, si la vieillesse pouvait.* That sort of stuff. But in this case, we hope to bring the savoir bit forward a great deal more than a smidgeon.

"So the Board, bless their cotton socks, have asked me to single out one or two to sit in with me. What do you think?" he asked with disarming diffidence.

She flushed with pleasure and mumbled assentingly. She'd join him, it appeared, one day a week and absorb what she could.

The first Tuesday went well, and the next. At the end of the third, he gave her a job.

"Here's an interesting letter to the editor. Response by a guy called Johnson to something by our man in East Africa – actually, of course, usually in Hampstead. That's where we find out what our readers want to hear. And you can find out quicker about Africa in Hampstead or Cambridge, and it saves a lot of flying!"

He smiled disarmingly – they well knew that the paper's correspondents were often enough where the action was. "See what you can do with it."

The original article spoke of "the myth of British Imperium as altruistic, benevolent and misunderstood". Out there, in the writer's estimation as a national subaltern doing his two years in the army:

"It stank. Whites of staggering insignificance behaved like the lords of creation."

Johnson's letter to the editor went:

"As a contemporary of his, I'm impelled to put an alternative to your writer's view. Having acquired similar views to his as a student and national serviceman, I resolved to get involved and joined the colonial service in Uganda. Most of us were liberal arts graduates from Oxbridge, leftish inclined, with good degrees and a tendency to go on International Voluntary Service work camps in the vacations.

"For me, as for many others who worked there, it's immensely pleasing to look back now, as one could reflect at the time, confident that almost nothing but good was achieved in our five key years there. Yes, the occasional settler was disgustingly arrogant (only one that I can recall). Galling for an itinerant national serviceman like your journalist, but insignificant against the realities as they affected the typical Ugandan.

"To avoid personal bias," Johnson continued, "I'd like to take someone I knew only from his reputation among the Bakiga tribe, Purseglove, to illustrate these realities. He was District Agricultural Officer, Kigezi – rolling, beautiful, overpopulated highlands, threatened with social and economic collapse because of the Pax Britannica, medical services, malaria eradication and civilisation in general.

"The danger arose from over-cultivation, and the sheet erosion of the hills which overtook the same terrain in neighbouring Ruanda. Purseglove's vision and his infectious enthusiasm led his department and his successors to create an agronomic revolution for half a million farmers; through bunding, terracing, tree planting and the introduction of appropriate cash crops. I had the exhausting job of accompanying his successors on extension safaris, day in and out, climbing up and down 3,000 feet from farmer to farmer and baraza to baraza. Purseglove is still known with affection and unconscious ambiguity among the Bakiga as 'Bwana Fertility'. Elsewhere his achievement is unknown, though agriculturalists know of his later research in the West Indies on breadfruit, for which he received the OBE. To misquote Schumacher in 'Small is Beautiful', Purseglove and many others were the people who really mattered. Why don't the Sunday broadsheets build on their, and similar, links, for the future; let the occasional boorish, irrelevant settler be forgotten."

Nadine came back with her work a week later. He scanned it.

"Hmm. Maybe we should get together about this this evening? I'm out all day at the Treasury – 'fraid you can't come. Not allowed to take fledglings!"

"Er well, I've unfortunately…"

"Early working dinner perhaps. That little place called 'á l'Écu de France'. Off St James's Square." His eyes glinted. "Six thirty prompt; I've got to get away by eight. And we've got to meet the weekend edition."

"Er well, er right. Thank you very much, BL." She smiled warmly at him. He seemed slightly bemused, then dismissed her peremptorily.

Later she dressed for the evening, and left for the "a l'Écu de France" She wore a swirling, dark blue skirt, a hip length jacket, a lovely deep red, sort of raspberry colour, and a wispy floating silk scarf. BL's "little place" turned out to be large, spacious and beautifully decorated in cream, jade and midnight blue, with much seemingly genuine Regency furniture. Known only to the cognoscenti. Rather reminiscent of the Mayfair in Washington, where her father had once given her a splendid American working breakfast, including hot waffles, bacon and maple syrup. It lay just between the bustle of the Strand and the quiet Roller-girt meg-affluence of St James's Square.

She went in diffidently, left her coat, and decided to go right through the ante-room, since BL would no doubt be in a hurry. A waiter came up questioningly.

"Yes, madame?"

"I'm meeting a Mr. Bubb."

"Ah, *bonsoir* madame. Monsieur Bubb, of course. It is Mme Humphrys Jones, *n'est ce pas*? He leaves a message, maybe perhaps a little late at the Treasury. Some wine perhaps?"

She ordered a Bloody Mary. Not her usual, but she felt like it. Later another. Then he arrived.

"So sorry, my dear. We'll have to rush I'm afraid."

They dickered through the ordering, and then he pulled out her work.

"No good at all, I'm afraid. This is just university stuff. Certainly readable, agreeable enough and so on. But not the paper's Weltanschauung, you know."

"Now, you should slash through all this stuff about Purseglove. We're not interested in colonial heroes, we're in business for the future."

"But surely Johnson's quite right."

Two agents sitting near tried to listen intensely and unobtrusively. Never get a finer meal again, and all on expenses. And just look at the popsey. Out with the directional mike. Caught a bit of the argument as voices rose. Would report it back to their infuriating boss in MI6. A Jock Rundle. A bleeding moaner. Have to say, though, he's a bright guy. Gets round all the restrictions on phone tapping just by placing a bog standard PC up to 20 metres away from your target. Back it up with a truck battery, load Nuance and you leave it to pick up every word.

"Right? Right? What d'you mean right? This is about the past. And the past's what we're in business to mould. To re-engineer. The world's going to have it in for us regardless, so let's get our retaliation in there first. The dear old Brits and their fond memories, we've got to erase all that garbage. Look."

He handed her an edited copy of the text, pruned and gutted, topped and tailed.

"Read that."

She read it, her heart gradually beating tightly.

"The impression we want to give is of a pompous, rather stupid ex-civil servant. A boring old fart of a colonialist. And we head it 'Proud Heritage'.[6] Invite the reader to conclude that the desperate woes of Uganda under Amin and Obote were attributable to thickies like this one."

---

[6] As in *The Guardian*, 1969.

"But surely," she said, "Purseglove was what the letter was all about. And Amin's atrocities were well down the track after eight years of independence and prosperity. And Amin came in because Obote tried a coup against the Baganda and got it all wrong. And there were hardly any settlers in Uganda, it was a protectorate. Land couldn't be alienated to foreigners directly, even the missions. Only 0.24 per cent of the land was alienated into the plantation sector. And our guy was just a callow, ignorant national serviceman in Jinja barracks."

"How d'you know that?" he asked suspiciously.

She started blinking rapidly and talked very fast.

"Well, my uncle worked and died of malaria there as an ADC, so I know something about it. What a drunken racist plantation manager said to our guy in a military garrison bar has no significance whatsoever. There were almost none of them, and their importance for the average Ugandan was vanishingly small. It's a peasant economy, like nearly all tropical Africa. Plantations didn't exist."

BL smiled faintly and laced his fingers together in a clerical steeple. Then his phone buzzed. "Sorry, I must just take this."

"Okay, go ahead and buy. Jack Kennedy stayed there. Mice Nayad or some such. In Kimrew or Kummry or whatever, C Y M R U in their funny orthography.[7]

---

[7] Cymru. Welsh orthography was standardised in 1870, and unlike English pronunciation, remains reasonably consistent. So, LlanBedr is anglicised as "Llan" – Hlun and "Bedr" – Bedder. Llan is a church or village, bedr is St Peter. The church pictured later.

Welsh has the longest literary tradition of any surviving European language, going back to the seventh century AD Brian Davies, Welsh place names unzipped.

Compare with English pronunciation, for example, "Nuneaton" – a French friend was unable to get a ticket at Euston station. She was asking for "Noon ay ah tong".

"I'll go down for the first bulldoze at Llanbedr, look you. Good to watch, look you. Get one of the drones onto it, look you... I'll be up there for the first shipments from the Windies. St Vincent. And for the start of the spaceport access road."

Then he thought further... I must get this girl.

BL picked up their conversation again. He laced his fingers together in the same persuasive clerical steeple.

"Sorry about that. Look, Nadine, my sweet. As far as we're concerned, our guy was there. Our guy knows his stuff. Full stop. Period. That's what real editing's all about. And that's the view our paper wants to paint."

"Well," she said, red spots on her cheeks, "your trashy so-called real editing's not for me."

"Look," he said, "let's talk this through. After all, we don't want to jeopardise your..."

She stood up dramatically and raised an arm.

"Waiter, my coat please," she said, and waited there, tapping her toe, while Bubb rose and tried to chat easily through the awkwardness.

"It's important," he said gently, "to unpack some of these grand phrases and see what they mean... Maybe when push comes to shove, we're basically in agreement..."

Her eyes crinkled and glinted, and she looked stonily across the restaurant, paying no evident attention. The coat was brought, and, not wanting to muddle herself by trying to put it on, she took it, laid it slowly and carefully across her left arm, and picked her way across the floor like a ballerina pirouetting on wet ice. She left without a backward glance, to the intrigued, admiring interest of the scattered diners nearby.

"Buggeration," said BL under his breath.

The head waiter came up with a slight, commiserating smile.

"The hunting tonight," he murmured. "Not so good, Monsieur Bubb, *n'est ce pas?*"

"*Vous avez raison, mon vieux. Mais je ne la laisserai pas la. Il y a encore de methodes.*"

"*Pas avec celle-la. Elle me semblait sauvage comme une lynxe.*"

"And all the better for it," muttered Bubb to himself.

And in due course his chance might come.

Chapter 3

The Comeuppance of Jock

This is from a report by a fellow officer which I found in the records for the No. 1 Training Regiment, Royal Signals, when they were at Catterick Camp in Yorkshire.
H. B. G-W

We are on the moors just above the River Swale and among the gorse and heather in the wilds between the Swale and the River Ure. It's a bitter December day, the sky is lowering, with the threat of hail and sleet.

A troop of trainee signallers stand with rifles at ease in a line across a long 10-foot high mound above the moor.

One hundred yards away are the butts, another even taller mound in front of which stand a series of 10 round targets.

Close to us and clearly commanding is a small dapper officer. He is Jock Rundle.

He is insufferable. He is five feet five and has a long narrow pointed nose and a warm smiling face, a face brimming with self-confidence.

The face dangles under a smooth officer's cap. Moulded carefully to his nut using special kit by the Officers' Hatter in Richmond town. Important that the officer's hat does not easily fall off. The town is improbably spectacular, set high on crags above the River Swale in North Yorkshire.

He comes from Fettes, the Scottish equivalent of Eton, and is going after his army service – brimming over with OQ (Officer Qualities) – to Trinity College Cambridge. A top chap. He is success in process personified, and he knows it.

He gives a command and the 10 signallers drop to the ground and lie with their rifles, Lee Enfield .303s, ready to fire.

Fire is commanded, and in the butts the signallers raise circular shapes on sticks to show where the rounds have hit.

They each fire off a full magazine of five rounds and are ordered to return to the at ease position.

As they do so, Signalman Foster drops his rifle, which somehow ends up barrel down in the earth. Bitterly cold, fingers frozen, and it had slipped from his hand.

Sgt Blandford comes up to see what's wrong, looks at the muzzle and sees it's blocked with mud.

He marches up to Rundle and reports.

Rundle strolls authoritatively across.

"What's up laddie?"

Foster explains.

"Give me your gun."

Foster does so. Rundle puts a round in the breach, closes the bolt, pulls the trigger pointing the rifle up.

The round probably lands somewhere in Catterick Camp.

"There we are laddie," says Rundle in a gentle tone, and with a smile. Sgt Blandford is impressed, Signalman Foster is impressed. Everyone is impressed.

Fast forward to the parade next morning at 0800 hours, the entire squadron of 200 is drawn up in three ranks and snappily carrying out the drill.

The command is given

"Squadron fix bayonets."

There is a sharp clatter of bayonets being slotted onto muzzles as the command is carried out.

But another sharp clatter as one bayonet falls to the ground.

It is Foster's bayonet.

"Sarnt take that man's name," snaps Rundle loudly.

The sergeant checks the bayonet and finds it won't fit on the muzzle.

The CO, commanding officer, asks, "What the hell is going on in three troop?"

Rundle reports, explains about the mud. The round must have blasted the barrel too wide for the bayonet to fix. Someone might have been injured if it had burst.

Rundle is reprimanded in due course in the court of enquiry which studies any damage to the regiment's weaponry.

Rundle returns to the mess at lunch.

I would like to say as a chastened and wiser Rundle.

But I would be wrong.

I tracked down the related records for the Royal Signals in Catterick camp.

As a general outline, they said that he was intensely interested in electronics, joined the radio mechanics course in No. 1 Training Regiment and passed out top of the class. Very rare for an officer.

Keen on athletics, a member of the Signals team which won the North Eastern counties and British Army team Championships.

As for the court-martial, it summarised the events above and at the bottom there was the customary signature:

I note this record

Jock Rundle,

2 Lt, R. Sigs

The customary words are "I accept", but no-one seems to have noticed his re-wording. Or perhaps ignored it. His commander, Colonel Reggie Atkinson, a ranker who had risen to seniority, his voice husky with humour, good living and whisky, valued liveliness and initiative in his young officers.

Rundle bought himself a light blue Triumph Thunderbird[8] at the end of his training. I'm surprised he could kick it over.

For Rundle it must have been a classic, and he loved tinkering about with old bikes, cars and boats.

---

[8] The Thunderbird was always light blue, an immensely attractive twin cylindered motorbike, introduced in 1955 by Edward Turner, MD of Triumph Motorcycles, directed at the avid American market. It had a bored out engine of 650cc.

Turner objected strongly when it was used as the base machine for the bike ridden by Marlon Brando in the film "The Wild One". The film has been a cult item for youth ever since. Like the Norton Dominator and the "Matchbox", it was popular with the "Ton up" boys in black leather jackets who made roads like the A20 out of London eastwards their own, often frightening, domain.

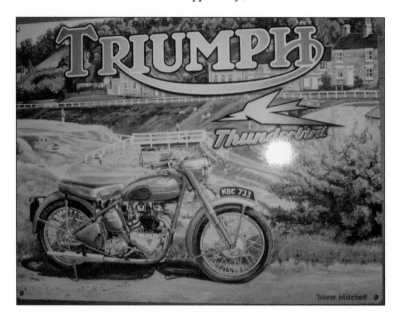

H. B. G-W

Chapter 4

The Llanbedr Spaceport is Mooted

In 2014, a British spaceport to rival others in Europe was proposed by the Westminster Government, to be in one of three locations.

The first was in Scotland. This was eventually ruled out because, perhaps, of the possibility of Scottish independence.

The second was in Llanbedr (also known as Llareggub), where there was already a massive airfield which had successfully been used by squadrons of Lancaster bombers during the Second World War. It had since been a fallback aerodrome for civil aircraft in distress. It was also used for a great range of activities to do with flying. The heritage of fascination with the Second World War, with flight and aircraft, was intense, with a base wing of the RAF, and a strong wing of local youngsters in a Cadet Force.

The third was in Newquay in Devon in the English South West.

For the Llanbedr option, the current road system would have needed massive development. A bypass over the River Artro and its lagoon to the west of the village was proposed to allow increased spaceport traffic greatly improved access from the north.

The fight by the people against this proposal, which would have virtually destroyed the loveliest village in Snowdonia, began with a letter in opposition from an environmentalist and lover of the area in Birmingham, England. The original County Council plan is shown below.

The process of opposition was eventually developed by the Llanbedr Lagoon Group. The key circular is shown below.

Help us save Llanbedr Lagoon

Issue 2, 27/1/19

From Graham Tottle, MA Emmanuel College Cambridge, Postgraduate Magdalen College, Oxford and Judy Rose, PhD. UEA

Thrumble Coombe, 2 Maes Artro, Llanbedr, Gwynedd LL45 2PZ

Simon Lewis Jones, St Catherine's, College, Cambridge, Gareth Williams, Archaeologist, Barmouth

Responses welcome to judy.rose103@gmail.com

We plan the following future issues

March: Views from the villagers and tourists, for whom the approved plan for a bypass and improved access to the Snowdonia Aerospace Centre cuts off the views out west to the lagoon and dunes. However, if the lagoon project goes ahead, all the objections can be resolved, with massive cost savings.

April: Timelines for global warming and its forecast effects and the SMPT.

May: Engineering aspects from advice by the Harbourmaster, Caernarfon and Conwy, with assessments from long experienced Marine Engineering and Civil Engineering professionals in Wales and South Africa.

Addressed to: The current groups for and against, plus: Pam Odam, Administrator, the Bro.; Richard Workman, Director of Shell Island; The Commodore/Secretaries, LPYC, RLSC, Cambridge University Cruising Club; Sir David de Dimbleby: Will Self; The Editor, *Cambrian News*; BBC Wales; John Humphrys, BBC Today Programme; Huw Edwards BBC News; Evan Davies BBC4 pm; Andy, Bishop of Bangor; The Royal Society for the Protection of Birds; The Ramblers; The Royal Yachting Association; the Lord Lieutenant for Gwynedd.

Chapter 5

Westminster and Cardiff Decide on Spaceport Access

Two syndicates were involved in the proposed location of the UK's spaceport. The most promising syndicate had selected Llanbedr, as will be shown later.

The rival syndicate favoured one of possibly two spaceports, one in Newquay, Cornwall, and one in Scotland.

The decision was pending when the campaign for the Llanbedr Lagoon was under weigh. Both syndicates had intense interest in, and influence on, the outcome.

Under the Freedom of Information Act (FoI), the details for the syndicates cannot be released until 2068.

Chapter 6

The Citizens' Advice Bureau

We are in Queenshampton where Nadine is working after leaving BLZ.
She is reviewing recent cases.

Nadine was at her desk, working on a debt case sheet. To the left breast of her sweater was pinned a snazzy-looking plastic tag:

"Nadine – Generalist and Debt Advisor"

Above her head was a minatory notice by the Youth Motivation worker who shared the office. It was in bright yellow:

TO ALL YOU YOUNG PEOPLE WHO USE THE YOUTH SHOP. THE STAFF ARE HERE TO HELP YOU, NOT CLEAN UP AFTER YOU.

SO TAKE NOTE, I'VE BEEN PUSHED AS FAR AS I'M PREPARED TO GO. I'VE SEEN CLEANER AND TIDIER FIVE-YEAR-OLDS!!!

"YOU HAVE BEEN WARNED."

On the desk, a notice to CAB advisors stressed: Social monitoring; full information including race, sexuality and disability, must be included.

An earlier case from the morning still worried Nadine, on a theme which had often troubled her before. The client was an unmarried mum, with a year-old daughter. Her current, young male partner wanted to move in with them and make things permanent – "Sort of like her father, like as well. You know?" The guy would father the infant. Nadine had gone through the financial side, the client's possible benefits. Calculating the one-parent premium, etc., for a single mum. Then the alternative, "what-if if the guy moved in". Net income less. No free this, no free that. Not so good.

"Ah, well," the client had said cheerfully, "that's him out then."

"It'll affect him not to see the kid, of course."

"See if I care."

Should Nadine have tried to argue? No, she concluded, the guidelines say don't be judgmental; just set out the options for the client to decide. Okay, it's tough on the guy, and much worse, it sets the scene for a disastrous upbringing for the child. But that's how it's got to be.

She dismissed it from her mind and finished off her last debt case sheet instead.

"He's thrown a sickie,"[4] she wrote on a covering pink sticker for her colleague at the top of the sheet, "to get away from the workbench and sort it all. He told them he's got to be off with his shoulder. The debts are on the sheet with the list of creditors, how much we recommend for each, the usual. See you. Nadine."

She put the case sheet in a basket, then completed the statistics for NACAB central office and sent them off down the Intranet. So many appeals against benefit decisions, Disability Living Allowance assessments, so many cases of sexual or police harassment, of debt, of employment law infringement, and so on. A crucial thermometer in measuring the happiness of the common weal.

She recalled an earlier case from the morning, when a young guy had come in. Unshaven, black haired, dirty T-shirt, holed jeans, rough trainers.

"What do you do on a daily basis?" she asked.

"What I do is I get up on a daily basis. Then I do sump'n. Then I do sump'n else. On a daily basis. Vat's what I do."

What else was there for him to do? Fill supermarket shelves? No manager would take him on.

Was she achieving anything?

She left the office still uneasy, slamming the door angrily.

Chapter 7

Escape from Baghdad – Robert McMichael and Dr Majid Dujaily

From *Computer Weekly*
Computer consultant Robert McMichael found himself working in the wrong place at the wrong time. Here he tells Computer Weekly Xtra! *how he escaped Baghdad before the bombs were dropped on Iraq.*

My former office in Baghdad is no longer standing – it was a prime target for cruise missiles in the Gulf War.

In Baghdad in June at noon, it is hot. Fiercely hot. 47 degrees. And dry. Fiercely dry. Breathe in through your mouth quickly and you blister your gullet.

From the dictator's office suite, high up, you can see most of the city. Two police Mercedes, a fading sun-battered green to the gunwales, topsides cream, dawdle truculently along Tigris Drive. The ancient river is low, a dirty, muddy, motionless brown. Even the water looks dry. Nothing else moves anywhere; everything crouches in dark corners, barely breathing, waiting for the sun to go away.

In 1990, a massively fortified skyscraper served as the heart of the Iraqi government. Outside are the extraordinary grey shutters four-inches thick of hardened Poznan steel, three massive, angled wedges of it for every office, wedges 30 foot by 5. They hang awaiting his command, like crocodiles' eyelids, to blink away prowling missiles and searching tyrannicidal shells.

This is where I worked, reporting to the Director of Planning, Dr Majid Dujaily.

Of the handful of foreigners allowed in, I was the only Westerner, admitted as a United Nations Food and Agriculture Organisation (FAO) consultant to help develop their sectoral database, predicting Iraq's agricultural production. My office was next to the lift shaft on which the cruise missiles were later to hone in on.

After joining, I was taken to the great Thursday meeting, for all the senior people in the Saddam HQ.

I stood in the background with my hosts.

From a group close by, their leader turned to me and said menacingly:

"You, consultant, remember Farzad Bazoft!"

His colleagues laughed in support.

Each morning I would sit with my counterpart, Dr Hamadi, an Iraqi professor, and chat over the day's plan. But on 17 April, he was like a burly bear with a sore head. I waited while he conducted a heated exchange in Arabic on the internal phone. He ended with a tirade and slammed the phone down. "These fucking idiots!" – the only time I heard him swear.

I was visited that evening by the FAO projects officer who described an extraordinary meeting he had just had. The Iraqi directors were due to give the forecast annual agricultural production data for the economy, but my counterpart had announced that, "Due to computing problems, this year's figures are not available." There was a sharp row and the meeting had broken up acrimoniously.

It was not my problem, but I knew that the computers were working perfectly. There were no computing problems.

By the morning of 2 August, we were well into the project. The news had been full of a fierce political confrontation between Iraq and Kuwait. "It's all okay," people insisted on telling me, "just the politicians."

I was miffed when the team, normally enthusiastic, kept disappearing in groups, clearly excited. I found out why that evening, when it was announced that the army had entered and taken Kuwait.

The director of the division, Dr Dujaily, was built like an Arabian James Bond, an acute statistician and agronomist, with immense charm and humour. Passionate in his descriptions of nights in the moonlit desert in a favourite oasis near Babylon. His easy leadership of his bunch of argumentative scientists was striking. A word of praise from him would bring a flush of pleasure to the recipient's face. When I entered his office each day, he'd greet me in broad Scots – "Och an' awa" or whatever – trained at Aberdeen University. Fluent and idiomatic in three languages, with a taste for the latest slang. As I left the first time, he disconcerted me by saying cordially, "Hallo, hallo." I found later that it was the in-way of saying goodbye in the upper reaches of the Iraqi Civil Service. A man, it was widely rumoured in the UN, who was tolerated by the regime for his vital role, but certainly mistrusted. Two smoothly dressed officials haunted the corridors, but I didn't know their functions.

After Saddam's invasion of Kuwait took place, I spent an uneasy night. What do you say to your friends and hosts the next morning when their country has suddenly gone berserk? I resolved to see Dujaily and to tell him the Iraqis were marching over a precipice. To make the point graphically, I'd walk my fingers across his desk and over the edge.

I went in.

"Hallo, Robert, take a pew." I sat opposite him, next to Ahmed, a humorous young statistician who was discussing a spreadsheet on egg production with him. My back was to an open archway into the smaller adjoining office.

I launched agitatedly into my prepared spiel, saying I feared the Iraqis faced military disaster from the West. Then did my finger-walking bit.

Dujaily's face froze, then he behaved quite extraordinarily. He rolled his eyes violently and continuously from side to side. As he did so, he ran into a long, heated tirade about Iraq's soldiery and rocketry, air force, secret weapons and so on – they were for sure, without question, invincible. Ahmed looked sideways at me, crinkling his eyes, giving a faint, quizzical smile. I twigged and hastily backed off. I hadn't realised, I said, that their technology was so advanced, and there were of course questions of Iraq's title to Kuwait and so on.

The tension eased; we chatted carefully and I left. As I did so, I glanced through the archway. There was one of the mystery men, but now in the military uniform of a full colonel. Dujaily's minder.

I withdrew my labour in accordance with the UN resolution, but against the strong advice of the British ambassador Harold Walker. "I will only have to try to get you out of jail like I did with Farzad Bazoft and his girlfriend."[9]

The United Nations debated the invasion and swiftly declared it illegal.

At this point, things became serious. Saddam rounded up his 3,000 foreign "guests" into various hotels, where they were held "for their safety".

A UN colleague, Nino Nicotra, head of peach research at the Italian institute near Rome, joined me in the city from the northern mountains. This made the whole operation more exciting and less alarming. We used to crouch on the rooftop at night with our shortwave radios, listening intently to Margaret Thatcher "vomiting poison like a spotted serpent", as Saddam Hussein put it.

As things worsened, the FAO decided to get us out.

We got clearance to cross the desert to Jordan in one of their Land Rovers, leaving Baghdad at 9am on 6 August. However, the driver protracted our departure by 10 hours, so we arrived at the frontier post at 2am. I was mentally rehearsing my interview for the BBC when our driver came up with a broad smile. "We go back Baghdad," he said. The border had been closed at midnight.

My escape plans foiled, I continued working in the ministry. The database I was working on looked very relevant to the possible UN sanctions, and my thoughts turned to espionage.

I described the database and a missile, which we had seen hidden under a motorway bridge on the way to Jordan, to an MI6 intelligence guy at the British Embassy. Jock someone –

---

[9] Farzad Bazoft was an *Observer* newspaper correspondent whom Saddam had recently had beheaded for suspected espionage.

tiny and not short of conceit. He was excited about the missile, which I identified from pictures – an Al Abbas, modified from North Korea, which provided the first concrete evidence that Iraq was moving armaments west to cover Tel Aviv in Israel. But he showed little interest in the database. A database written in a standard computer language, he said dismissively.

But a database which might have been vital to the allies' plans. How far might the Iraqis be defeated by sanctions on food imports alone, resulting in famine? Was a military campaign needed?

That night I thought about the dangers that spying posed to me and the team, and about abusing their friendship. Skulking around the corridors slipping spreadsheets on to diskettes would undoubtedly be seen as betrayal.

As I have found on other remote assignments, you get deeply involved with your colleagues, and take an astonishingly different view of the world. I decided to do no more about the database.

The prat, Jock Rindle or something, had showed no interest. He had impressed Harold Walker, the ambassador.

The MI6 guy was Jock Rundle. Made his name with the ambassador by handling a mass protest against the Brits.

The Iraqis had laid on busloads of protesters from Mosul. But when they arrived at the Embassy, the lane was blocked with people applying for visas, invited by Rundle via his agents to the public the night before. H. B. G-W

I was joined by Nino Nicotra from FAO Rome. He had been studying the possibilities for improving peach cultivation in the north-west.

The pressure intensified when UN Resolution 661 instructed us to withhold further consultancy. This was debated at one of the regular meetings for the three thousand Brits held by Harold Walker.

Walker was clearly worried by his experience with the beheading of the *Observer* reporter Farzad Bazoft, and when I said I'd withhold my labour, he advised against it.

"I'll only have to try to get you out like I did for Farzad Bazoft and his girlfriend."

However, at work the next day, since the Iraqi minister refused me permission to leave as and when I wished, I asked my Iraqi counterpart to come with me to UN FAO. There I said I would work no more. He assured me I could stay safely with him, but I refused.

That night, at 2am, the police raided my flat. Lights flashed, people screamed, but I was hiding in an empty apartment nearby. When the vehicles left, Nino and I moved on to hide in the FAO library.

In the days that followed, I did some work developing

a peach database for Nino's outfit – texture, colour, habitat, etc. In the evenings, we listened to the news on the roof and twiddled the cursors on MS Flight Simulator 4. But finally we took refuge in the Educational Social and Cultural Centre of West Asia (ESCWA), the UN's Middle East headquarters. Here our escape plans turned to putting pressure on the decision-makers.

Nino phoned Rome and New York to great effect, "Our situation here is desperate", while I worked on ESCWA's top guys, who were all highly politicised and pro-Iraq. We would be sitting in an ESCWA officer's anteroom before he arrived in the morning, and stay there, courteously embarrassing, throughout the day and the next until we got another level up the hierarchy.

Astonishingly, I was occasionally able to get through to the UK by phone in the small hours. At the sound of a Western voice, the Iraqi operators would usually just cut the connection, but once in a while I got through.

The UN used its influence to get its people out. Saddam Hussein needed the UN's goodwill, and the 200 UN expatriates dwindled, arguing fiercely about allowances, compensation, etc., until just Nino and I were left.

"Look at these persons' passports. These persons must of course stay."

We slept on sofas in various areas, our favourite spot being the rather fine mezzanine. There was no cooking equipment except for mass meals. But people left us their frozen delicacies when they left and we cooked strawberries and spaghetti in a coffee percolator.

Then on 24 August we got to meet ESCWA's top man, Tayseer Abdel Jaber. We pressed him, and he assured me that there was no way he would leave until he had got us out. We rejoiced – cautiously.

We sat in Abdel Jaber's office the next morning to make sure the promise stuck. He came in and announced that he was leaving at midday and handing us over as refugees to the UNHCR.

Things got very heated and we threatened his UN future. Then a softly-spoken middle-aged Ghanaian came in, one of two deputy UN secretary-generals who had arrived under resolution 661 to sort the UN staff's situation out.

The man had an extraordinary capacity to analyse a situation and pour oil on troubled waters. Could we seek shelter with friends? No, they would be executed. Move to a hotel? No, random snatches were commonplace. Stay at our homes? We had none. So, Abdel Jaber needed to do this, the foreign ministry that and Iraqi Airways the other; a resolution meeting would be held with the following agenda.

We watched the spellbinder with hope and more than a tad of scepticism. "I'll have you out on Wednesday," he said.

But he held a meeting of the three ambassadors and us in his tenth floor hotel room in the Rashid to announce his success. A brilliant eye for dramatic publicity.

I went to the director for final clearance (they were now safely ensconced in the city). Dujaily said with a twinkle in his eyes:

"For sure, Graham, I cannot sign this release because you have not completed your project."

"For sure, Majid, I could not complete our project because you had taken away my hardware." We laughed with pleasure.

The army had taken over their high-tech novel networking system, forbidden to them by NATO, which enabled them to connect all their key defence computers together.

They were not to meet again for many years. H. B. G-W

We left as promised in a diplomatic limo, flags flying, and were escorted to the front two seats in an unscheduled waiting Boeing 737. Nino and I clicked on the pins, as if flying the plane with Microsoft Flight Simulator 4.

And so we reached Jordan. Picked up by a US army full colonel. He radioed as we went: "VIPs now at Wedonga… now at Shebira," and so on.

Later, in my hotel room in Amman, I managed to phone my sister.

"Hello, Robert," she said. "Still in the capital, are you?"

"Yes." Lump in the throat. "But a different capital."

The courteous Ghanaian magician? Kofi Annan, later UN Secretary General.

Chapter 8

Oldman Dosses Down

I have always believed a theory also propounded by Evelyn Waugh – For example, the Brigadier and Captain Apthorpe's thunderbox – that if you are particularly content, Fate or God waits round the corner to biff you one. And so it was. A thunderbox is a wooden portable lavatory, as often carried by a porter on African safaris. H. B. G-W

The ketch, *Lady Amanda*, lay in Porth Penrhyn, Bangor, a paradise for lovers of old wooden yachts in a real working port. Under the mountains of Snowdonia. The aged owner falls asleep in quiet contentment. "We don't stop playing because we grow old, we grow old because we stop playing" – George Bernard Shaw
But contentment brings its penalties. God is lurking round the corner. Heavily grantinated. Just as with Waugh's Brigadier and poor old Apthorpe's thunderbox.[10] Lurking and waiting. Lurking and waiting to biff the old man one.

Will he save the lagoon? As the Malaysians say, "Who can tell?"

---

[10] Evelyn Waugh in the Second World War trilogy.

On Sunday they had launched the ketch, *Lady Amanda*, with immense success – water poured in for twenty minutes until the caulking between the planks took up, but after that, hardly any leaks at all – and Scott Metcalfe and the old man motored her up to her new mooring in Porth Penrhyn, Bangor, just below the pink trawler – mud flat as a pancake, just what she needed for her flat keel to sit on and hold her upright at low water. And as accessible as you might wish.

He falls asleep.

Chapter 9

The Lagoon Plan Key Events Circulated

Help us save Llanbedr Lagoon

Issue 2, 27/1/19

From Graham Tottle, MA Emmanuel College Cambridge, Postgraduate Magdalen College, Oxford and Judy Rose, PhD. UEA

Thrumble Coombe, 2, Maes Artro, Llanbedr, Gwynedd LL45 2PZ

Simon Lewis Jones, St Catherine's, College, Cambridge, Gareth Williams, Archaeologist, Barmouth

Responses welcome to judy.rose103@gmail.com

We plan the following future issues

March: Views from the villagers and tourists for whom the approved plan for a bypass and improved access to the Snowdonia Aerospace Centre cuts off the views out west to the lagoon and dunes. However, if the lagoon project goes ahead, all the objections can be resolved, with massive cost savings.

April: Timelines for global warming and its forecast effects and the SMPT.

May: Engineering aspects from advice by the Harbourmaster, Caernarfon and Conwy, with assessments from long experienced Marine Engineering and Civil Engineering professionals in Wales and South Africa.

Addressed to: The current groups for and against, plus: Pam Odam, Administrator, the Bro.; Richard Workman, Director of Shell Island; The Commodore/Secretaries, LPYC, RLSC, Cambridge University Cruising Club; David Dimbleby: Will Self; The Editor, *Cambrian News*; BBC Wales; John Humphrys, BBC Today Programme; Huw Edwards BBC News; Andy, Bishop of Bangor; The Royal Society for the Protection of Birds; The Ramblers; The Royal Yachting Association; the Lord Lieutenant for Gwynedd.

Chapter 10

Jock in North Korea

*This piece in the FAO (UN Food and Agriculture Organisation) library in Rome is an informal narrative from Jock Rundle, a consultant who worked in North Korea when it was seen as a viciously dangerous pariah state, the "axis of evil". It's rather long, but it gives clues to the world's history ever since. We don't yet know for certain the roots of our disasters; terrorists most believe. But I have a gut feel where they lay. It was contained in many letters from Rundle to the UK and US press. It's a good example of the press working in unison to ignore the truth in those times, to ignore reality. **Post Truth** they called it.*

And the nadir of the BBC's descent into the abyss of Post Truth was to be reached when the North Korean President Kim Jong-Un made a first, remarkable, step towards friendship with the West.

The BBC derided it, and did not recognise the corporation's heavy responsibility in doing so until it was goaded to do so by a UN consultant who had worked in the country. This took four letters from him to the director-general, letters dismissed initially as being trivial viewer complaints.

Only when President Kim Jong-Un acquired noticeability by his development of nuclear weapons did the international

community wake up and take notice.
   An example of the Post Truth disease:

The Letters editor,
The Observer

Dear Editor,

Your readers may welcome a different view about North Korea, which has dominated the national headlines recently. Bearing in mind that, as a BBC commentator once put it, "North Korea is impossible for me to report. It is like trying to report on a football match from **outside** the stadium."

But I was inside the stadium.

I was on the pitch!

My view is from a mission which I carried out as an agricultural computing consultant for the UN's Food and Agriculture Organisation.

I was there for six weeks, probably the only Westerner in the Republic. The barriers to getting there, even with full UN accreditation, were astonishing. I only got in because they had a problem with their Korean database system which they could not solve, and it affected the fertiliser planning and production process for the entire nation. To analyse and record fertility levels in every field in the country using PCs and an X-ray spectrometer which analysed and recorded samples of **each field's fertility.** To use this information to control production of all fertiliser and distribution for every field throughout the country. And so, to achieve a level playing field of fertiliser production for every commune in the entire country.

Using the French revolutionary critique for civilised living, I know that they scored zero points for democracy, but maximum points on the two key characteristics, equality and fraternity.

I could give you many examples like that above, and perhaps the most human was the fact that we all had to go and work in the fields all day every Friday, **from director level down** – good for the work ethic, good for togetherness. More broadly, the range of salary differential between the top brass and the workers was, by all Western standards, extraordinarily narrow. And similarly for accommodation and lifestyle. No problem with obesity, they were all immensely fit and keen.

As regards fraternity, the scenes which the BBC have written off as "manipulated", were genuine. I was there for the congress of foreign supporters of the regime, and I experienced the depth of commitment. And this commitment applied throughout the country. When we succeeded in our fertiliser allocation program, we were given a four-day holiday in the lovely mountains of Kum Gang San. And there we were, climbing from a comfortable hotel (equivalent to British three-star) among one worker from every commune. Each was given a splendid full week's holiday.

As a general conclusion, let me quote a BBC correspondent who pointed at a satellite-based picture of the Korean segment of the globe at night. She pointed to the brilliant light being thrown out by South Korea and Japan, the faint light from China and the total blackness from North Korea.

"There," she said in condemnation. "That blackness shows the hardship and poverty of this pariah republic."

What she neglected to say is that it showed also that the republic's lifestyle is **sustainable**, whereas the blazing lifestyle of ourselves in the West is not. Only systems like those in North Korea and Maoist China could achieve sustainability for our planet.

Yours sincerely,

Jock Rundle

MA Cambridge, UN Consultant in IT, FAO, Rome

I attach a detailed report which I circulated. The major media, including *Private Eye*, did not wish to know.

The presenter finally showed a satellite view of the area at night. China, South Korea and Japan were a blaze of light. North Korea was in total darkness apart from a brilliantly lit statue of the leader OGLPKIS.

"There you are," she said. "Contrast the bright civilisation of the West with the pariah state in pitch darkness."

But, I thought, maybe the pariah state has it right.

Only systems like those in two modern states might have safeguarded our future on the planet:

North Korea under Kim Jong-Un and China under Chairman Mao Tse-Tung:

Limited family children, or the dispersal of industry to the communes. Problematic engine parts not replaced from Shanghai, but machined on site in the commune, for example.

The affection for his Korean friends, as we will see, lasted right through Jock's life, through to the Scottish Referendum and beyond. H. B. G-W

Chapter 11

The Inshallah Factor

This account is copied from the World Bank records. It is Robert McMichael's description of his consultancy in Sudan. A massive setback to a promising career – it was three years before he gained another assignment. It was also the document which showed the characteristics which were later to persuade Dr Dujaily to recruit him in the drug tracing. Robert's full report is given in Appendix 3.

My project, SKADP (South Kordofan Agricultural Development Project, World Bank) was situated in the Nuba Mountains in this area, the war zone south of the Sahara desert. The war had been in constant ebb and flow for thirty years, a confrontation between the socialist Arab regime and culture in the north and the Nilotic and Nilo-hamitic Bantu tribes in the south. A confrontation fomented by religious differences, between Islam in the North and Paganism – spirit worship – and Christianity in the South. The Sudanese had (and have, as the crises in neighbouring Darfur show) no wish to have interfering Westerners in those parts. But they needed the SKADP money, $40 million, desperately, and World Bank HQ demanded independent monitoring and evaluation to ensure their funds were being well-spent. The

Bank was dissatisfied to put it mildly, and the warlords, who ran Kordofan and similar parts, refused to grant the Bank officials access to check what was going on. So, we three Brits had been brought in to carry this out:

One (Robinson), the Management Engineer, looking at transport and equipment (tractors were being blown up by mines, and Land Rovers were being commandeered and converted into war vehicles with heavy machine guns mounted on tripods in the body).

One (Tom Mangan), Team Leader, a General Agriculturalist looking at overall project management.

And one, myself, Head of the Information Systems Unit, to define and secure "M&E", as the jargon has it, Monitoring and Evaluation of planning, progress and resources across all the project's disciplines. The project's prime target was agriculture, but water conservation, crop storage facilities, factory processing facilities, transport and infrastructure improvement were all included.

Significantly, although Tom was the team leader, it was specified that "each team member would report directly to the director general", and this would prove crucial.

The hotel hosted us among the tall office blocks in the centre of the city. Dominated at this time of the year by the thundering individual generators for each building, which made the night air foul, spouting diesel fumes into the narrow canyons of the streets. Hydroelectricity from the Nile was at its lowest ebb now, in summer, just when it was most needed. But only two blocks away from this inferno, to the north, were the banks of the White Nile which rolls down from the Ethiopian Mountains, and the banks were graced by various sprawling colonial ministries. The buildings were surrounded by green gardens, unbelievably attractive in the middle of the harsh desert. I took to wandering round these parts in the pleasing hours through sunset and twilight.

For me, these walks became a very necessary antidote to heated frustration. I remember my introduction to SKADP and its building, part of a large private house with no air conditioning but gallons of delicious chilled water, out toward the edge of the desert. It was so hot and dry that in all my time there, I never sought out the toilet to pee.

I went into the building for the first time with Tom, who, rather oddly, failed to introduce me. I found a meeting of maybe twelve people in progress, and a white-robed Sudanese at the chair behind the main desk. I fear that white robes for me signified a lower status than the grey-suited others, and I failed to recognise the Director General, "The Sheikh", who ran the project. The sort of mistake at which you squirm in the early hours of the night, though happily in this case it didn't matter at all.

I got little guidance from Tom Mangan, who just had me tagging along with him as he went from one chancellery to another, sitting waiting in grubby offices, clearing various items like our long-range radio transmitter/receivers. This kit indicates the colossal difficulties that the project endured. There was no postal/telecomms system to Kordofan, water was short. There were no local supplies of diesel, so our fuel had to be transported across 1,300 miles of deeply rutted desert tracks from the Red Sea coast in our five big tankers. Kordofan in 1992 was more backward than most African countries in 1930. Our project was to cover 138,000 square miles, twice the area of the UK, of savannah, desert and mountains, for polyglot people ranging through nomad pastoralists, transhumant pastoralists (the Nuer mentioned earlier), to livestock (camels, cattle, chickens, sheep, goats) and to some "sedentary" agriculture, cultivating primarily sorghum, the local cereal crop. The Project Proposal is, I think, a fascinating document. A strictly factual, matter of fact, definition of an impossible objective. And all this to be achieved with a vicious irreconcilable civil war in progress. Concluding eventually with the creation of a new independent nation, South Sudan.

However, I was slow to take this on board; head down to get on with my job. I was fascinated by the project, sat in on progress meetings and got to know the key people, notably the chief of finance, the head of extension, and a tall gangling southerner with a broad forehead and wide, staring eyes, Atif Rantendi, who was Head of Progress and M&E.

Most of the PMU (Programme Management Unit) team were very friendly, though given to sharply argumentative and often excitable behaviour. Though, one key man, Hambin, however, the leading agricultural extension specialist, was immensely persuasive, charismatic and highly respected. I had some doubts about his objectives.

The Sudanese refused any permits for foreigners to enter the war zone until the person had served sufficient time in Khartoum for them to evaluate him (on top of careful scanning of CVs and so on before his arrival) and required a bewildering chain of documents, permissions and stamps. I used 23 passport photos and saw countless bureaucrats, sometimes warmly welcoming – one paid my fee for me when I was short of change! Sometimes hostile, one actually shouting at me for several minutes. In this process, I rapidly realised that the central government's remit ran thinly in many parts, and that people like the Governor of Kordofan, our region, had often complete, autocratic authority over their regions. The writ of the Khartoum government ran exceeding small. This is a familiar picture in development – the central government are often not wilfully obstructive; they lack authority, as shown in the horrifying civil war in Kordofan's neighbour, Darfur.

So, I spent six weeks first familiarising myself with the project, and meeting the key people. Since Tom Mangan was an agriculturalist of long-standing and would cover that key area, I took a particular interest in the Water Management side. Tom and Robinson, the Engineering Management specialist, got on not at all, and Robinson used the let-out clause in the Proposal, with regard to the reporting, to communicate nothing to him. Nothing at all. I talked to Robinson occasionally. He spent every evening writing to his wife.

"Why don't you phone her?" I asked – the lines out to the UK were fairly good, and the salaries from the World Bank excellent. Understandably – Sudan was reckoned the worst post in the whole developing world.

"If I did, she'd realise from my voice what a dreadful place this is."

Sounds glum, but he was dead right. Cooped up often in an office just outside Kadugli with a suspicious workforce who were scared stiff to move their vehicles out of the compound, with chances of getting blown up (two tractors of the six) or shot up. He set-up procedure manuals and gave training in the operation and maintenance of all the machinery, but that was the limit of his range of action, and soon after my arrival he returned to the UK.

As Tom and I toured government offices for permission to import this and that item of equipment – rain gauges, for example – I started to explore what Tom saw me doing, and how my M&E (Monitoring and Evaluation) role would monitor the agricultural development for which he was responsible. Some casual pointers to his attitudes worried me.

"What about the Bagara?" I asked. "Why is there no plan for the Bagara?" The Bagara were a mysterious nomadic tribe. They spent the "winter" wandering with their herds in the south, then when summer rains brought the biting flies which drove their cattle mad, they all assembled and trekked 800 miles over track-free desert and mountains to rough country west of El Obeid oasis in the desert for the summer. What kept them all alive there through that region's dreadful summers, I never found out. Their tents and leather ornaments and so on were really superb, and they themselves were cheerful, humorous and truculent.

I particularly liked Areit, the only Bagara tribesman on the project as a manager. To see this spare, hawk-eyed nomad looking at a spreadsheet on the screen, his face and eyes crinkled from years of looking over vast distances in the desert sun, and to see his pleasure dawn as some complex equation was solved in an instant, was unforgettable.

From my notes:

"I worked one morning in our offices five miles along the road into the bush, working on training notes. I heard gradually increasing pandemonium and went out to the gates. And there were the Bagara on the march at the start of their annual migration away from the dangerous flies, which gradually swarmed around the Southern swamplands, and into the desert for their annual migration up to the oasis of El Obeid. It was like the annual migration of the London cockneys, out to pick autumnal fruit in the Kentish orchards. Men in the lead with spears, then the matrons sitting cross-legged astride large cows, with massive yokes carrying domestic implements, food, leather tents, carpets, chickens and what have you. And then the children scampering around alongside playing games and full of the joys of life.[11]

"Oh, the Bagara," Tom Mangan said. "Give it another ten years and there won't be any."

But what on earth were we, the development project, to do with such splendid races, was and is a very valid question, and one without a lot of answers.

"Leave them to enjoy their lives, and help them only by vaccinating their cattle," was the response from their British vet, as they passed through the desert. And does this not apply very widely in the developing world?

---

[11] You could say the same of the Nuer tribe: in the last twenty years, the focus of appalling civil war, genocide and massacre in South Sudan.
The great 1930s sociologist, E. P., Evans Pritchard, spent a year living among them. He found them truculent, confident, humorous and happy. And how was it that, with no evidence of any sort of government, they carried out their 80-mile annual migration across the Sudd and the Nile marshes without any of the clashes between one clan and another, which you would expect.

I became increasingly suspicious that Tom Mangan wanted me to stay in Khartoum. What I would do there, he wouldn't specify, but he didn't want me in Kadugli. He certainly didn't. In fact, he assigned my bungalow there – we had five bungalows in a compound on the edge of town – to a fellow mission, a ten-man World Bank "Land Utilisation Survey".

From my end, this was totally unacceptable – you can't "monitor and evaluate" progress on a massive project from the far side of the Sahara desert! Meanwhile, visa clearances slowly accumulated. The officials were sometimes warm and friendly, chatting easily about their country and its past links with the Brits, and sometimes curt and hostile – after independence, their government had swerved firmly to the communist world.

Tom had gone south to Kadugli, and all my permissions had at last come through, so after a word with the Sheikh, I set arrangements in hand for my journey south. I went to the British Embassy – not the International splendours of Baghdad, but an attractive modern building feeling cool with the surrounding trees and vines – to see the First Secretary (Commercial) to get his view of the region:

"We have no information except of the gravest kind. We advise all British citizens not to go there. However (with a smile), if you do go, and you're clearly determined to do so, do let me know how you find it. Come and tell me about it."

We took off for the south before dawn, and at daybreak were skirting the bank of the Victoria Nile, then away across the desert. The tarmac road had mostly deteriorated to impassability, and our diesel-powered Land Cruiser followed the edges of the ruts cut by lorries, swerving and rolling to prevent the axles grounding. It was a rough ride, and after a night stopover in El Obeid oasis, we reached Kadugli around dusk the following day. Tom Mangan was hostile and bitterly angry at my arrival, and tried to move me out to stay at the project enclave five miles out. But servants, food, water and fuel were lacking there, so I moved in with him.

Things improved gradually, and I started courses for the project management on the PCs in DOS, Peachtree Accounting, Norton Antivirus, Laplink, Lotus spreadsheets and WordPerfect word processing, then the world leaders. It was a fascinating experience. I particularly recall teaching Areit, the only Bagara tribesman on the project. To see this spare, hawk-eyed nomad looking at the screen, his face and eyes crinkled from years of looking over vast distances in the desert sun, and to see his pleasure dawn as some complex equation was solved in an instant, was unforgettable.

Kadugli was a hilly, sprawling town. We, the World Bank project, were all in a large compound surrounded by euphorbia and flimsy brushwood fencing, and blessed – unlike in Khartoum – with generated electricity, and hence air conditioning in the evenings and refrigeration. I enjoyed the experience greatly, and often picked up my own food from the market – the meat was roughly chopped and fly infested, so overcooking was essential. Since we were south of the desert fringe, there were sometimes fresh vegetables, local mangoes and their delicious pinkish grapefruits.

More ominously, sprawling across the open hillside by us, were the provincial military barracks. At 5am on Easter Day, we were awakened by heavy gunfire from the barracks, followed by more gunfire from one sector in the distance first, then another, then another. Not just small arms fire, serious stuff. They came round later in the day and explained that it was all just a celebration, because the new Governor was visiting.

Curtis Pastik's Land Evaluation team from the World Bank were allowed out to selected areas (we were confined to the 5km main road from Kadugli to the Project HQ), and came back with useful pointers. Most worrying were the occasional big open trucks crowded with people who seemed to overnight at transit camps out in the savannah en route north. We were told they were refugees. We suspected they were slaves en route to Arabia, as had been the practice a century earlier. Two years later, a detailed report in *The Observer* showed we were right. The Pastik team's most fascinating discovery was that the remains still existed of tanks (dams) built by the engineers of the Meroitic kingdom in the fifth century AD, left disused and abandoned for twelve hundred years. Their rehabilitation was built into the Water Development plan on which I was working. On the agricultural side, Tom's pigeon, the difficulties were massive, notably in agricultural extension. The security situation even in Kadugli was serious. Tom's progress meeting was broken up by a sudden burst of gunfire – the army next door were pouring machine gun fire up into the hills, perhaps with some reply – hard to tell. And if this was true in the town, how much more dangerous might it be for the extensionists? Their remit was to tour in pairs on foot or by bike, and encourage and exhort the villagers to adopt new plant varieties, etc. – all the activities we saw carried out under SCAPA, for example in RISDA and Malawi. The risks of death or kidnap by the SPLA were unacceptable – just as they are now in 2006 in Iraq.

Tom decided the only thing to do was to pull out of this area and base the Project in Dilling in the east, but I don't think this was taken seriously. Politically and militarily, I think the government would regard such a move as a humiliating defeat.

We set up a system for regular progress review with the various government departments, to be chaired and driven by the Sheikh on the second Tuesday of each month. Then Tom and the Pastik team left for Khartoum, and I settled into my personal bungalow, doing my own cooking, and following the agreed training programme. It was immensely pleasing, and I particularly recall working one greatly peaceful Saturday morning out at the HQ, to hear a rising hubbub on the road. Cockerels crowing, cattle lowing, children shouting, dogs barking. I walked outside to see the head of a long clan of Bagara nomads, starting off on their annual migration north. Large, fat mothers sitting cross-legged on top of cows, gesturing imperiously at their offspring, family paraphernalia tied to the cows' flanks, children skipping around and laughing, goats and sheep herded along, chickens tied upside down to the flanks of spare heifers.

I failed to notice points of importance. Water of course, and diesel, were essential to our very existence in Kadugli, and Curtis Pastik and Tom, the two team leaders, spent much of their time driving these apparently simple issues. Continuous checks were made as to the location of the five project tankers in the 3,000-mile grinding, rolling return journey over the desert eastward to the coast. What was the level of the water in the compound's two big tanks? Where to replenish it? Some of the sources were badly polluted – we found one spring was a hundred yards below a public urinal! Though, I suppose, urine is aseptic.

The morning after they all went, I did a check. For water, there were a few gallons left in one tank, the other empty, and the fuel was very close indeed to exhaust. How had this happened? They had used vast quantities. Was someone trying to get rid of me?

I tried to radio the Sheikh in Khartoum to get some action, but our set, brand new, was u/s (unserviceable). Atif and I eventually got through via another project's radio, and in due course the supplies were replenished, so I relaxed. I finished the first stage training – Lotus Spreadsheets for planning, and dBase and Wordstar – and returned with Atif and others to Khartoum.

But deeper questions worried me. A World Bank review of the project was due immediately. How could it possibly survive, given that almost none of the objectives were being met and half the funds had been spent? Tom and I had helped prepare papers for submission at the meeting, to be held at El Obeid, a desert city halfway across the Sahara – the Governor would not even let the World Bank Head enter his province! Even though $40 million was at risk.

I got there for the meeting. The World Bank guy turned out to be a Brit, Oxbridge trained, and a National Twelve dinghy sailor against whom I might have raced on our local lake. So we had some very friendly prior discussions. I urged him to consider that the funding needed for the project was desperate, even though so little had been achieved. We'd now been assured the security situation was coming under increasingly firm control, and then progress might leap forward. The project should be given a chance in view of its massive problems and the desperate needs of the people. Tom stayed carefully absent at the local cinema, arriving just in time for the formal discussions, and left without saying anything. I flew back together to Khartoum in the World Bank plane.

My sister arrived in Khartoum and joined me in giving IT training to the HQ people. It was a familiar assignment for us, and they enjoyed the training. The World Bank review concluded that the project should continue providing a set of criteria, for example, for effective management, were met by the one following a year later. Tom went on leave to the UK, and actions were due to be taken on his first monthly progress meeting.

I resolved to go down to Kadugli by the time the next monthly meeting was due, and see what happened. That might be an acid test for me – was the whole business a whitewash for Tom's consumption, or were SKADP now in serious mode?

I had noticed an "Inception Report" by Robinson on the files, summarising the position on his engineering project, when he arrived. Copied to Masdar and, crucially, to the World Bank. This seemed a way of getting through to the PMU management, so I drafted my own "Inception Report" and included an accurate but fairly damning summary of progress on the project to date – providing much of the background I'd given informally for the World Bank review. In casual discussions among expats, I'd suggested a major problem in Sudan was "The Inshallah Factor". Inshallah is the Arabic and Islamic word for "God willing". And their God, as described brilliantly in the article I'd given to Kofi Annan, is a God who is incalculably powerful and remote, symbolised by the fierce heat, blinding sun and the harshness of the desert environment. Good intentions signify nothing if they do not suit His irresistible and inscrutable will.

This word "Inshallah" came into any discussion on progress and plans, as it does in many Arab countries. To me it conveyed the lack of confidence and determination which, I thought, contributed greatly to project problems. No-one would rely on anything happening, hence the mentality of the Soukh. Trust no-one and make your bargain while you can. Yesterday's friend may well be tomorrow's enemy.

I terminated my report urging the need for attitudes to change, and for us to be aware of the "Inshallah Factor" as a source of uncertainty, knowing this phrase might, for religious reasons, give great offence to Muslims. Alison typed it and I sent it off as a "draft for discussion" to the Sheikh, to Masdar, but also to senior people in the project and key contacts, to provoke a response.

The Sheikh called me in:

"Graham, this has been seen by many people, and has given offence."

"But it is a serious problem."

"Maybe so. But it has given offence."

Masdar in the UK were never to receive their copy.

I left word quietly for the Sheikh that I was going to attend his monthly meeting at Kadugli in two days' time.

Would the meeting be held, I wondered? Would he be there or not? This was the acid test of their commitment. Exciting stuff!

But my plan was to fail desperately.

So, Atif and I went on my second visit across the desert

with team members.

On the way south, we met up with a large team from the Project going north. They all tumbled out of the vehicles, shaking hands with each other and slapping and roaring with laughter. In retrospect, I guess they had all been ordered by the Sheikh to return to Kadugli and hold the progress meeting as Tom had specified

Later, we arrived in wooded and savannah land near near Kadugli, only to be stopped by a friendly young army commander "because there is fighting ahead".

During the night I woke up, wandered around and got lost. I saw the glow of a fire, made my way towards it. There were two old people. I greeted them:

"Salaam aleikum!"

"Aleikum Salaam."

"Al hamdulilla."

"Al hamdulilla."

And then I waited with them by their home till dawn, and then left.

I told Atif and he was horrified.

I felt a sort of worried detachment. After we reached the project offices, we sat at a desk in the open for a while.

"The Sheikh is worried about him," I heard.

Then I went to our compound.

When I'd settled in, there was a sudden burst of heavy machine gun fire from the barracks close by. I dived to the floor, recalling the experience of some friends in a similar situation in Kampala under Idi Amin. Forget your dignity, concentrate on surviving!

Like on the foredeck of a yacht in a gale – crouch down, hang on and crawl around – much more effective than standing up in dignity as the rise of a wave hurls you over the side!

The firing went on desultorily for maybe a quarter of an hour. Then there was quiet. I settled down, then heard stealthy noises outside. I flung the door open, and there was a fit, heavyset young army officer with my cook. I flung a punch at him, thinking he was persecuting the little cook. He parried it with ease, smiling as he did so, and grabbed me. I was taken down to stand at an office window I was to get to know later. And interrogated. All I would give was my name and affiliation – as in "name, rank and number" – as one was told to give to the army if captured. Nothing else.

The next incident I recall was sitting at a long table in the open, evening time, with about six officials interrogating me, and I sensed numerous people behind me. I was in the open before a long low building, and with a low euphorbia hedge behind me. I felt that I was under deep threat, refused to answer many questions, then suddenly flung myself upwards, flinging my arms outwards and letting out a colossal shout. They might well kill me, I thought, but rumours might survive for my son to track down in years to come. I was bundled onto a stretcher and trundled to a hospital ward. There I was awakened in the night by the sound of many people coming past my bed. Just visible in the light from dim oil lamps. A bit like being the corpse with mourners filing past.

An educated voice said:

"He talked to them in their own tongue, they say. Just

like one of them."

"Nonsense."

"Of course. Of course. But that's what they say."

For a week I was guarded by a soldier with a Kalashnikov in a corner in my room.

I refused to see Atif Rantendi. I believed that would protect him. He was pressing daily, but was ordered back across the desert to Khartoum. "And now I will never see the UK," he said, deeply troubled. A splendid guy.

I vaguely remember talking to a group in the project and asking if I could start the course on spreadsheets now.

Not yet, I was told, we have not finished with you yet.

Then many days later, I was invited to send a message home.

I wrote: "Happy birthday to my brother Bartholomew".

I had no brother Bartholomew. Bartholomew was the name of our much loved Labramatian.

My sister realised the telex was a plea for help, that something strange was up. She got on to MASDAR consultancy in the UK and set in train actions which eventually had me moved back across the desert, affected by acute psychosis, to a hospital in Khartoum. Thence they moved me to the American Embassy, where a formidable doctor fixed electrodes around my head and torso and shouted imprecations which I didn't understand. After he was satisfied with whatever he was doing, he relaxed and put me in a cot in his office. The next morning I was taken by a psychiatric nurse to the airport and hustled across a waiting zone towards a plane.

"This is a very ripe fruit cake indeed," I overheard him saying.

He had to take me off the first plane home because I was too violent, and kept me in the US security compound till the next day. Thence I was admitted to the splendid cavernous Parkside mental hospital in Macclesfield. There, it took a month of gentle treatment, experiments with various drugs and the healing effects of its lovely green parkland, to bring me back to partial sanity. Halfway through, I rolled out of bed in the morning twilight, crawled underneath all the beds, out onto the main road and started walking home. They picked me up after three miles and put me in a padded cell for half a day. There was a recurrence and I was sectioned, which means that you can be held in a mental hospital until cleared by two doctors.

My doctor, a splendid Dr Wareing, said I could have been drugged.

The Victorians understood mental illness in many far better ways than they did in 2018, when the grassland and healing coppice was replaced by desirable detached residences. A major factor in healing many mental afflictions is for a loved one to make love to the patient. You don't make love in a hospital ward. H. B. G-W

Chapter 12

The Villagers' Views and Engineering Comments from South Africa

The villagers

The two governments' proposals will place large structures and a causeway which will block off the view from our houses across the entire lagoon. This will have significant depredations for us and the tourist industry, right into the Rhinog mountains, some of the most rugged and least visited in Snowdonia. Including Lake Cwmbychan, the Roman Steps and the famous waterfalls. The much-loved Welsh Coast Path will be affected drastically.

To quote one of our member's experience of recent tidal effects:

"We were in our log cabin in Llanbedr and drove to the harbour to safeguard our boat as the great spring tide came swirling in. The sight was unbelievable, the huge slate quay was underwater. The road was flooded, and a quarter mile long waterfall of sea water cascaded down onto the fields. When the tide ebbed, great swathes of bank were carved away. It took three days' work by a helicopter just to plug the hole with mud."

This was the situation four years ago, and recent forecasts are of a further foot and a half rise in global tides in a few years to come.

The proposed engineering by the local lagoon protection group can easily take care of this, as will be detailed in October

The village's cultural background is delightful:

There is the annual raft race down the river – the crowds are sometimes so dense, they block off the railway line for half an hour.

There are two active choirs, one the Cambrian Coast Choir, the other that for St Peter's Church, where Sir John Black who created the Triumph Stag is buried.

The Cardiff Bay sailing clubs' annual long-distance race: the Squirrel trophy. So named because Eric Tutton, Chief Engineer of a Liverpool sweet manufacturer, had a wonderful ancient Vertue sloop called *Squirrel*, with a double diagonal wood hull. He fixed her up with an automatic wind vane steering system, locked it in place at the start gun of a race, then disappeared below to make a cup of tea, letting the wind decide on the course. The yacht often led at the first buoy, sometimes accompanied by a pod of the local dolphins.

The fishing inshore and offshore was splendid and once a 56lb tope was caught off the ten mile long St Patrick's Causeway.

The level causeway was believed by medievals to be the pathway along which St Patrick walked to convert the Irish to Christianity. Actually, the rocks are the terminal moraine from millennia of glacial melt from two conjoining rivers.

Wreck markers abound, and there is an East Passage inside it which was used for the drone tests.

A massive 24-gun ship from 1709, carrying 76 blocks of Carrara marble, lies in five metres at the apex of the passage, and is crucial to our account.

Engineering comments from South Africa

These notes were made by Graham Tottle in Cape Town on 14 February 2019. They cover his friend's, Eivind Thesen's, memory of contracts many years ago, and should be taken only as comments, but very relevant comments.

They describe a fairly typical "Iceland" spillway in the Cape. The security requirements in South Africa for dams are intense, hence the unlikely name we have chosen.

The spillways are large barriers which are raised and lowered to maintain chosen water levels in the vital dams, which is fundamental to South African agriculture and exports.

There is a rising gate on a massive horizontal hinge. It is balanced by a counterweight, similar to lift systems, to minimise the energy which is needed to raise and lower the gate. The dam contains about 55,000m³ of water, vastly greater than Llanbedr lagoon. Unlike the lagoon proposal, it cannot handle pressure from the outside in terms of wave effects. Unlike the dangerous open seas in Llanbedr, wave effects are not a problem as there is about half a mile of fetch inside the dam. It is about 8 miles across from one wing to the other.

Regarding construction, it is vital that the concrete is well vibrated as the concrete brackets are required to take a massive strain. The maximum depth of the water at the spillway is 30 feet – very similar to what's proposed for Llanbedr.

The keynote in design must be simplicity and, later, rigorous construction.

(From Eivind Thesen, a Civil Engineer graduate from Cape Town University with a 30-year long career in civil engineering. The notes are from his and his colleagues' memory of contracts many years ago, and should only be taken as comments.)

Chapter 13

Aberystwyth

I constructed this account from Lady Amanda's log book. H. B. G-W

On 5 June, the ketch, *Lady Amanda*, lay with easy grace at one of the pontoons at Aberystwyth, a picturesque snug seaside town and university city halfway down the 60-mile stretch of Cardigan Bay. Wide open like all the other little ports to the Irish Sea's wild south-westerlies, it was only safe to enter approaching high water, and even then it is a potential death trap when the south-westerly gales build the seas up.

It was 0800 and the crew were getting the boat ready for sea. Forecast wind only force 4; not much sea likely.

Later: it was 0820 and Robert McMichael called to Gareth apBews to clear the warps. Engine on and bow off downwind, they dropped down towards the entrance. On the pier head above them, a young woman walked, watching them head out to sea. Slender, dark-haired, probably Welsh, and fine skinned. Her gold sparkled grey eyes brightened with interest when she saw the turbulent sea state, invisible to the yachties. Then the figure on the foredeck caught her attention. Steadily, methodically and stylishly coiling in the warps. Perhaps a bowman, the sort of loner who swings easily way out above the waves and up onto the end of a spinnaker pole in a rolling seaway, retrieving halyards or some other foul up when normal mortals would blench and crawl aft on hands and knees into the cockpit.

Leaving Aberystwyth, you drop down river about a hundred yards from the pontoons, then take a sharp right angle turn to the west into the narrow channel. Eighty yards later you're out in the open sea. There it can be very rough and confusing as the high swells curve in and bounce back off the harbour walls. Before the turn, a sixth sense prompted McMichael to call to Gareth.

"Be ready with the jenny, Gareth. We may need it to push us through."

They swung round the end of the channel, and he saw heavy foaming crests right across the entrance ahead of them. Gareth was behaving with infuriating deliberateness, and waving nonchalantly to a young woman who was waving both arms vigorously from the pier head in return. He had his back to the line of the course, pulling in the fenders.

"For Christ's sake, Gareth, we can do that next year. Get the bloody genoa."

Gareth turned, saw the breakers romping across the entrance, then rushed to the cleats to let the genoa out and give the boat more power. But the wind, a good force 6, snatched the sail as it unrolled, and whipped the control lines out of his hands. The great foresail ballooned out to its full extent with a tremendous crack. The boat heeled sharply and the bow was thrust away to leeward towards the rocks, just ten yards off them.

No need to yell. Gareth had seen his mistake and was cranking away at the furling winch like a madman to get the sail back to a manageable size. McMichael had to choose whether to ram the throttle full ahead with the helm hard a-starboard using wind and engine to their max to turn and haul them off, or to slow down to get the sail under control. Caution might leave them pounding on the rocks, while speed might just get the hull and rudder biting the water in time to luff up and away from danger. Or drive them more violently to disaster.

He opted for speed. Throttle hard forward. They thumped into the first breaker, sliced it away in a shower of spray, but she maintained her speed and turned towards the port-hand boulders. But the weight of the sail gradually eased, and the bow crept a little towards safety. Four more combers and she was through. Both men were panting with shock and exertion, and they kept heading out westward.

Not for five minutes did either speak or change the sail trim.

It was an experience to live yourself away from in absolute silence, without moving any muscle unnecessarily.

Then rationality returned.

"Made a pig's ear of that, didn't I?" said Gareth.

"You could say that again. What I always say. Confidence is no substitute for competence."

"Bastard," said Gareth cheerfully. "All that woman's fault anyway."

The young woman on the pier head had watched, enthralled. Then turned to trot back along the front to the university. She skipped occasionally, hinting deliciously at a brim-full of joie de vivre. <u>Her name was Nadine. Nadine Humphrys Jones.</u>

Chapter 14

Robert McMichael's Background

I have constructed this account partly from the Bishops and Hurstpierpoint school records. Robert was a strange mixture of rigorous discipline and commitment, insensitivity in human relations, fascination with linguistics and an affection for African legends like the Xhosa tale of the Dassie's tail in Appendix 7. H. B. G-W

Robert McMichael was a good-looking 35-year-old, bred in Kalk Bay near Cape Town, South Africa.

Jackass penguins, Robert's home, Kalk Bay, in the distance.

A source of hope for the planet. In the 1990s, the penguins suddenly arrived from no-one knows where. The group must have swum together for a hundred or so miles through shark infested waters, settled and multiplied, and thrived.[12] Robert was educated at Hurstpierpoint College, UK and Bishops (Diocesan College) in the time of Clive van Ryneveld, at Cape Town University.

Clive was an extraordinarily gifted sportsman. He used to spend one year captaining South Africa at cricket and the next to earn enough as a lawyer to defend black victims of Apartheid. A leg spin bowler like Shane Warne, he took six for 57 against England's touring team under Doug Insole.

At Hurstpierpoint, Robert had been guided and goaded, goaded and guided, like many of his fellow historians, by Ken Mason, "Magpie", to question anything and everything. To question orthogonally. And these young historians moved on to Oxbridge and then to service. One to become ambassador to Russia, another to fly the Fairey Swordfish, a lumbering vulnerable biplane, one of which torpedoed the battleship *Bismark* as she entered the Western approaches to the English Channel, another to earn the Military Cross in Malaysia to help prevent a Chinese takeover and stop their southern Asia

---

[12] The jackass penguins, knee high to us, make a braying noise. This colony of fifty or so suddenly arrived near Mounts Bay, no-one knows whence. Explorers like humans perhaps, and swimming fast enough to outpace the predatory sharks.

According to some accounts, a pair were placed in Boulders in 1992, and thrived thereafter.

Sounds unlikely that a single pair could do so. If they were all descended from a single pair, there would be no new DNA entering the colony, they would be susceptible to new diseases and die out.

drive and another to develop IT systems for farms to develop agriculture in the Third World. And so on.

Flight Lt Arnold Robin served as a pilot in the Fairey Swordfish, a slow old biplane strung together with wires and carrying a single enormous torpedo underneath. Churchill ordered a squadron to join in the battle of Britain, and as expected they were all shot down and killed.

However, some time later, after much provocation by the Brits, part of the German fleet set out from safety in Kiel. Their greatest battleship, the *Bismark*, sank HMS *Hood*, broke through our blockade and disappeared into the Atlantic. It was picked up by a Swordfish when trying to enter the Channel – immensely menacing. The Swordfish were ordered to attack. Happily, one of their torpedoes hit the *Bismark's* steering gear and locked it over hard to port. So all it could do was circle until the destroyers finished it off.

Arnold was not involved in that battle, but he had some skirmishes with the Luftwaffe Messerschmitt fighters. Slowly trundling at a third of their speed, and so an easy target. The Swordfishs's response was to load up their cockpits with toilet rolls, and as the fighters came in, the toilet rolls were hurled out. The Messerschmitts sheered away to avoid this new British technology.

A dedicated cyclist, Robert annually took part on his Holdsworth Cyclone de Luxe in the great 14-day circuit in South Africa's Cape Province. Lightly bronzed, freckled, curly red hair, four years in the Zambian police and eight years with British DIFID – Department for International Development. He was on the same course as Nadine, but as a mature recruit to the UN Drugs Control Service.

The lecturer described skinnerism and an experiment with captive colobus monkeys, to train them to copulate with specially shaped tree trunks. The dark head and shoulders flinched slightly in a gesture delightfully expressive of feminine distaste. He absorbed with pleasure the precise inclination of the head, the forward movement of one shoulder. Robert's mind drifted further, a negligible conscious element jotting notes on his pad, the remainder tracking off down more vivid highways to pastures fresh and new. He assured himself that both lines of thought were under close control. That eyes, ears and writing hand were safely linked, leaving the rest free to wander.

"Skinnerism" took him back to the strangely unreal world of the late nineties and early noughties. Had they really believed it all? Serial monogamy. Rationality in international relations. What about Serbia? There are more things in heaven and earth, Professor Giddins, than are dreamt of in your global utopia. And the language. Depriving the kids of an understanding of grammar and syntax when it was fundamental to the technology of the times. What could be more structured and logical than an operating system, a database or a computer program? That was why classicists, particularly Latin classicists, had been so good. And yet there we were, following the Yanks, collapsing our language into participle-free, adjective-free, preposition-free, conditional-free strings of words. Shave cream, sail boat, whoop cough, box match, exit windows, click run. A language as unstructured, decayed, collapsed, pictorial and imprecise as Chinese.

His mind drifted further. The dark-haired girl. He remembered Yvonne. He'd set about to forget Yvonne and search for another girl. An astonishing rippling river of dark hair, she'd have. Unlike this one, whose hair was far too short. A concealing dark cascade to reveal a long, slender white neck. Sitting demurely at the helm yet letting his hands rove sweetly unseen. Like John Donne. He'd need to get another boat to replace his old boat. Something long-keeled, classic, wooden, a finely panelled main cabin, green enamelled charcoal-burning stove, double bunk upholstered in yellow silk? Irresistible. If only you can get her there.

Try Soulmates in *The Observer* perhaps?

"Womanly woman required by manly man with large yacht. 36, 29, 7."

No, not "required" – too abrupt. Too imperative. Important to convey how gently sensitive he was.

"Longed for", maybe. Might get confused with the boat's length.

"Needed", perhaps?

Or "Sought"? Conveys a yearning.

"Yearned for"? No, no. A manly man wouldn't yearn for anything. Even a yacht. Or not in public anyway.

"Sought" was good. Sounds Old English. I seek, thou seekest. He, she or it seeks. We, you or they…

His hand tried desperately to cope with parallel meandering streams of consciousness.

He found out that the woman came from the eastern counties. That she liked swimming. And that other men on the course found her attractive. This attention she had obviously met and parried before. Nevertheless, standing in a group and watching some demonstration or other, he half consciously moved to where the light caught her face, where he could glance unobserved at the fall of her lashes on her pale cheeks. Or where the gentle thrust of her breasts was outlined by some fortuitous interplay of light and shade against the gadgetry, a sweet curve in a white sweater against the four-foot high angular 2970 computer. He watched and waited patiently for her to sigh with boredom, for the clinging sweater to move slightly with the shift of her breasts beneath.

The following Sunday, Robert went with his colleagues to the crowded Cathedral for the mandatory matins – this is an un-Britishly religious outfit evidently.

Robert suddenly saw the dark-haired girl process in with the sopranos. To his intense pleasure, the sopranos were diagonally alongside him; forward a little and maybe 30 feet away, and that entrancing woman was nearest to him. He watched her unconscious mannerisms: tilting her head to one side for passages of beseechment, and, most appealing, her swinging her shoulders slightly side to side while her head stayed still as she sang the familiar responses, as her mind and soul perhaps drifted free along some celestial off-piste powdered snows. Then the psalm:

O let my tongue cleave to my mouth if I remember thee not!

By the rivers of Babylon, there we sat and wept / remembering thee Zion; on the poplars that grow there / we hung our harps

O let my tongue cleave to my mouth if I remember thee not!

The dean's sermon starts. Pere Dil preaches with conviction.

Pere Dil, at the helm in his pulpit, fails to hold the girl's attention. She has unusually long lashes; they lay a dark curved curtain across her cheeks.

"And now, Congregation, in the name of the Father…"

The sermon ends. At the end of the service the choir processes out to a final soaring descant. Iced water trickles down your spine, making the down tingle. That silvery timbre might be her voice. Tricky though. He would see her. He is determined to. He slips out as politely as possible, but still rudely, through the throng waiting to shake Dil's massive paw, and those of his smiling associates. Round through the Lady Chapel. There she is. But also a man, obviously close to her; came to fetch her. Sod's law. But maybe not amatorially close. And there she is, gone off with the bugger. In an Aston as well.

Nadine. Nadine Humphrys Jones.

Walking inattentively down the cloister after one course session, and admiring the swing of her kilt ahead of him, he was startled when she spun round and faced him.

"Will you stop staring at me during lectures?"

Not a request, more of a broadside. The "Will" was hardly more than whispered, more hissed with burning intensity, through lips spread thin beneath tight nostrils and flashing eyes. Shattering.

Dumbfounded with surprise and something else – elation? Hope? – he tripped and fell flat on the flag-stones. As he hit, he gasped out:

"No."

She looked down concernedly:

"Oh dear. I'm so sorry."

"Or yes," he said. "Yes, if you'll have coffee with me."

A flicker of suspicion, then she relented and walked with him to the refectory.

They collected their cups from the urn and talked rather like strangers in a railway buffet car.

He noticed the way her chin puckered slightly when she talked on certain issues. Rather like a child's chin, quivering as tears approach.

Unprepared for his good fortune, he dredged his mind for something significant to say.

"What do you think of the course so far?"

Don Juan Robert, not on his most sparkling form. She looked unimpressed.

"Quite a key step in your career progression," she said. "Like the old army Staff College, only in Government Information Systems."

Still, he'd talked to her.

Chapter 15

Death Death Death

The approach by the group to all of Wales attracted massive media support, but not enough to persuade the governments to pull out. So the appeal to the UK and worldwide took off.

But, to illustrate the level of some Welsh hostility to the English in Gwynedd, below is a report from Porthmadog, near Llanbedr, and correspondence between Graham Tottle and Lord Cecil Parkinson:

An Englishman turns into the pub on Porthmadog Main Street. He picks up a drink at the bar and slips into a position on the left at the back. The guy next to him turns towards him.

"You English?" he asks. Hostile voice.

"Yes."

The Welshman moves away in revulsion.[13]

The Welsh are playing England in the Rugby Six Nations cup. England are tipped to win the grand slam.

---

[13] According to Tudor archaeologists, the English are in fact Welsh, and the Welsh are in fact English.

As his eyes become attuned to the darkness, the English man sees that the pub is full of well-built men, all dressed in Welsh rugby jerseys.

The preliminary anthem is sung passionately:

Land of our fathers

The English anthem,[14] *God save the Queen*, is greeted with derision.

The game starts. It's immensely physical, with scores even towards half-time. Each time Wales scores, a leading Welshman on the left in the pub stands up and punches the air.

"Death… Death… Death,

Death to the English bastards."

The entire pub stands up, punches the air and howls:

"Death… Death… Death,

Death to the English bastards."

At half-time the Englishman slips away, sickened, and listens to the remainder of the game on the radio on his boat.

What poison is it, he reflects, that generates this hatred of the English. I'm an Anglo-Scot. I've worked for, alongside and under lots of Welshmen. Easy-going, happy, bright, never a racial break, occasional fun and banter. But get them in their superb homeland round Porthmadog, and from the yobboes the bile spills out. Never mind the friendliness of the Tal-

---

[14] Now replaced by the moving spiritual: "Swing Low, Sweet Chariot".

y-Bont Gardening Club, never mind Shakespeare's Captain Llewellyn, these few people are frightening. Frightening and threatening. Frightening, threatening and burning.

The Welsh win triumphantly.

Following this account from Graham's book, below is a letter from him to Lord Parkinson, a much loved key advisor to Prime Minister Margaret Thatcher over many years, followed by Parkinson's reply. He can be seen on the Falklands video at the window of number 10, waving with her and Dennis Thatcher to a rejoicing crowd, celebrating victory in the Falklands War. He was the leader of the war cabinet. Parkinson was the son of a railwayman in Lancashire who won a scholarship to Emmanuel College, Cambridge. He was a brilliant quarter miler and Secretary of the University Athletics Club

Personal

Thrumble Coombe
2 Maes Artro,
Llanbedr, Gwynedd LL45 2PZ
07866852079 (No BT available)
tottles111@gmail.com
1/10/13

Dear Cecil,

You may remember that we rowed together in the Emmanuel banana boat[15] in the 1950s. Very memorable. And Peter Hunt who also rowed with us for the Emanuel

---

[15] A 1930 design, banana boat because the seats were staggered transversely and it steered like a banana. It was a notorious assignation which never qualified for the races even with four Cambridge blues aboard.

athletics club: is still a close friend with whom I have worked with in Uganda.

I write now because I, like you, I am sure, am deeply concerned at the drift towards independence for Scotland and Wales.

I have recently moved from Cheshire to Harlech in North Wales, and find that the antipathy towards the English and towards the Westminster government has grown deeply, sometimes to the extent of real hatred. Watching Cameron on television recently, I had the clear impression that he is completely unaware of this.

A suggestion, which may be daft, is that HS2 could be authorised, but it could span from London to Glasgow. The economic costs would of course be fantastic, but the results in terms of tying the UK together again seem even more important. And you as a railway enthusiast, a railwayman's son and a creator, might be the guy to do it.

Like you, I had an adventurous life, greatly relished. In my case, the adventure carried me around the world in Third World countries and perilous times in Iraq, Uganda and Sudan. I have written a near future sci-fi novel based around all this, which you may find entertaining. It features Emma, the IT industry, North Wales, the US and Uganda. It's called "Point of divergence" on Amazon, et al.

I have done what little I can to oppose the trend to devolution, including the letter to large numbers of Scottish local newspapers, which I give below.

I hope you flourish as I do, writing and carrying out various functions like museum curator, secretary ship of Our

Dunes preservation group, and keeping splendid old wooden boats afloat.

Best wishes,
Graham Tottle

****

Dictated by LORD PARKINSON and signed by Susan O'Donnell, Lord Parkinson's Personal Assistant:

Dear Graham,

It was a really pleasant surprise to hear from you. I remember our times at Cambridge very well and I particular remember Peter Hunt. If you are in touch with him, please give him my warmest best wishes.

I am now the proud possessor of your book, which I intend to take to our home in Spain when we go there for our next break.

North Wales has always been a problem area for the Conservative Party and if we were ever inclined to forget the antipathy of parts of North Wales towards us, then we have the Welsh Nationalists as a continuing reminder.

Scotland is another matter. In my early days in the Commons, we had a substantial body of MPs, but there was a gradual decline and now we have virtually no representatives at Westminster. The Thatcher Government is often blamed for this, but I can assure you that during her time in office, we fell over backwards to pump money into Scotland and to support Scottish industries which, had they been located in England, would have been closed years before. We could, however, never outspend Labour and I'm afraid that Scotland now is more of a public sector responsibility than a country!

When I went back to Central Office as William Hague's Chairman, I met the leaders of the Scottish Conservative Party to discuss its future. They stressed that they must not be seen as a branch of the English Conservative Party and that they needed effectively to be independent except in one respect: London should continue to fund them! I found your letter to the Scottish press really interesting and persuasive. I only hope it is striking a chord with those who read it. I certainly feel we can win the Scottish referendum and I earnestly hope we do.

If you ever come to London, with or without Peter Hunt, I would love to see you both again, and to entertain you to lunch in the House of Lords. This is a serious invitation!

Kindest regards,

Cecil

The lunch was eventually cancelled through Parkinson's advanced cancer, and he returned to his home in Spain to die. The Guardian obituary was unbelievably hostile. Never mind that as a Lancashire railwayman's son, a scholarship boy, he led the war cabinet in the Falklands War. That he nearly became Prime Minister. Fine for guys to have mistresses aplenty. But going home to wife and family? Verboten.

Chapter 16

Gors-y-Gedol

Following up on his drug line as discussed in l'Écu de France,
BLZ came to Maes-y-Neuadd in the north-west of Llanbedr.
It's a fine mansion, overlooking the area. The Kennedys had
stayed there on their trip to the UK and Ireland, soon before US
President John Kennedy was assassinated. Jacqueline Kennedy,

---

[16] Two red kites are often seen circling high over Llanbedr. Fierce predators with five-foot wingspans. Approach one when it's on its prey, and it will turn and glare at you. Come closer and it will truculently fly slowly away.

later the jet setter of jet setters, loved it. One of her letters sold for about a hundred thousand pounds. The Harlech choir sang for them in the church of Llanfihangel-y-Traethau, ever since a special place for American visitors and poets.

Recalling the jagged, slatey, car-scraping walls of Gwynedd, Jock seems to have brought west the Thunderbird, as well as the Stag. A bikers' paradise, swinging and belting around the winding hillside, lakeside and mountain roads from Dolgellau into Snowdonia. Preserve the Stag and its British Racing Green hard top; keep it safe off the lanes.

My source for this is a background note in the police files in Macclesfield, Cheshire. It arose from discussions they had with a firm called MSS, Macclesfield Surveillance Services. The firm had delivered and installed complex surveillance equipment, including eight readouts. This is the engineer's report:

We drove south from Llanbedr on the A496 to Tal-y-Bont, then turned left at the North Lodge and climbed a straight road high up the hill a good mile or so to this great manor place, Gors-y-Gedol.[17] It was already open for us and we installed all the kit and tested it out. A well-chosen site, the signals from all around the area were good. The place was a fine old mansion, really fine. Someone must have never had it so good, and there was a Triumph Stag, yellow and green, standing in the courtyard. Bonnet open; tools on the ground.

The one with the two engines bolted together was a V8. Cool. Totally unreliable at first, but better every year since.

---

[17] Probably "bog of the people" – higher above the mansion was a lake and a bog in which various flora, notably orchids, flourish.

Twin exhausts. V8. So probably a '78 or so model. Spent the night in the Victoria Inn, see invoice, and returned to Macclesfield the next day.

Gors-y-Gedol.

Chapter 17

Amygdala

In Uganda's riverine town of Masindi Port, you notice a strange phenomenon. The far bank of the Victoria Nile, which is half a mile away, seems to be gradually sliding past. Sliding past about 1.5 knots, say 2mph. But you are looking not at the far bank of the river, but at one of the massive islands of papyrus which have been peeled off upstream in the vast swampy Lake Kyoga.

Several miles away downstream, the longest, fattest and happiest crocodiles in this world are basking on platforms of pureed papyrus. Their breakfast lunch and supper are passing by, plus nibbles.

In between them and Masindi Port upstream is the first wonder of the world. Foaming white and roaring. The Murchison falls.

Go back and up 150 feet, and you walk along a little sandy path through the flat bush. Then you round a bend. To see the river, the entire River Nile, suddenly slipping away through a gap only 19 feet wide, cutting down to hammer against a diagonal cliff, to bounce off and hurtle down. Given a straight run up, a good long jumper could clear it easily. The jumper would need considerable confidence. This is not a feat which could be accomplished as it can in the Niagara Falls or the Victoria Falls by a chap in a padded-out barrel.

Go up to one of the basking crocodiles below with a 410 elephant gun and blast its brains out. It will turn and scramble down into the water. This is the crocodile's amygdala taking control from a centre 2 feet away from its brain. In warm-blooded animals, the brain structure has been compressed and the amygdala is at the centre of the brain. But it has the same function, immensely fast access direct from the visual cortex in response to disaster situations. It overrides the much slower normal processing of information through the area where images and sounds are processed and actions are taken. Similar to the top priority processes in computers – IBM 360 and ICL System 4 – their P4 routines take care of events like fire and turn on sprinklers or whatever.

A man is climbing up from Kirstenbosch Botanical Gardens to the plateau of Table Mountain in South Africa. Slung over his shoulder in a grey bag is a tourist kit, and hidden in the kit, a Kalashnikov. The vast plateau is topped with small mountains which Afrikaners call kopjes. He makes his way around or through them, and through a narrow gap which leads out to a vertiginous ledge hovering over a two-thousand-foot drop. On the road below is a grey Volkswagen. He gets out a searchlight and flashes twice. The VW also flashes twice. He assembles the Kalashnikov and settles down to watch the cable car station.

The cable car starts winding its way up and he lies flat.

Down, crawl, observe, sights, fire.

Nothing seems to happen. He loses off a whole magazine and then another. Then the cable car is safe in the top station. No-one seems to have noticed. He eases himself back along the ledge. A white man is blocking his way, viewing the panorama. His name is Robert McMichael. He is watching a dassie[18] and its young.

The assassin waits and waits. The VW flashes, and flashes insistently. Eventually he reaches out and grabs McMichael's belt to try and throw him off the cliff. But McMichael's amygdala clicks in.

He swings round and thumps the assassin in the jaw as he had been taught by Ronnie Karstad, some time middleweight champion of South Africa. The assassin slips down and away, screaming. 2,000 feet. Accelerating at 108 feet per second. Tumbling into the brittle, grey protea.

McMichael is horrified and hastens down to Kirstenbosch and phones the police.

The police investigate. They find a broken Kalashnikov, two magazine's full of cartridge shells and a great swathe in the brittle protea which has been smashed down. But no body. The assassin has been carried away alive after a very successful exercise. Didn't kill the High Commissioner but Al Qaeda had made their point.

---

[18] The dassies are delightful, intelligent rabbit-sized creatures, next of kin to the elephant. Also called coneys in the Bible.

Chapter 18

Westminster and Cardiff Decide

Despite worldwide appeals, the Welsh Assembly and the UK government authorised implementation of the Spaceport Access plan. Detailed planning of the airfield access road started.

Dawkinsism was just taking off.[5]

Timeline

In 2023, following Boris Johnson's election on the 12th December 2019, these occurrences were during the second Trump Presidency, and Theresa May's third as Prime Minister in the UK, but before the first Agricultural war.

It was the time after the extraordinary first election of Theresa May, which is still now, decades later, a fascination for historians.

Striking was the deep hostility of the leading BBC commentator, Laura Kuenssberg. Clearly she was extremely well educated and experienced, yet she persisted in highlighting allegations, notably using the word "GAMBLE", when she must have known, as most media people did, that the reason for the election was not a GAMBLE. It was the developing hostile sniping of all the other parties, which would seriously have jeopardised the Brexit process.

Other presenters, especially David Dimbleby, failed to draw out the obvious weaknesses in the debate, for example, against the development of the Trident nuclear missile launcher. He should have pointed out, especially to youthful watchers, that the threat of nuclear holocaust had world wars. They should recall that there were no world wars in the second half of the twentieth century. And that the nuclear bombs on Japan had shortened WWII by three years and saved millions of lives.

***

In 2020, in parallel with starting the construction of the northern access road to Llanbedr, the UK's planned spaceport, and its airfield, manufacturing facilities were set-up to produce the VEM, what the public came to call dronebots (*raised previously*). The UK lead in this technology continued with massive worldwide interest. Much was centred on Manchester and Macclesfield in the north-west. The prototype VEM eventually passed production trials and manufacturing commenced. The standard acceptance tests involved the usual QA tasks, ranging from bump tests, etc., to the much dicier aspects of software development, high level simulation, orthogonal diagnostics, independent validation, beta tests and so on. Finally, each VEM was demonstrated,[19] taking off from a rolling platform on the airfield simulating the sea, flying out at low-level, six miles west out to sea, focusing on Harlech Castle's left most tiny

---

[19] Amazing how many products, allegedly covered even down to Quality Assurance, collapse at simple demonstration. IBM once issued software to support a new and important, but fairly simple, device. It was unusable! What were the top managers doing?

octagonal aperture. The image was relayed back to base and analysed. Meanwhile, if it passed, the VEM was returned to base for packing and transport to the purchaser.

Boeing's car swaps the highway for a skyway

Castle's left most tiny octagonal aperture. The image was relayed back to base and analysed. Meanwhile, if it passed, the VEM was returned to base for packing and transport to the purchaser.

(Picture from *The Times*)

Chapter 19

Dujaily and the Drugs Administration

Dujaily escaped during the savagery after the second Iraq War. He was eventually appointed as director in the Drugs Surveillance Commission of the UN.

World production of hard drugs had amounted to over $400 billion. South America's military elite now made drugs not war. Countries unable to grow their own were offering sophisticated forms of transportation as a means of getting into in the business. Quoted from Chapter 6 in John le Carre's Single and Single.

This describes a most important drug surveillance project:

It is based on a report from Dujaily's files, which was submitted by a Graham Tottle, an EU consultant.

St Vincent, like most of the other Windward Islands in the West Indies, but on a vaster vertical scale, is a towering volcanic island, rising straight out of the deep Atlantic into its prevailing winds. Its jungle and banana-girt on the lower slopes; tropical rain forest among the high crags. The volcano, La Souffriere, is occasionally live. "Found" by Columbus on his third voyage. "Windward" because they are the islands the Europeans first reached, to windward of the rest. Not at all popular with tourists, for it has only one tiny strip of yellow tourist-friendly sand and much dark coarse volcanic sand fringing many precipitous coves. So deep you can't anchor yachts, and they have to use shore lines to palm trees from one side of a cove to another. At substantial rental to the tree-owners!

St Vincent's only harbour is dominated by Young Island. It's a pinnacle of rock atop which six British marines and a gun once held the French blockaded for several months. There you feel as if you are in a naval yarn of the 1790s by the incomparable Patrick O'Brian. The French and Brits fought over St Vincent for two centuries, in which the island changed hands 14 times. Escaped slave communities lived 6,000 feet up in the peaks and raided both sides effectively and impartially. The tropical semi-paradise is the scene of an ICL IT drama because IT was one of the keys in the economic struggle between the independent, impoverished smallholders of the islands and the powerful mechanised US-owned estates, Chiquita and Dole, on the South American mainland – the prize being the banana slots in European householders' pantries. The key issue is whether the smallholders, with only up to 3 acres of hillside apiece, can excel the quality of the produce of the big South American estates despite the estates' great advantages of flat land (the Vincentians have to cultivate on slopes as steep as the flanks of the English downs), size, mechanisation, capital and large-scale production.

The EU consultant, Graham, flew in and settled into one of three hotels in Umbrella Bay by Young Island Cut, the channel between Young Island and the mainland. Exquisitely beautiful. Then he went into Kingstown to work at SVBGA, the St Vincent Banana Grower's Association. It was in sombre dark green two-storey offices in the south of the town, in a vast factory and shipping area dominating the port, and also in dispersed extension and processing centres under the mountains among the growers. Bananas were by far and away the island's premier industry.

On his morning pre-breakfast snorkelling, once or twice through the crystal-clear water, Graham saw a Danforth anchor lying on the sand thirty or so feet below him. Once it had a small packet up a line floating just six feet from the surface. He snorkelled on, mildly curious, but thinking of the day's work to come.

It was widely known that drug runners from Colombia sailed up to West Indian latitudes at dusk one day, and that at the next dawn they were all setting off due south again. What did they do in the 12 hours of darkness. Who can tell – there are all manner of little islands to which they might have gone.

As Graham scrambled one dusk along a low, broken narrow wall just above the beach, round the deeply curved bay hung over with great jungle trees over the water, there was a thudding of steady footsteps behind him.

"You Mr Tottle?" a deep, slow and threatening voice demanded.

"Yes."

"Mr Tottle from Umbrella Beach Hotel?"

"Yes."

"I don't got nothing against you. Not personally I don't. But you should know this is a dangerous place for you to walk. A very dangerous place. Not a good place at all."

He was a big man. A very big man. The size of Viv Richards. Graham turned off and up to the nearest hotel and a nervous beer, then set the incident back in his mind, too absorbed in his own concerns. Only after the end of the assignment did the realities sink in. Graham then went for a day's scuba diving at nearby Bequi Island. And as he followed the dive leader through a forest of swaying kelp – it wasn't good diving terrain, claustrophobic tendrils of kelp reaching out at you – the skin on his back suddenly crawled. He felt an overpowering instinct to get away, maybe from the murderers following him through the weed. The amygdala section of his brain in action perhaps. He gestured to the dive leader to go up to the boat. Somewhat annoyed, the dive leader refused at first, then did so.

He recalled then that all the other consultants had been told very firmly that Umbrella Beach Hotel was full.

But it wasn't. Far from it.

But someone didn't want inquisitive morning-snorkelling consultants around. Tourists OK. Test teams OK (England were then touring and everything stopped in the island to watch it). But curious consultants, no.

Should Graham have reported all this further? Perhaps so, but who knows what threads might get drawn from it, and leading to whom? He let it lie.

***

Years later, Dujaily met Graham, talked through his report and looked through his staff availability lists. BLZ was known to be involved in the West Indies and had just acquired a property in North Wales. Dujaily was told to liaise with a Jock Rundle from MI6, the UK's Intelligence Service in the international druggist and terrorist identification organisation. They'd met, he remembered, in Baghdad.

Rundle briefed him. Inside the UK, he said, the track led from the Welsh market town of Shrewsbury to Birmingham. But how did the drugs get to Shrewsbury from the West Indies?

BLZ's property was in Llanbedr. Was this a pointer?

So Dujaily decided to set up his headquarters in Llanbedr and chose the splendid old Victoria Inn just alongside the bridge over the Artro, across the road from Hen Fecws, the old bakery, and the Wenallt tea rooms and delicatessen.

He took over the restaurant as their work room, and the new team would use the very fine traditional rooms individually. Communications access was appalling, as it was in most of Gwynedd, and so they set up a new mast on the hilltop.

He looked at McMichael's background. A tad aggressive, but well committed. Educated in Cape Town, trained in the Royal Corps of Signals, British Army, and five years in the Zambian Police, though a strange report on Sudan. Had worked with DIFID.[20] Sounded promising as a leader.

He recruited also a Gareth apBews, trained more recently. Local guy, spoke Welsh, athletic, principled and ambitious. They would be the two to get action.

So Dujaily assigned Robert McMichael and Gareth apBews to track the drug activities, and follow up on any links to BLZ. Dujaily was informed that it was suspected that BLZ ran a vast drug-running network in the area.

---

[20] Department for International Development, UK.

Chapter 20

Scottish Independence

I unearthed these descriptions among information just released under the Freedom of Information act.
H. B. Goulding-Williams, Emmanuel College, Cambridge, 23 July 2039.

Three miles south of the famous or infamous Sauchiehall Street[21] in Glasgow is a bowl in the hills containing a reddish brown 400m running track. Three runners are taking the circuit, bounding along as if their legs were taut springs. Grinding the ash with their spikes. Fine, straight black hair, high cheekbones, slitty eye sockets, bronzed faces. Might have been cousins to Man United's fine inside left, Jee Sung Parc.

They work at EKB, Motorola Corporation,[22] peoples' affectionate term for their main Glasgow computer and systems development centre in East Kilbride.

They are the East Asia Software Team, something

---

[21] This area on a Saturday night is crowded out with aggressively nationalist inebriated gangs, many with frightening careers in the Black Watch and Royal Corps of Signals, as pictured in books by McCall Smith.
[22] Motorola invented the first in-car radios and have pioneered micro-miniaturised systems ever since, including the Apple computer processors.

of a mystery to their colleagues, and they are writing the software with Koreanised versions of dBase, Linux, Java, PHP and an obscure assembler. The beautiful Korean script is not widely understood.

They are hacking. They are hacking the leading bit of the PC's twenty-four hour clock. And from it they are hacking leading bits of a very large number of twenty-four hour clocks in the Internet.

They are also writing little apps. The little apps skulk around in dark corners. The little apps are kicked off by assorted twenty-four hour clocks in assorted ways.[23]

Six miles out from the centre of Edinburgh to the East beyond Arthur's Seat, lies the seat of the Duke of Buccleugh. High up on rugged hills, it's called the Dalkeith Palace. Below it, dark woods and turbulent streams cascade down to the Firth of Forth and the sea.

You enter the palace into a splendid, sprawling, marble atrium, with a broad spiral staircase leading to the mezzanine floor. As you go in, you may also enter one of several fine doors, probably of Honduras cedar.

One door leads to a large reception centre, occupied by managers, PAs and clerks using numerous computer terminals. On the far side, in the corner where the wooden mouldings dovetail, is a discreet small round brass knob a centimetre across. Press this knob down and a section of the wall swings open. Go through it and you are in the Duke's personal private centre of operation.

---

[23] A common problem in all operating systems. On ICL's System 4, the vital MTBF (mean time between faults) stuck just below 24-hrs. Reason? The software and hardware disagreed on the bit setting.

From here the activities to control the process of Scottish and British severance are directed.

The walls between Scotland and Britain are in place. Many had been built under the Roman Emperor Hadrian. The standard EU immigration controls are crucial, and have already been developed as on the more normal passport and other checking systems at Britain's external frontiers. Seven lane passport channels on the M6 and A74(M) and the A1, standard overseas clearance procedures are applied, with thistle to sterling to euro currency conversion desks, for example, for passengers at the big airports. On the trains, the expresses offer immigration clearance en route from Edinburgh and Glasgow to the border and the British cities to speed things up. But scrutiny at the border takes place for those on stopping trains.

Prime Minister May now faced the same decision as was faced by the British Governor, Earl Mountbatten, at independence for India in 1946. Mountbatten had had to decide whether to cut the Gordian[24] knot and grant independence immediately, or to work through the situation politically to try to circumvent the bitter determination of Pandit Nehru and the Indian Hindus, against the totally inflexible Liaquat Ali Khan leading the Pakistan Islamic movement. In the end, Mountbatten sliced the Gordian knot almost immediately, the national boundaries were defined

---

[24] The Gordian knot – it was said that this complex knot had to be unravelled by any possible ruler before he could take power.
Alexander the Great solved the problem with a single blow, slicing through it with his sword.

and train loads of people crossed the two new countries' frontiers in the face of hostile populations who often raided the coaches, raped the women, stole the belongings and slaughtered the men. Mountbatten's action in this has often been assessed, and the common judgment is that, as with the use of nuclear bombs over Japan which ended WWII, the death roll and the agonies were appalling but minimised. Two years of violent war and deaths were avoided.

Diary note by TM

Meeting in Dalkeith went well. Present were Nicola Sturgeon and Dewar for the Scots, and Jock Rundle and me for the Brits. Professor Stag was our technical advisor in view of his status and background.

Found him incomprehensible. Big burly fellow. Dominated everything in a cheerful way. Strings of pauses, stammers and jargon. "Chuch… chuch… eckpoint Hub… bub… h-ump h-estart… bu… bub… bub." Professor of Computation, University of Manchester. Professor Directing Communication Systems, UK. Visiting Professor of this in Singapore. Visiting Professor of that in Beijing. How on earth does he do it? Does he exploit his stammer to gain respect and attention? What's he like at home? But the bagpipes were splendid. Moving. Soon we'll not hear them like that again.

Jock Rundle was, as usual, particularly effective, a tower of strength. He insisted on resumability for all Information Technology and urged us all not to make Margaret Thatcher's mistake in imposing the Poll Tax in 1987, the mistake which brought her down. We will instead start with "Beta tests" as they call them, and full system trials to ensure that the management of immigration at the airports, the M6 and lesser borders and the railways would work effectively. As well as give the public familiarity and confidence.

So, we agreed to warn the public and to have a TST, a total system trial, on Saturday and Sunday.

Should be exciting. I'll travel back from Westminster to see the show.

Jock wanted me to ride pillion on his Triumph Thunderbird. Seemed like fun, but inappropriate.

"Cocky wee fella wi' a pointy ney" is how one of the Scots described him.

TM

The TST was a great success, so the Prime Ministers ordered full Independence to be applied on Saturday and Sunday, 11 and 12 September 2021. All road, rail and air services had to stop at the borders, where people had to go through the usual EU, UK and Scottish immigration checks for whichever of the countries they were entering. Come and wave your passport. Change yourself some Thistles or Sterling. Buy some haggis. Buy our Kendall mint cake.

Worldwide media coverage would be intense. Come and see the fun. Brits at their best. Nearly as good as the Falklands War.

Top army and police officials had attended discussions as to how the new procedures would be managed. It was all going to happen.

Just like that.

The three months of chaos which followed and led to the Reunification, are widely written up of course. The occasional language changes on the motorway, and road signs, were rather pleasing. People soon grasped the meaning of "PAN SEFWCH OLAU COCH SEFWYCH YMA".

But most effective, I think, was the randomness of the interrupts. The M6, for example, would sometimes open all lanes then inexplicably close some or all after drivers had hastened and queued for the slots, and ATMs would open and close apparently randomly. Even the public toilets would run out of paper or lock solid with someone inside. Compared with the damage that could have been done, of course, this was fairly benign. The messing up of all British people's dental records, appointments and so on caused pain for many who had teeth. But do the same for medical records – easily done – would have caused deaths.

I would add that the detail of the Motorola East Asia project has only just come to my notice from a friend in Google Motorola's HR department who wishes to be nameless. They seem to have left for Seoul just before the total systems trial.

A US CIA agent tracked three Koreans from Seoul Airport at Inchon. They made for the beach, waved cheerily to him and sprinted to a far distant inflatable and were carried off. He puffed after them, but they were well offshore and taken on board what may have been one of the North Koreans' new stealth submarines.

He returned through a gate to his bike.

A Brit on a Triumph Thunderbird was watching. Number plate JR999.

"Nice Bike," said the Yank.

The Brit enthused.

"Not a patch on a Harley," said the Yank.
"Fine if you're fit, fat and over 40."
H. B. G-W

Chapter 21

Friendly Debates Between Gareth and Robert

Dujaily listened in occasionally to keep in touch, and recorded a few for interest.
They were talking about languages and their complexity.

Robert:

My service in Uganda necessitated learning Luganda, and Runyankore/Rukiga, using the Rukiga in normal daily work in the Sazas and Gombololas, and this prompted a great interest in the Bantu languages. How was it that many millions of people speaking over 1,000 languages, all got to use the same complex grammatical strucures, with the same grammatical rules as applied in the 1920s England, and in Latin? Active and passive moods, reflexive, imperative, subjunctive, etc. No Academie Francaise to keep it all under control.

Gareth: Interesting, but what's that got to do with us now?
Robert argued that as an Anglo-Scot, a citizen of the UK, he had a right to feel at home anywhere. Gareth arguing that the four countries were different, and had the right to fight for their identities: different histories, different geographies,

different geologies,[25] different languages, different temperaments. Take Scotland – brilliant thinkers, brilliant engineers, but entirely lacking the intuitiveness and subtlety to succeed in marketing. For that you needed other talents: Empathy, charm and confidence. Attitudes bred in the south-east and the English and Welsh "public schools".

Take, as an example, the way in which people greet each other. There were comments by people who went to church services and were then overwhelmed by unwanted hugs. The Hugathon.

"My partner, five foot one, in a charming bright red jacket, was surrounded at the rear of the crowded church at the communal harvest service for our large area."

Later on in the service, we came to the frequent stage:

"Let us now show to each other the sign of peace."

At this, it is customary to handshake with people around.

But she was trapped, trying to avoid contact with complete strangers, and was hauled to the chests of two men, about six feet tall, complete strangers.

"That convinces me," she said later. "I'll never become an Anglican."

There has been much talk recently in the press, for instance Sean Hagan in *The Observer*, about our dwindling "Britishness". And about our "loss of identity".

Let's bring our identity back. To strangers, a handshake and a warm smile are what to do. Remember the explorer H. M. Stanley's meeting with Dr Livingstone in the heart of unexplored Eastern Africa. A handshake.

---

[25] Scotland is shown by skeletal microorganisms to have drifted east across the Atlantic from America, and thumped into the north-west of the English coast in the UK.

And let's recall that there is a political dimension in our purchasing. Don't buy Chinese if you can get Indian.

"Doctor Livingstone, I presume."

If it was good enough for them, it's good enough for us. There is a statue of Stanley in his home village, hand held out beguilingly.

Robert suggested there was a political aspect of consumption. Don't buy Chinese stuff if you can get Indian.

Moving on, he described what he called the toilet test. The Brits had a highly-structured society, and you can illustrate this by looking at the various words for the toilet:

Lavatory, bog, loo, toilet, shithouse.

And in most conversations, the use of certain words enabled you to immediately place the speaker in a certain category. For example, if a guy talked of the bog, he was probably from one of the so-called public schools. And between people who use the same word, there was an immediate feeling of empathy.

The structuring was immensely effective. The leading groups in the society recognised each other, trusted each other and tended to select new colleagues with similar backgrounds. The groups had entirely different views of life, and lived happily at their own level. Witness the frequent, humorous series in "That was the week, that was".

A very tall man, a medium height man and a very small man.

The tall man:

"I am upper-class. I look down on them both."

The medium height man:

"I am middle-class. I look up to him, but I look down on him."

The very smallman:. "I know my place."

What was essential, Robert said, was that a system provided for individuals to work their way upwards, but only with considerable difficulty.

Not unlike the Indian caste system, though the Indian caste system had the massive disadvantage that one's caste was defined for life, and movement upwards and downwards was greatly restricted.

Gareth picked up on the subject:

What about equality of opportunity and fairness? Look at the differentials between top management and the average in the 1960s; it was a factor of 20. Now it is a factor of 120. How is that for fairness and equality? How are you to bind together a society where the gap in wealth between rich and poor is massive? The problem did not exist in the 1950s after the Second World War. And perhaps it didn't exist because everyone had to do national service. Two years, and during the first nine weeks, you were all together regardless of background. And that is what helps society to gel. Any chance that the Britain of 2020 would have withstood a Hitler? Doubt it.

In Thailand, the normal practice is for students to complete their education and then spend a year in National Service by donning the orange robes of Buddhists and then working their way round the country trying to do good.

In Ghana, the students, immediately after they graduate, spend three months in an appropriate organisation, for example the Ghana Association of Industry. This rule infuriates the people who actually work there, who have to hand over their desks and equipment to the privileged immigrants.

In Gareth's view, race rather than language dominated our lives. He quoted a widely admired racist letter from the local *Cambrian News* attacking so-called "English immigrants". No matter that they were all citizens of the United Kingdom. They were forcing up Welsh property prices, buying second homes when Welsh people had nowhere to live, and placing colossal burdens on the local services, particularly the health service.

But, as in a letter in response in the *Cambrian News*, average house prices were lower, not higher, in England.

"Go down to Barmouth and look at that wonderful bridge. Designed by Brits, funded by Brits, built by Brits. We're all one nation. And a world leader."

In another example, on a BBC TV programme, a local lady accused the English "foreigners": "Not only do they steal our houses, they even steal our blackberries." Humorous, but underneath deeply felt. And totally unjustified.

Robert responded that, for language, throughout the European Union you needed to master the local language to get employment in the public sector, and often in the private sector as well. So the European Union's proud boast of "uncontrolled movement of people" was a myth. You can't get jobs in Lithuania if you don't speak Lithuanian. You can't get public sector jobs in Wales, or join the army, or police, unless you speak Welsh. There was a case for Scotland, England and Ireland to join together as the only countries in Europe where to speak English sufficed for you to get employment. Call the country "UKEire".

They got onto religion, and Robert discussions he had had while in Baghdad. In particular a paper by an American academic who had lived and worked for 40 years in Iran. Why was it that Islam produced so many terrorists?

This academic's theory was that, in the pitilessly hostile environment of the desert, with summer temperatures over 47 degrees, people thought of God as remote, incomprehensible and all-powerful. The daily routine of five prayers, the first before dawn, crouching and bowing the head to the floor to Allah. The haunting prayers by the muezzin from minarets echoing around the city. This routine created deep devotion. And this led to the conflict between the Sunnis and Shia, and the idea that a jihad against all unbelievers was an imperative. A jihad that would lead the jihadis to salvation and immortal bliss.

Well-meaning Christian Anglicans like Archbishop Justin Welby could not take this obvious truth on board.

Immanuel Kant's "Categorical imperative" was a better guide to human action. Effectively, in any situation, do as any civilised human would. In 2020, act to reverse global warming.

Gareth summed up with a quote:

"We're killing millions of people every day with killing machines

But you can't kill an ideology with a gun" – Ben Ferencz.

Time for a coffee!

Behind my back they said they liked me, my Hello Hello and occasional Aberdeen accent!

Chapter 22

The Llanbedr Airfield

The Haskoning map shows the area which was central to the access road development. The hatched area indicates the way the estuary was expected to extend as a result of global warming and rising sea levels before the end of the first Trump Administration.

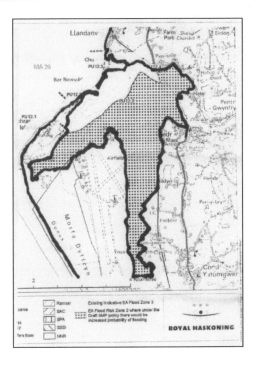

Chapter 23

Dujaily and His Team Trace The Drug Trail

I found this diary note by Dujaily in the files. They relate to the third Theresa May administration after her predecessor was impeached, but before the Zika pandemic.

I was contacted by MI6; they wanted me to liaise with a Jock Rundle. I remembered him from my days in Baghdad. A short fellow with a pointy nose, very assertive, who had made his number with the ambassador. Rundle passed me a report from two agents who had been trying to monitor BLZ in London.

The project was given top priority from Rome and Rundle had moved somewhere into this area. He got around on a rather fine motor bike. A Triumph Thunderbird classic.

Another diary note:
At Rundle's suggestion, I looked at the background of a young woman, Nadine Humphrys Jones, who had just joined our administration. She had been on the same course as Robert and might join our team. I had my doubts, but Rundle said he had just asked her previous

employer for a reference, and it had been fine. Rundle was very insistent. Not sure how far to trust him.

"I urge you, Dr Dujaily, get her with the Welsh boy." Then he muttered to himself, something like sprat for our mackerel. But I don't go much for fish.

I saw her and assigned her to the project.

Another diary note:

Nadine has now joined us, and I introduced her. Robert made as if to hug her, but she just shook hands.

Tension seems to be building up between Robert and Gareth. Started with friendly banter about the nations. Robert said the Anglo-Scots had seawater in their veins. Look at their history, look at the Saltire of Scotland, diagonal blue cross on white, look at the flag of St George, red cross on white. Civilised, friendly. Then look at the Welsh Dragon, red and green, scaly, eagle's claws and red cavernous mouth, just like the Welsh, battlers out for a fight.

But the joining of an attractive woman, Nadine, adds a whole new unpredictable dimension. Does she favour one of them – I guess the young lad.

At coffee, I had to intervene in an increasingly bitter argument about citizenship rights.

I broke in: Why don't you two swap handbags – Prime Minister Margaret Thatcher was reputed to have thumped her ministers with her handbag – and let's get on?

I ended the coffee break.

And in any case, avoid using the two guys – two rivals – in tandem.

Recall the way Professor Hunt was treated for stating the obvious. That mixed sex projects introduce all manner of powerful and uncontrollable variables. The politically correct outcry was so vicious, this great researcher left and settled in Japan.

Chapter 24

Garth Moves Lady Amanda to Pensarn

Taken from the 2020 brochure. Pensarn village lies just to the north of Llanbedr, and was pictured in the Save the Lagoon leaflets.

Pensarn is one of Wales's most jealously guarded gems. Lying in a valley between mountains called the Rhinogs, its river, the Artro, is fed by hanging valleys from above, and falls past the "Roman Steps", where allegedly the Legions used to forage through and thump troublesome Celts into a semblance of peaceful tax payers, into a lovely lake called Cwm Bychan. Then down through woods of dwarf oak and beech into coastal meadow land, and on into its own vast sandy lagoon. And thence, like no other Welsh river, straight out into the sea. The river had broken sideways out of its own sandbank riddled estuary into the "New Cut" around 1860. As a result, in the space of 50 yards, you could come in from perhaps viciously turbulent seas in the bay into a flat calm lagoon under the lee of high dunes. Just the spot to keep your yacht, with only one drawback. But a substantial one: the famous Sarn Padrig, or St Patrick's Causeway.

The Causeway is a strange, straight jumbled line of heavy rocks stretching 10 miles offshore, believed by medieval

Christians to have been a divine pathway, along which St Patrick walked to and from Ireland in the Dark Ages to Christianise the Irish. Less improbable is the rival account, that he sailed the 80 miles in a miraculous boat which looks something like a modern coracle, but was, they said, made of solid stone. Less prone than a feather-light Welsh coracle to scud along before the slightest wind. Perhaps the first forerunner of a ferroconcrete hull.

Anyway, the rocks of Sarn Padrig lurk just below the low water mark, and like other sarns further south, are one of the reasons why boating, pleasure and commercial variants, are rare in these waters.

Between the Sarn and the mainland, close to where a Spanish galleon from the Armada was wrecked in 1588, lies the East Passage. Also here is a more mysterious wreck from the 1660s or so. It carries a full cargo of expensive Carrara marble, the marble which was then being imported to build St Paul's Cathedral. How did it come to be 300 miles away from its destination on the opposite side of the UK? Perhaps a seventeenth century insurance job, the swindle having been scuppered by St Patrick and his causeway. Anyway, it has a key role in our account as described later.

East Passage is a shallow, unbuoyed gap a quarter of a mile wide between the Sarn and the mainland. A major problem is that there is no easy way of deciding where the quarter mile gap starts and ends, because the beach shelves very gradually. This leaves the navigator uncertain where he is.

These notes are from Gareth's account in a published article.
Gareth had bought _Lady Amanda_ from an old man who found that reefing the mainsail lying flat on his back under

the boom in stormy weather had become beyond him. The 1957 winches had become heavier, the sheets took a jamming riding turn fiendishly difficult to release, the wheel he could only turn with both hands, so he tumbled around in the cockpit, the boat plunged around viciously in heavy seas, and picking up moorings or anchoring were somehow tougher. The US comedy writer, James Thurber, as he aged, had had similar problems in modern phone booths. You had to stand outside to read the dials or digits and the operators' voices had become ridiculously faint.

Gareth found the fees for *Lady Amanda* in Pwllheli vastly more than he could afford. He looked at the long deep narrow cutting in Pensarn and resolved to move her there despite the local rules – it was an SSSI (Site of Special Scientific Interest) and no development whatsoever was allowed. Not even, so they said, to lower an anchor.

But what a spot. The only deep water mooring in all the 80 miles of Cardigan Bay. Get there and who is to move you?

In Pwllheli, Gareth worked with Robert to load the ketch with two special triangular anchor-like objects ready to slice into the mud in the river, and lots of other heavy weights including an old truck engine. And they set off for Pensarn in warm sunshine.

The morning tide slid in over the sands and mudflats where the turnstones turn the stones for crabs on a sleepover in their passage from Greenland to Morocco. And the oyster-catchers swoop in in racketing echelons searching for crabs and worms – no oysters in Pensarn – or just enjoying the view while libelling a neighbour.

They reached the entrance, motored carefully into position and dropped the anchors 80 feet apart at the very edge of the channel. Arguably inside, arguably outside. The tide left and *Lady Amanda* keeled over on her side like a massive beached whale. But preparations continued as planned, and over the next tide she rose slowly just before the cockpit filled and, to their delight, stayed in position. *This position was to be fundamental in the final stages of the drugs battle.*

The LPYC (Llanbedr and Pensarn Yacht Club) committee met, with most of its members in high dudgeon at how so many rules of so many outfits had so arrogantly been transgressed. But the secretary, David Robinson, was a man of imagination and principle. In the debate, he disputed the committee's views forcefully, and worded the minutes carefully. And so the old ketch stayed to grace the lovely lagoon. Ready for her future. As she still is today, still watched by otters and a single vicious predatory mink.

Chapter 25

Love in the Dunes

The 2039 records include any assignments of the MI5 drones. One was assigned to Rundle, but the mandatory records have been mislaid. H. B. G-W

At Llanbedr, Nadine and Gareth drive to Shell Island on the south side of the Artro estuary, and stride off a half mile or so. Then they slow and walk up a dune. She reaches out a hand and lightly caresses Gareth's palm with her fingers.

Later, over the crest, Gareth draws Nadine to him and they kiss and hold each other. Trembling, he slips his right hand over her breast.

"Gareth," she asks softly, "is this going to take a long time?"

"For ever."

She looks up at him, takes his hand to her lips, kisses it and presses it to her breast again.

"Me too."

She sighs, leans against him, then jumps away.

"It's just that I've got this hair appointment."

"Come here, beauty."

Later, they were walking peaceably eastwards back to the village, she on the crest of a dune, he a few feet down inland below her. Beyond the marram grass and sand, the countryside to the west spreads away from them, out to the misty green sea. He looked up at her: skirt swirling, silhouetted against the noon sky. The dreaded one-eyed trouser snake stirred insistently. He dropped to the ground saying, "I'm really tired you know?"

"Oh. You poor thing; let me kiss you better."

She spun round and slipped down to lie with him, legs curled sideways the way only females can.

He reached up tenderly and undid her blouse again.

Later he said dreamily, "You're wearing a skirt. I've never seen you in a skirt. Why are you wearing a skirt?"

She looked at him innocently, fluttered her eyelids like a fifties film star and said:

"I can't possibly think."

That evening they rowed out to the *Lady Amanda*, cooked and settled down to sleep. Sleep was slow coming and they rolled together. Later there was a sudden bright light through the skylight. They didn't notice. An MI5 drone had got a snap. Then hopped over the boom for another, different, angle. Merge them with Photoshop for a 3D effect.

The drone made off. Got what it was told to get. A snap to catch the mackerel. It clicked on a shroud and woke Gareth up.

He coughed.

"What was that?" she asked, startled.

"Just me."

He placed a gentle hand on her warm leg.

"Love you," he said.
"See if I care."
"Oh yes you do."
"Love you too."

Chapter 26

Barmouth Bridge

Extract from the curators' notes in the Ty Nyi museum.
H. B. G-W

The drug research had led from Birmingham west towards Barmouth, ten miles south of Llanbedr. It's on one of the most famous railway lines around the UK, the Cambrian Coast Line. In spite of Dr Beeching's attempt to close it in 1965 – allegedly, the attempt stopped because it ran through so many marginal parliamentary constituencies![26] – it waggles around 60 lovely miles on the west coast of Cardigan Bay in Wales. It has to cross a deep valley, the valley of the River Mawddach,[27] and it's a dramatic U-shaped crossing, with the lonely, gaunt, sharp mass of Mount Cader Idris towering a thousand metres above. The railway skirts the valley, cuts into precipices, and then swings hard left to cross the valley and river to the harbour and seaside town of Barmouth, whence

---

[26] Dr Beeching was assigned from ICI – International Chemical Industries – to rationalise the UK's rail network. The "Beeching Axe" chopped off thousands of miles of track and hundreds of stations.
An in joke at the time: "Why did he axe Llanfairpg… gogoch? It's hard to say."

[27] Mawddach, internationalised: Mow as in cow, and thach as in loch.

came the first Tudor, Henry VII, in 1485, summoning his 20,000 men at Ty Nyi house to march east and conquer the last English king, Richard III.[28] Up the valleys, gathering men, herders and fighters, to meet the alleged hunchback villain at the battle of Bosworth field in 1485.

"My kingdom, my kingdom, my kingdom for a horse," cried the Englishman as he was surrounded. But none came and he was slain, and the English crown was found hanging on a gorse bush.

Or so Shakespeare would have it. Tudor propaganda at its peak, to endear him to Queen Elizabeth I.

The Barmouth bridge is spectacular, with 113 spans covering half a mile, way above the water level. This allows a 30 feet clearance at high tide springs, but is nevertheless too low for the slate ships that used to go up the valley for loading. The Victorians built a swing bridge in 1857. It's a massive structure with two balanced wings, brilliantly engineered, and rotating on a colossal single steel spindle. To turn it and let ships through, four men are needed to wind the capstans, as if for a ship's anchor.

In the middle of the seventeenth century, in a lovely rural town in Kent, a Presbyterian minister conceived a new problem in mathematics. His name was Bayes.[29] He worked on it for many years, published papers and, in due course, the approach, known as Bayesian statistics, was recognised, established and stashed away as an interesting curiosity.

---

[28] Later, monarchs were Welsh, Scots and Germans.
[29] Thomas Bayes, 1701-1761. His work and findings were in manuscript notes, published after his death by his great friend Richard Price.

Though, two centuries later, as interest in "expert systems" or "fuzzy logic" and Artificial Intelligence developed, Bayesian statistics were found to be central to a major problem. This problem concerned the weakness in computing systems that demand "yes" or "no" answers. To give an example, take a computing application in agriculture. In Kenya and Uganda, it is widely ruled that Arabica coffee should not be grown at altitudes less than 4,000 feet. But what if the target smallholding is 3,999 feet, and therefore unfairly disqualified? Bayesian statistics make it possible to blur such boundaries and to take in numerous variables. For example, in this case, it is held to be bad practice to plant coffee on east-facing slopes because the night's dew will concentrate the rays of the rising sun and burn the leaves. But what if the slope faces east north-east by east? Nearly east, but not quite.

Bayesian logic was what was used for the dronebots software. The details are still not published, but at the time, AI products like Deep Mind and SwiftKey were attracting worldwide attention to various teams in London and Cambridge, the centre of AI research and robot controls for vehicles, which were instituted for trucks in 2022.

***

Dujaily was prompted by MI6, probably by Jock Rundle (the MI5 and MI6 files will not be accessible until 2068). He sent Nadine and Robert to monitor what happened, how the drugs were carried from Llanbedr, perhaps, to Shrewsbury. Are are picked up off the Sarn and loaded with the new drones on the train? He picked a possible contact point, Barmouth station. He loved railways. That splendid bridge. And the loco. Might go myself, he thought.

The airfield train was going though, the old school's class steam locomotive "Hurstpierpoint College", hissing gently downhill in the moonlight. Full moon, high water springs. Hauling this month's load of VEMs for testing.

Lh Lunn Luh lun Luh lun Luh Lun

In the rear viewing coach were dronebots, their single eyes waving on the cantilevered arms rather like humans conversing.

The lead dronebot swung her stalk imperiously.

"Restore Active Desktop!" she yelled.

"A one, a two, a three and a half, four."

They sang together. First a faint solo treble:
Click the start button Click the start button
Click the start button to start. Trala
Click the start button Click the start button
Click the start button to stop. Trala
(**They were still using Windows Professional Version 7.3)**
Then a resounding chorus:

Click the start button Click the start button

Click the start button to start. Trala

Click the start button Click the start button

Click the start button to stop. Trala

It was all great fun. They were having a whale of a time, and as the bridge drew close, they crowded to the left side to see it all swing by. The train ran on into the station. A mechanical voice came from the PA:

"Apologise for any inconvenience caused. Like to apologise your next station-stop. Your hand baggage."

"Good God," Robert said. "They're playing trains. They're bloody playing trains."

One dronebot sidled along the platform carrying what looked like a massive key. A second dronebot sidled up from the guard's compartment and accepted it. Then it continued forward to the driver's cab and climbed in while its colleague clearly took over as guard for the next section. No sign of a human driver.

"Sandwiches and light refreshments station-stop."

"Where this train will terminate," announced the PA metallically with a dying fall.

The engine hissed and the train continued on its way to the airfield.

The two reported back to Dujaily. They discussed what might be going on.

"They go on to the airfield. Then what?"

Majid said,

"So, for sure. They go out to sea and do their stuff. And then they bring something extra back. Something that's been stowed somewhere. How about as in St Vincent and the drugs. Failings of criminals – they keep doing the same thing. As with Newham Council's anti-crime system. Feed in the location they've gone to, not too far from home, not too close, method and type of crime, etc. Up come some matches. Up come some pictures. Pop them into boxes, and bingo, there are the suspects and out go the arrest warrants. 80 per cent hit rate. Tough on the other 20 per cent, but a case of omelettes and eggs.

"We'll follow the next one through and we'll catch them."

Chapter 27

Ty Gwyn and the Wreck Off Llanbedr

This wreck in 1709 proved to be the key three centuries later, as we will see, in tracking the drug shipments in 2020. The Barmouth Wreck Museum (Ty Gwyn), has fascinating display cases, Carrara marble, anchor, swivel guns, clothes, silver, and diving articles from the ship wrecked in 1709 on the sands near the famous Sarn Padrig off Shell Island in Llanbedr.

What on earth was a ship loaded with 41 tons of the finest marble doing in this remote part of Wales?

A ship sunk off Sarn Padrig in Llanbedr in only two metres at low water springs. A massive 500 ton ship armed with 24 cannons and ten carronades. A ship carrying wealthy passengers, living in luxury off splendid pewter plates. Some say the skipper mistook Wales for Brittany, some that it was a very early insurance scam. We still don't know her name, and we don't know where she was going. No records anywhere, except the graves of Genoese sailors in nearby Dyffryn Ardudwy.[30] They must have swum ashore.

---

[30] Since challenged by Tom Benett. He believes the wreck happened not in a gale, but in calm weather. And all survived and were shipped home, but the truth was concealed by the local Lord of Gors-y-Gedol.

Chapter 28

Tracking the Shipment

Dujaily remembered Graham's account of the drops in St Vincent and realised that the druggers were following the same strategy. The wreck from 1709 was a necessary pinpoint in the vast areas of sand and rock around the East Passage inside Sarn Padrig. Only 10m deep, and easy for a sub aqua vehicle to come in from the sea, identify, drop off its load and buoy it. Tricky waters, with Sarn Padrig stretching eight miles off shore,[31] visible only at low water springs. Not many boats around at midnight. Just the odd night fisherman out to catch tope.

The team resolved to track the next cargo at the next full moon.

The objective would be to get the coordinates of the location for which the dronebots were making. Nadine and Robert would act in tandem. They were to climb onto the last wagon, using a special container to hang on the top exit link and the buffers. A dangerous task, but the best they could

---

[31] The medievals believed the Sarn, "St Patrick's Causeway", was the way that St Patrick walked on his move to Ireland to convert the Irish to Christianity. In fact, the Sarn was created by the confluence of two glaciers melting during a period of global warming, and dropping rocks and sand.

think up. They would drop off at Llanbedr station, where the train would reverse to the spaceport.

They would monitor the VEM drones, which would probably be taking off, flying ou six6 miles, looking at and recording the content of a window in Harlech Castle.

Boeing's car swaps the highway for a skyway

Flying cars may still be the stuff of science fiction, but Boeing is a little closer to bringing one to the masses (Tom Knowles writes).

The aircraft maker completed its first outdoor test of an electric flying, autonomous car that it hopes will one day whisk people away from congested roads and along a highway in the sky. A prototype stretched limousine completed a controlled vertical take-off, hovered for 60 seconds, then successfully landed during a test in Manassas, Virginia.

Boeing is in a race with its rival, Airbus, and a number of smaller companies to create small self-flying vehicles capable of vertical take-off and landing. Intel is working on its own flying car, while AeroMobil is designing a stretchable limousine that can turn into a fixed-wing aircraft. The investment, which are being fuelled by significant leaps in autonomous technology and concerns about gridlocked cities, have the potential to change the face of the aerospace industry.

Boeing's push into this field has been boosted by its acquisition in 2017 of Aurora Flight Services. This is what revolution looks like, and it's because of autonomy," John Langford, Aurora's chief executive, said.

Aurora is one of five companies working to future of mobility — moving goods, moving cargo, moving people — that future is happening now and it's going to accelerate over the next five years and ramp up even more beyond that," Dennis Muilenburg, Boeing's chief executive, told a for the company. The car will have a 50-mile range and carry up to four passengers. The aircraft have only a few feet during its test, but it is a significant advance for the company. The car will have a 50-mile range and carry up to four passengers. The aircraft have only a few feet during its test, but it is a significant advance flying car will have a 50-mile range and carry up to four passengers. The under Uber's Elevate division, Uber is so confident that it says it will test its first flying taxis in Los Angeles and Dallas in 2023. Boeing's 300 by 250.

Boeing's prototype electric flying car performed a vertical take-off in Virginia and powered for 60 seconds before landing at the World Economic Forum in Davos, Switzerland.

However, Boeing and others will have to overcome significant regulatory and safety obstacles before flying cars are cleared for take-off.

Extract from The Times

Each would then return to the airfield. Dujaily had checked with Production, and this was the standard acceptance test on each drone following production – bump tests, rotor checks and so on. Nadine and Robert would use a GPS device to record the compass bearings of a drone as it flew.

They would wait till morning and walk back along the coast to their base to report to Dujaily.

The night arrived, and the train came. Nadine and Robert followed up and hung the container by the rear buffers as the announcement system went through its standard rigmarole. They hooked successfully onto the coach. A drugdrone[32] dropped onto the platform, went across to the booking hall and smashed the window. She rummaged around and came back with a paper – possibly the *Cambrian News*. As she climbed back she saw some line dangling from the back of the coach and seemed to stop and think, then get on board. "Light refreshments your next station-stop," the PA rigmarole finished, and the train took off for Llanbedr.

The pair got off at Llanbedr station while the drugdrones were fixing the points for the train to reverse into the airfield. The drugdrone followed them. She called in an Assasin.[33].

---

[32] Probably a marinised version of the Phantom 5 which was recognised to be king of consumer drones. Emulating the US "Predator", which monitored the Canadian border. Incredibly simple to pilot and almost impossible to ditch disastrously. It bristles with sensors and cameras to keep it steady in the air and helps to avoid collisions. The commercial version had 28 minutes flying time per charge. It had the ability to be gently returned home when the juice ran low, and a fully stabilised camera (Observer, 30/10/18).

[33] Probably the Assassin6. But, as for the English Electric Lightning fighter (used to frighten off the USSR Bear atom bombers), the details have never been revealed.

Nadine set off west for the dunes, and Robert north-west for the river. The Assassin had to choose; it selected Robert and followed him.

For Nadine, it was alarming to find her way across the airfield perimeter and causeway in the moonlight, but she reached the viewing point. She had to wait a while – no doubt preparing the target VEM for the night took a while. Then she heard the buzzing, noted the coordinates, which had a strange kink in them, and settled down for the night on soft grass in a dip in the dunes. The following morning she went along the coast and back to base to report to Dujaily.

Dujaily, Nadine and Gareth waited for Robert, and they waited with ever increasing anxiety. Dujaily spread out Imray chart C51 and plotted the dronebot's course. It had a kink in the middle going to the West, then followed a straight line out to the 6-mile point off Harlech. Then they bethought themselves of the Wreck museum and checked the point where the 24-gun ship had sunk in 1709. That was it, that was where the marble was, and that was the pickup point where the drones were picking up their cargoes of drugs. The museum even had a Channel 4 TV video of a diver exploring the 71 blocks of Carrara marble in astonishing detail.

No sign of Robert. Nadine and Gareth looked increasingly distressed.

Dujaily said:

"Look, you two. I'll get on to the police. You just go home, leave it to me and we talk tomorrow morning. Meanwhile, I'll be in touch."

Chapter 29

Dujail's Battle

No way I could call in the police – they would want to know what the guy was doing out in the estuary at midnight.

Contacted Rome and got clearance for collaboration with UK Drugs Administration (MI5). Special Branch would check the area. And, in fact, Robert was never seen again. Was this hostile action or did he, in kayaking out to the point, capsize and drown? Or even get taken by an orca? These killer whales were moving northwards as global warming took effect.

Also, got on to the top VEM drone Production boss and asked him to scan the estuary. In the mud they found an Assassin6 with one damaged prop stuck in the mud. Really deep mud in that area – fall down and you can't get up. You've got to crawl a hundred yards to the sea wall, and even then it's not easy to progress. What was the drugdrone doing? Following Robert in a kayak? Robert hit the drone, downed it, perhaps, and then he and the kayak were swept out to sea? Perhaps. We don't know. A great guy, a great loss.[34]

The dronebot Production boss later reported that his QA guy had suddenly resigned in writing, and left. The QA guy will have been the one who controlled the dronebots as they lifted the drugs.

Resolved to let it all run. Monitor BLZ activities as the Council do the first cut on the lagoon.

---

[34] See Appendix 2.

Chapter 30

Oldman 4

In the Second World War, the Japanese and Commonwealth prisoners were building the "Railway of death".

The prisoners in one cutting were digging out the foundations using shovels. On completion of a day's work, the Japanese commander at the cutting ordered that the shovels were counted. One was missing. He had the guards surround the prisoners with loaded guns. "One of you admits the crime or you will all be shot."

A prisoner stood up and said, "I did it."

He was shot.

They returned to camp and counted the shovels. None were missing.

***

The grass is starting to grow on Llanbedr hill. The old man is staggering from side to side up the hill from the houses. Your sense of balance goes. Grey face like an inverted rain drop, broad forehead, narrow chin warmed by a long beard. Wispy white hair. Really seriously old.

He's in Fergie time.[35] Slung round his shoulder is a heavy file. <u>On the lid, "FoI aspects of the environmental costs of the Llanbedr lagoon."</u>

Right foot up.
"And the one,"
Left foot up
"I loved the most,"
Right foot up
"Was little Willy Wee,"
Left foot up
"Who is six feet de."[36]

Not long to go anyway, he thinks. Better to go with a bang than a whimper. For the ashes of my fathers and the temples of my Gods. Or whatever.

Hard going for the old guy, getting up the gradient from the houses, past the copse, the ever-yellow gorse and the grazing. He staggers again, falls and crawls, but he makes it. He lies down shivering by the bulldozer lade, on the soft, sheep-grazed grass in the lee of a bank of gorse.

Stanford's setting of the Nunc Dimitis drifts through his mind and soul:

"Lord, now lettest thou thy servant… Depart in peace."

---

[35] Fergie time is still widely known among soccer lovers as the last minutes of add-on time in a match; when his Manchester United teams used to crack in a last-second, winning, goal.

[36] Polly Garter in *Under Milkwood*. Polly Garter's song, *Under Milkwood*.

Rejoice, rejoice, rejoice at the dying of the light.[37]

The old man is in front of the bulldozer. The bulldozer is positioned to make its first cut for the access road. Southerly gale just picking up, with the odd flake of snow.

Is he busy dying?[38]

As we will see, in the end, he may save the lagoon.

---

[37] Unbelievably, as it now seems, doctors were compelled to prolong their patient's life, "striving officiously to keep alive", causing distress to many hundreds and thousands. The obvious fact that, for normal families, an easy death for the elderly when they so decided, was something they all wished for. But against this, cynics set the danger of exploitation. After a campaign by a cross-bench bishop in the House of Lords in 2020, it was agreed that for the greatest happiness of the greatest number, the risk of occasional abuse should be accepted.

[38] Rev Wilfred Meyer, Vicar St Davids, Kalk Bay, Cape Town, RSA.

End

At the top of the bypass, the bulldozer driver is sitting in his seat for the first cut. It's a Sunday, no-one around, double time. Deep snow, no sign yet of his mate. An hour or more before the press will be able to get through in this.

Using the Maes-y-Neuadd camera, BLZ is watching. From the Victoria Inn camera, Dujaily is watching. He is also watching BLZ watching. He is recording BLZ watching. Rundle must have been watching them all.

The bulldozer driver settles down with a cup from a flask. BLZ is excited, he turns to the fire, slips his zip down and pees into the grate. A splendid sizzle. Then zips up. Slaps his thighs with delight.

"Next, the girl."

The sun slides up slowly over the Rhinogs and bathes the hillside. Slowly the snow melts. The driver finishes his sandwiches. His mate arrives. Hangs around a bit. A while yet before the press arrives through the snow. Then he puts the dozer in gear. Check it out, ready. A black mound appears before the blade. The old man.

It was expedient that the old man should die for the village. And for the druggies. And so he has.

Epilogue

After immense popular pressure, the governments and the Snowdonia Park Authority authorised the implementation of the lagoon proposals in 2021.

The governments decided to delay the proposed southern access road "through lack of funds". The concrete structures following the South African guidelines and the Snowdonia Enterprise Zone's design were laid at the lagoon entrance in 2024.

The governments have decided to delay the proposed southern access road through lack of funds.

BLZ escaped from police custody, it was never clear how.

Dujaily took a hammering in the media and people pressed for him to be charged as an accessory to murder. But in his defence, the footage of BL peeing into the fire was excellent.

The police investigated, and an autopsy revealed that the old man had been dead for several hours.

Dujaily now lives, greatly honoured, retired, in a little village out on the desert in Kurdistan.

Colin Leakey had a fascinating career, communicating

ideas and criticisms in many countries. For example, in Malaysia, RISDA, the rubber smallholder's development authority was responsible for 3,000 smallholders. "Not only the rubber trees, but also the men women and children behind the rubber." (Dr Mohammed Nor.)

The latex from a rubber tree tails off after 25 years, and then it is necessary to educate the farmers to cut down and replant. The standard procedure was to clear everything except for the tiny rubber seedlings. So, for five years while they matured, there was an opportunity. Tropical sun, fertile soil, adequate rainfall. Colin picked this out and persuaded them to introduce inter-planting with various crops, for example with yams. Eventually these were developed into 50 stage action lists in Bahasa, the name of the Malay language, which helped greatly in advising each smallholder, and in managing every stage from the provision of seedlings or whatever to the provision of credit, and to the final marketing of the crops.

The benefits of his work are incalculable.

Jock Rundle became Lord Rundle of Shapinsay. I could find no background.

Nadine and Gareth married, and she took on assignment in Barmouth, helping to find refugee children foster parents in the area. Their first son was an immensely promising cricketer at Llandovery. A wayward young guy, rather like David Gower. His mum writes to the cricket master, Duncan Craik, asking him to keep an eye on the young lad while the team go on tour in Holland. Duncan fails in the task. But he keeps the letter, might be nice to have around.

I used to visit St Vincent and stay in a lovely little hotel, the Umbrella Beach hotel (described earlier), opposite Young Island Cut.

One morning at the landing stage, I saw a smart, pulling pinnace being rowed ashore from a fine ketch, probably mahogany on oak, fine reverse tumblehome – 70 footer or so. Freeman perhaps. Rowed by four men in white and blue sailors' uniforms. In the stern was a red-faced cheery individual, at the helm. A top, top guy, I thought, no doubt a member of the Royal Yacht Squadron. Deep navy blue blazer, brass buttons probably engraved, white silk scarf. He stepped out onto the landing stage and walked past me in his brown brogues. As he did so, I heard him singing quietly:

> *"I must go down to the sea again*
> *to the lonely sea and the sky,*
> *and all I ask is a tall ship and a star to steer her by."*

As he came past, he turned and gave me the broadest and most infectious of smiles, lips lifting way up at the corners, and eyes crinkled warmly with friendliness. But from the side, his smiling mouth seemed tautened upwards and opened as if poised to cackle, the jaws becoming shark-like and voracious, the nose probing predatorily forward. BLZ.

I did not do anything – not my task. After all, I am an historian.

H. B. G-W, 30/4/39

Author

APPENDIX 1

North Korea

(Young Jock Rundle's report to FAO)
This piece in the FAO (UN Food and Agriculture Organisation) library in Rome is an informal narrative from a consultant named Rundle who worked in North Korea in 1992, when it was seen as a viciously dangerous pariah state, the "axis of evil". It's rather long, but it gives clues to the world's history ever since. We don't yet know for certain the roots of our disasters; terrorists most believe. But I have a gut feel where they may lie.

I eventually flew in from Beijing at sunset to see a rather striking city dominated by a strange 600 foot high pyramid like an upturned dart. With a tiny rusting crane on top – they'd run out of money to finish it.

We got off the plane an hour later to a seemingly unenthusiastic, suspicious welcome from my host Dr Han, the head of the Soil Research Institute. He came with two others whom he didn't introduce. Later in the evening, he said they had three Chinese consultants to help them on a problem, a problem which he didn't explain. I went to bed in the Potonggang

Hotel, glumly thinking of frying pans and fires – the set-up seemed too similar to my previous assignment in Baghdad, in Iraq, which had ended with a spell as one of Saddam's reluctant "guests". Another great dictator, "Our great leader President Kim Il-Sung". And on top of this, three inscrutable Chinese who would no doubt muddy the waters. I turned on the TV to see a great crowd being addressed by the people who had been on the plane with me. Formidable-looking people with allegedly scintillating academic records from India, Greece, or South America. Each gave, in turn, a tedious paean of fulsome praise to DPRK and the "Great Leader Kim Il-Sung", and his political vision of the "Juche Idea" and of a united Korea. "One nation, two systems." Roars of adulating applause.

The next morning dawned sunny and chilly, and I saw the hotel was surrounded by lovely wooded parkland alongside a river. Rather fragile-looking trees, mostly birch, with crystal clear water flowing slowly by, rowing dinghies for hire, tracks winding into the capital, where there were wide squares and impressive architecture. My growing assurance took a bit of a dip when my hosts whisked me into the city to join a queue at the national airline offices. Ten hours into the country and they were wanting to book me out again!

But from then on, things improved rapidly. We shot off in an official limo through wide empty streets to the National Agricultural Research Institute,four4 miles out into the countryside, and I was introduced around the place, and to our own laboratory of soils sciences. I asked about my Chinese "colleagues". Ah, they had left yesterday – presumably, I hoped, having been stumped by the undefined "problem"!

Together, we explored the apparently insuperable problems which they had hit. They were to do with the performance of their national database of fertiliser applications. Their system tried to do for fertiliser what Frank Cope's system had done for two hundred farms in Suffolk, as we saw earlier, and for which, I think, he received the Chemical Society's very rare gold medal.

In outline, from every "field" in the country, a soil sample was provided once every four years. All these samples were sent to the laboratory for analysis in an X-ray spectrometer. The process added water to the sample and stirred it to dissolve the soil. It then heated the liquid to boiling and blasted it, then analysed the optical spectrum of the steam. The colours in the spectrum revealed which minerals were present. The resultant data was fed into their PC. Here, soils software designed by Dr Han listed the number, amounts and timings of fertiliser applications to be made to each field, increasing the allocation where nutrients were deficient and vice versa. The system attempted to create a level playing field of fertility for every field in every commune so that all were nearly equal. It's an astonishing, egalitarian process which would never be attempted in "supply-led", free Western agriculture. (But, has it a role perhaps for us in the future when, through global warming and climate change, our traditional, profligate use of resources will have to be circumscribed, for example by carbon rationing?) However, the system's performance was plainly crucial to the nation's agriculture, and its performance was so slow that allocations were falling behind, and crude manual approaches were being used.

The programs were written and ran in Korean, in their rather beautiful script. They used their own counterfeit of Ashton Tate's dBase, then the world's foremost database programming language, interfacing to Korean BASIC for scientific calculations. So, I was faced with 44 modules of complex analytical software in an incomprehensible language with an incomprehensible character set!

However, we came to some clear conclusions:

The problem almost certainly lay with the modules of code which drove input and output on the discs.

Miss Li would enable me to comprehend the code by converting it to standard English dBase.

We would create a model concentrating on the input/output (i/o) programs.

We would simulate the scientific calculations by just imposing slight delays in the model's running at the related stages.

This took us about two weeks, working long days. Fridays were different. The national custom was for all top brass and white collar workers to leave their desks and work in the fields. Even our institute director! Though, some alleged that he scheduled key journeys across the country for the fifth day! Miss Li and our limo driver had special dispensation, and she and I were the only occupants of the entire sprawling institute.

After the two weeks, we had our first runs of the model, and were able to observe the timings. No joy at first, but then I noticed one of the modules performing strikingly badly. So I delved into it and came to the conclusion that Miss Li had carried out the i/o transfers clumsily. To put it simply, in fact to over-simplify, you can visualise the database as a massive book. You can either read it from cover to cover a page at a time. Or you can read in the sequence of the first word on page one, then the first word on page two and so on, to the first word on the last page. Then back to the second word on page one, and so on. If you do it the latter way, you are going to take a phenomenal amount of time.

Eureka! I announced my discovery. Miss Li set to work to reprogram as needed, and at the end of the next afternoon, we watched as she kicked off the programs as amended. Time passed. In the end, they took a marginally longer time than before! We all laughed ruefully, and I returned, consultant confounded and chastened, to the hotel.

The next morning, I got back in to be met by a bleary-eyed smiling Miss Li. She had worked all through the night rewriting the real, Korean, software modules, and ran them, and found the timing problem had gone away. My theory had been right, but we had only been using a small sample from the database. And the operating system had been quietly "caching" this sample into the store (memory) for efficiency. This is unbelievably faster than going back and forth to the disc. So then, once the sample data was all in the cache, it made no difference which way you read the data. Fine, but with a full large database, caching was not feasible. And without caching, computing speed was crippled.

We all rejoiced, and Dr Han called the Research Institute's Director. He congratulated us, winding up by asking me to go and pack for a special trip for four days to the mountains of Kum Gang San. We left Pyongyang station – no Miss Li – in the sleeper for the big eastern seaport of Won San. I got my camera out but was instructed to put it back again. We went through the night and arrived at Won San at daybreak.

An attraction of computing is the intense pleasure of intractable problems which are jointly solved. Getting friendly with Dr Han, Mr Ho ("hardware") and Miss Li ("software"), we talked ("you and I are scientists; we may speak of these things") increasingly openly of the differences between our countries. Dr Han's view of the UK was the usual communist caricature – a country of unfettered exploitation of downtrodden masses, unemployment, violence, drugs and decay, ruled over by a Queen in a way which symbolised the backwardness of a once great country. My feeling for DPRK was less stereotyped, because I'd read Simon Winchester's book "Korea". This dispelled the current British view – of a country of stern Orientals, terrorists and assassins, of bitter cold and pickled cabbage, of barren hills and paddies, savagely fought over in the drawn war in the fifties, dominated since then by a dictatorship to be named among the worst with Ceauşescu and Saddam. A country shortly to collapse, the Westerners believed, with so many others into the arms of the severe but welcoming west. Winchester had not been allowed to cross the truce line from South Korea into DPRK, but had the impression that the rampant excessive capitalism and corruption which disfigures the south had, in the north, been tempered by care and generosity. (His recent articles have been less approving.)

Looking back, my first impressions had been very pleasing. As I hinted earlier, the capital stretches among hills along two winding rivers backed up with shallow weirs and dotted with occasional clusters of communal rowing boats, cheap and much-used. The river sides are fringed with occasional benches, fishermen and miles of parkland, woods, lily ponds and fountains. The parks merge in and out of formal squares with large, no doubt very costly, but often imaginative public buildings. Most of the city is very clean, with wide streets, firm whistle-blowing women traffic-police and negligible traffic. Everywhere there is an emphasis on youth and students, typified by fine new buildings like the Mangyongdae Students and Childrens' Palace. In the squares, the communal exercise sessions, which all ages love, take place – like open-air aerobics involving lines of people, often 1,000 in a square, bending, dancing, stretching and doubling back and forth to the instructions of a leader who stands atop a platform using a megaphone. After the sessions, people spill enthusiastically into the parks doing handstands, arguing and chatting amicably. (There is a strong emphasis on art also, and the sculpture and architecture of the capital seems finer to me than that of most equivalents – say Seoul or Singapore or Hong Kong.) One sees crocodiles of schoolchildren walking purposefully and swiftly to school singing songs of their mountains and of praise for "Our great leader President Kim Il-Sung" – henceforward OGLPKIS – (the phrase rolls infuriatingly off everyone's tongue) and with similar but more muted reverence for his son and grandson, now successor, Kim Jong-Un.

As we walked outside the Childrens' Palace, Mr Ho told me with shiny eyes, "OGLPKIS he loves all our children. At New Year he gives EACH child a special present." Driving out to the institute once, my exasperation at OGLPKIS broke loose. A visiting scientist and I had been discussing our tax systems, and he said proudly, "In Korea, we have no taxes at all." I responded, "No; with us we earn our money and then the state takes some. With you, the state takes first and then gives a little back." More warmly: "Take Mr Ho – he says that OGLPKIS loves every child, gives them each presents… But I tell you it's not the President who gives them the presents! It's you." He glanced at those in front quickly to see if they had heard, giggled, looked hard at me and said, "Yes of coss, of coss. But you must not say!"[39]

The strength of popular support among young and old for the system and OGLPKIS: "You can see nowhere – nowhere – in the world," Dr Han told me after we saw a fervent mass demonstration which must have involved more than a million, seemingly the entire capital, welcoming Kim Il-Sung back from a key visit to China. To confuse this real fervour with the rent-a-mob antics in favour of Saddam which I saw in Baghdad, gatherings would be very dangerous. My feeling was that the north was brimming with confidence, was taking the initiative in the bridge-building process with the Koreans in the South, and believed with some reason that it had the support of the majority, especially the youth in the south. To his people, OGLPKIS was succeeding – for example, while I was there, he launched an International Crusade for Korean re-unification and the removal of US nuclear missiles, supported, his people were told, by "318 million people worldwide" – and shortly, the US missiles were on their way out.

---

[39] For a balanced view of Kim Il-Sung, see the Swedish satirical novel "The hundred year old man". His achievement for his people ranks alongside that of Churchill for the British and Americans or Mao Tse-Tung for the Chinese.

Dr Han and others at his level were more cautious. When we discussed IT, they were well aware of their backwardness. On privatisation versus state enterprise, they were very conscious of evidence that the infrastructure was decaying – notably the railways (pretty good), which I rode overnight to visit the lovely Mountains of Kum Gang in the east, but was forbidden to photograph. They had no doubt their political system was better, but had obvious misgivings at communist collapses elsewhere.

Their system is encapsulated in the "Juche idea", OGLPKIS's philosophy, derived from Marxism but a distinctive brand propagandised vigorously everywhere. The emphasis on youth, art and gracefulness is one strand; others are a refreshing egalitarianism. Everyone has a job; nearly all live in similar rooms in reasonably attractive apartment blocks where "only the old hanker for the cottages of the past"; every Friday, senior management and white collar workers all have to work all day in the fields or equivalent – hospitals only offer emergency cover because doctors are out planting rice. Professionals like scientists or doctors earn only 40 per cent more than the average manual wage. Egalitarianism permeates all – the objective of our soils/fertiliser system is to achieve a uniform fertility level across the entire national field (30,000 units) so that all co-operatives have equal productive potential. All must produce either rice or maize – pre-revolutionary alternatives like wheat, barley, etc. are banned (and with ecologically sound justification).

A strong feeling for communal activity and discipline – individualism is seen as perhaps dangerous and sinful. If

I asked who designed a building, the response was "what does that matter?"; when we went in the mountains, there was invariably only one path, often up sheer cliffs, which we climbed on steel companion ladders, as on ships, from Won San shipyards. Often, we queued with a stream of workers from the communes who made their way up and down. Each member had been voted by his/her fellows to be the holiday person or group of the year. (Sometimes a group would stop with us and sing and dance the rather haunting ballads of the "Sky Goddesses" who live in some mountain pools – though not the pool which celebrates the spirit of OGLPKIS.) The social pressures at work sounded formidable; the elected group leader gathers his group together each evening and announces who has earned how many work days (usually .8 to 1.3) and why. Eddie Grundy be warned! Their group tasks and targets have been set from the County Co-operative Management Committees; their targets, in turn, were set by the national soil database system on which I had worked. Here lies the rub, because without a price system, no-one can assess what levels of fertiliser are the economic optimum – production cost and benefit ratios cannot be assessed since neither can be evaluated without a market mechanism.

Western media reports suggested appalling hardships in the countryside. I saw none round the Institute or en route east across the entire peninsula to Kum Gang Sang.

Finally, when I left, Miss Li bid me goodbye in a prepared speech as we left the institute, and Han and Ho took me to the airport. There was a long straight corridor from the departure point. I looked back as I left it. There they were, hands raised formally in farewell. I expect that, like me, they felt this had been a fine, rare experience. That we were friends who were never ever going to see each other again.

But, cogently, Dr Han must have known the truth. And if the Westerners' reports were right, why was he so confident in the rightness of his cause? Westerners, including two of only four I met there, generally commented with hostility, and expected the system to collapse on OGLPKIS death – it hasn't. I suspect the dice are loaded heavily that way. But DPRK offers much in the balance against lost liberty and grossly sycophantic totalitarianism:

Fairness; absence of violence, aids and drugs; full employment, no poverty (in 1992), astonishingly low pollution (contrast Pyongyang with Seoul in South Korea), social confidence, much apparent happiness. And, maybe, the key quality which the West cannot claim for itself, leave alone the rest of the world: **sustainability**. It's a challenging alternative. Personally, I favour the Western approach, though with increasing doubt. But humanity will gain if the other approach also survives. We worship at the shrine of biodiversity; why not also socio-diversity and political diversity, and welcome the Juche alternative.

In a nutshell, taking the famous French revolutionary causes **liberty, equality and fraternity.**

North Korea scores zero **for liberty**, but nine for **equality** and nine for **fraternity.**

In a BBC2 hour-long documentary, the presenter used only material from people who had escaped after vicious torture. None of the beauties of the country, of the evident pleasure if not joy of those who had won their commune's annual competition for a holiday in the mountains, living in hotels comparable with Holiday Inns in the West, climbing up wide stairways built in the shipyards, stopping to sing in groups at the stages in the ascent. (No-one, I fear, was allowed to roam, and the great mountains were devoid of footpaths.) The presenter finally showed a satellite view of the area at night. China, South Korea and Japan were a blaze of light. North Korea was in total darkness apart from a brilliantly lit statue of the leader OGLPKIS.

"There you are," she said. "Contrast the bright civilisation of the West with the pariah state in pitch darkness."

But, I thought, maybe the pariah state has it right: Kim Il-Sung and Chairman Mao were the only leaders with policies which might stop global warming.

APPENDIX 2

Robert is found

I bought *Lady Amanda* many years after all this. She lay in Pensarn still, and people loved to come and photograph her against the Rhinogs.

The mussel beds to the north of the boat produced large, juicy shellfish, and I used to dive down and pick them. Eighteen for a good meal, cooked in onion, garlic butter and cider. And the juice soaked up in crusty bread from Hen Fecws.

One day after heavy rains, I swam down and noticed that crystal clear cold water streamed underneath the hazy tidal salt. The orange bottom material had been newly scoured out and opened up, and there were bones. We had them analysed, and it is pretty sure that the remains were those of Robert McMichael. There were pieces of alloy paddles, and it seems likely that Robert fought off the Assassin with some success, but was eventually killed.

A fine man killed in a fine cause.

Rejuvenation
Protea on Table Mountain
It has to burn off periodically, about eight years.
And then the flower Lily, Cyrtanthus elatus, grows and
flowers.

Appendix 3

The Sudan

The Sudan was then the largest country in Africa, and I remembered the adage in the Colonial Service as: "A country peopled by blacks and ruled by blues."

My project, SKADP (South Kordofan Agricultural Development Project; World Bank) was situated in the Nuba Mountains in this area, the war zone south of the desert. The war had been in constant ebb and flow for thirty years, a confrontation between the socialist Arab regime and culture in the north and the Nilotic and Nilo-hamitic Bantu tribes in the south. A confrontation fomented by religious differences, between Islam in the North and Paganism – spirit worship – and Christianity in the South. The Sudanese had (and have, as the crises in neighbouring Darfur show) no wish to have interfering Westerners in those parts. But they needed the SKADP money, $40 million, desperately, and World Bank HQ demanded independent monitoring and evaluation to ensure their funds were being well-spent. The Bank was dissatisfied, to put it mildly, and the war lords, who ran Kordofan and similar parts, refused to grant the Bank officials access to check what was going on. So, we three Brits had been brought in to carry this out:

One (Robinson), the Management Engineer, looking at transport and equipment (tractors were being blown up by mines, and Land Rovers were being commandeered and converted into war vehicles with heavy machine guns mounted on tripods in the body).

One (Tom Mangan), Team Leader, a General Agriculturalist looking at overall project management.

And one, myself, Head of the Information Systems Unit, to define and secure "M&E", as the jargon has it, Monitoring and Evaluation of planning, progress and resources across all the project's disciplines. The project's prime target was agriculture, but water conservation, crop storage facilities, factory processing facilities, transport and infrastructure improvement were all included.

Significantly, although Tom was the team leader, it was specified that "each team member would report directly to the Director General", and this would prove crucial.

I recalled the adage quoted in the colonial service about Africa's largest country, the Sudan:

A country populated by Blacks and governed by Blues.

My entry was not propitious. It was in a vast cavernous and grimy airport complex, together with a bunch of rather unhappy-looking fellow passengers waiting with me in the immigration area. Slowly they were documented and released until only I and one other waited.

The hotel hosted us among the tall office blocks in the centre of the city. Dominated at this time of the year by the thundering individual generators for each building, which made the night air foul, spouting diesel fumes into the narrow canyons of the streets. Hydroelectricity from the Nile was at its lowest ebb now, in summer, just when it was most needed. But only two blocks away from this inferno, to the north, were the banks of the White Nile which rolls down from the Ethiopian Mountains, and the banks were graced by various sprawling colonial ministries. The buildings were surrounded by green gardens, unbelievably attractive in the middle of the harsh desert. I took to wandering round these parts in the pleasing hour through sunset and twilight. On one bank of the Nile I saw a pump drawing water up into fields. And sometimes the pump attendant. He explained to me that he just had to pour in some diesel, roll the pump on and leave it to pump until the diesel was used up.

"This was the wonderful gift from the Soviet Union to us."

I crouched down and looked at the emblem on the side.

It said English Electric 1920.

For me, these walks became a very necessary antidote to heated frustration. I remember my introduction to SKADP and its building, part of a large private house with no air conditioning but gallons of delicious chilled water, out toward the edge of the desert. It was so hot and dry that in all my time there, I never sought out the toilet.

I went in to the building for the first time with Tom, who, rather oddly, failed to introduce me. I found a meeting of maybe twelve people in progress, and a white robed Sudanese at the chair behind the main desk. I fear that, for me, white robes signified a lower status than the grey-suited others, and I failed to recognise the Director General, "The Sheikh", who ran the project. The sort of mistake at which you squirm in the early hours of the night, though happily in this case it didn't matter at all.

I got little guidance from Tom Mangan, who just had me tagging along with him as he went from one chancellery to another, sitting waiting in grubby offices, clearing various items like our long-range radio transmitter/receivers. This kit indicates the colossal difficulties that the project endured. There was no postal/telecomms system to Kordofan, water was short, there were no local supplies of diesel, so our fuel had to be transported across 1,300 miles of deeply rutted desert tracks from the Red Sea coast in our five big tankers. Kordofan in 1992 was more backward than most African countries in 1930. Our project was to cover 138,000 square miles, twice the area of the UK, of savannah, desert and mountains, for polyglot peoples ranging through nomad pastoralists, transhumant pastoralists (the Nuer mentioned earlier), to livestock (camels, cattle, chickens, sheep, goats) and to some "sedentary" agriculture, primarily cultivating sorghum, the local cereal crop. The Project Proposal is, I think, a fascinating document. A strictly factual, matter of fact, definition of an impossible objective. And all this to be achieved in the war zone with a vicious irreconcilable civil war in progress.

However, I was slow to take this on board; head down to get on with my job. I was fascinated by the project, sat in on progress meetings and got to know the key people, notably the Chief of Finance, the Head of Extension, and a tall gangling Southerner with a broad forehead and wide, staring eyes, Atif Rantendi, who was Head of Progress and M&E.

Most of the PMU (Programme Management Unit) team were very friendly, though given to sharply argumentative and often excitable behaviour. About one key man, Hambin, however, the leading agricultural extension specialist, immensely persuasive and highly respected, I had some doubts.

The Sudanese refused any permits for foreigners to enter the war zone until the person had served sufficient time in Khartoum for them to evaluate him (on top of careful scanning of CVs and so on before his arrival) and required a bewildering chain of documents, permissions and stamps. I used 23 passport photos and saw countless bureaucrats, sometimes warmly welcoming – one paid my fee for me when I was short of change! Sometimes hostile, one actually shouting at me for several minutes. In this process, I rapidly realised that the central government's remit ran thinly in many parts, and that people like the Governor of Kordofan had often complete, autocratic authority over their regions. The writ of the Khartoum government ran exceeding small. This is a familiar picture in development – the central government are often not wilfully obstructive; they lack authority, as shown in the horrifying civil war in Kordofan's neighbour, Darfur.

So, I spent six weeks first familiarising myself with the project, and meeting the key people. Since Tom Mangan was an agriculturalist of long standing and would cover that key area, I took a particular interest in the Water Management side. Tom and Robinson, the Engineering Management specialist, got on not at all, and Robinson used the let-out clause in the Proposal, with regard to the reporting, to communicate nothing to him. Nothing at all. I talked to Robinson occasionally. He spent every evening writing to his wife.

"Why don't you phone her?" I asked – the lines out to the UK were fairly good, and the salaries from the World

Bank excellent. Understandably – Sudan was reckoned the worst post in the whole developing world.

"If I did, she'd realise from my voice what a dreadful place this is."

Sounds glum, but he was dead right. Cooped up often in an office just outside Kadugli with a suspicious workforce who were scared stiff to move their vehicles out of the compound, with chances of getting blown up (two tractors of the six) or shot up. He set-up procedures manuals and gave training in the operation and maintenance of all the machinery, but that was the limit of his range of action, and soon after my arrival he returned to the UK.

As Tom and I toured government offices for permission to import this and that item of equipment – rain gauges, for example – I started to explore what Tom saw me doing and how my M&E (Monitoring and Evaluation) role would monitor the agricultural development for which he was responsible. Some casual pointers to his attitudes worried me.

"What about the Bagara?" I asked. "Why is there no plan for the Bagara?" The Bagara were a mysterious nomadic tribe They spent the "winter" wandering with their herds in the south, then when summer rains brought the biting flies which drove their cattle mad, they all assembled and trekked 800 miles over track-free desert and mountains to rough country west of El Obeid for the summer. What kept them all alive there through that region's dreadful summers, I never found out. Their tents and leather ornaments and so on were really superb, and they themselves were cheerful, humorous and truculent.

I particularly liked Areit, the only Bagara tribesman on the project as a manager. To see this spare, hawk-eyed nomad looking at a spreadsheet on the screen, his face and eyes crinkled from years looking over vast distances in the desert sun, and to see his pleasure dawn as some complex equation was solved in an instant, was unforgettable.

From my notes:

"I worked one morning in our officesfive5 miles along the road into the bush, working on training notes. I heard gradually increasing pandemonium and went out to the gates. And there were the Bagara on the march at the start of their annual migration away from the dangerous flies, which gradually swarmed around the Southern swamplands, and into the desert for their annual migration up to the oasis of El Obeid. It was like the annual migration of the London cockneys, out to pick autumnal fruit in the Kentish orchards. Men in the lead with spears, then the matrons sitting cross-legged astride large cows, with massive yokes carrying domestic implements food, leather tents, carpets, chickens and what have you. And then the children scampering around alongside playing games and full of the joys of life.

"Oh, the Bagara," Tom had said. "Give it another ten years and there won't be any."

But what on earth were we, the development project, to do with such splendid races, was and is a very valid question, and one without a lot of answers. I became increasingly suspicious that Tom Mangan wanted me to stay in Khartoum. What I would do there he wouldn't specify, but he didn't want me in Kadugli. He certainly didn't. In fact, he assigned my bungalow there – we had five bungalows in a compound on the edge of town – to a fellow mission, a ten-man World Bank "Land Utilisation Survey".

From my end, this was totally unacceptable – you can't "monitor and evaluate" progress on a massive project from the far side of the Sahara desert! Meanwhile visa clearances slowly accumulated. The officials were sometimes warmly and friendly, chatting easily about their country and its past links with the Brits, sometimes curt and hostile – after independence their government had swerved firmly to the Communist world.

Tom had gone south to Kadugli, and all my permissions had at last come through, so after a word with the Sheikh, I set arrangements in hand for my journey south. I went to the Brbassy Embassy – not the International splendours of Baghdad, but an attractive modern building feeling cool with the surrounding trees and vines – to see the First Secretary (Commercial) to get his view of the region:

"We have no information except of the gravest kind. We advise all British citizens not to go there. However (with a smile), if you do go, and you're clearly determined to do so, do let me know how you find it. Come and tell me about it."

We took off for the South before dawn, and at daybreak were skirting the bank of the Victoria Nile, then away across the desert. The tarmac road had mostly deteriorated to impassability, and our diesel-powered Land Cruiser followed the edges of the ruts cut by lorries, swerving and rolling to prevent the axles grounding. It was a rough ride, and we reached Kadugli around dusk the following day. Tom Mangan was hostile and bitterly angry at my arrival, and tried to move me out to stay at the project enclave five miles out. But servants, food, water and fuel were lacking there, so I moved in with him.

Things improved gradually, and I started courses for the project management on the PCs in DOS, Peachtree Accounting, Norton Antivirus, Laplink, Lotus spreadsheets and WordPerfect word processing, then the world leaders. It was a fascinating experience. I particularly recall teacammedAreit, the only Bagara tribesman on the project. To see this spare, hawk-eyed nomad looking at the screen, his face and eyes crinkled from years looking over vast distances in the desert sun, and to see his pleasure dawn as some complex equation was solved in an instant, was unforgettable.

Kadugli was a hilly, sprawling town. We, the World Bank project, were all in a large compound surrounded by euphorbia and flimsy brushwood fencing, and blessed – unlike in Khartoum – with generated electricity, and hence air conditioning in the evenings and refrigeration. I enjoyed the experience greatly, and often picked up my own food from the market – the meat was roughly chopped and fly infested, so overcooking was essential. Since we were south off the desert fringe, there were sometimes fresh vegetables, and local mangoes and their delicious pinkish grapefruits.

More ominously, sprawling across the open hillside by us was the provincial military barracks. At 5am on Easter Day we were awakened by heavy gunfire from the barracks, followed by more gunfire from first one sector in the distance, then another, then another. Not just small arms fire, serious stuff. They came round later in the day and explained that it was all just a celebration, because the new Governor was visiting.

The Pastik team were allowed out to selected areas (we were confined to the 5km main road from Kadugli to the Project HQ) and came back with useful pointers. Most worrying were the occasional big open trucks crowded up with people who seemed to overnight at transit camps out in the savannah en route north. We were told they were refugees. We suspected they were slaves en route to Arabia, as had been the practice a century earlier. Two years later, a detailed report in *The Observer* showed we were right. The Pastik team's most fascinating discovery was that the remains still existed of tanks (dams) built by the engineers of the Meroitic kingdom in the fifth century AD, left disused and abandoned for twelve hundred years. Their rehabilitation was built into the Water Development plan on which I was working. On the agricultural side, Tom's pigeon, the difficulties were massive, notably in agricultural extension. The security situation even in Kadugli was serious. Tom's progress meeting was broken up by a sudden burst of gunfire – the army next door were pouring machine gun fire up into the hills, perhaps with some reply – hard to tell. And if this was true in the town, how much more dangerous might it be for the extensionists. Their remit was to tour in pairs on foot or by bike, and encourage and exhort the villagers to adopt new plant varieties, etc. – all the activities we saw carried out under SCAPA, for example in RISDA, Malaysia and Malawi. The risks of death or kidnap by the SPLA were unacceptable – just as they are now in 2006 in Iraq.

Tom decided the only thing to do was to pull out of this area and base the Project in Dilling in the north, but I don't think this was taken seriously. Politically and militarily,

I think the government would regard such a move as a humiliating defeat.

We set up a system for regular progress review with the various government departments, to be chaired and driven by the Sheikh on the second Tuesday of each month. Then Tom and the Pastik team left for Khartoum, and I settled into my personal bungalow, doing my own cooking, and following the agreed training programme. It was immensely pleasing, and I particularly recall working one Saturday morning out at the HQ, greatly peaceful, to hear a rising hubbub on the road. Cockerels crowing, cattle lowing, children shouting, dogs barking. I walked outside to see the head of a long clan of Bagara nomads, starting off on their annual migration north. Large fat mothers sitting cross-legged on top of cows, gesturing imperiously at their offspring, family paraphernalia tied to the cows' flanks, children skipping around and laughing, goats and sheep herded along, chickens tied upside down to the flanks of spare heifers.

I failed to notice points of importance. Water of course, and diesel, were essential to our very existence in Kadugli, and Curtis Pastik and Tom, the two team leaders, spent much of their time driving these apparently simple issues. Continuous checks were made as to which of the five project tankers was where in the 3,000-mile return journey to the coast. What was the level of the water in the compound's two big tanks? Where to replenish it? Some of the sources were badly polluted – we found one spring was a hundred yards below a public urinal! Though, I suppose, urine is aseptic.

On the morning after they all went, I did a check. For water, there were a few gallons left in one tank, the other empty, and the fuel was very close indeed to exhaust. I tried to radio the Sheikh in Khartoum to get some action, but our set, brand new, was u/s (unserviceable). Atif and I eventually got through via another project's radio, and in due course the supplies were replenished, so I relaxed. I finished the first stage training – Lous sSpreadsheets for planning, and dBase and Wordstar – and returned with Atif and others to Khartoum. I should have asked myself how supplies for these twelve people had suddenly come on exhaust, simultaneous as soon as they left.

But deeper questions worried me. A World Bank review of the project was due immediately. How could it possibly survive, given that almost none of the objectives were being met and half the funds had been spent? Tom and I had helped prepare papers for submission at the meeting, to be held at El Obeid, a desert city halfway across the Sahara – the Governor would not even let the World Bank Head enter his province! Even though $40 million was at risk.

I got there for the meeting. The WB guy turned out to be a Brit, Oxbridge trained, and a National Twelve dinghy sailor against whom I might have raced on our local lake. So, we had some very friendly prior discussions. I urged him to consider that the funding need for the project was desperate, even though so little had been achieved. We'd now been assured the security situation was coming under increasingly firm control, and then progress might leap forward. The project should be given a chance in view of its massive problems and the desperate needs of the people. Tom stayed carefully absent at the local cinema, arriving just in time for the formal discussions and leaving without saying anything. I flew back together to Khartoum in the WB plane.

In Khartoum, Alison arrived and joined me in giving IT training for the HQ people. It was a familiar assignment for us, and they enjoyed the training. The WB review concluded that the project should continue providing a set of criteria, for example, for effective management were met by the one following a year later. Tom went on leave to the UK, and actions seemed to be being taken on his first monthly progress meeting. I resolved to go down to Kadugli by the time the next monthly meeting was due, and see what happened. That might be an acid test for me – was the whole business a whitewash for Tom's consumption, or were SKADP now in serious mode?

I had noticed an "Inception Report" by Robinson on the files, summarising the position on his engineering project when he arrived. Copied to Masdar and, crucially, to the World Bank. This seemed a way of getting through to the PMU management, so I drafted my own "Inception Report" and included an accurate but fairly damning summary of progress on the project to date – giving much of the background I'd given informally for the World Bank review. In casual discussions among expats, I'd suggested a major problem in Sudan was "The Inshallah Factor". Inshallah is the Arabic and Islamic word for "God willing". And their God, as described brilliantly in the article I'd given to Kofi Annan, is a God who is incalculably powerful and remote, symbolised by the fierce heat, blinding sun and the harshness of the desert environment. Good intentions signify nothing if they do not suit His irresistible and inscrutable will.

This word, "Inshallah", came into any discussion on progress and plans, as it does in many Arab countries. To me it conveyed the lack of confidence and determination which,

I thought, contributed greatly to project problems. No-one would rely on anything happening, hence the mentality of the Soukh. Trust no-one and make your bargain while you can. Yesterday's friend may well be tomorrow's enemy. But burnt into my experience was that our ICL computer operating systems could never have been created if this attitude had prevailed. In ICL, you stated your dependencies on others, for example, for a disc file driver to such and such a specification and date. They signed it off as a commitment, and woe-betide them if they failed to meet it. And woe-betide you if, when it was provided, you didn't immediately fall on it and use it. That was the attitude needed for this project. Of course, agriculturalists would respond that agriculture was "not like that". Too many imponderable variables – climate, disease, cultivations, planting materials, supplies, labour, credit, marketing and so on and so on. Even so, look at the success of the Malays in RISDA, and of the new smallholder tea and coffee organisations in East and Central Africa, where SCAPA was doing its stuff, and where long-established estates in India and Sri Lanka were being outperformed.

I terminated my report, urging the need for attitudes to change, and for us to be aware of the "Inshallah Factor" as a source of uncertainty, knowing this phrase might, for religious reasons, give great offence to Muslims. Alison typed it and I sent it off as a "draft for discussion" to the Sheikh, to Masdar and also to senior people in the project and key contacts, to provoke a response.

The Sheikh called me in:

"Graham, this has been seen by many people, and has given offence."

"But it is a serious problem."

"Maybe so. But it has given offence."

Masdar in the UK were never to receive their copy.

I left word quietly for the Sheikh that I was going to attend his monthly meeting at Kadugli in two days' time.

Would the meeting be held, I wondered? Would he be there or not? This was the acid test of their commitment. Exciting stuff!

Atif told me that seventeen people had been killed in Kadugli in a battle the week before – a matter too trivial, or perhaps too divisive, to get into the national press. He suggested we delayed our departure – but this would negate the acid test. So I set off with him for the South. Towards nightfall, we reached the transition between desert and the savannah, only 40 miles to go, when we encountered a convoy of SKADP vehicles coming in the opposite direction. I was greeted courteously, but peripherally. The project team walked around on the road, grasping each other by hands and slapping the forearms, hilariously amused by something. They all turned around and followed us towards Kadugli.

We were stopped at an army road block in the savannah and scrub ten miles on. A very educated and courteous young captain came to see me. There was an "operation" in progress and we must camp in his perimeter for the night. He, Atif told me, was one of "us" and could be trusted.

We pulled off the road at an encampment and I tried to settle down for the night. Visited by one or two of the team, who found my low-slung mosquito net hilariously funny. There was little sign of Atif, but I guess he was renewing friendship with others in the team. I felt laughed at and annoyed.

Then came an episode which was to colour my future for many years. I slept fitfully, and at about five – pitch dark in the tropics – I got up and started to stroll round the area. Suddenly, I looked around and found I couldn't identify my hut. Lost. But there was a faint glow of a fire in one direction. I wandered slowly towards it. I came up to a grass hut, or rather open shelter, and there by the side of a glowing smouldering fire were an old man and his wife. I felt a sudden sense of immense peace, of a permanent significance in this moment. Quite uncanny. I greeted them as usual:

"Salaam aleikum."

"Aleikum salaam!"

"Alhamdulillah."

"Alhamdulillah."

I stood for a long moment, and they looked at me. Then I drifted away and sat down on the sand to wait for dawn.

When it came, Atif came up and greeted me, smiling. But he seemed thunderously annoyed when I described my meeting with the old people.

We moved off to have breakfast along the road. Small pieces of liver simmered in a sauce, and eaten with your hands from a communal tureen. Not appetising when eaten for the third day in succession!

I felt a sort of worried detachment, and after we reached the project, sat at a desk for a while, then went to the compoundfive5 miles away.

When I'd settled in, there was a sudden burst of heavy machine gun fire from the barracks close by. I dived to the floor, recalling the experience of some friends in a similar situation in Kampala under Idi Amin. Forget your dignity, concentrate on surviving!

Like on the foredeck of a yacht in a gale – crouch down, hang on and crawl around – much more effective than standing in dignity as the rise of a wave hurls you over the side!

The firing went on desultorily for maybe a quarter of an hour. Then there was quiet. I settled down, then heard stealthy noises outside. I flung the door open, and there was a fit, heavyset young army officer with my cook. I flung a punch at him, thinking he was persecuting the little cook. He parried it with ease, smiling as he did so, and grabbed me. I was taken down to stand at an office window I was to get to know later. And interrogated. All I would give was my name and affiliation – as in "name rank and number" one was told to give in the army if captured. Nothing else.

The next incident I recall was sitting at a long table in the open – evening time – with about six officials interrogating me, and, I thought, numerous people behind me. In the open, before a long low building and with a low hedge behind me, I felt that I was under deep threat, refused to answer many questions, then suddenly flung myself upwards, flinging my arms outwards, and letting out a colossal shout. They might well kill me, I thought, but rumours might survive for people to track down in years to come.

I was bundled on a stretcher and trundled to a hospital ward. There I was awakened in the night by the sound of people coming past. Just visible in the light from dim oil lamps. A bit like being the corpse with mourners filing past. An educated voice said:

"He talked to them in their own tongue, they say. Just like one of them."

"Nonsense."

"That's what they say."

After this, delirium set in, with apocalyptic visions – one included thundering engines, military sounding, as of tanks in some battle between good and evil – another a confrontation between the advanced nations – the "West" and the "East" – in a search for goodness in at least one human being – a search which failed at first, and yet again, even after both had been substituted for by the innocence of Africa. It was a terrible time, during which I was fed on a drip, on my own in a small ward with just a guard with a Kalashnikov standing on duty in the corner.

My interpretation of all this is that my meeting with the two old people, and the public interrogation and my gesture of defiance, had become enmeshed in the conflict between the Arabs and Africans. For the latter, I'd been seen as a saviour, sent to them by God. So I aimed to relieve this perception by behaving as a demonstrably fallible human. At the same time, I did strange things like crawling around the wards under the beds at night, and on one occasion, outside – bidding to crawl off across the Sahara!

Two incidents stand out. In the first I was talking to three of the team, led by the Sudanese Agricultural Advisor.

"Can we now start the Lotus spreadsheet course?" I asked.

"No. We have not finished with you yet," was the grinding answer.

And another day, I was taken to the Land Rover with my kit to stand in front of them on a grassy patch.

"Now we will say goodbye to you," he said in a hostile tone. Then he turned triumphantly to the others:

"First Robinson," he said, "then Mangan. And now Tottle."

They laughed. They'd got rid of the WB Brits. We roared off down a very rough track northwards, perhaps, I think, to get past hostile road blocks, until we reached the provincial boundary. Then more sedately to El Obeid for the night, and on to Khartoum.

My hallucinations continued throughout. I particularly remember watching out of the Land Rover window as herds of camels stretching to the far desert horizon, strode forward step by step in unison. Line after line.

My sister had realised the telex was a plea for help, that something strange was up. She got onto MASDAR and set in train actions which eventually had me moved back across the desert, affected by acute psychosis, to a hospital in Khartoum. Thence, they removed me to the Amebassy Embassy, and there a formidable doctor fixed electrodes around my head and torso, and shouted into my face imprecations which I didn't understand. After he was satisfied with whatever he was doing, he relaxed and put me in a cot in his office. The next morning I was taken by a psychiatric nurse to the airport and hustled across a waiting zone towards a plane. "This is a very ripe fruit cake indeed," I overheard him saying. He had to take me off the first plane home because I was too violent, and keep me in the US security compound till the next day. Thence, I was put in the splendid cavernous Parkside mental hospital in Macclesfield. There it took a month's gentle treatment, and the healing effects of its lovely green parkland, to bring me back to partial sanity.

Appendix 4

Nuclear Power Station. The problem with the station had been embrittlement of the reactor steel due to the cold temperature at the base – rather like the welded ships in the Second World War; on arctic convoy runs to Murmansk, the steel became dangerously brittle, particularly when the hulls were stressed in storms. And unlike traditional riveted craft, a welded hull could fracture right through without warning. Liberty ships, they were called, but often they were crowded cruising coffins, biding their moments to plunge or founder.

Liquid CO_2, not prone to nuclear contamination, circulated from the reactor to the boilers, where water was steamed up in heat exchange to drive the turbines. The steam screamed past the honed blades with unbelievable power. Tiny residual droplets slammed the leading edges with such violence that the titanium was gradually pierced to become a paper-thin honeycomb where once it was solid tempered metal.

Appendix 5

From Julius Caesar

SCENE II. The Forum.

ANTONY
Moreover, he hath left you all his walks,
His private arbours and new-planted orchards,
On this side Tiber; he hath left them you,
And to your heirs for ever, common pleasures,
To walk abroad, and recreate yourselves.
Here was a Caesar! when comes such another?

First Citizen
Never, never. Come, away, away!
We'll burn his body in the holy place,
And with the brands fire the traitors' houses.
Take up the body.

Second Citizen
Go fetch fire.

Third Citizen
Pluck down benches.

Fourth Citizen
Pluck down forms, windows, any thing.

Exeunt Citizens with the body

ANTONY
Now let it work. Mischief, thou art afoot,
Take thou what course thou wilt!

Enter a Servant

How now, fellow!

Servant
Sir, Octavius is already come to Rome.

ANTONY
Where is he?

Servant
He and Lepidus are at Caesar's house.

ANTONY
And thither will I straight to visit him:
He comes upon a wish. Fortune is merry,
And in this mood will give us any thing.

Appendix 6

ON ILKLEY MOOR BAHT 'AT

Wheear 'as ta bin sin ah saw thee,
Where have you been since I saw you
On Ilkla Moor baht 'at!
On Ilkley M-moor without a hat
Wheear 'as ta bin sin ah saw thee,
Where have you been since I saw you
On Ilkla Moor baht 'at!
On Ilkley M-moor without a hat
<u>On Ilkla Moor baht 'at!</u> <u>baht 'at</u>
<u>On Ilkla Moor baht 'at!</u> <u>baht 'at</u>
<u>On Ilkla Moor baht 'at!</u>

Tha's been a cooartin' Mary Jane
You've been courting Mary Jane
On Ilkla Moor baht 'at
On Ilkley Moor without a hat
Tha's been a cooartin' Mary Jane
You've been courting Mary Jane
Tha's been a cooartin' Mary Jane
You've been courting Mary Jane

<u>Chorus</u>

Tha's bahn t'catch thi deeath o'cowd
You's bahn t'catch thi deeath ong.

.On Ilkla Moor baht 'at
On Ilkley Moor without a hat
Tha's bahn t'catch thi deeath o'cowd
You's bahn t'catch thi deeath ocold
Tha's bahn t'catch thi deeath o'cowd
You's b tt to catch your death of cold

Chorus

Then we shall ha' to bury thee
Then we shall have to bury you
On Ilkla Moor baht 'at
On Ilkley Moor without a hat
Then we shall ha' to bury thee
Then we shall have to bury you
Then we shall ha' to bury thee
Then we shall have to bury you

Chorus

Then t'orms' 'll cum and eat thee oop
Then the worms will come and eat you up
On Ilkla Moor baht 'at
On Ilkley Moor without a hat
Then t'orms' 'll cum and eat thee oop
Then the worms will come and eat you up
Then t'orms' 'll cum and eat thee oop
Then the worms will come and eat you up

Chorus

Then ucks' 'll cum and eat oop t'worms
Then the ducks will come and eat up the worms
On Ilkla Moor baht 'at
On Ilkley Moor without a hat
Then ucks' 'll cum and eat oop t'worms

Then the ducks will come and eat up the worms
Then dcks "ll cum and eat oop t'worms
Then the ducks will come and eat up the worms

<u>Chorus</u>

Then we shall go an' ate oop ducks
Then we will go and eat up the ducks
On Ilkla Moor baht 'at
On Ilkley Moor without a hat
Then we shall go an' ate oop ducks
Then we will go and eat up the ducks
Then we shall go an' ate oop ducks
Then we will go and eat up the ducks

<u>Chorus</u>

Then we shall all 'ave etten thee
Then we will all have eaten you
On Ilkla Moor baht 'at
On Ilkley Moor without a hat

Then we shall all 'ave etten thee
Then we will all have eaten you
Then we shall all 'ave etten thee
Then we will all have eaten you

<u>Chorus</u>

Appendix 7

How the Dassie lost its tail – Xhosa legend

A long time ago, long before man was created, the Lion was king of all the animals.

A most distinguished king he was indeed with a massive tail. Sure he was very proud of his tail and liked to parade it before all his subjects. But there were moments when he felt sorry for the other animals. He realised that a tail was not only something beautiful, but also very useful. Sometimes he even felt the odd one out, sensing that the other animals stirred with jealousy. The King decided one fine day that he would make tails for all his subjects and present them personally. How his eyes glitter in anticipation; what a wonderful surprise it would be.

He busily set to work crafting tails in all sorts of wondrous shapes and sizes. When it was accomplished, he contentedly looked at his work. Then he summoned Baboon, ordering him to call all animals to appear before him.

Far and wide, Baboon passed on the Royal order, and the animals set off to the Lion's Court, and by night fall, all had arrived, except the Dassie. Dassie asked Baboon to collect his present for him and let the king know that he felt too ashamed to appear before him. Being good-natured, Baboon agreed.

The King warmly greeted his subjects, standing expectantly around him, and began to hand out the presents. Despite the bright moon, the ageing King with his failing eyesight could not always distinguish the size and shape of tail which he pulled out from the bag. Thus, the mighty elephant stood expectantly before him and the King pulled out a curly little tail to give to this animal. Of course the elephant was far too polite to protest and trotted off. And when it was squirrel's turn, the King handed him a big bushy tail far too big for him. But the squirrel hopped off gratefully. The sack emptied and the Lion noticed that the Dassie was missing and roared at them all. In the excitement, Baboon had forgotten to pass on the Dassie's apology. Lion was furious, but in the end agreed for Baboon to take the present to the Dassie. He picked up a long tail for the Dassie, and as the festivities drew to an end, Baboon set off. But the road was rough, the day had been long and he was exhausted. He rested on a rocky ledge.

He does not deserve a present, lazy fellow that he is, he thought.

Nevertheless, he wanted to teach Dassie a lesson, so he sauntered off to the Dassie's rocky ledge and showed off his tail, mocking poor little Dassie. Of course, Dassie was upset that he had no tail at all but was far too lazy to do anything about it.

"See if I care," he muttered under his breath.

Acknowledgements

My warmest thanks go to many people, whom I have quoted, with great thanks to them, but I'd like to mention particularly:

Gareth Williams, Welsh archaeologist, who has contributed immensely, Jenny Ratcliffe who read drafts from the earliest, and kept the plot on track, Dr Judy Rose who provided the horticultural detail and vetted the IT pieces, Callum Hughes and his aunt, responsible for most of the Welsh, Cemley Griffiths for the Russian translation, and, foremost, my old friend, Dr Majid Dujaily.

This book owes an immense amount to critique, suggestions and editing by Shirley (editor), Gabriel, James and A N Other (cover design). Also Granada for the picture of Dylan Thomas and *The Times* for the picture of the drone.

(c) Graham Tottle

Endnotes

1 Who's there? Stop matey!

2 Stop at once. Freeze

3 "Mischief, thou art afoot,

take thou what course thou wilt."

Julius Caesar

Marc Antony, having kidded Brutus, Cassius and others who slew the "tyrant" Caesar, that he will only make a brief funeral speech to the populace: "So are they all. All honourable men." Antony has turned the populace around and incited violent revolution.

4 This was among the key issues upside in the noughts, part of the male backlash against overweening feminism. The move was triggered particularly by a book by one Anthony Clare, "Masculinity in Crisis". Clare had made his name as the psychologist in the chair, conducting perceptive interviews on BBC Radio 4 with the famous, notorious or interesting, exploring their lives, motivation and so on. From this plank, he became a media guru on psychology, and then published the book, which became widely debated. In Clare's Weltanschauung, the male in the global society was a dangerous source of instability and aggression, against a picture in which the female could carry out

all the functions needed, and do so tenderly, empathetically and with a deeply tuned capacity for relating to others. In fact, what had happened in society was an upsurge of feminism, which the scrawls on the CAB wall had mildly satirised. You could take the old adage "sticks and stones may break my bones, but words can never hurt me". In crumbling relationships, physical violence, the sticks and stones were usually the males' offence. But what Clare and his colleagues adequately failed to suss out was that the "words" of the adage, perhaps the continual abuse or nagging or criticism, could also be poisonously effective. And they were the province of the female.

The CAB was among the organisations to pull some of these chestnuts out of the fire, especially in the context of breaking families. As the marriage or partnership broke up, each parent drew away and formed a new view of life; these views inevitably diverged, and in the harrowing business of break-up, partitioning the possessions, resolving the home ownership, and most of all, custody of the children, each partner's attitudes typically hardened at the kids' expense.

In principle, society held that the childrens' best interests must be paramount. But in practice, chief custody went to the woman, access occasionally going to the man for set hours on set days. For quite natural reasons, a political element crept into the relationship, and the men were gradually squeezed out, the weekly access visits with Dad became more and more harrowing. You could see them out, say, at the local zoo or wherever, working hard to give the youngsters a good time, and slowly finding it harder and harder, until the whole thing collapsed.

Until the nation's children acquired a complement of 30 per cent of single mums, where previously they'd had dads as well. The correlation between this and the violence, ignorance, low self-esteem and so on of the youngsters, was widely documented.

Part of the very successful answer was to strengthen the court's jurisdiction and determination when access orders were flouted by self-centered mothers. Until then, a mother who ignored court orders to allow a father reasonable access was effectively unchecked. Almost without exception, the dads eventually gave up in immense pain, and formed a new childless life.

Even in cases where access was equal, and the children spent half the time with the mum and half with the dad, the law was woman-biased – sometimes the mums would actually put Social Security onto the dads, and get them dunned for child maintenance.

Interestingly, the "amateurs", like the volunteer workers in the NGOs, were much more aware of these realities than the clinical psychiatrists and social workers. The Christmas round-robin from the National Womens' Register in one issue gave this wry analysis of the feminine viewpoint:

RULES.WOM **The RULES**

The FEMALE always makes the rules

The rules are subject to change at any time without notice

No MALE can possibly know all the rules

If the FEMALE suspects the MALE knows all the rules, she must immediately change some of the rules

The FEMALE is never wrong

If the FEMALE is wrong, it is a result of something the MALE said or did wrong

The MALE must immediately apologise for causing said misunderstanding

The FEMALE may change her mind at any time

The MALE must not change his mind without the express written consent of the FEMALE

The FEMALE has the right to be angry or upset at any time

The MALE must remain calm at all times, unless the FEMALE wants him to be angry or upset

The FEMALE must, under no circumstances, let the MALE know whether she wants him to be angry or upset

The MALE is expected to mind read always

If the FEMALE has PMT, all the rules are invalid

The FEMALE is ready when she is ready

The MALE must be ready at all times

Any attempt to document the rules could result in bodily harm

The MALE who doesn't abide by the rules can't take the heat, lacks backbone and is a wimp.

The answer was, in part, education, education, education, to quote what was called a sound bite of the time. For hosts of reasons, not least the immense economic costs incurred through one-parenting and father-free families, society ceased to stand back and let the woman have her way. And so, ongoing training in citizenship came to include, for those whose relationships were being sundered, mandatory sessions for the partners picking out how important the relationships were for the children, and the way the partners had to control their natural feelings of growing apartness and lean over backwards to make access agreements, and so on, work caringly and smoothly. And, imitating Henry VII's splendid practice towards the overweening barons, the arrangements were enforced not by confrontation and sledgehammer action in the courts, but by simple economics – slight deductions in family allowances, slight penalties in taxation deducted automatically through PAYE, for example.

But more importantly, society and its key institutions – the four estates, the religions, the arts, medicine, commerce, industry and agriculture, regained their confidence in the rightness of family relationships. Political rectitude became as derided as was McCarthyism in the US. The process of returning to marriage and gender roles some of the legislative and revenue and other privileges, which had helped bolster the nuclear family as the norm of gender relationships, without losing the increased freedoms for women and gays, was an exciting one.

5 Named after a Richard Dawkins, a brilliant biologist.

In Britain, of course, actions like sloshing out large tractor loads of cattle dung on approach roads for the big events worked effectively. Man United vs Arsenal, the opening of Parliament at Westminster or Belfast, the Welsh Eistedfod, the Edinburgh tattoo, a state visit to the Prime Minister's residence at Chequers in Wendover.

Political theorists held sway. Notably Dawkins. In the following, I give a recent critical view of his work and influence. H. B. G-W

The Dawkins delusion

I'm an agnostic Anglican Christian. Doubting and hoping vaguely, like Doubting Thomas in the upstairs room, before Christ perhaps reappeared, and I have probed Dawkins's background, message and motivation, expressed, for example, in his best-selling book "The God Delusion", or in his half page article in *The Observer* newspaper deriding Christianity as

"militant" and destructive, and selective from the rarely sung hymn "Onward Christian Soldiers" marching AS IF TO war. Delete the "as to" and he was right. But dishonest.

Here is a man who, as a youngster and a teenager, was brought up as a devout Christian Methodist. The overwhelming messages of this education must have been built into his mind and his soul. Peacefulness, love, forgiveness, compassion, etc., as in the Christian Beatitudes.

"Blessed are the peacemakers, for theirs is the kingdom of heaven."

Or the lovely bucolic hymn at harvest time:
"We plough the fields and scatter
The good seed on the land"
Or the message from the angels at the birth of Christ:

"And on earth, peace, goodwill toward men."

Or the Book of Common Prayer:
"Bless and succour all those who in this transitory life are in sorrow, need, sickness or any other adversity, and grant them a happy issue from all their afflictions."

Imagine the hope and solace this and so much more has brought to billions of people. Hope which Dawkins dismisses so deliberately and misleadingly. Goodness and loving kindness are absent from his vocabulary. How far should we trust him?

Only, I suggest, trust Dawkins as a biologist. And there he emphasises the importance of the cell boundary in containing and controlling the developments within it. Does that marry with the emphasis in those days on uninhibited transit across national frontiers? Global financial meltdowns? Global gluttony of the planet's resources? Global extinction of non-human species? Global slopping and sloshing and swilling around of human talent? He didn't say. But these ideas about boundaries gave rise to the dramatic political theory often called Dawkinsism. Closing boundaries and keeping people inside them. To quote Enoch Powell's much reviled diatribe against uncontrolled immigration from the Commonwealth into the UK in the 1960s:

"I see the river Tiber foaming much blood."

What the people of the UK failed to grasp was that for millions of people overseas, for then as in 2020, the UK was a Mecca of unbelievable prosperity.

Worth risking even the sacrifice of your life to attain.

We now have a sustainable world, and the extraordinary pronunciations of the mediacrats in the early 2000s are discredited, often derided. My favourite example is from the UN consultant, Rundle, in Pyongyang. It is worth repeating:

A BBC commentator showed a satellite view of East Asia at night. China, South Korea and Japan were a blaze of light. North Korea was in total darkness. There you are, she said, contrast the shining civilisation around it with the pariah state and darkness within.

But, I thought, maybe the pariah state has it right. Is there any other state in the world that can claim to be

sustainable in the face of globalisation and democracy? Not since the exit of the "Gang of Four" in China and the death of Chairman Mao. He was responsible for thirty million deaths. But his country was sustainable as a result, for example, with his "one child per family" policy limiting the escalation of the population. If you will keep on increasing the world's population, it will cost you.

About North Korea, Robert Galucci, US chief negotiator in the Korean unification talks, said:

"These people are committed Stalinists. They know what they're about. We mess with them at our peril worldwide."

As my Malaysian friends would say:
"Who can tell?"

Self-Assessmer

Resp
Medicine
Second Edition

Stephen G. Spiro BSc, MD, FRCP
Head, Division of Respiratory Medicine
Clinical Director of Medicine
University College London Hospitals, London, UK

Richard K. Albert MD
Professor and Vice-Chair
University of Colorado Health Sciences Center
Chief of Medicine
Denver Health Medical Center, Colorado, USA

David Fielding FRACP, MD
Visiting Respiratory Physician
Royal Brisbane Hospital, Queensland, Australia

Angshu Bhowmik MBBS, MRCP
Specialist Registrar in Respiratory Medicine
University College London Hospitals, London, UK

MANSON
PUBLISHING

Acknowledgements

For their help in preparing this book we thank Dr Simon Abel (Registrar, Papworth Hospital, Cambridge, UK), Dr J. Bomanji (Department of Nuclear Medicine, University College London Hospitals, UK), Dr Merryl Griffiths (Department of Histopathology, University College London Hospitals, UK), and Dr Martin Hetzel (formerly of Department of Respiratory Medicine, University College London Hospitals, UK).

Copyright © 2004 Manson Publishing Ltd
ISBN 1–84076–046–X

A CIP catalogue record for this book is available from the British Library.

For full details of all Manson Publishing Ltd titles please write to:
Manson Publishing Ltd, 73 Corringham Road, London NW11 7DL, UK.
Tel: +44(0)20 8905 5150
Fax: +44(0)20 8201 9233
Website: www.manson-publishing.co.uk

Printed by: Grafos SA, Barcelona, Spain

Preface

Students and practitioners of respiratory medicine are aware that it covers many diverse areas and encompasses about 25% of all general medical problems. The questions and answers in this book aim to present key points on topics across this spectrum of diseases. There are proportionally more problems on the common disorders, including lung cancer, obstructive airways disease, and pulmonary infections. Other topics include lung function testing, occupational medicine, sleep medicine, intensive care, interventional techniques, thoracic surgery, pulmonary vascular disease, immunological disorders, nasal pathology, and pulmonary fibrosis. Pulmonary manifestations of systemic disease and human immunodeficiency virus are also covered.

The aim of this book is to increase the reader's understanding of clinically relevant topics by providing explanatory answers; it is more than a book of spot diagnosis questions or a catalogue of rare conditions with interesting radiological featurs which the reader simply knows or does not.

The contributors have extensive experience in their specialized fields and have described situations which reflect actual practice, in so far as is possible. Several have just completed their specialist training and have provided questions that they consider of particular value to those undergoing specialist accreditation. Furthermore, by presenting the questions in pictorial form we hope that the problems become more interesting and the material easier to remember for the reader.

Stephen G. Spiro
Richard K. Albert
David Fielding
Angshu Bhowmik

Contributors

Richard K. Albert, MD
Professor and Vice-Chair
University of Colorado Health Sciences Center
Chief of Medicine
Denver Health Medical Center
Denver, CO, USA

Roger Allen, FCCP, FRACP, PhD
Consultant Respiratory Physician
Clinical Associate Professor
Prince Charles Hospital, Brisbane, Australia

Angshu Bhowmik, MBBS, MRCP
Specialst Registrar in Respiratory Medicine
University College London Hospitals
London, UK

Griffith M. Blackmon, MD, MPH
Kitsap Chest Consultants
Bremerton, WA, USA

M. Gary Brook, MRCP
Senior Registrar in Genitourinary Medicine
University College London Hospitals
London, UK

Feroza M. Daroowalla, MD, MPH
Clinical Assistant Professor
Stony Brook University, NY, USA

David Fielding, FRACP
Visiting Respiratory Physician
Royal Brisbane Hospital
Brisbane, Queensland, Australia

Rebecca Fox-Dewhurst, MD
Issaquah, WA, USA

Vishesh K. Kapur, MD
Assistant Professor of Medicine
University of Washington
Harborview Medical Center, Seattle, WA, USA

Margaret Krieg, MD
The Doctors Clinic/Pulmonary Medicine
Bremerton, WA, USA

Alan W. Matthews, MD, FRCP
Consultant Physician
Queen Alexandra Hospital, Portsmouth, UK

Robert F. Miller, MRCP
Senior Lecturer and Consultant Physician
University College London Hospitals
London, UK

David R. Park, MD
Assistant Professor
University of Washington
Harborview Medical Center
Seattle, WA, USA

Wilfred B. Pugsley, FRCS
Consultant Cardiothoracic Surgeon
Middlesex Hospital, London, UK

Stephen G. Spiro, BSc, MD, FRCP
Head, Division of Respiratory Medicine
Clinical Director of Medicine
University College London Hospitals
London, UK

Eric J. Stern, MD
Professor of Radiology and Medicine
University of Washington
Harborview Medical Center, Seattle, WA, USA

Yoke Khim Tan, M. Med
Visiting Senior Registrar
Middlesex Hospital, London, UK

David F. Treacher, MRCP
Consultant Physician
Director of Intensive Care
St Thomas' Hospital, London, UK

William Walker, FRCP
Consultant Cardiothoracic Surgeon
City Hospital, Edinburgh, UK

Bennet M. Wang, MD
Pulmonary & Critical Care Medicine
Group Health Cooperative of Puget Sound
Seattle, WA, USA

A. Kevin Webb, MRCP
Consultant Chest Physician
Wythenshawe Hospital, Manchester, UK

Mark Woodhead, MRCP
Consultant in General and Respiratory Medicine
Manchester Royal Infirmary Manchester, UK

Abbreviations

2D	two-dimensional
ABPA	allergic bronchopulmonary aspergillosis
ACE	angiotensin converting enzyme
ACTH	adrenocorticotrophic hormone
AFB	acid fast bacilli
AHI	apnoea–hypoapnoea index
AIDS	acquired immune deficiency syndrome
ANCA	anti-cytoplasmic antibodies
AP	anteroposterior
ARDS	acute respiratory distress syndrome
ATS	American Thoracic Society
BAL	bronchoalveolar lavage
BMT	bone marrow transplant
BOOP	bronchiolitis obliterans organizing pneumonia
CF	cystic fibrosis
CFA	cryptogenic fibrosing alveolitis
CMV	cytomegalovirus
CNS	central nervous system
COAD	chronic obstructive airways disease
COPD	chronic obstructive pulmonary disease
CPAP	continuous positive airways pressure
CRP	C-reactive protein
CSF	cerebrospinal fluid
CT	computed tomography
CTPA	computed tomography pulmonary angiogram
CWP	coal workers' pneumoconiosis
CXR	chest X-ray
DIC	disseminated intravascular coagulation
DIOS	distal intestinal obstruction syndrome
DIP	desquamative interstitial pneumonia
DL_{CO}	diffusion coefficient for carbon monoxide
DNA	deoxyribonucleic acid
DOT	directly observed therapy
DRSP	drug resistant *Streptococcus pneumoniae*
DTPA	diethylenetriamine penta-acetate
DVT	deep vein thrombosis
ECMO	extra corporeal membrane oxygenation
ECG	electrocardiogram
EEG	electroencephalogram
EMG	electromyogram
ERV	expiratory reserve volume
ESR	erythrocyte sedimentation rate
ET	endotracheal
FEV	forced expiratory volume
F_IO_2	inspired oxygen fraction
FRC	functional residual capacity
FVC	forced vital capacity
HCG	human chorionic gonadotropin
HDI	hexamethylene diisocyanate
HIV	human immunodeficiency virus
HLA	human leukocyte antigen
HP	hypersensitivity pneumonitis
HPOA	hypertrophic pulmonary osteoarthropathy
HRCT	high-resolution computed tomography
ICS	inhaled corticosteroids
ILO	International Labour Organization
IPF	idiopathic pulmonary fibrosis
JVP	jugular venous pressure
KS	Kaposi's sarcoma
LAUP	laser-assisted uvulopalatoplasty
LEMS	Lambert–Eaton syndrome
LTOT	long-term oxygen therapy
LVF	left ventricular failure
MAC	*Mycobacterium avium-intracellulare* complex
MDI	(diphenyl) methane diisocyanate
MDP	methylene diphosphonate
MHC	major histocompatability complex
MIC	minimum inhibitory concentration
MRC	Medical Research Council
MRI	magnetic resonance imaging
MSLT	multiple sleep latency testing
MST	morphine sulphate continus
NOTT	Nocturnal Oxygen Therapy Trial
NSIP	non-specific interstitial pneumonia
OCS	oral corticosteroids
OLB	open lung biopsy
OSA	obstructive sleep apnoea
PA	posteroanterior
PAN	polyarteritis nodosa
PAS	periodic acid–Schiff
PCP	*Pneumocystis carinii (jiroveci)* pneumonia

Abbreviations

PCR	polymerase chain reaction	RV	residual volume
PDT	photodynamic therapy	SCLC	small-cell lung cancer
PE	pulmonary embolism	SIADH	syndrome of inappropriate
PEEP	positive end-expiratory pressure		anti-diuretic hormone secretion
PEFR	peak expiratory flow rate	SLE	systemic lupus erythematosus
PET	positron emission tomography	SVCO	superior vena caval obstruction
PIE	pulmonary infiltrates with	TDI	toluene diisocyanate
	eosinophilia (syndrome)	TLC	total lung capacity
PIOPED	prospective investigation of	TNM	tumour classification system
	pulmonary embolism diagnosis	UAWO	upper airway obstruction
PLMS	periodic limb movement in sleep	UIP	usual interstitial pneumonia
PMF	progressive massive fibrosis	UPPP	uvulopalatopharyngoplasty
PTE	pulmonary thromboembolism	VATS	video-assisted thoracoscopic
RAP	right atrial pressure		surgery
RBILD	respiratory bronchioloitis-	VA	alveolar volume
	associated interstitial lung disease	VC	vital capacity
REM	rapid eye movement (sleep)	VD	dead space
RLS	restless leg syndrome	VO$_2$	maximal oxygen uptake
RQ	respiratory exchange ratio	V/Q	ventilation perfusion (scan)
	(quotient)	YAG	yttrium aluminium garnet (laser)

Bacterial, fungal, and other organism abbreviations

A. fumigatus	*Aspergillus fumigatus*	*M. tuberculosis*	*Mycobacterium tuberculosis*
B. cepacia	*Burkholderia cepacia*		
C. albicans	*Candida albicans*	*Myc. pneumoniae*	*Mycoplasma pneumoniae*
C. burnetti	*Coxiella burnetti*	*P. carinii*	*Pneumocystis carinii*
C. neoformans	*Cryptococcus neoformans*	*P. aeruginosa*	*Pseudomonas aeruginosa*
		P. pseudomallei	*Pseudomonas pseudomallei*
C. psittaci	*Chlamydia psittaci*		
E. coli	*Escherichia coli*	*S. haemotibia*	*Schistosoma haemotibia*
H. influenzae	*Haemophilus influenzae*	*S. japonica*	*Schistosoma japonica*
		S. mansoni	*Schistosoma mansoni*
K. pneumoniae	*Klebsiella pneumoniae*	*Staph. aureus*	*Staphylococcus aureus*
L. pneumophila	*Legionella pneumophila*	*Str. pneumoniae*	*Streptococcus pneumoniae*
M. avium	*Mycobacterium avium*		
M. intracellulare	*Mycobacterium intracellulare*	*T. gondii*	*Toxoplasma gondii*
M. kansasii	*Mycobacterium kansasii*		

1 This HIV-positive man has developed several new lesions, as that in **1a**.
i. What is the diagnosis?
ii. How and when may the lung be affected by this condition and what is its therapy?

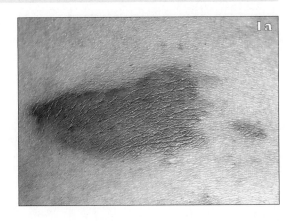

2 **i.** What stain has been employed on this endobronchial biopsy (**2a, 2b**)?
ii. Is this positive staining specific for this condition?
iii. Are these tumours usually confined to within the bronchial lumen?

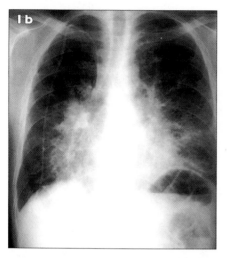

1 i. 1a shows a typical lesion of Kaposi's sarcoma (KS). KS is usually purple but can be red and is either papular or nodular, or less commonly macular or forms plaques. Lymphoedema of the surrounding tissue is often marked. There are often several lesions which can appear at different parts of the body. ii. KS can remain localized for months or even years in patients with high CD4 counts. Lung involvement is most commonly seen in patients with lower CD4+ lymphocyte counts ($<0.2\times10^9$/l) when the cutaneous lesions often become more widespread and the disease may involve lymph nodes and viscera. Endobronchial involvement can lead to bronchial obstruction with distal collapse or infection. Parenchymal lung disease (**1b**), often associated with surrounding oedema, may cause dyspnoea with reduced gas transfer. Endobronchial lesions may cause an obstructive pattern on spirometry and frequently present with cough. The chest radiograph can reveal interstitial shadows, nodular shadowing that may coalesce, hilar or mediastinal lymphadenopathy and pleural effusions. Endobronchial lesions may be seen at bronchoscopy. More peripheral or interstitial lesions can be identified on high-resolution CT (spiral) scanning. Localized KS is usually treated with radiotherapy. Vincristine, bleomycin, liposomal doxorubicin or daunorubicin, paclitaxel, and interferon alpha are treatment modalities used for disseminated KS. It is now recommended that patients with AIDS-related KS who are receiving effective anti-retroviral therapy begin receiving low-dose interferon-[alpha] alone or after induction chemotherapy with an anthracycline or paclitaxel. Experimental treatments such as anti-angiogenesis compounds, interleukin-6 monoclonal antibodies and anti-human herpesvirus-8 agents are being evaluated.

2 i. The histological features of islands and ribbons of cells with uniform nuclei and cytoplasm are consistent with a carcinoid tumour and the stain chromogranin has been used to verify the neuroendocrine nature of this tumour (**2a**). Other stains which could have been used for this purpose include neurone-specific enolase and synaptophysin.
ii. The stain is specific for cells of neuroendocrine origin; however, other lung tumours of neuroendocrine origin including small cell carcinoma and atypical carcinoids will also be positive for neuroendocrine staining.
iii. Carcinoid tumours often infiltrate the bronchial wall and the part of it visible at bronchoscopy may be the 'tip of the iceberg'. **2b** shows the tumour bulging into the bronchial lumen and deforming it. They also tend to be highly vascular and, if suspected by its macroscopic appearance, are preferably biopsied with rigid bronchoscopy.

3 This low-power photomicrograph (3) of a Wright–Geimsa-stained cytospin has been prepared from bronchoalveolar lavage (BAL) fluid from a normal volunteer.
i. Describe a typical protocol for performing BAL.
ii. What is the expected cell recovery from normal subjects?

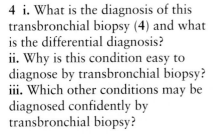

4 i. What is the diagnosis of this transbronchial biopsy (4) and what is the differential diagnosis?
ii. Why is this condition easy to diagnose by transbronchial biopsy?
iii. Which other conditions may be diagnosed confidently by transbronchial biopsy?

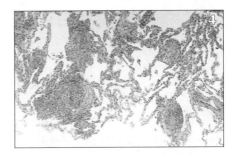

5 The chest radiographs in 5a , 5b are of the same 38-year-old man, both taken in full inspiration 2 weeks apart. He presented with ocular symptoms, then bulbar weakness and finally dyspnoea. The vital capacity was 1.2 l. Over the 4 days before the second film was taken he received treatment that required brief daily admissions to the intensive care unit.
i. What is the likely cause of the radiographic abnormalities?
ii. What degree of muscular weakness results in respiratory failure?

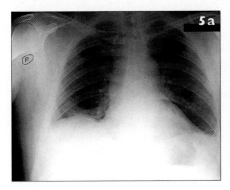
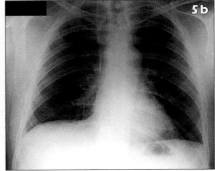

3 i. BAL is performed by wedging the tip of a flexible fibre-optic bronchoscope into a segmental or subsegmental airway until the lumen is occluded. Sequential 30–50 ml aliquots of physiological saline are then instilled through the working channel of the bronchoscope and withdrawn. The total volume of saline used is typically 150–200 ml and approximately 50% is recovered. The remainder is rapidly absorbed or expectorated. It is estimated that BAL fluid represents an approximately 100-fold dilution of alveolar epithelial lining fluid.

ii. Approximately 10×10^6 cells are normally recovered, of which >85% are alveolar macrophages, 7% are lymphocytes (predominantly T-cells), 3% are airway epithelial cells, and <5% each are neutrophils, eosinophils, basophils and mast cells. Greater numbers of cells are commonly found in cigarette smokers and urban dwellers.

4 i. The compact granulomas with a paucity of interstitial inflammation are typical of sarcoidosis.

ii. The granulomas are situated adjacent to bronchi, making them amenable to diagnosis by bronchial or transbronchial biopsy. Only four separate biopsies are usually needed to obtain typical granulomas. A transbronchial lung biopsy may be positive, even when the chest radiograph shows only hilar lymphadenopathy without parenchymal shadowing. The main differential is extrinsic allergic alveolitis, though here the granulomas are not so tightly formed and are overshadowed by an interstitial inflammatory cell infiltrate.

iii. Other conditions which can be readily diagnosed with transbronchial lung biopsy include lymphangitis carcinomatosa and alveolar proteinosis. Conditions such as idiopathic pulmonary fibrosis may be suggested by transbronchial biopsy, but definitive diagnosis usually requires large samples such as from an open lung biopsy.

5 i. The first chest radiograph (5a) shows small lung fields with bilateral atelectasis most marked on the right. The second (5b) is normal except for the presence of a multiple lumen catheter in the superior vena cava.

ii. The small lung volumes could be due to poor patient effort, but this is, in general, unlikely. A restrictive process should therefore be considered and would include intrapulmonary disease, pleural disease or structural chest wall deformity but there is no radiographic evidence to support these diagnoses. The other possibility is a failure of the muscle pump. As the condition was successfully treated over 2 weeks and the presence of the intravenous catheter noted on the second radiograph suggests the possibility of plasma exchange, it suggests either Guillain–Barré syndrome or myasthenia gravis. The diagnosis was myasthenia gravis.

Acute respiratory failure due to alveolar hypoventilation develops when the vital capacity (VC) falls below 800 ml in an 80-kg individual, but inability to cough and clear secretions would occur earlier. This is particularly relevant when bulbar symptoms are present with the risk of aspiration and pneumonia. The patient had a thymoma and plasma exchange was therefore indicated before surgery.

6 The owner of this bird (6) presented with a 1-week history of cough, fever and myalgia. Her chest radiograph showed patchy shadowing in the right lower zone.
i. What unusual pathogen may be the cause of her illness?
ii. How would you confirm the diagnosis?
iii. What is the treatment of choice?

7 As well as dyspnoea, this man also complains of multiple floating spots across his field of vision for several weeks and on examination has retinal haemorrhages and exudates (7a).
i. How commonly would such eye and pulmonary problems be connected?
ii. What is the appropriate management of this situation?

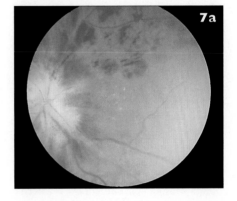

8 This asthmatic man (8) presented acutely with increasing dyspnoea and retrosternal discomfort.
i. What has happened?
ii. How should he be treated?
iii. What other causes of this condition are there?

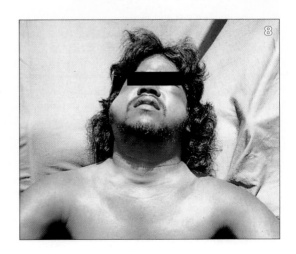

6 i. Infection by *Chlamydia psittaci* (psittacosis) is a possibility, although statistically pneumococcal infection is still most likely. If the bird had been recently acquired or recently bred, or was itself ill, the chances of psittacosis would be increased.
ii. The diagnosis is usually made by serology looking for a four-fold rise in complement-fixing antibodies to the type II antigen of *C. psittaci*. Direct fluorescent staining of respiratory tract secretions can be used to look for chlamydial antigen.
iii. The treatment of choice is tetracycline. A macrolide would be second choice.

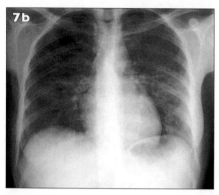

7 i. The retinal problem is due to cytomegalovirus (CMV; **7a**). The differential diagnosis of interstitial pneumonitis is as in the answer to **195**, with *Pneumocystis carinii (jiroveci)* pneumonitis (PCP) still being the most likely cause (**7b**). Other than the eye, this organism also causes disease of the gut, nervous system and biliary tree. Rarely, CMV may be implicated in HIV-related pneumonitis when other pathogens, such as PCP, have been excluded as a cause.
ii. Initial management would be as in **195**; that is, therapy for presumed PCP until the result of bronchoscopy is obtained. In the rare case of CMV pneumonitis, the patient would be treated with intravenous ganciclovir at high dose for 2–3 weeks. Foscarnet is an alternative if ganciclovir cannot be tolerated. Due to the myelosuppressive effects of ganciclovir and zidovudine, caution is required if both drugs are to be given simultaneously. If the CMV pneumonitis occurs without concomitant eye involvement no further therapy is necessary.

8 i. The upper chest and face is grossly swollen. The skin is indented easily and contains palpable crepitus. He has 'surgical' or subcutaneous emphysema. He has either a pneumothorax with mediastinal emphysema which has tracked up and out of the mediastinum, or he has ruptured an airway causing mediastinal emphysema which again has tracked upwards. Usually the condition is self-limiting but can be most uncomfortable and painful especially around the eyes.
ii. A careful check for a pneumothorax should be made with, if necessary, inspiratory and expiratory chest films. Interpretation can be difficult due to extensive extrathoracic gas being present. A CT of the thorax may be necessary. The asthma should be treated as usual. If a pneumothorax is present a large intercostal drain should be inserted. Oxygen should be given by mask to minimize the amount of nitrogen entering the tissues, as nitrogen resorbs more slowly than oxygen.
iii. Other causes include: (1) A partially dislodged chest drain; a side hole may become extrathoracic allowing air to pass into the extrathoracic tissues. (2) A traumatic pneumothorax with a rib fracture. A chest drain should be inserted and a pressure bandage applied. (3) Rupture of a main airway following a deceleration injury or a seat belt injury, which can cause a large pneumo-mediastinum and surgical emphysema.

9 i. Describe the different types of exercise apparatus used for progressive exercise testing.

ii. What is a progressive exercise test and why is it done?

10 i. A 30-year-old man was admitted with fever, cough with haemoptysis and dyspnoea. A few red blood cells but no microorganisms were noted on sputum Gram-stain.

i. What does the lung function test (Table) show?

ii. What does this chest radiograph (**10**) show?

iii. What is the cause?

iv. Name three important conditions associated with this and the laboratory investigations that would differentiate them.

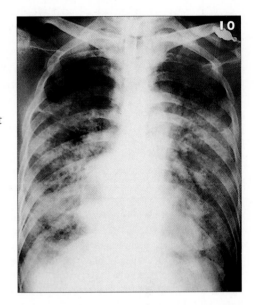

Test	Predicted	Range	Result	% Predicted
PEFR (l/min)	450	383–518	470	104
FEV_1 (l)	2.75	2.34–3.16	1.47	53
FVC (l)	4.05	3.45–4.66	2.23	55
FEV_1/FVC (%)	69	58–79	65	55
DL_{CO} (Hb corrected)[a]	7.88	6.70–9.06	11.07	96
VA (l)	1.47	1.25–1.69	3.72	140
K_{CO} (Hb corrected)[b]	3.09	2.63–3.55	2.97	202

[a]DL_{CO} = transfer factor; [b]K_{CO} = transfer coefficient in DL_{CO}/VA

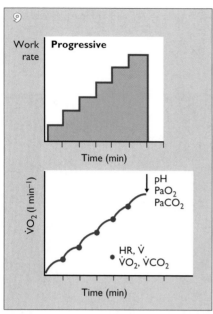

9 i. The different types of apparatus used for progressive exercise tests are a stepping test, or more commonly a treadmill test, or a cycle ergometer test. During these tests, the workload is increased by small increments at regular times. The workload will gradually increase until the patient reaches his/her maximum exercise capacity or maximal oxygen uptake (9).

ii. The main purpose of a progressive exercise test is to measure the work capacity achievable by the individual. Several measurements can be made including heart rate, minute ventilation, mixed expired gas concentration by capturing the expired gases with the patient breathing through a two-way valve box via a mouth piece. It is mandatory to measure the ECG during exercise and, from it, the heart rate. Minute ventilation can be measured by collecting expired gas volumes or by sampling the expired gas volumes for the expired CO_2 and oxygen concentration and, from this, the oxygen uptake per unit time (usually minute-by-minute) is measured. The progressive exercise test is commonly used in the investigation of heart disease (e.g. Bruce protocol) where chest pain, ECG abnormalities or breathlessness are looked for. In patients with lung disease, exercise is usually stopped by maximum exercise ventilation being achieved, causing breathlessness. It is also possible to measure arterial blood gases during exercise, either by an indwelling arterial cannula or from arterialized capillary blood collected from an earlobe. Measurements of arterial/arterialized blood gas tensions will allow the alveolar arterial oxygen gradient to be calculated.

10 i. A high K_{CO}, i.e. increased diffusion capacity across the alveolar–capillary membrane. Additional carbon monoxide uptake occurs in the lungs because of the presence of alveolar haemorrhage.
ii. Bilateral alveolar filling pattern.
iii. Pulmonary haemorrhage.
iv. Three important associated conditions and the laboratory investigations that differentiate them are:
- Goodpasture's disease: anti-glomerular basement membrane antibody.
- Wegener's granulomatosis: c-anti-cytoplasmic antibody (c-ANCA).
- Systemic vasculitis: anti-nuclear antibody, anti-double-stranded DNA antibody.

11 This chest radiograph (**11a**) is from a middle-aged man who presented with a cough 3 months after a renal transplant for polycystic kidney disease.
i. What is the differential diagnosis?
ii. How would you investigate this?
iii. What is the treatment of choice?

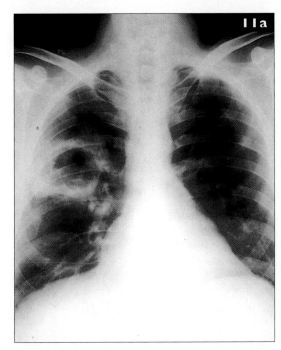

12 This man was referred for consideration of resection of a mass in the left lower lobe. The CT scan (**12**) showed an irregularly shaped lesion with streaky shadowing extending into the depths of the right lower lobe.
i. Of what are these appearances characteristic?
ii. With what are they associated?

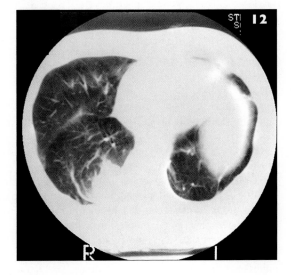

11 i. The chest radiograph shows a large right mid-zone cavity which has a thick, rather irregular wall. Fungal infection, tuberculosis, Gram-negative or anaerobic bacterial infection or a cavitating pulmonary infarct are the most likely causes.
ii. Bronchoscopy with lavage of the affected area, and/or percutaneous needle aspiration of the cavity. CT scanning will delineate the margins of the cavity and its

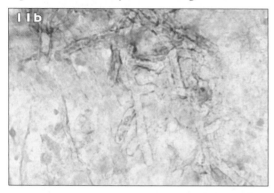

exact position with greater clarity. Recently a halo sign on CT scanning has been suggested to be specific for fungal infection. In this patient both needle aspiration and bronchoscopy revealed *Aspergillus*. **11b** and **11c** are low-power photomicrographs of a histological section of a medium-sized airway obtained at autopsy. Numerous dark-stained branching hyphae can be seen invading the airway wall. Submucosal glands and cartilage are present in the adjacent tissue. Necrotizing aspergillosis can also occur in the larger airways and in the same clinical setting as invasive aspergillosis, although this is less common.

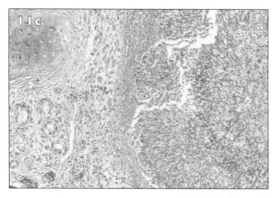

iii. Amphotericin B is the treatment of choice although new lipid-based preparations, such as liposomal amphotericin B, have been introduced to minimize the high incidence of side-effects with this agent.

12 i. The CT shows a peripheral mass, inseparable from the pleural surface, with tongues of dense tissue that extend medially into the pulmonary parenchyma. This appearance is known as 'folded lung', Blesovsky's syndrome or 'rounded atelectasis'. It is due to part of the dorsal surface of the lung becoming adherent to the parietal pleural surface and causing that segment of the lung to twist and become densely consolidated; this often contains an air bronchogram which can be seen on CT.
ii. This appearance occurs mostly in subjects exposed to asbestos with pleural plaques that become adherent to the visceral pleura, immobilizing the dependent pulmonary segment. The CT appearances are characteristic and require no biopsy or other action.

13 A 24-year-old male motor-cyclist was admitted as an emergency after being involved in a road traffic accident.
i. What abnormality can be seen on the plain chest radiograph (13a) and what diagnosis must be suspected?
ii. What is demonstrated on the subsequent vascular imaging films (13b, 13c)?
iii. Where is this lesion normally encountered, what is the mechanism of injury and what are the possible consequences?

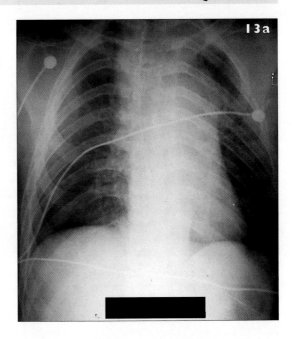

14 A young man presented to the emergency department complaining of left chest pain and breathlessness after a kick to the left side of body.
i. What does the chest radiograph (14) show?
ii. What is the differential diagnosis and what surgical treatment should be offered?

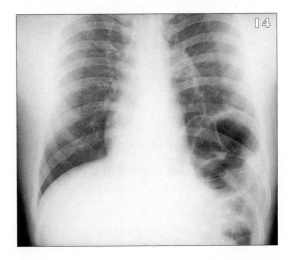

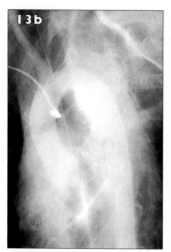

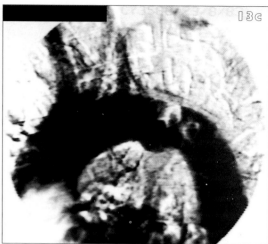

13 i. There is gross widening of the mediastinum on the plain chest radiograph (**13a**), even allowing for the AP nature of the examination. The severity of the injury and the mediastinal widening make traumatic aortic transection a definite possibility.

ii. The aortogram (**13b**) shows a bulge in the region of the distal aortic arch/proximal descending aorta. This is clearly shown on digital subtraction angiography (**13c**) to be due to disruption of the aortic wall.

iii. This lesion is characteristically seen at the aortic isthmus, i.e. the junction between the aortic arch and the descending aorta. This injury is believed to occur because the arch can move forward with deceleration whereas the descending aorta is relatively fixed. Immediate exsanguination will occur in many cases. Those that reach hospital can undergo repair of the ruptured segment, usually with the insertion of a short length of prosthetic graft. Either before or during surgery, spinal cord ischaemia can occur with consequent lower-limb paralysis.

14 i. The left hemithorax contains gas-filled loops of intestine.

ii. The differential diagnosis includes a raised hemidiaphragm, enventration of the diaphragm, congenital diaphragmatic hernia and, given the history of trauma, traumatic rupture of the diaphragm.

Eventration of the diaphragm results from paralysis, hypoplasia or atrophy of the muscle fibres. It can be difficult to diagnose even on CT scan and often is only confirmed at surgery. The aim of surgery in eventration is to incise the thinned-out diaphragmatic leaf and to repair the diaphragm by imbricating one layer over the other. In diaphragmatic hernia or traumatic rupture the diaphragm is repaired either by direct suture or by the placement of a 'patch' (Marlex Mesh) across the defect.

15 This radiograph (**15**) of a 25-year-old man was taken on admission to hospital via the accident and emergency department. How is ARDS managed?

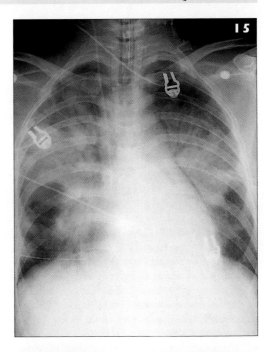

16 Fibreoptic bronchoscopy in this patient revealed a squamous cell carcinoma in the right lower lobe (**16**). Apart from an increase in dyspnoea, the patient is well. The FEV_1 is 1.8 l. How would you stage for possible thoracotomy?

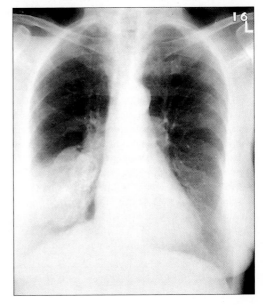

15 The management of ARDS includes:

- Maintenance of adequate arterial oxygen saturations (SaO_2) so that oxygen delivery is not compromised – in this case SaO_2 of 90–92% would be adequate and would allow the inspired oxygen concentrations to be kept below 80% thereby reducing the risks of oxygen toxicity.

- The goal of ventilating patients with ARDS should be to maintain adequate gas exchange and avoid ventilator-induced lung injury. Ventilation directed at preventing cyclical opening and closing of alveoli by adjusting PEEP (currently usually set at about 15 cmH_2O) to maintain alveolar recruitment helps to maintain oxygenation and may have a role in preventing lung injury. Further studies are underway to clarify this issue. Recently 'permissive hypercapnoea' has been used as part of lung protective ventilatory protocols. $PaCO_2$ levels of 2–3 times normal seem to be well tolerated for prolonged periods. Whatever mode of ventilation is used, the tidal volume should be set in the region of 6 ml/kg rather than the traditional 10–12 ml/kg and the peak pressure should be limited to 30–35 cmH_2O to prevent lung overdistension. Extracorporeal membrane oxygenation (ECMO) has proven mortality benefit in neonatal ARDS but studies in adults are required. High frequency ventilation, including a recruitment protocol, may offer the ultimate lung protective ventilation, but further clinical studies are required.

- Inhaled vasodilators and methylprednisolone (after excluding infection) may have a role.

- The patient should be well sedated. If the patient is hyperpyrexial, cooling could be considered to minimize oxygen consumption and CO_2 production. On occasions, paralysis may be necessary, but paralytic agents may adversely affect diaphragmatic function.

16 The chest radiograph (**16**) shows consolidation or an intrapulmonary mass with an additional mass at the lower pole of the right hilum. The mediastinum looks normal. Initial tests include a full blood count and biochemical screen. Abnormal liver function tests would require a liver ultrasound or CT to exclude metastases. An elevated serum calcium requires a bone scan, although the primary tumour (if squamous) may cause ectopic secretion of peptide hormones.

If tests are normal, then a CT scan of the thorax and upper abdomen is performed. If this shows no signs of inoperability, the chances of a CT brain or a bone scan identifying an isolated occult metastasis is 1–4%. However, a PET scan should be performed, if available, at this stage to rule out metastatic spread. If the CT thorax shows mediastinal lymph nodes enlarged to over 1 cm in shortest diameter, trans-oesophageal endoscopic ultrasound-guided lymph node sampling and/or mediastinoscopy may be required.

17 Parts **a–c** of Figure **17** are segments of a polysomnogram [LEG(R)(L), leg movement; THOR/ABDO RES, thoracic and abdominal movement]. Which of these shows:
i. Obstructive apnoea;
ii. Central apnoea;
iii. Mixed apnoea?

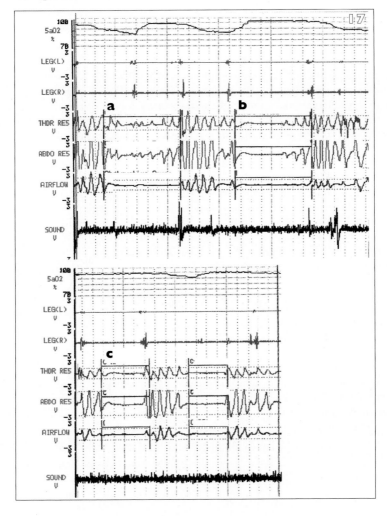

18 i. Describe four distinct clinical presentations of silicosis.
ii. What infection is of particular concern in patients with this disease?

17 i. Obstructive apnoeas (**17a**) are characterized by cessation of airflow with continued evidence of respiratory effort on the chest and abdominal traces, often in a paradoxical fashion. Arterial oxygen saturation decreases during the episodes, periodically reaching a nadir at the end or just after reinitiation of airflow.
ii. Mixed apnoeas (**17b**), a variant of obstructive sleep apnoea, consist of a central event followed by an obstructive portion (respiratory effort begins before airflow does).
iii. Central apnoeas (**17c**) result in a cessation in airflow with no evidence of respiratory effort on the chest and abdominal traces. This event was terminated by an EEG arousal.

18 i. Silicosis is diagnosed by radiographic and clinical criteria in the setting of an appropriate exposure history. The radiographic appearance is classified according to standardized International Labour Office (ILO) criteria. Four distinct forms exist: chronic simple silicosis, progressive massive fibrosis (PMF), accelerated silicosis, and acute silicosis. Chronic simple silicosis is the most common. It is usually recognized as a radiographic abnormality in asymptomatic patients. Small (<1.5 mm) rounded opacities with an upper lobe preponderance slowly develop after 5 to 10 years of exposure. Pulmonary function abnormalities are rare. More severe disease is manifested by more extensive and larger opacities and may be associated with airflow limitation and reduced lung volumes. PMF presents with progressive coalescence of discrete opacities into large, irregular masses, generally in the perihilar regions of the upper lobes. Severe restriction, hypoxaemia, and disabling dyspnoea are often present. The course is often insidious and can progress without ongoing exposure to silica. Accelerated silicosis is uncommon but may develop within 2 to 5 years of intense exposure. In contrast to the upper lobe involvement characteristic of simple silicosis, diffuse, irregular reticulonodular infiltrates are the usual radiographic finding in this form of the disease. The prognosis is poor as progressive disease culminates in death within several years. Acute silicosis occasionally develops following exposure to very high concentrations of silica such as may occur with sandblasting.
ii. Tuberculosis complicating silicosis was first recognized in the 19th century. Silicosis is associated with an increased incidence of infection by *M. tuberculosis* and by atypical mycobacterium. Although symptoms respond readily to therapy, sputum cultures may remain positive. Chronic suppressive therapy with isoniazid following standard multidrug (e.g. isoniazid, rifampicin, pyrizinamide with or without ethambutol) therapy is required in some cases. A tuberculin skin test is mandatory in all patients with silicosis.

19 i. Would you expect any abnormality of the vital capacity of this 18-year-old male patient whose lateral and PA chest radiographs are shown (19a, 19b)?
ii. What associated clinical abnormalities might this patient have?

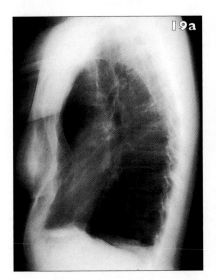
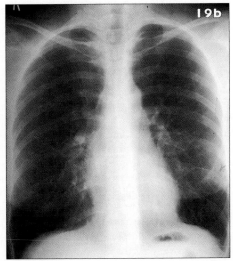

20 A 17-year-old patient complains of paroxysms of sneezing, nasal pruritus, nasal congestion, clear rhinorrhoea and palatal itching. The mucosal surfaces of her eyes and ears were indurated and an examination of her nose revealed a wet reddened mucosa.
i. What is the diagnosis?
ii. What is the treatment?
iii. What are some preventive strategies?

21 i. What is shown in **21**?
ii. How does it work?
iii. What is it used for and how useful is it?
iv. What are its side effects?

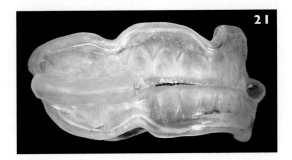

19 i. The lateral chest radiograph (**19a**) shows pectus excavatum, inward displacement of the sternum which has probably been present from birth. Despite what is occasionally a striking physical abnormality it does not cause reduction of the vital capacity, except in a minority of cases. Also, such patients do not have breathlessness due to the sternal deformity.

ii. Associated features include thoracic kyphosis and scoliosis. Cardiac effects include right axis deviation on ECG (due to leftward displacement of the heart), supraventricular tachycardias, mitral valve prolapse and, rarely, reduction of right ventricular filling due to cardiac compression.

20 i. Allergic rhinitis. It is recognized by the greyish appearance of the nasal mucus membranes.

ii. Treatment varies with the severity of the condition but can include some of the following: (a) allergen avoidance; (b) antihistamines for nasal, ocular, and/or palatal itching, and for sneezing and/or rhinorrhoea; (c) nasal topical corticosteroids; (d) oral decongestants in combination with antihistamines; (e) intranasal cromolyn sodium or ipratropium.

iii. The condition may be prevented by avoiding specific antigens (particularly the house dust mite) and by nasal administration of cromolyn. It is also important to exclude the possibility of rhinitis medicamentosa (i.e. overuse of topical nasal α-adrenergic decongestant sprays for more than a few days leading to rebound nasal congestion on withdrawal). Prolonged topical decongestant use might also lead to nasal mucosa hypertrophy and inflammation. When this problem is diagnosed, topical or oral steroids should be initiated as the decongestant spray is tapered.

21 i. A mandibular advancement splint.

ii. Oral appliances are used by dentists for many purposes, including correction of various occlusal disorders. The techniques often modify the position of the mandible within the restricted mobility defined by the temporomandibular joint and the pterygoid muscles. In snoring and obstructive sleep apnoea, these devices are designed predominantly to advance the mandible and pull the base of the tongue forward, thus preventing it from falling backward to occlude the pharynx during sleep.

iii. A review of 21 publications describing 320 patients treated with oral appliances for snoring and obstructive sleep apnoea showed that, despite considerable variation in the design of these appliances, the clinical effects are remarkably consistent. Snoring is improved in almost all patients and is often eliminated. The studies show that OSA improves in the majority of patients. Approximately half of those patients who improve achieve an AHI of <20, but as many as 40% are left with notably elevated AHIs. Sleep is generally improved, although significant sleep disturbance persists in the patients with residual apnoea.

iv. Limited follow-up data indicate that oral discomfort is a common but tolerable side effect, and that dental and mandibular complications appear to be uncommon.

22 The biopsy shown in **22** is from the lower trachea in a 35-year-old male who complained of increasing breathlessness. Chest radiography showed numerous large opacities bilaterally. What is the likely diagnosis?

23 i. Describe the appearances in this chest radiograph (**23**) from a man with a long history of gastrointestinal symptoms.
ii. What are the most likely causative organisms?
iii. What is the treatment of choice?

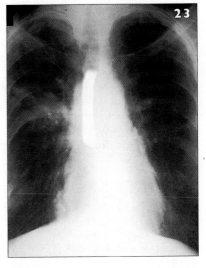

24 This flow–volume loop (**24**) was obtained from a 56-year-old patient with marked respiratory distress and audible wheeze and in whom the initial diagnosis was 'status asthmaticus'. The patient had recently been discharged from hospital after 4 weeks of treatment in intensive care for acute respiratory distress syndrome (ARDS).
i. What does the flow–volume loop demonstrate?
ii. What is the likely diagnosis?
iii. What inhalation treatment might be helpful?

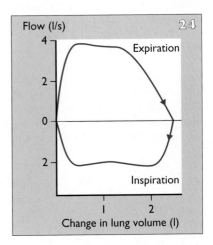

22 There is granulation tissue in the mucosa, and ulceration of the epithelium at the upper left of **22**. These changes are most suggestive of Wegener's granulomatosis. Tracheal and endobronchial involvement are well described in this disease along with lung parenchymal involvement, as manifested by infiltrates or masses on chest radiography. Tracheal involvement may eventually result in stenosis which, if not resolving with anti-inflammatory therapy, may require laser resection. Such therapy may need to be repeated in the event of recurrence. Monitoring endobronchial involvement is best achieved with flow–volume loops and spirometry; the use of anti-neutrophil cytoplasmic antibody titres is less helpful here.

23 i. The chest radiograph shows patchy shadowing in the right mid to upper zone. In the upper mediastinum the oesophagus is outlined by a column of barium, the appearances therefore suggesting oesophageal obstruction and aspiration pneumonia.
ii. The most likely causative organisms would be normal oropharyngeal commensal organisms which are typically anaerobes such as bacteroides or peptostreptococcus. If the patient had spent more than 4 days in hospital before aspiration occurred then Gram-negative enterobacteria would also need to be considered.
iii. The treatment of choice for anaerobic lung infections is either a combination of penicillin plus metronidazole or alternatively, clindamycin. The oesophageal obstruction should also be treated (see **97**).

24 i. The flow–volume loop demonstrates a reduction in the maximum inspiratory and expiratory flows which both plateau over a large proportion of the Forced Vital Capacity (FVC) manoeuvre and a low FVC <3 l. The reduction in flow is more marked during inspiration and this is typical of narrowing of the extrathoracic trachea (see **142, 190**).
ii. The initial diagnosis of asthma should be avoided on the basis of the physical signs which, in addition to stridor, are most marked in inspiration but often audible during expiration. A simple test to detect upper airway obstruction (UAWO) is the ratio of FEV_1 to peak flow, i.e. FEVml/PEFR l/min. Normally this is less than 10 but in UAWO the peak flow is affected most, e.g. 2000 ml/150 l/min = 13.
   The data would be compatible with a high tracheal or laryngeal area of narrowing/collapse, the most likely cause in this case is tracheal narrowing following a tracheostomy due to a mass of friable granulation tissue at the tracheostomy site. This was the diagnosis and the problem was effectively treated by diathermy.
iii. A mixture of oxygen (21%) and helium (79%) as helium is less dense than nitrogen, allowing greater flow of gas.

25 A 57-year-old non-smoking man, with no respiratory symptoms, began to behave in an uncharacteristically aggressive and uninhibited manner early in the morning. What is the likely cause of the radiograph shadow (**25**) and what is the explanation of his behaviour?

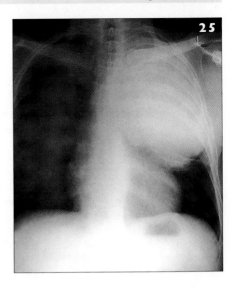

26 A 20-year-old patient complained of severe breathlessness each time after he roller-blades. The result of exercise testing revealed is shown in **26**.
i. What does the exercise test show?
ii. What is the diagnosis?
iii. How would you manage this condition?
iv. What is the pathogenesis of this condition?
v. What drugs are allowed by the Olympic committee before competition?

27 This worker (**27**) is properly attired to perform sandblasting safely.
i. Which pneumoconiosis is associated with this occupational exposure?
ii. What other occupations pose similar risks?

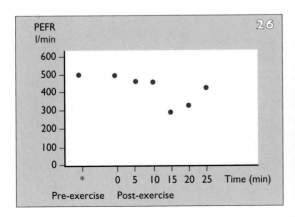

27

25 Massive pleural fibroma, with spontaneous hypoglycaemia. The huge size of the tumour in an otherwise healthy patient suggests that it is benign in nature. The diagnosis is easily confirmed by percutaneous needle biopsy. Large mesenchymal tumours may produce insulin-like growth factors. It is probable that these peptides both stimulate the growth of the tumour itself, which may attain great size, and lead to spontaneous hypoglycaemia. Insulin-like growth factors are normally produced under the control of growth hormone and their abnormal production leads to its suppression by a negative feedback mechanism. Plasma insulin and C-peptide levels are also low. Despite their large size, these tumours can be removed quite easily surgically as they usually arise from the parietal pleura on a finger-like stalk. Resection leads to complete resolution of the biochemical abnormalities.

26 i. A 40% fall in peak flow reading after exercise compared with pre-exercise value.
ii. Exercise-induced asthma. This diagnosis requires a minimum change of 25% in PEFR from the pre-exercise value to the lowest measurement – usually found 10–20 minutes post-exercise.
iii. Advise the patient to inhale beta-agonist 15 minutes before exercise and to warm-up adequately.
iv. Exercise results in isocapnic hyperventilation and inhalation of cold air which results in water loss from the airway lining, causing airway cooling and hypertonicity. These result in vasoconstriction and mast-cell activation and stimulation of the neural reflexes which cause rebound vasodilatation, oedema and bronchial hyperreactivity. Mucosal thickening and smooth muscle contraction will then occur, leading to bronchoconstriction of the airways. Current research shows that leukotrienes may also play an important role in exercise-induced asthma.
v. Beta-agonists and sodium cromoglycate.

27 i. Silicosis is a chronic, fibronodular interstitial lung disease caused by inhalation of free crystalline silica (SiO_2). Silica occurs both complexed with other elements and in isolation as a 'free' form. The latter, occurring primarily as quartz, tridymite and cristobalite are associated with fibrotic lung disease. Tridymite and cristobalite are more fibrogenic than quartz.
ii. Sandblasting is widely used to clean and etch stone and metal surfaces. Highly pressurized air or water drives a stream of abrasive sand into the workpiece. Very high concentrations of respirable silica are present in the resulting dust cloud. Non-siliceous particulates are increasingly used to minimize this risk, but if the target surface (e.g. stone) contains silica, significant exposure may still occur. Because silica is a major constituent of the earth's crust, mining, tunnelling, quarrying and stone cutting may also entail significant exposure to silica-containing dust. Finely powdered quartz, known as silica flour or tripoli, is another common source of exposure as it is used as a polishing agent, as a dry lubricant in the rubber industry and as a thickening agent in paints and plastics.

28 These arterial blood gas tensions (Table) are from a 25-year-old man with nocturnal confusion 24 hours after the pinning of a fractured femur sustained in a motor vehicle accident. No abnormality was detected on physical examination or chest radiography. What is the likely diagnosis and management?

Test	Result	Reference Range
FIO₂	0.3	–
pH	7.54	7.35–7.45
pCO₂	3.7 kPa (28 mmHg)	4.6–6.0 (35–46mmHg)
pO₂	9.1 kPa (69 mmHg)	12–16 (91–122mmHg)
HCO₃	18 mmol/l	22–30

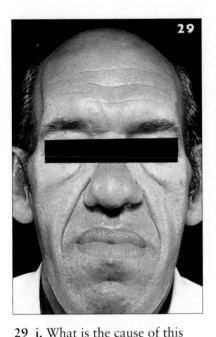

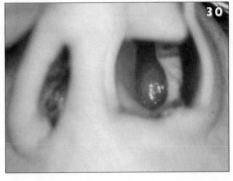

30 i. What condition is seen in 30?
ii. How is it treated?
iii. What is the common association of this when it occurs in patients with asthma?

29 i. What is the cause of this patient's (29) obstructive sleep apnoea?
ii. How would you treat this condition?
iii. If the sleep apnoea is severe, what precaution would you take prior to and after surgery?

28 Fat embolism syndrome. Acute lung injury arises due to deposition of fat globules displaced from the marrow of the fractured bone into the pulmonary arteries, with subsequent release of free fatty acids. The syndrome begins with tachypnoea very soon after the trauma or orthopaedic surgery. Chest radiographs may initially be normal but may progress to show a pattern of acute respiratory distress syndrome, at which time chest examination will reveal widespread fine crackles. Treatment is with oxygen and is supportive as for any other form of acute lung injury. Corticosteroids are of no benefit, except possibly if given early. Other features of the syndrome include central nervous system effects ranging from mild disorientation to seizures and coma, usually 12–36 h after injury. Petechiae may be present, particularly in the conjunctivae and over the upper extremities and axillae. Both of these features are the result of microvascular injury.

29 i. Acromegaly – there is typical frontal bossing with prominent supraorbital ridges, prognathism, coarse skin and thickened lips. Another endocrinological cause for obstructive sleep apnoea is myxoedema.
ii. Transphenoidal removal of the pituitary gland. Octreotide, which is a somatostatin analogue, has also been reported to improve obstructive sleep apnoea in some patients with acromegaly. Despite successful surgery, most acromegalic patients continue to have significant sleep apnoea which requires treatment with nasal CPAP.
iii. The patient should be put on nasal CPAP before and immediately after surgery, even if the surgery is potentially curative. This is because anaesthesia and opiates can cause a further reduction in upper airway tone and a suppression of their arousal response to obstruction. Once the patient has recovered from the surgery, a repeat sleep study should check whether there is still significant obstructive sleep apnoea.

30 i. A nasal polyp, a red mass in the region of the middle turbinate. These occur when oedematous sinus mucosa prolapses into the nasal cavity. They are often associated with perennial rhinitis and low-grade sinusitis.
ii. Nasal polyposis should be treated medically with a short course of oral steroids or local steroid drops followed by topical steroid sprays. If this is not successful, intranasal or endoscopic polypectomy can be considered for polyps that occlude the nasal cavity. Surgery is not curative, however, and the recurrence rate is greater than 40%. For polyposis that occurs in the setting of chronic rhinosinusitis the allergic disease should be treated with antihistamines, topical nasal corticosteroids and immunotherapy.
iii. Some 20–40% of patients with asthma have nasal polyps and many of these patients are allergic to aspirin; 10% of all chronic asthmatics respond to aspirin or other non-steroidal anti-inflammatory drugs with an exacerbation of asthma and acute rhinoconjunctivitis. Some 30% of asthmatics with polypoid rhinosinusitis have aspirin sensitivity. Patients with nasal polyposis and asthma may have eosinophilia; in those being treated with leukotriene receptor antagonists, Churg–Strauss syndrome and other vasculitides should be considered.

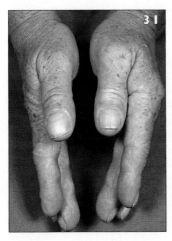

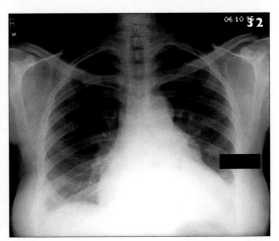

31 Shown (31) is a para-malignant syndrome.
i. What is this condition? How can the arms and legs be affected and how is the latter recognized?
ii. With what else is it associated?

32 What is the major abnormality on this chest radiograph (32)? What further investigations should be carried out to investigate this abnormality?

33 Lung function data are shown in the Table for a patient with rheumatoid arthritis on low-dose methotrexate. The lung function was normal when the drug was commenced 2 months previously and a chest radiograph showed bilateral alveolar shadowing. Could the abnormalities be due to methotrexate?

Test	Predicted	Range	Result	% predicted
FEV_1 (l)	3.32	2.83–3.82	2.24	67
FVC (l)	4.17	3.54–4.79	2.53	61
FEV_1 (%)	81	68–93	88	110
FRC (l)	3.53	3–4.06	1.7	48
TLC (l)	5.8	4.93–6.67	3.34	58
VC (l)	4.17	3.54–4.79	2.23	54
RV (l)	1.6	1.36–1.84	1.11	69
DL_{CO} (mmol/min/kPa)[a]	9.58	8.14–11.02	5.87	61
VA(l)	–	–	3.05	–
K_{CO} (mmol/min/kPa/l)[b]	1.88	1.6–2.16	1.92	100

[a]DL_{CO} = transfer factor; [b]K_{CO} = transfer coefficient in DL_{CO}/VA.

31 i. The hands show clubbing with loss of nail fold angles. This is associated with non-small-cell lung cancers. It can be associated with pain and swelling of the distal forearm and shins which can become red, oedematous and the bones themselves very tender to pressure. Radiography will show new bone formation or periostitis. The condition is known as hypertrophic pulmonary osteoarthropathy (HPOA). Bone scintigraphy with Tc-99m MDP may reveal increased tracer uptake along the distal fingers and toes due to clubbing. Treatment is with non-steroidal anti-inflammatory medication and, if possible, treatment of the primary tumour.

ii. HPOA occurs primarily with lung cancer but has also been reported in association with pulmonary sepsis, thymic carcinoma, chronic myeloid leukaemia, thyroid carcinoma, Hodgkin's disease, adenocarcinoma of the oesophagus, primary lymphocarcinoma of the lung and bronchial carcinoid tumour. Benign associations include cyanotic congenital heart disease, pleural fibroma, Grave's disease, oesophageal achalasia, portal cirrhosis, inflammatory bowel disease, leioma of the oesophagus, cystic fibrosis and idiopathic or familial HPOA.

32 The left heart border is obscured by an opacification which protrudes in the aortopulmonary area. The features are consistent with an anterior mediastinal mass but the differential diagnosis includes a large left atrial appendage.

Further investigation should consist of a CT scan to delineate the extent of any mediastinal mass. If the abnormality arises from the heart or pericardium, lateral chest radiography and then further investigation by echocardiography should be carried out. In this case the abnormality was confirmed, on CT scan, to be a large anterior mediastinal mass which descended to involve the pericardium; it surrounded all the great vessels including the arch of the aorta. To obtain tissue for histological diagnosis, combined video-assisted mediastinoscopy and video-assisted thoracoscopy is an alternative procedure which, where available, is likely to supersede mediastinotomy in terms of diagnostic efficacy. Histological diagnosis revealed an enlarged thymus gland with lymphoid hyperplasia and cyst formation.

33 The lung function data suggest a moderately severe restrictive defect with reduced gas transfer and this, along with the radiographic picture, suggests an acute pneumonitis, which has been associated with the use of methotrexate. The pathogenesis may be either a hypersensitivity or an idiosyncratic drug reaction. In general, elderly patients and those with poor renal function (reducing renal drug clearance) are at risk of methotrexate side effects. Data on lung function disturbances with methotrexate are confounded as patients with rheumatoid arthritis develop interstitial shadowing and opportunistic infections. Indeed, *P. carinii* pneumonia should always be excluded in both suspected acute or chronic toxicity before assuming that the drug is the cause. Lung biopsy findings in methotrexate lung toxicity range from lymphocytic infiltrates to interstitial fibrosis. Milder cases usually respond to stopping therapy; however, corticosteroid therapy would be warranted in the case described here.

34 This is a chest radiograph (34) from a 45-year-old man who presented with a 2-week history of cough, fever and sweats.
i. Describe the appearances.
He was treated with an aminopenicillin for a week but with no influence on his symptoms and he was referred to hospital.
ii. What simple test could confirm the clinical diagnosis?
iii. What is the treatment of choice?

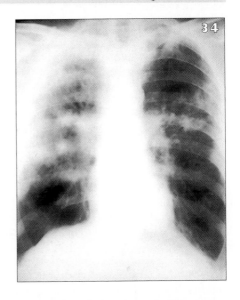

35 What are the indications for use of each of these three oxygen delivery devices (35) in the acute setting?

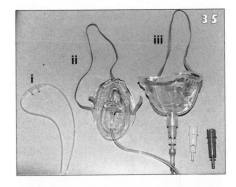

36 This scan (36) was taken 5 years after the patient, a 55-year-old man, presented with a blood-stained pleural effusion. At that time examination of the fluid and bronchoscopy were negative. What is the abnormality shown and what are the possible causes?

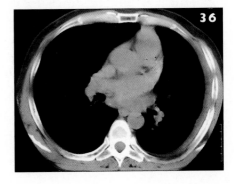

34 i. The chest radiograph (34) shows the presence of patchy shadowing in the right upper and mid-zones with smaller area of shadowing in the left mid-zone.
ii. Ziehl–Nielsen stain of the patient's sputum showed the presence of acid-fast bacilli, confirming the clinical suspicion of tuberculosis. Tuberculosis can mimic simple community-acquired pneumonias, although the symptom duration is usually longer and patients usually lack the acute toxic features of a bacterial pneumonia.
iii. In view of the increasing prevalence of isoniazid resistance, treatment should be with four drugs (isoniazid, rifampicin, pyrazinamide, and ethambutol) for the initial 2 months followed by a further 4 months of isoniazid and rifampicin in most cases. If positive culture for *M. tuberculosis* has been obtained but susceptibility results are outstanding after 2 months, four drugs should be continued until susceptibility is confirmed. If there is a delayed response to treatment, further investigations should be carried out to identify multi-drug resistant organisms and the course of treatment should be prolonged. Directly observed therapy (DOT) is recommended if there is any doubt at all about adherence to the treatment regimen.

35 i. Nasal prongs are useful at flow rates of 2–3 l/min for mild hypoxaemia.(SaO_2 <88–90%). They allow the patient to eat or drink and there is no CO_2 re-breathing. Higher flow rates can be achieved, although this may cause discomfort and dry the nasal mucosa and the inspiration of oxygen delivered is variable and uncontrolled and therefore potentially harmful.
ii. Hudson, or MC face mask. These can deliver oxygen at flow rates up to 15 l/min corresponding to an approximate FiO_2 of 0.7. The amount of delivered oxygen is dependent on the rate and depth of the patient's respiration and is not safe in patients with reduced hypoxic drive who require controlled oxygen therapy.
iii. Venturi mask. This enables controlled oxygen (24, 28, 35%) to be delivered at high flow rates. Entrainment of air occurs through the holes in the coloured fittings at the neck of the mask to give the high total flow rate which may be needed in severely dyspnoeic patients. It is indicated in hypoxaemic patients with reduced hypoxic drive where oxygen delivery must be constant to prevent uncontrolled respiratory depression with subsequent hypercapnia. A range of fittings is available giving a range of inspired oxygen concentrations. Each fitting requires a different oxygen flow rate from the wall oxygen outlet.

36 Benign pleural thickening. In contrast to the scan of malignant pleural mesothelioma, the pleural thickening is smooth and diffuse, with only slight constriction of the hemithorax. A blood-stained pleural effusion is always suggestive of malignancy, but the long history makes this unlikely and this case was, in fact, due to benign asbestos-related pleurisy. Diffuse asbestos-related pleural fibrosis usually follows organization of episodes of pleurisy with effusion and is often bilateral. It tends to progress slowly, leading to a constrictive defect of ventilation with reduction in static and dynamic lung volumes and increasing dyspnoea, but the gas transfer factor remains normal or may be elevated. There is a significant incidence of malignant mesothelioma developing at a later stage and the patient should be followed-up regularly.

37 i. What does the open lung
biopsy in 37 show?
ii. What is its pathogenesis?
iii. What conditions predispose to
this appearance?

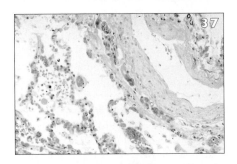

38 Enumerate types of mediastinal
involvement by lung cancer and how
they may present. What is the cause
of this radiological appearance (38)?

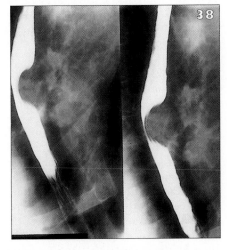

39 A patient with bronchial asthma has persistent nocturnal attacks of
cough and wheezy breathlessness which are not controlled despite inhaled
steroid therapy and long-acting beta-2 agonists. The cause of the nocturnal
attacks was found when 24-hour oesophageal pH monitoring (39) was done.
i. What is the cause of the persistent nocturnal attacks?
ii. How can this patient's asthma be controlled?

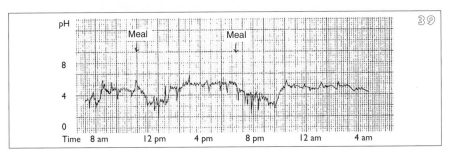

37 i. The lymphatic channels next to the large vessel are infiltrated by tumour cells. There is some vascular congestion. Both are typical of lymphangitis carcinomatosa. **ii.** Tumour enters the lungs via the pulmonary arteries and embeds in the vessel wall from where it penetrates into the adjacent lymphatics with subsequent permeation throughout the lung. Some patients may only have spread within the vascular tree. Marked reduction in carbon monoxide gas transfer may be demonstrated in these cases of vascular permeation. **iii.** The most common tumour that gives rise to this condition is adenocarcinoma; primary sites include breast, stomach, prostate, ovary, endometrium, pancreas and colon. When these tumours are known to be present the diagnosis is relatively simple. However, lymphangitis carcinomatosa may be the presenting symptom of these tumours so the cause of breathlessness may be confused with pulmonary oedema or benign causes of interstitial lung disease until transbronchial or open lung biopsy is performed.

38 Mediastinal involvement includes:
- Left recurrent laryngeal nerve palsy presents as hoarseness, and poor cough. It is due to metastases in the subaortic fossa.
- SVCO is caused by tumour compression by the right paratracheal lymph nodes.
- Dysphagia can be due to mediastinal lymphadenopathy of the subcarinal nodes. Barium swallow identifies the location of the obstruction (38).
- Arrhythmias, usually atrial fibrillation, can be caused by direct pericardial invasion by tumour, particularly from the left lower lobe.
- Pericardial effusion – as above, is due to direct invasion by tumour. Tamponade can ensue with dyspnoea and appropriate physical signs.
- High hemidiaphragm due to phrenic nerve entrapment in the mediastinum.

Horner's syndrome results, usually, from a primary apical tumour extending on to the posterior mediastinal surface entrapping the sympathetic chain. It is characterized by a small pupil with enophthalmos on the affected side. There is partial ptosis due to paralysis of the sympathetically innervated portion of orbicularis occulis muscle (Muller's muscle). Also, there is unilateral absence of sweating on the face and forehead.

39 i. Gastro-oesophageal reflux. This figure shows numerous episodes of increased oesophageal acidity, especially after meals. Continuous oesophageal pH monitoring can yield a temporal profile of acid reflux and acid clearance. Variables for measurement include the number of reflux episodes, acid clearance times and oesophageal exposure to acid. Possible pathophysiological factors include reflex vagal bronchoconstriction due to nerve fibre stimulation in the lower oesophagus and microaspiration. **ii.** In addition to an inhaled steroid and a beta-agonist, oesophageal reflux should be minimized by instructing the patient to sleep with the head elevated, take smaller but more frequent meals, and to take regular H_2 receptor antagonists or proton pump inhibitors. The patient should also avoid factors which can reduce the gastro-oesophageal sphincter tone such as caffeine, chocolate, cigarette smoking and medication such as theophylline.

40 i. What abnormality is shown on this radiograph (40)?
ii. What is the differential diagnosis?
iii. What additional radiological study can be done to assess the abnormality?

41 i. The material in 41 was obtained from whole lung lavage of a patient with what disorder?
ii. What is the appropriate treatment for this condition?
iii. Do corticosteroids have a therapeutic role?

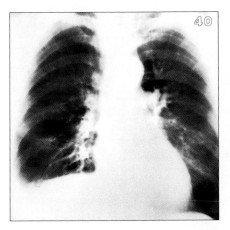

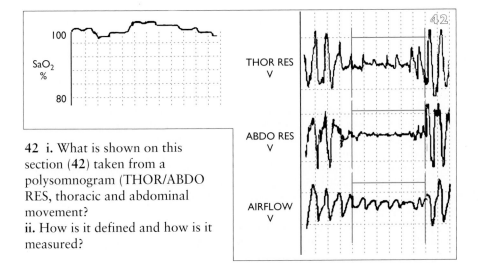

42 i. What is shown on this section (42) taken from a polysomnogram (THOR/ABDO RES, thoracic and abdominal movement?
ii. How is it defined and how is it measured?

40 i. The radiograph (40) demonstrates unilateral diaphragmatic elevation.
ii. This problem is most commonly caused by phrenic nerve paralysis. The nerve originates from the third, fourth, and fifth cervical roots. The most common causes of phrenic nerve paralysis include: (a) invasion by bronchogenic carcinoma; (b) disruption from thoracic trauma; (c) cold thermal injury associated with cardiac surgery; and (d) idiopathic (some of which may represent peripheral neuropathy). A less common cause is compression from a thyroid goitre or aortic aneurysm. Diaphragm elevation may also result from atelectasis, subphrenic abscess, hepatomegaly or subpulmonic effusion, and a similar radiographic pattern can also be produced by diaphragmatic eventration.
iii. A 'sniff test' done under fluoroscopy in the supine posture can aide in assessing the integrity of the phrenic nerve. The patient is asked to abruptly and strongly sniff while the diaphragm is observed. A paralysed diaphragm will paradoxically move up into the thorax as intrapleural pressure becomes more negative.

41 i. The lavage fluid shown is characteristic of pulmonary alveolar proteinosis, a disorder in which a phospholipid-rich proteinaceous material is deposited in the alveoli and bronchioles without associated lung fibrosis. Lung fluid obtained from whole lung lavage or BAL is milky in appearance and contains large macrophages with prominent cytoplasm.
ii. Whole lung lavage is the only treatment that is consistently successful. Often lavages of as much as 20 litres are performed at one session under general anaesthetic. The procedure is generally well tolerated and may be repeated as necessary, generally at 6- to 12-month intervals.
iii. Corticosteroids have not been shown to have a beneficial effect in this disorder and may be harmful. Inflammation does not appear to play a role in the pathogenesis. The condition is often self-limiting, with spontaneous remission after lavage clearance on radiography.

42 i. A hypopnoea.
ii. Apnoea is defined as complete cessation in airflow of 10 s or longer. Hypopnoea is more difficult to measure and is less precisely defined. Although there is wide agreement that hypopnoea occurs when there is a reduction in ventilation during sleep, opinion on how it is best measured and what degree of reduction is significant is very diverse. However, the reduction in ventilation must be accompanied by oxygen desaturation, arousal or both.

A decrease in ventilation can be documented directly by measurements of airflow and indirectly by measurements of thoraco- and/or abdominal movement. A wide range of devices which vary in both precision and reliability has been used to measure these parameters.

One definition of hypopnoea is a reduction of airflow of 50% or more, accompanied by a decrease in blood oxygen saturation of 4% or more. Another uses a 50% reduction in the thoracoabdominal movement as measured by inductive plethysmography.

43 The polysomno-gram in **43** shows abnormal EMG traces, leg movement traces labelled LAT and RAT (left and right anterior tibial), together with an EEG recording (top six traces).

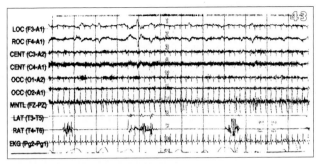

i. With what symptoms might this patient present?
ii. What is the relationship between this disorder, narcolepsy and/or obstructive sleep apnoea?

44 This 50-year-old lady presented with gradually progressive dyspnoea over the course of 6 months. Her mother had become unwell at that time and she had started visiting her mother daily to look after her.
i. Describe the appearances seen on the HRCT of the lungs (**44**).
ii. What important history would you obtain?
iii. What is the likely diagnosis?
iv. How would you treat this condition?

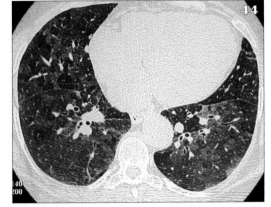

45 A number of medications have been associated with the development of interstitial lung disease.
i. What pulmonary disorder is classically associated with nitrofurantoin?
ii. Name other medications associated with interstitial lung disease.

43 i. Periodic limb movement in sleep (PLMS) is a condition in which patients experience stereotyped repetitive movements once they are asleep. Patients can present with insomnia as there may be an irresistible urge to move the legs and excessive daytime somnolence. In addition, many patients with PLMS have restless leg syndrome (RLS) which manifests as discomfort in both legs accompanied by irresistible movements of the limbs during the day.

ii. PLMS can occur secondary to narcolepsy, central and obstructive sleep apnoea, and REM sleep behaviour disorder. It is more common in older patients, occurring in up to 30% of patients over 60 years old. Polysomnography with measurement of periodic leg movements by EMG is required to diagnose PLMS. Often period leg movements during drowsy wakefulness are seen, as in **43**. During sleep, leg movements are followed by an arousal. Treatment is primarily that of the underlying cause, or where none is apparent, hypnotics suppress the arousal.

44 i. There is diffuse ground-glass shadowing with some areas of centrilobular nodularity.

ii. Ask about exposure to any pets or unusual dusts or chemicals. This lady's mother had a cockatoo which she had been feeding since her mother became unwell.

iii. Extrinsic allergic alveolitis or hypersensitivity pneumonitis may be caused by exposure to a variety of dusts and antigens and may be confirmed by avian precipitins in the serum and removal of the source, i.e. the bird.

iv. Patients have to be instructed to avoid the allergen or precipitant. Oral prednisolone may be used during the initial few weeks until the patient feels better, although there is no definite evidence on optimal dose and duration.

45 i. Both acute and chronic forms of drug-induced interstitial lung disease can occur in association with use of nitrofurantoin. The acute form begins within days (sometimes hours) of initiating therapy. Patients develop bilateral alveolar–interstitial infiltrates, fever, rigors and cough. Pleurisy may also occur. Symptoms resolve a few days after the drug has been stopped. The chronic form of disease can occur as long as 7 years after starting long-term antibiotic therapy and presents with an alveolitis and/or with interstitial fibrosis. Nitrofurantoin is the most common antibiotic associated with interstitial lung disease.

ii. Many additional medications are known to cause interstitial lung disease. The most common include various cytotoxic chemotherapeutic agents (e.g. bleomycin, cytoxan, methotrexate, nitrosoureas); and hydrochlorothiazide, gold and aspirin (acetylsalicylic acid). Other drugs causing pleural disease include bromocriptine, methysermide and methotrexate.

46 A 55-year-old man has had a large right pleural effusion (46) aspirated using a cannula on two occasions. Cytology has revealed malignant cells and he remains breathless. How would you proceed with the management of this patient?

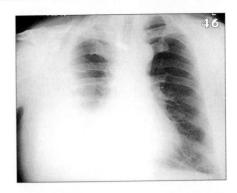

47 What device has been deployed in this patient's trachea (47)?

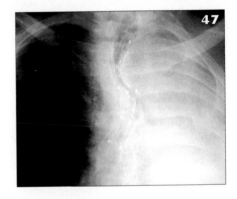

48 This chest radiograph (48) of a 58-year-old female ex-smoker presents with lethargy, a non-productive cough and mild generalized arthralgias. Her chest film shows bilateral hilar lymphadenopathy and an abdominal CT showed paraortic lymph nodes. Her serum ACE, biochemical profile and full blood count was normal, but her ESR was 80 mm/h
i. What is the differential diagnosis?
ii. What other investigations would you do?

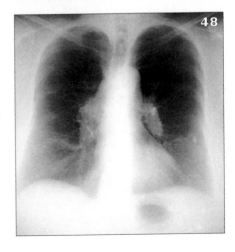

46 Management of large, recurrent, malignant pleural effusions should be aimed at palliation of symptoms which include dyspnoea. Video-assisted thoracoscopic surgery with pleurodesis by talc poudrage is, where available, the treatment of choice for those patients fit enough for a general anaesthetic. The pleural cavity may be drained to dryness and an accurate diagnosis can be made if necessary. Any loculations in the fluid can be broken up and if the lung re-expands, pleurodesis can be effected by insufflation of 5 g of sterile talc into the pleural space. Alternatively, a chest drain can be inserted under local anaesthetic and once the pleural effusion has completely drained, a talc suspension can be introduced into the pleural cavity via the drain. The chest radiograph performed after chest drain insertion in this case showed the lung had not re-expanded. Therefore, pleurodesis could not be performed as the pleural surfaces were not apposed. In this situation palliation can be effected by the introduction of a pleuro-peritoneal shunt. This allows the patient to drain the pleural effusion into the abdomen through a manually operated one-way valve sited under the skin of the lower chest wall.

47 An expandable metal stent. The patient's trachea was narrowed by extrinsic compression due to a tumour. Stents are used to palliate breathlessness due to extrinsic compression of major airways. They are deployed under general anaesthetic with the use of a rigid bronchoscope. Laser resection may precede placement if there is additional endoluminal disease. Problems with this type of airway stent include the fact that they cannot be removed, ingrowth of tumour between the wires, and long-term penetration of the bronchial wall with possible stent fracture. None of these problems occur with silastic stents, which are flexible and remain in place due to small protuberances on their outer surface. The relative thickness of silastic stents lowers the maximum achievable luminal diameter. The migration rate of the Dumon stent has been reported as 18.6%.

Patients with stents must regularly check peak flows to monitor for the effect of blockage of the stent by secretions or tumour ingrowth, although obstruction may be quite severe before peak flows start to fall. They should also have 3-monthly check bronchoscopies to look for these complications.

48 i. A normal serum ACE does not rule out sarcoidosis. A very high ESR is not common in sarcoidosis and although para-aortic lymphadenopathy may occur in sarcoidosis, metastatic carcinoma and lymphoma must be excluded.
ii. Although a transbronchial biopsy may be useful in a younger patient, a mediastinoscopy is more likely to obtain a diagnosis here. Her mediastinal lymph nodes showed adenocarcinoma and no primary was found. Sometimes mediastinal lymphoma may be misdiagnosed as sarcoidosis if there is no biopsy confirmation and even with a lymph node biopsy misdiagnosis can occur as regional lymph nodes draining carcinomas and lymphomas can show granulomatous reactions which mimic sarcoidosis. An elevated serum ACE occasionally occurs in Hodgkin's disease and non-Hodgkin's lymphomas – especially histiocytic lymphomas – and may lead to misdiagnosis.

49 These lung function results (Table) are from a 40-year-old woman 18 months post-allogeneic bone marrow transplantation (BMT) for acute myeloid leukaemia. There was no acute change in the results after bronchodilator. She had developed skin and gastrointestinal graft-versus-host disease at 12 months post-BMT.

i. What is the likely cause of the lung function abnormalities?
ii. What are the common pulmonary complications of bone marrow transplantation?

Test	Predicted	Range	Result	% predicted
PEFR (l/min)	374	318–430	122	33
FEV$_1$ (l)	2.31	1.96–2.65	0.85	37
FVC (l)	3.04	2.58–3.49	1.84	61
FEV (%)	75	64–86	46	62
DL$_{CO}$ (mmol/min/kPa)*	7.61	6.47–8.75	5.90	78
VA (l)	–	–	3.05	–
K$_{CO}$ mmol/min/kPa/l)**	1.70	1.44–1.95	1.94	114

*DL$_{CO}$ = transfer factor.   **K$_{CO}$ = transfer coefficient, i.e. DL$_{CO}$/VA.

50 A 40-year-old man presented with marked lethargy, cough, polyuria and thirst and this skin lesion on his elbow. His serum ACE is markedly elevated.
i. What is the skin lesion (50)?
ii. What is the cause of his polyuria and thirst?
iii. What is the role of serum ACE in the management of sarcoidosis?

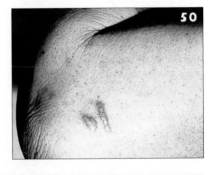

51 i. This 30-year-old man complained of a chronic cough for 3 months. His chest radiograph was normal.
i. Interpret the lung function test (Table).
ii. What is the diagnosis?

Test	Predicted	Range	Result	% predicted
PEFR (l/min)	531	451–611	344	65
FEV$_1$ (l)	3.16	2.69–3.63	1.78	56
FVC (l)	4.03	3.43–4.65	3.02	75
FEV$_1$/FVC (%)	71	61–82	58	83
Post-bronchodilator				

Test	Predicted	Range	Result
PEFR (l/min)	–	–	430
FEV$_1$ (l)	–	–	2.22
FVC (l)	–	–	3.10
FEV$_1$/FVC (%)	–	–	71

49 i. There is severe airflow obstruction. The likely cause is bronchiolitis obliterans, a progressive irreversible fibrosis of small airways. It may stabilize, leaving the patient with severe breathlessness or, in a significant number, it may be fatal. Treatment with immunosuppressive drugs may slow the rate of progression but increases the risk of opportunistic infection. Risks for the development of the condition include chronic graft-versus-host disease, and episodes of preceding pulmonary toxicity.

ii. Idiopathic interstitial pneumonitis is well described occurring at approximately 1–2 months post-transplant and is almost always fatal. This may be a drug toxicity effect of the common agents used for pre-transplant chemotherapy (conditioning), Busulfan and cyclophosphamide. CMV pneumonitis may occur later and is diagnosed by viral detection in broncho-alveolar lavage fluid by PCR, antigen detection, viral culture, or shell vial methods. The prognosis is poor although treatment is attempted with ganciclovir and i.v. immunoglobulin as well as supportive care. Bacterial and fungal pneumonias also occur. A less common fatal complication is pulmonary haemorrhage.

50 i. The skin lesion is cutaneous sarcoidosis which looks like keloid.
ii. His polyuria and thirst are from hypercalcaemia. His 24-hour urine calcium shows marked hypercalciuria also caused by the overproduction of calcitriol by sarcoid granulomas and pulmonary macrophages. He should be rehydrated and commenced on high-dose prednisolone.
iii. World-wide an elevated serum ACE has a sensitivity of 57% with a specificity of 90%, a positive predictive value of 90% and a negative predictive of 60%. The serum elevation in sarcoidosis is due to the epithelioid cells of sarcoid granulomas and pulmonary macrophages. It is elevated also in silicosis, severe diabetes, hyperthyroidism and cirrhosis and is always markedly elevated in Gaucher's disease. ACE inhibitors used in cardiac failure and hypertension markedly depress serum ACE. Serum ACE is more likely to be elevated in severe active sarcoidosis especially with hypercalcaemia and falls as the disease remits or is treated with corticosteroids. It is an invaluable test for the long-term monitoring of disease activity.

51 i. A 25% improvement in FEV_1 following bronchodilator therapy. A difference of more than 12% between two efforts at spirometry is considered significant. The greater the improvement after inhaled bronchodilator and the faster the spirometry returns to normal, the more likely is the diagnosis to be asthma. Some patients with chronic obstructive airways disease will show improvement in spirometry, usually after large doses of bronchodilator. An acute change may not be seen in asthmatics if they have been taking regular bronchodilators before testing or if their treatment is optimal with inhaled corticosteroids, thus stabilizing their condition, or with severe or persistent asthma.
ii. Bronchial asthma. (Marked post-bronchodilator changes such as these indicate poor control of asthma in patients who are already on treatment.)

52 This chest radiograph (52) in a 36-year-old male smoker who presented for a routine life insurance medical examination. He is in good health with a normal physical examination.
i. What is the provisional diagnosis?
ii. What radiographic stage is the disease?
iii. What investigations would you suggest to confirm the likely diagnosis?

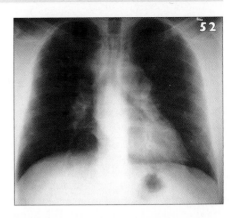

53 Shown is the chest radiograph (53) of a 61-year-old man with symptoms of high fever, headache, cough and pleuritic chest pain of 3 days' duration. He smoked cigarettes, drank 40 units of alcohol a week and took prednisone on alternate days for rheumatoid arthritis. He appeared obtunded and tachypnoeic and was hypotensive. A Gram stain of sputum obtained by nasotracheal suction showed many polymorphonuclear leukocytes but no apparent bacteria.
i. What are the radiographic findings?
ii. What is the most likely diagnosis?
iii. What is the most appropriate treatment?

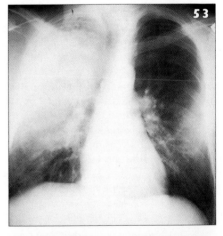

54 This woman of 58 has had similar appearances on her chest radiograph (54) for over 5 years. She does not have significant respiratory symptoms. What is the differential diagnosis?

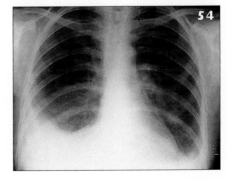

52 i. Sarcoidosis is the most likely diagnosis in a fit young male, although it is less common in smokers.
ii. This patient has stage I disease. Sarcoidosis is staged as follows: normal chest radiograph, stage 0; bilateral hilar adenopathy, stage I; bilateral hilar adenopathy and parenchymal infiltrates, stage II; parenchymal disease only, stage III; and irreversible pulmonary fibrosis and/or bulla formation, stage IV. Stage I disease occurs in about 50% of patients. A diffuse reticulonodular pattern is the most common parenchymal abnormality. Involvement of the anterior mediastinal lymph nodes and unilateral hilar lymphadenopathy is less common in sarcoidosis and raises the possibility of lymphoma or malignancy.
iii. A markedly elevated serum angiotensin-converting enzyme (ACE) alone may be sufficient in patients with classic clinical features. It is sometimes advisable if the presentation is unusual to obtain histological confirmation by fibre-optic transbronchial lung biopsy or mediastinoscopy to exclude other possibilities. Serum calcium and a 24-hour urine calcium are recommended to identify unsuspected hypercalciuria or hypercalcaemia.

53 i. There is dense consolidation of the right upper lobe with prominent air bronchograms.
ii. This patient has a severe community-acquired pneumonia which is most often caused by *Str. pneumoniae*, *Staph. aureus* or Gram-negative bacilli including *Legionella* sp. In this setting, a Gram stain demonstrating a purulent exudate but no organisms is highly suggestive of *Legionella* infection. Legionellae are facultative, intracellular pathogens which infect alveolar macrophages and cause a pneumonic illness which is often accompanied by systemic manifestations which can be severe. Corticosteroid-treated patients, cigarette smokers and heavy drinkers are particularly susceptible. The organisms are poorly seen on Gram-stains of sputa but can some-times be visualized using basic fuchsin-based stains or direct fluorescent antibodies. Isolation requires special culture medium and several days of incubation. Serological testing can confirm infection after the fact but cannot guide antibiotic therapy.
iii. A macrolide (erythromycin or clarithromycin) or a fluoroquinolone (such as levofloxacin) is preferred for treating *Legionella* infections. For life-threatening infections where *Legionella* could be present, the addition of rifampicin is recommended.

54 The chest radiograph (54) shows moderate bilateral pleural effusions. The absence of cardiac enlargement and significant dyspnoea should exclude left ventricular failure (LVF) although cardiac failure can occur with a normal cardiac silhouette in patients with mitral stenosis or constrictive pericarditis. It is most likely that she has an inflammatory pleurisy, probably due to autoimmune disease such as systemic lupus erythematosis or rheumatoid arthritis. The patient shown here suffered from chronic rheumatoid arthritis. Other possible causes include vasculitides such as polyarteritis nodosa, Wegener's granulomatosis and, polyserositis, drug reactions, e.g. hydralazine, phenytoin, phenothiazines and practolol, lymphatic hypoplasia (yellow nail syndrome) and hypothyroidism. In general, bilateral effusions suggest a systemic cause and unilateral fluid a local cause.

55 A previously well patient presents with mild, gradual-onset left pleuritic pain. The lung scan [55 – KR, krypton (ventilation) image; TC, technetium (perfusion) image] is reported as showing intermediate probability for pulmonary embolism (PE). How would you proceed?

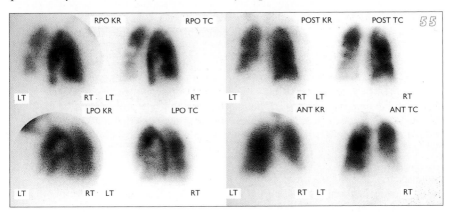

56 This 16-year-old girl presented with myasthenic symptoms and underwent routine evaluation for thymectomy which included a normal plain chest radiograph.
i. What abnormality was found on the CT scan (56)?
ii. What are the usual characteristics of the thymus in myasthenia patients?
iii. What treatment should be advised? What is the significance of the lesion present?

57 i. What is the likely cause of this (57) gastrointestinal complication in a CF patient?
ii. What is the best treatment.

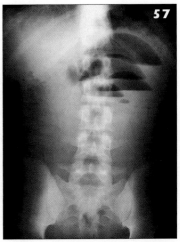

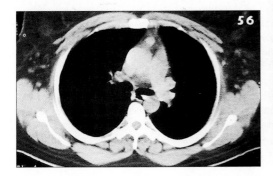

55 Based on PIOPED criteria, intermediate probability scans had a likelihood of pulmonary embolism (based on pulmonary angiogram) of between 16–66%. On the other hand, high-probability scans with high clinical probability have a 96% chance of having PTE and normal scans even with high clinical probability effectively rule out PTE. Therefore, intermediate and low probability scans can be regarded as being of indeterminate probability and patients require further investigation. Since the PIOPED study, some studies have recommended CT as a first-line investigation while others have used it in combination with V/Q scanning and venous Doppler ultrasound. The use of multi-slice helical CT scanners has greatly increased the value of CT scanning ('CT pulmonary angiography') in the diagnosis of pulmonary embolism; some studies have demonstrated specificity and sensitivity approaching that of pulmonary angiography, although sub-segmental emboli may still be more difficult to diagnose. The other chief value of CT scanning is that it allows diagnosis of conditions other than pulmonary embolism that cannot be detected by V/Q scanning.

56 i. A small (2 cm) thymoma can be seen in the retrosternal space.
ii. Most myasthenia cases (90%) occur after puberty. Thymoma is present in only 10–15% of these adult cases and is exceptionally uncommon in juvenile onset cases. Approximately 10–25% of adult cases have a normal gland but the majority exhibit lymphoid follicular hyperplasia.
iii. It is usual to recommend thymectomy for all cases of myasthenia except those which are very mild or confined to the occulomotor muscles. It should be performed in all patients with a thymoma.
   The available data regarding outcome are confused as more severe cases proceed to surgery whereas less severe cases are managed by anticholinesterase medication. Thymectomy appears to be associated with better long-term survival and clinical result than medical therapy. For those with hyperplasia, 15% are drug free following surgery, 25% are in drug-maintained remission, 50% are clinically improved and 10% are unchanged. The presence of a thymoma is associated with a significantly poorer result from surgery.

57 i. The radiograph in 57 illustrates the typical features of the distal intestinal obstruction syndrome (DIOS) with dilated loops of small bowel. It is due to inspissated intestinal contents in the distal ileum and proximal colon.
   The more common causes are insufficient prescription of pancreatic enzymes or patient non-compliance with enzyme treatment.
ii. Treatment of the acute event involves rehydration and the administration of oral gastrograffin (100 ml in 400 ml of water in older patients). It may also be given as an enema. For resistant cases, large volumes (5–6 l) of a balanced electrolyte intestinal lavage solution administered by a nasogastric tube is very effective.
   Surgical treatment should be avoided.

58 A patient with severe, stable COPD has stopped smoking and bronchodilator therapy has been optimized (**58**). He continues to be dyspnoeic. Corticosteroid therapy is now considered.

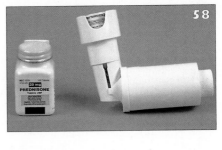

i. When should corticosteroids be used in the long-term management of COPD?
ii. How should a steroid trial be conducted in stable patients with COPD?

59 The cytology specimen in (**59**) was obtained by fine-needle aspiration of a peripheral mass seen on chest radiograph. What does it show and how accurate is this procedure in predicting the histology of masses removed by surgery?

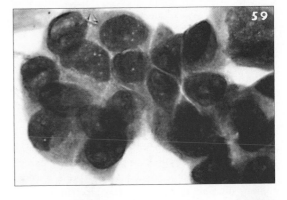

60 **i.** Describe the appearances in this chest radiograph (**60**).
ii. What are the likely causative organisms?
iii. What are the causes of a swollen lobe in the presence of pneumonia?

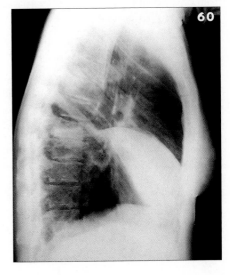

58 i. There is still some controversy about the use of inhaled corticosteroids in COPD. However, a review of several large studies (Copenhagen City Lung Study, ISOLDE, EUROSCOP, Lung Health-21) concludes that exacerbation frequency, and probably severity, are reduced by high-dose inhaled corticosteroids. This is important because a high exacerbation frequency is associated with a reduced health-related quality of life. However, there is no evidence that inhaled steroids slow the rate of decline of FEV_1 with time.

ii. The effect of corticosteroids should be assessed by spirometry (with and without bronchodilators) and a walking distance test obtained before and after the steroid trial. Most recommend starting systemic corticosteroids (e.g. prednisone at approximately 0.5 mg/kg daily, or equivalent) for 2 weeks. An improvement in the FEV_1 of at least 20% and an absolute increase of at least 0.2 l are regarded as evidence of steroid responsiveness. If a response is observed the steroids are then tapered to the lowest effective dose and/or the patient should be switched to inhaled steroids.

59 This shows non-small-cell carcinoma. The features are not specific enough to differentiate between squamous cell carcinoma and adenocarcinoma; however, they do show large hyperchromatic cells with abundant cytoplasm and nuclear atypia. When removed surgically the final histology may be squamous cell or adenocarcinoma, or if no specific features are shown it may be termed large cell carcinoma, a diagnosis of exclusion. Cytologically, small cell carcinoma shows cells with minimal cytoplasm and uniformly hyperchromatic and moulded nuclei. They are not always truly small on smears and nuclear changes are not constant. Also there may be a number of cell types expressed to varying degrees within a single tumour since all lung tumours most likely arise from a single stem cell rather than from cells which have already differentiated into for example squamous cells. In general, cytological samples obtained by fine-needle aspiration are able to distinguish small-cell from non-small-cell lung cases very accurately – but are cell type-specific in up to 70% of non-small-cell carcinomas.

60 i. This lateral chest radiograph (60) shows homogeneous consolidation within the middle lobe. The horizontal fissure is bowed upwards, suggesting some swelling of the lobe.

ii. *Str. pneumoniae* is the most common cause of community-acquired pneumonia and is the most typical cause of lobar pneumonia. However, it is often unappreciated that most other common bacterial causes of pneumonia can also cause lobar consolidation including legionella, *Staph. aureus* and as many as 50% of *Myc. pneumoniae* pneumonias are lobar.

iii. *K. pneumoniae* is also a cause of a swollen lobe on the chest radiograph but as in this example, which is due to *Myc. pneumoniae*, any bacterial pathogen can potentially do this.

61 The mediastinum may be divided into three compartments for classification of mass lesions: anterior, visceral and paravertebral (61). The anterior compartment lies between the sternum and the anterior surface of the pericardium and the great vessels which forms the anterior border of the visceral compartment. This contains the intrathoracic organs and therefore extends posteriorly to the vertebral column. The paravertebral compartment comprises the paravertebral spaces. List the more common lesions found in each compartment.

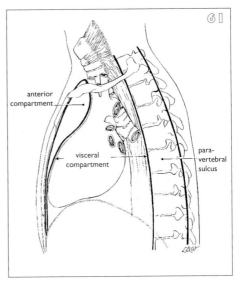

62 The abnormalities seen in the chest radiograph (62) developed suddenly in a patient with history of recent intravenous drug use.
i. What is the differential diagnosis?
ii. How might information obtained from the pulmonary artery catheter affect the differential diagnosis?
iii. How might the history of heroin use relate to the abnormalities shown?

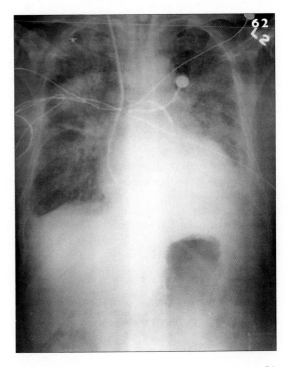

61 Clearly, any tissue element may give rise to a tumour so that rarities such as sarcomas are possible but the more common lesions are :

- Anterior: lymphoma, thymoma, thymic hyperplasia, germ cell tumours (teratomas, dermoid cysts, malignant germ cell tumours).
- Visceral: secondary mediastinal tumour, lymphoma, retrosternal thyroid, aortic aneurysm, hiatus hernia, lymphadenopathy, enterogenous cyst, bronchogenic cyst, pleuropericardial cyst, ganglionoma.
- Posterior: neurogenic tumour, lymphoma, haemangioma.

Note that the older classification of superior, anterior, middle and posterior mediastinum may be encountered. This can be confusing as it utilizes arbitrary boundaries between these areas. The superior mediastinum lies above a line drawn from T4 to the manubrial–sternal junction and thus includes elements of the three compartments described above. Similarly, the posterior mediastinum includes both the paravertebral compartment and that portion of the visceral compartment which lies behind the trachea and heart. This older classification leads to the same lesion potentially appearing under several descriptive areas. For example, a moderate retrosternal thyroid would be a superior mediastinal lesion which might easily extend through the middle mediastinum into the retrotracheal section of the posterior mediastinum. The compartment classification would place this lesion entirely in the visceral compartment.

62 i. The differential diagnosis of acute interstitial infiltrates can be divided into cardiogenic causes and conditions resulting in increased vascular permeability. Cardiogenic causes include congestive heart failure, myocardial infarction or coronary insufficiency, acute valvular heart disease, severe volume overload and acute diastolic dysfunction. Increased permeability can result from near drowning, heroin or other drug overdose, sepsis, chest trauma, burns or exposure to toxic gases. The oedema that develops at high altitude may result from abnormalities in both intravascular pressure and permeability.

ii. A pulmonary artery catheter allows measurement of the pulmonary arterial occlusion (wedge) pressure as a reflection of the left ventricular preload and/or the intravascular hydrostatic pressure in the pulmonary capillaries (ignoring the effects of possible venoconstriction) and can frequently separate cardiac from permeability problems. A wedge pressure of >18 cm H_2O suggests cardiac abnormalities.

iii. As stated above, heroin and other opiate drugs – illicit as well as conventional use – can cause acute non-cardiogenic pulmonary oedema. Intravenous drugs are also associated with alterations in consciousness leading to widespread aspiration, to acute myocardial dysfunction (cocaine) or to valvular incompetence (acute bacterial endocarditis).

63 This middle-aged male patient complained of mild dysphagia. A barium examination and endoscopy both showed only smooth mild extrinsic compression of the oesophagus. A CT scan was obtained (63).
i. What abnormality is present?
ii. What is the differential diagnosis?
iii. How may this be treated?

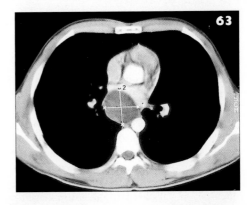

64 A 60-year-old female patient underwent major abdominal surgery for a non-malignant condition; she spent some days on the intensive care unit. Her chest radiograph at follow-up, some weeks later, showed a wide mediastinum; the subsequent CT scan is shown here (64).
i. What is the abnormality?
ii. What is the likely cause and how would you further investigate the patient?

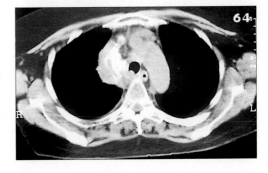

65 Shown (65) is a CT scan from a 75-year-old Chinese man who has chronic sputum production which has not increased over the past 4 years. Sputum cultures have grown *Mycobacterium intracellulare*.
i. Should antituberculous chemotherapy be given?
ii. Should isolation procedures be used?

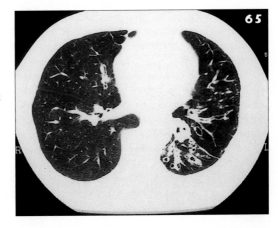

63 i. The lesion is a smooth-walled cyst in the visceral compartment.
ii. This is most likely a foregut cyst. During the development of the tracheobronchial tree from the foregut, cells may be sequestered which subsequently give rise to foregut cysts, i.e. a bronchogenic or enterogenous cyst. It is not possible to say accurately without histological examination of the lining epithelium and even then the features may be non-specific.

In a child other possibilities would exist. A neurenteric cyst connects with the meninges and is normally found in young children with associated spinal deformities. These occasionally also communicate with the gastrointestinal tract. A gastroenteric cyst is lined by gastric mucosa and may communicate with the stomach below the diaphragm. It is also normally encountered in children and associated with spinal abnormalities.
iii. Opinion varies regarding best management of foregut cysts. Small cysts which are asymptomatic chance findings can be observed but if bronchial or oesophageal compression symptoms are present they should be removed or marsupialized to the pleural cavity.

64 i. The CT scan (**64**) shows a mediastinal mass in the right paratracheal region.
ii. This could indicate mediastinal lymphadenopathy but the patient is likely to have had a radiograph before her abdominal surgery. Was this normal? If it was, taking into consideration that the patient spent time on the ITU, were any central lines inserted in the perioperative period? If internal jugular lines were used then it is likely that the apparent mass on the current CT scan represents haematoma and follow-up with plain chest radiography is indicated. If doubt remains as to the aetiology of the 'mass' then the investigation of choice would be mediastinoscopy.

65 i. This organism – which is ubiquitous in the environment – is usually regarded as a colonizer of damaged airways, such as the extensive area of bronchiectasis depicted in the CT scan. This patient's plain chest radiograph had features of previous tuberculous infection which may have been the cause of the bronchiectasis.

Clinically a typical mycobacteria, of which *M. intracellulare* is one, can cause disease indistinguishable from typical *M. tuberculosis* infection. Along with the other opportunistic mycobacterial organisms it may also arise in patients with altered immune function.
ii. The decision to treat would be based on isolating the organism in at least two sputum samples (as it may be a contaminant) and the presence of radiograph abnormalities consistent with tuberculosis, particularly where those abnormalities are progressive. The decision to embark on treatment should include consideration that the length of treatment will be 2 years, that the response rates to therapy may be as low as 50%, and that the most effective drug regimen is yet to be determined.

66 An elderly patient with severe COPD has the following room air, arterial blood gas tensions when breathing room air: pH, 7.38; $PaCO_2$, 46 mmHg (6.0 kPa); PaO_2, 54 mmHg (7.1 kPa).

i. Is supplemental oxygen (**66**) appropriate for this patient?
ii. If oxygen is to be prescribed, for how many hours a day should it be used?
iii. What are the benefits of long-term oxygen therapy?

67 i. What is the allergen likely to be present in high concentrations in normal living environments?
ii. How can environmental control be achieved?
iii. What is the role of immunotherapy in this type of allergy?

68 i. What is the diagnosis from the CXR (**68**)?
ii. What treatment option may be considered when this patient's dyspnoea becomes irreversibly severe? What factors would influence this decision?

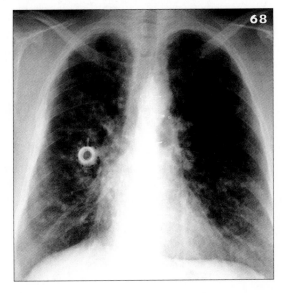

66 i. Yes. Indications for long-term oxygen therapy include: (a) resting room air PaO_2 <55 mmHg (7.3 kPa) or O_2 saturation <88%; (b) resting room air PaO_2 56–59 mmHg (7.3–8.0 kPa) or O_2 saturation 89% plus evidence of end-organ dysfunction due to chronic hypoxia [e.g. P-pulmonale on the ECG (P waves >3 mm in II, III, aVF), right heart failure (pedal oedema), erythrocythaemia (haematocrit >55%)].
ii. Continuous, 15–24 hours per day. The improvement in survival with long-term oxygen therapy is proportional to the number of hours per day the O_2 is used. The NOTT study in 1981 showed improved 2-year survival in patients having nasal oxygen continuously, compared with 12 hours per day (40.8% versus 22%). Similar improvements were shown in the MRC study 1981 where 5-year mortality in COPD patients receiving 2 l nasal oxygen for 15 hours per day was 45.2% compared with 66.7% in non recipients of O_2.
iii. Long-term oxygen therapy improves survival, pulmonary haemodynamics, exercise capacity, and neuropsychological performance in patients with COPD.

67 i. House dust mites thrive in the environment pictured. The allergens involved include the *Dermatophagoides* species of mite (*D. pteronyssinus*, *D. farinae*, *D. microceras*). *D. pteronyssinus* has four allergens, I–IV. Development of atopy to the mite is genetically linked. If one parent is allergic there is a 50% chance that the child will be allergic; if both parents are allergic the chance is 80%. The intensity and duration of exposure in early childhood correlates with subsequent sensitization.
ii. The mites live and die in bedding, carpeting, curtains and upholstered furniture. Central heating and limited ventilation also predispose to mite build-up. Aggressive reduction of mite numbers can be accomplished by:
- Washing the bedding at >55°C at least weekly.
- Vacuuming the carpets.
- Replacing the carpets with vinyl or hardwood floors.
- Keeping the relative humidity <50% with air conditioning.
- Enclosing the mattress in a vinyl cover.

iii. Immunotherapy involves the administration of increasing amounts of allergenic extracts with the idea of reducing clinical reactivity. It works in a small number of patients. A very small risk of death due to anaphylaxis with this treatment should always be discussed first.

68 i. Cystic fibrosis.
ii. Lung transplantation may be considered when the FEV_1 falls to less than 30% predicted and the life expectancy falls to <2 years. Females and children under 10 years of age may need to be referred earlier. Resting tachycardia, anaemia, low serum albumin, and desaturation on exercise may also be factors prompting earlier referral.

69 This chest radiograph (**69**) is of a 26-year-old man who had repeated syncopal episodes and required permanent pacemaker insertion for complete heart block. He also had experienced several months of lethargy and intermittent dull retrosternal chest pain.
i. What diagnostic possibility does the radiograph show?
ii. What investigations would you suggest?
iii. What is the cause of the pain?
iv. When are corticosterioids indicated?

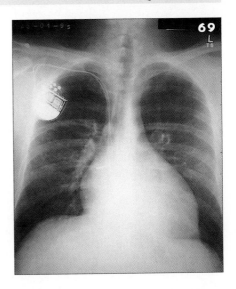

70 i. How is the maximum exercise ventilation predicted in patients with chronic airflow obstruction?
ii. Ventilation for a given oxygen uptake is often excessive in patients with airflow obstruction. What factors contribute to an excessively high ventilation during exercise in these patients and others with pulmonary disease?

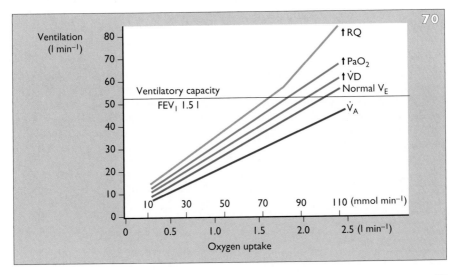

57

69 i. This patient has stage III sarcoidosis with cardiac involvement. Cardiac disease in this condition may cause a range of ventricular and supraventricular arrhythmias and conduction defects. Cardiomyopathy may develop rarely.

ii. ECG and Holter monitoring to document arrhythmias; 2D echocardiography may show ventricular septal thinning, localized regional wall abnormalities or a generalized cardiomyopathy. Thallium scintigraphy may show regions of abnormal perfusion. Endocardial biopsy may yield positive histology in less than 40% of cases.

iii. Chest pain in sarcoidosis is common (at least 25%) and may be pleuritic or dull and retrosternal. It may be severe and sometimes mimic a myocardial infarct. Cardiac sarcoidosis is a difficult diagnosis to establish without a myocardial biopsy. Even then, a clear association with an arrhythmia and sarcoidosis is difficult unless the sarcoidosis is clearly active in other sites.

iv. Arrhythmias and cardiomyopathy should be treated in the usual way. Corticosteroids would be indicated if standard treatment was ineffective or if the sarcoidosis was active at other sites. Monitoring of the response of cardiac sarcoid to corticosteroids is difficult.

70 i. The maximum exercise ventilation is predicted as the $FEV_1 \times 35$ in litres.

ii. The ventilatory response to exercise is linear until anaerobic metabolism stimulates ventilation further by a decrease in the pH.

Minute ventilation is a combination of alveolar ventilation and dead space ventilation. In patients with airflow obstruction, the contribution from the dead space (VD), both anatomical and physiological, increases. The worse the airflow obstruction, the higher the minute ventilation has to be in order to maintain a normal rate of gas exchange.

Other factors that will increase minute ventilation are:

- Hypoxia – this will add to ventilatory drive and ventilation will rise.
- Respiratory exchange ratio (RQ) – if the patient makes an anaerobic contribution to exercise, either due to an abnormal diet, e.g. high fat, low carbohydrate, or because the anaerobic mechanisms 'kick in' early due to poor aerobic metabolism.

70 shows an idealized scheme where minute ventilation comprises alveolar ventilation, dead space ventilation (VD) and contributions due to hypoxia (PaO_2) and an increase in respiratory exchange ratio (RQ). The horizontal line shows the predicted maximum exercise ventilation for an FEV_1 of 1.5 l and it can be seen as the various factors cause the minute ventilation to rise, the curves will move to the left, limiting exercise prematurely.

71 This man was treated with six courses of cytotoxic chemotherapy for small-cell lung cancer 18 months ago. He returned to the clinic feeling well, but had noticed some lesions in his neck.

i. What is illustrated in **71**?
ii. How should this be treated?
iii. What is the value of chemotherapy in relapsed small-cell lung cancer?

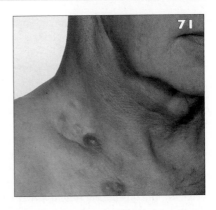

72 An HIV-antibody positive man (CD4+ count of 0.06×10^9/l) has worsening cutaneous Kaposi's sarcoma (KS) which also involves the palate. The chest radiograph showed fine bilateral reticulonodular shadowing. A bronchoscopic alveolar lavage, taken at the same time as the baseline pulmonary function tests, was negative for pathogens, but tracheal and bronchial KS were seen. He received cytotoxic chemotherapy with bleomycin and vincristine in 3-weekly cycles. Eight weeks later he reported increasing exertional dyspnoea and a non-productive cough. There was partial regression of the skin and palatal tumours but the chest radiograph was unchanged. Repeat pulmonary function tests were performed (Table).

i. What is the likely cause of the change in the lung function?
ii. How would you confirm the diagnosis?

Test	Baseline (% predicted)	After 8 weeks (% predicted)
FEV_1	98	73
FVC	101	70
TL_{CO}^*	86	47
K_{CO}^*	88	63

*Corrected for haemoglobin

73 **i.** What is shown in **73**?
ii. What is it used for?
iii. How useful is it?

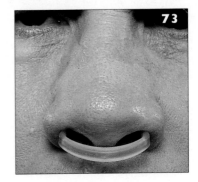

71 i. The lesion shows supraclavicular lymphadenopathy and a further lesion just below the head of the right clavicle. Fine-needle aspiration confirmed small-cell lung cancer.

ii. The treatment of these lesions is with palliative radiotherapy.

iii. Relapse chemotherapy in small-cell lung cancer is generally disappointing. Although chemotherapy as initial treatment may produce response rates of up to 80%, the response rate in relapsed disease is usually less than 20%. There are no clear guidelines as to what chemotherapy to use in relapse. It is reasonable to repeat the initial chemotherapeutic schedule or to use alternative drugs. Most patients who relapse are usually not well enough or unwilling to receive full doses of intravenous 3-weekly cycles of chemotherapy. They may be best treated with single-agent chemotherapy or may be suitable for phase II studies of new cytotoxic agents. In general, the greater the time that has elapsed from the completion of initial treatment to relapse, the greater the chance of the patient responding to further chemotherapy. This is unlikely to be substantial in more than 20% of individuals.

72 i. Possible causes include:
- Progressive Kaposi's sarcoma, but this is unlikely as the skin and palate lesions are regressing on treatment and the chest radiograph is unchanged.
- Bleomycin pulmonary toxicity, but the patient has only received two courses.
- Intercurrent *P. carinii (jiroveci)* pneumonia or other infection including pyogenic or mycobacterial causes.

ii. Fibre-optic bronchoscopy. This showed regression of the tracheobronchial Kaposi's sarcoma; cytological examination of the lavage fluid confirmed *P. carinii (jiroveci)* pneumonia.

A single reduced TL_{CO} recording cannot distinguish *P. carinii (jiroveci)* from other opportunistic infections. A low TL_{CO} can occur in asymptomatic HIV-positive individuals, as well as those with infections and pulmonary KS. A fall in TL_{CO}, from baseline, of >5% when used to predict the presence of *P. carinii (jiroveci)* pneumonia has a sensitivity of 75% but a specificity of only 28%. A normal TL_{CO} value is very useful because of the high negative predictive value (98%) which would make *P. carinii (jiroveci)* pneumonia unlikely.

73 i. A Nozovent.

ii. Treatment of snoring

iii. It is useful in about 5–10% of snorers, especially in those whose examination shows a substantial opening of the anterior nares on inspiratory nasal flow. Unfortunately it can fall out during the night. It has not been of proven benefit in OSA as most patients with this condition have airway obstruction at sites distal to the anterior nares.

74 i. A 60-year-old man had progressive dyspnoea and bilateral ankle swelling. He was admitted several times over the past year and diagnosed to have 'chronic obstructive airway disease'. Arterial blood gas tensions showed hypercapnic respiratory failure. His chest radiograph was normal. A flow–volume loop was done.

i. What do the spirometry (Table) and flow–volume loop (74) show?
ii. Was the diagnosis correct?
iii. What are the possible causes?
iv. What test would confirm the diagnosis and what does this test involve?

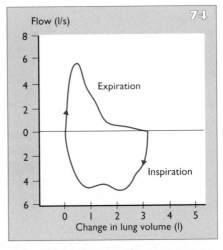

Test	Predicted	Range	Result	% Predicted
PEFR (l/min)	531	451–611	361	68
FEV$_1$ (l)	3.16	2.69–3.63	2.13	67
FVC (l)	4.03	3.43–4.65	3.25	81
FEV$_1$/FVC (%)	71	61–82	65	92

75 This photomicrograph (75) of a Wright–Geimsa-stained cytospin was prepared from BAL fluid obtained from a 54-year-old Middle-Eastern woman with a chronic cough, wheezing and peripheral blood eosinophilia. Her chest radiograph showed mild, diffuse interstitial infiltrates.

i. What cells are present in the BAL (arrows)?
ii. What diagnoses should be considered?

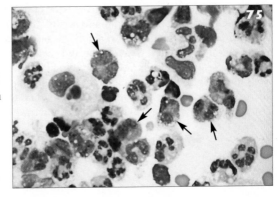

74 & 75: Answers

74 i. Mild volume-dependent airway collapse with a FEV_1/FVC of 65%.
ii. No. The mild obstructive airway disease seen on the flow–volume loop by itself is unlikely to explain the respiratory failure.
iii. Central or obstructive sleep apnoea. Respiratory failure usually does not occur in sleep apnoea unless there is concomitant chronic obstructive airway disease, even though this may be very mild.
iv. Polysomnography – this includes continuous monitoring of the electroencephalogram, electro-oculogram and chin electromyogram for sleep staging, continuous monitoring of arterial oxygen saturation with a finger probe using a pulse oximeter, ribcage and abdominal movement to measure apnoeas and hypopnoeas using inductance plethysmography, continuous measurement of nasal airflow using a nasal thermistor, monitoring of body position, monitoring of leg movement and measurement of snoring using a microphone. There is no respiratory effort during the period of absent airflow at the nose and mouth in central sleep apnoea in contrast to obstructive sleep apnoea.

75 i. The BAL shows numerous eosinophils (in addition to neutrophils and alveolar macrophages) suggesting an allergic process such as asthma, allergic bronchopulmonary aspergillosis or chronic eosinophilic pneumonia.
ii. The patient's tropical origin makes parasitic infection an important consideration. Occult filariasis is also called pulmonary infiltrates with eosinophilia (i.e. the PIE syndrome) or tropical pulmonary eosinophilia. It manifests as intermittent coughing, wheezing, and vague systemic symptoms. Lymphadenopathy may be seen but massive lymphoedema is absent. Radiographic features are variable and include interstitial, miliary or focal consolidative patterns. Eosinophilia is routinely present and serum IgE levels are markedly increased. Occult filariasis is thought to represent an allergic reaction to the circulating microfilaria of the mosquito-borne nematodes, *Wuchereria bancrofti* and *Brugai malayi*. A sustained hypersensitivity reaction leads to interstitial lung injury, eosinophilic and granulomatous infiltration, and fibrosis. The diagnosis of occult filariasis is supported by findings of eosinophilia, elevated IgE levels and positive serology in a patient with a compatible clinical presentation. Microfilariae may be seen in the lung or lymph nodes but, if the diagnosis is suspected, a therapeutic trial of diethylcarbamazine is preferable to biopsy.

76 Over the preceding 6 months this patient has complained of chronic cough which temporarily improved somewhat on antibiotics. He now complains of fever, breathlessness and a productive cough with purulent sputum for 2 weeks. The CD4+ lymphocyte count is 0.02×10⁹/l.
i. What are the abnormalities in the two radiographs 76a and 76b?
ii. Are these two conditions related and if so what is the likely aetiology?
iii. Describe an appropriate management plan for the acute condition.
iv. How commonly is the condition in radiograph (76b) seen in HIV-positive patients and what are the causes?

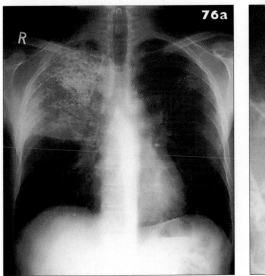
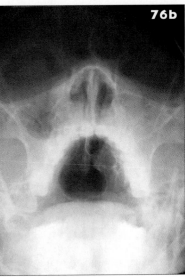

77 What are some broad predictors to identify patients who may be successfully weaned from a ventilator?

76 i. The chest film shows lobar shadowing consistent with acute infection. The sinus views in (76b) show mucosal thickening and sinus opacification indicative of chronic sinusitis.

ii. The history of chronic cough in this setting is probably due to a post-nasal drip related to chronic sinusitis and rhinitis. The more acute illness is suggestive of a bacterial chest infection, although other aetiologies such as *P. carinii (jiroveci)* should still be considered. Chronic inflammation of the frontal, maxillary and ethmoid sinuses is increasingly associated with acute or sub-acute pneumonia due to *P. aeruginosa*.

iii. The aetiology of the chest infection should be confirmed by sputum culture or bronchoalveolar lavage if necessary, and treated with an anti-pseudomonal antibiotic such as ceftazadime or ciprofloxacin for 2 weeks. There is a high (35%) rate of relapse in these very immunocompromised patients.

iv. Chronic sinusitis is being increasingly recognized as an HIV-associated condition with approximately 5% of patients with a CD4 count under $0.02 \times 10^9/l$ complaining of sinusitis and 15% of AIDS patients having sinus thickening on MRI scanning. The sinusitis is usually related to chronic rhinitis, which should be treated with nasal decongestants and topical steroids. Secondary infection of the sinuses can be acute and related to *H. influenzae* or *Str. pneumoniae*, or indolent and due to pseudomonas. There are recent reports of sinus infection with *Microsporidia* sp.

77 The best validated index designed to assess the patient's readiness to breathe without the assistance of a mechanical ventilator is the ratio between the respiratory rate and the tidal volume (in ml) measured while the patient is breathing spontaneously, the rapid-shallow breathing index. An index >100 predicts weaning failure. Other predictive variables include a vital capacity >10 ml/kg (needed to prevent atelectasis), a minute ventilation of 6–12 l/min (indicating an intact ventilatory drive on the low side and resolution of the primary process driving hyperventilation on the high side), and a maximal inspiratory pressure >30 cmH$_2$O (indicating adequate inspiratory muscle strength). Prior to measuring these, the primary problem for which the patient was receiving ventilatory support should be largely or completely resolved, and the patient should not require >50% oxygen to maintain adequate oxygenation.

78 Shown are the chest radiograph (**78a**) and chest CT (**78b**) of a 34-year-old man with symptoms of a non-productive cough and occasional, scant haemoptysis. He had received a full course of treatment for pulmonary tuberculosis 2 years earlier.

i. What are the radiographic findings?

ii. What is the most likely diagnosis?

iii. What management approach is indicated?

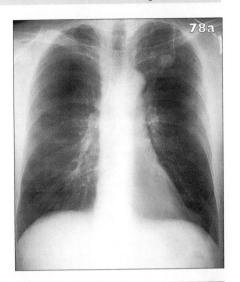

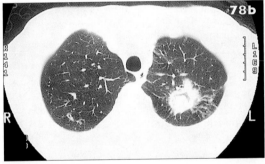

79 An elderly patient with COPD is planning a trip involving air travel. He asks if he will need oxygen during the flight.

i. What is the effective cabin altitude inside most pressurized commercial aircraft when cruising at peak altitude?

ii. If, at sea level breathing air this patient's arterial blood gas showed a pH of 7.39, a pCO_2 of 6.5 kPa (41 mmHg), and pO_2 of 8.5 kPa (62 mmHg), would you prescribe supplemental O_2 for his flight?

78 i. 78a and 78b show an irregular, thin-walled cavity containing a nodular density in the dependent position. There are some linear streaks extending toward the hilum but no surrounding infiltrates.

ii. This is most likely an aspergilloma (also called a mycetoma or a fungus ball) growing in a pre-existing lung cavity. Classically the mass is described as having an 'air-halo'.

iii. Aspergilloma are common, and a complication of tuberculous cavities and patients with chronic sarcoid cavities. Most are asymptomatic and the problem may be discovered as an incidental radiographic finding. Serum precipitins against *Aspergillus* species are usually elevated. Haemoptysis can be the presenting manifestation and, on occasion, may be life-threatening. Although most aspergillomas are saprophytic, rather than invasive infections, immunosuppressed patients may develop a locally invasive form of the disease extending into the lung tissue adjacent to an aspergilloma, a form of chronic necrotizing aspergillosis. Most aspergilloma require no treatment. Excision is very difficult due to adhesions around the affected lobe and because of the underlying chronic lung disease. Angiographic embolization is another option for haemoptysis, but is also difficult as the bronchial artery supplying the cavity is not hypertrophied – as in cystic fibrosis. Selected patients may benefit from intracavitary amphotericin B or oral itraconazole. Systemic antifungal treatment with amphotericin B should be instituted promptly in patients with chronic necrotizing aspergillosis.

79 i. Most commercial aircraft cruise at between 22 000 ft (6706 m) and 44 000 ft (13 411 m) above sea level. Pressurization is added to the cabin to yield an effective cabin altitude of 5000 ft (1529 m) to 8000 ft (2438 m) at most cruising altitudes. The P_IO_2 is approximately 21 kPa (150 mmHg) at sea level and falls to 17 kPa (118 mmHg) at 8000 ft (2438 m). At 8000–10 000 ft, the corresponding arterial partial pressure of oxygen (PaO_2) is 6.5–7.9 kPa (50–60 mmHg) in most healthy individuals at rest.

ii. Yes. Supplemental O_2 should be prescribed because his pre-flight, sea level, room air PaO_2 is <10 kPa (70 mmHg). Ideally it is difficult to arrange for flows of 4 l/min of oxygen on intercontinental flights.

Altitude simulation tests may be performed to assist in O_2 prescription. Patients inhale FiO_2 of 0.18 or 0.16 either at rest or with light exercise, to determine if any oxygen desaturation can be corrected by 2 or 4 l/min of oxygen.

80 This 30-year-old man complains of mild exertional dyspnoea.
i. Of what condition is the chest radiograph on inspiration (80a) and expiration (80b) suggestive, and what is the possible aetiology?
ii. From what else should the condition be distinguished?

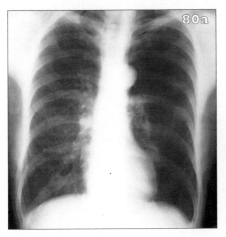 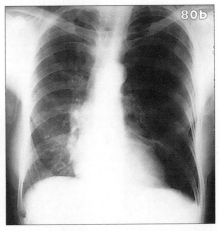

81 A patient with known carcinoma of the bronchus presents with a 2-day history of progressive mid-lumbar back pain and numbness on the anterior surface of the left thigh. Shown (81a) is his lateral lumbar spine radiograph.
i. What is the likely cause of the symptoms?
ii. How would you investigate them?
iii. How would you treat the patient?

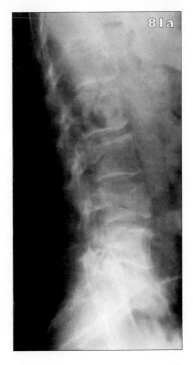

80 & 81: Answers

80 i. The radiographic finding of a unilateral radiolucent lung was described by Macleod and is also known as Swyer–James syndrome. The syndrome is ascribed to neonatal or early childhood bronchiolitis obliterans. The lung is usually otherwise normal and well-preserved, but with small pulmonary vessels. Large air spaces can develop, with poor ventilation of the affected lung, which may remain fully inflated on an expiratory film (**80b**). The prognosis is good.
ii. Other causes of a radiolucent appearance to a lung include congenital absence of the chest wall muscles or mastectomy, obstruction to a pulmonary artery by embolus or tumour, compression of the pulmonary artery by tumour or nodes and congenital abnormalities. Partial obstruction of a main bronchus by a tumour or a foreign body can occasionally produce unilateral hyperlucensy.

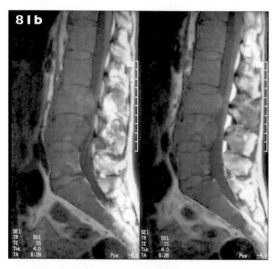

81 i. The back pain is most likely to be due to metastatic disease. The vertebral column is one of the most common sites of metastatic spread.
ii. The numbness of the thigh may indicate a root lesion (lower motor neurone) compatible with early corda equina compression. Enquiries as to bladder and other sphincter function is essential. The patient needs plain radiographs of the lower thoracic and lumbar spine. Even if normal, further investigation is needed. If the radiographic changes are suggestive of metastatic disease, i.e. loss of height of a vertebral body or loss of a pedicle, one should proceed to examination of the spinal column, ideally by MRI scan to see the spinal cord, the bony structures and any soft tissue mass due to tumour (**81b**).

If the plain spinal radiographs are normal, then a bone scan should be performed and, if abnormal in the area under suspicion, one should then proceed to MRI scan. If the MRI is not immediately available, then myelography is an excellent investigation to perform.
iii. Suspected paraparesis needs urgent treatment. Paraplegia, once established, rarely improves. Primary treatment is radiotherapy together with steroid cover. There is no advantage from surgical decompression.

In patients with small-cell lung cancer, if the cord lesion is the presenting symptom, then chemotherapy can be added following radiotherapy if the clinical response appears adequate.

82 Shown (**82a**) is the chest radiograph of a 29-year-old, non-smoking woman with severe steroid-dependent asthma. She had symptoms of dyspnoea, wheezing, and a cough which was productive of thick mucous and small plugs. A left upper lobe pneumonia occurred 3 months earlier during an exacerbation of asthma and cleared with a course of antibiotics and an increase in her steroid dose.

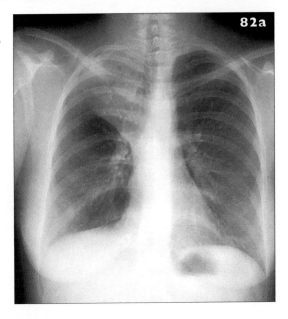

i. Describe the radiographic findings.

ii. Discuss the most likely explanation for this clinical presentation.

iii. Outline an appropriate diagnostic and therapeutic approach.

83 A patient is receiving nebulized 3% saline.

i. What type of nebulizer is being used (**83**)?

ii. What are the indications for the use of 3% saline?

82 & 83: Answers

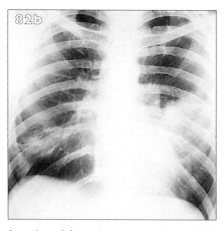

82 i. The chest radiograph (82a) shows some hyperinflation of the left lung with right upper lobe consolidation and collapse. There is some peribronchial cuffing.
ii. The radiographic changes, together with the clinical history, should suggest the diagnosis of allergic bronchopulmonary aspergillosis (ABPA). ABPA is characterized by reversible airflow obstruction, recurrent lung infiltrates and fever, eosinophilia, mucous plugs and central bronchiectasis. Often, eosinophils and mould hyphae are present in the sputum, and moulds may be cultured from the sputum. Serum IgE levels are usually markedly elevated and aspergillus-specific hypersensitivity can be confirmed by skin reactivity or by specific anti-aspergillus IgE titres. Bronchiectasis occurs at a relatively late stage of the disease. Subsequent exacerbations can cause extensive damage (82b).
iii. The evaluation of patients with asthma and lobar collapse and/or pulmonary infiltrates should include a differential blood count and serum IgE level. Sputum should be examined for eosinophils and for hyphae, and cultured for fungi. Specific anti-aspergillus IgE titres and skin testing can be confirmatory. Bronchiectasis can be identified with greater sensitivity by high-resolution CT scanning than by plain radiographs. The treatment of ABPA typically requires systemic corticosteroids. Once the pulmonary infiltrate has cleared the patient's medication should be determined only by the severity of the asthma and oral steroids stopped if possible.

83 i. This is an ultrasonic nebulizer. It uses high-frequency sound waves from a piezoelectric crystal impacting on the surface of the liquid in the reservoir to generate a fountain of droplets. A baffle above this fountain collects the larger droplets, leaving a mist of smaller droplets to be inhaled by the patient. Usually no driving gas is used. The solution is warmed by the effect of the sound waves. The output of drug from this nebulizer is usually greater than for jet nebulizers so that the same quantity of drug can be delivered more quickly. The size of particle generated is larger with this type of nebulizer (5–10 μm), and the fraction of particles likely to be exhaled (up to 2 μm) is less than with jet nebulizers.
ii. As 3% saline is hypertonic it draws fluid into alveoli and peripheral airways, as well as facilitating expectoration by an irritant effect on major bronchi. It is therefore useful for sputum induction, usually for diagnostic purposes, for example in detecting *P. carinii*, although it is not as sensitive as bronchoscopy for this purpose. Problems in some patients include nausea, bronchospasm, and oxygen desaturation.

84 i. Describe the CXR appearance (84).
ii. What is the likely diagnosis?
iii. What further investigations are necessary?

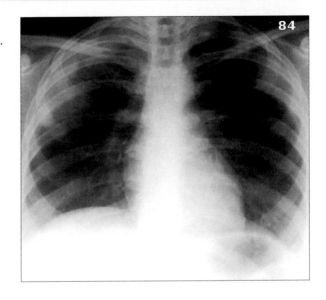

85 This radiograph (85a) of a 25-year-old man was taken on admission to hospital via the accident and emergency department and a second film (85b) was taken 3 weeks later in the intensive care unit. From the changes seen on the two chest radiographs, what is the most likely diagnosis?

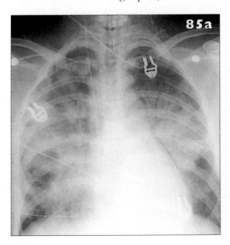
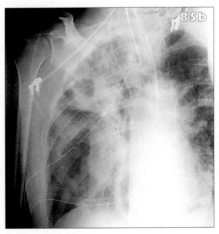

84 i. There are bilateral, diffuse, peripheral infiltrates, predominantly in the upper zones. The appearances are often described as being the 'photographic negative' of pulmonary oedema. It may be confused with tuberculosis.
ii. Eosinophilic pneumonia (Loeffler's syndrome).
iii. Usual tests include: blood count for eosinophilia, sputum eosinophil count, and stool for ova or parasites. Microbiological specimens should be obtained. CT scanning of the chest and serology for parasites may be required. Broncho-alveolar lavage and sometimes even lung biopsy may be required to confirm the diagnosis.

85 Radiograph 85a shows multiple rib fractures on the right side with a chest drain *in situ*, bilateral alveolar infiltrates and a pneumo-mediastinum as indicated by the rim of gas outlining the left heart border.

The unifying diagnosis in this case is trauma and the patient was a victim of a road traffic accident 36 hours earlier. The lung infiltrates could be due to aspiration but more probably represent ARDS resulting from increased permeability of the pulmonary alveolar capillary membrane, as a result of blunt trauma. Pulmonary contusion is another possibility. Other causes of pneumo-mediastinum include penetrating chest injuries, damage to the upper airway during instrumentation and tracheostomy formation, oesophageal rupture or perforation and, rarely, gastrointestinal tract perforation below the diaphragm with air tracking up to the mediastinum via the retroperitoneal tissues. However, the most common cause is alveolar rupture due to high alveolar pressures. Air may track up the mediastinum to produce surgical emphysema of the face, neck, supraclavicular areas and upper chest. This particularly applies during intermittent positive-pressure ventilation in severe asthma and in ARDS where poor compliance of the lungs results in increased alveolar pressures. It is also reported after vomiting, straining at stool, parturition and performing a Valsalva manoeuvre. It is frequently symptomless but may cause central chest pain and auscultation may reveal a clicking sound during systole (Hamman's sign). The mediastinal air can often be seen more impressively on a lateral chest radiograph.

86 i. Of what is this appearance (86) a part? In which cell type of lung cancer does this occur and what is the treatment of choice?
ii. What other hormone-secreting effects are seen commonly in lung cancer?

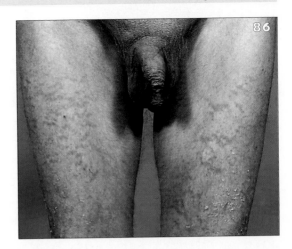

87 The worker shown (87) is filing a tungsten carbide saw.
i. What respiratory diseases are associated with 'hard-metal' exposure?
ii. What is the causative agent?
iii. What is the usual clinical course of this disease?
iv. What other metals are associated with interstitial fibrosis?

86 i. The illustration (86) is of pigmented striae, in a man with small-cell lung cancer who has ectopic ACTH secretion. The plasma ACTH levels are elevated in up to 30% of patients presenting with small-cell lung cancer, but the natural history of the disease is too short to allow florid Cushing's syndrome to develop. Occasionally, pigmentation – as shown here – is seen together with thirst, proximal myopathy, hypokalaemic alkalosis, and elevated plasma cortisol. The treatment is of the underlying tumour with cytotoxic chemotherapy.

ii. The most common syndrome is inappropriate anti-diuretic hormone secretion (SIADH) and is exclusive to small-cell lung cancer. The patient initially retains water but eventually becomes clinically dehydrated. The serum urea, sodium and osmolarity are low with a concentrated urine with a osmolarity at least 2.5-fold that of the serum. It occurs as a clinical problem in 10–15% of new cases of SCLC. A water loading excretion test is abnormal in 60% of patients. Hypercalcaemia also occurs from the secretion of a parathormone-like peptide from primary squamous cell tumour.

87 i. Hard-metal lung disease classically refers to interstitial lung disease occurring in individuals manufacturing or working with cemented tungsten carbide tools. In addition, these workers may also develop occupational asthma, hypersensitivity pneumonitis, giant cell interstitial pneumonitis and bronchiolitis obliterans. There may be a continuum of disease with components of several processes present simultaneously in an affected individual.

ii. Cobalt, a binding agent used in the manufacturing process, rather than tungsten carbide is the causal agent. Tungsten carbide is relatively non-toxic in animals and characteristic hard-metal lung disease occurs in workers exposed to cobalt alone. The presence of tungsten but occasional absence of cobalt in lung biopsies of hard metal workers reflects the high solubility of cobalt and rapid transit out of the lung.

iii. A minority of exposed workers develop disease. Cough, wheezing and dyspnoea are typical early symptoms though fever, chills and malaise suggestive of extrinsic allergic alveolitis may be present. Initially, patients improve when removed from the workplace but continued exposure leads to chronic, progressive impairment. Reduced lung volumes and diffusion capacity are typical pulmonary function abnormalities of patients with chronic disease. The latency between first exposure and onset of disease may range from 6 months to 4 years.

iv. Metals are associated with numerous pulmonary airway and parenchymal disorders. Interstitial fibrosis may occur following exposure to aluminium, barium, beryllium, cadmium, copper, gold, mercury, nickel, thallium, titanium, zinc, and the rare earth metals (cerium, yttrium, terbium).

88 Shown (88) is the result of a surgical procedure on the oropharynx.
i. Which procedure was performed and what does it treat?
ii. What are the non-surgical methods available to treat this problem?

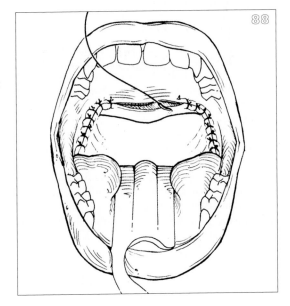

89 These radiographs (89a, 89b) are of a 32-year-old man with cough, sputum, recurrent chest infections, sinusitis and partial deafness.
i. What are the abnormalities shown?
ii. What is the condition and what is the major defect?
iii. Describe the management.
iv. What is the mode of inheritance? Name other similar conditions.

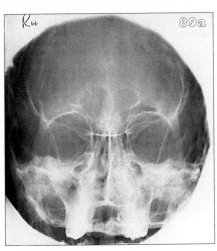

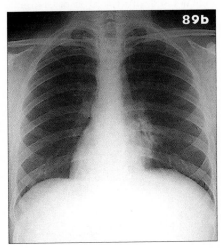

88 i. Uvulopalatopharyngoplasty (UPPP) increases the size of the oropharyngeal lumen by removing redundant soft tissue. Laser-assisted uvulopalatoplasty (LAUP) has been found to be useful in the treatment of some patients with mild OSA and has been shown to decrease the CPAP pressure required to treat it, but reductions in apnoea/hypopnoea index and symptomatic improvement are minor. LAUP is most useful in the treatment of snoring without OSA, however. Improvements in snoring have been demonstrated on follow-up for 4 years.

ii. Non-surgical methods which can be effective in treating snoring include: weight loss, avoidance of sedatives (including alcohol) before sleep, and the wearing of a carefully fitted mandibular advancement splint.

89 i. The facial radiograph (**89a**) shows no air in the frontal sinuses and gross mucosal thickening of the maxillary sinuses, especially the left. The chest radiograph (**89b**) shows dextrocardia.

ii. The patient has Kartagener's syndrome (also known as the ciliary dyskinesia syndrome) with poorly developed or absent frontal sinuses, chronic sinusitis, situs invertus (in 50% of cases), eventual bronchiectasis and immotile cilia – both in the respiratory tract and sperm immotility. The structural defect in the cilia include absence of dynein arms, radial spokes or microtubules. Because of abnormal ciliary movement, mucus collects in the bronchi, sinuses and Eustachian tubes causing cough, infected sputum, ultimately bronchiectasis, sinusitis and deafness. Infertility is common in males.

iii. The treatment is that of chronic bronchial sepsis with broad-spectrum antibiotics when necessary, postural drainage of bronchiectatic areas; grommets and antrostomies for the ear and nasal problems. The prognosis is good.

iv. Primary ciliac dyskinesia is autosomally recessive with incomplete penetrance, and occurs with a frequency of 1 in 15 000 to 1 in 30 000. Young described a syndrome in males of obstructive azoospermia, sinusitis and bronchiectasis. Secondary ciliary dyskinesia occurs when normal cilia beat more slowly; this can occur in severe asthma, viral infections, bacterial infections and with heavy tobacco consumption.

90 Shown is a representative high-power photomicrograph (**90**) of a Wright–Geimsa-stained cytospin prepared from BAL fluid from a patient with interstitial lung disease.
i. What cell types are present?
ii. Discuss the interaction of these cells in lung inflammation.

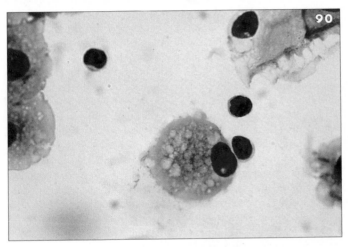

91 i. What is the diagnosis of the condition shown in **91** and what are the symptoms?
ii. What are the predisposing factors?
iii. What is the relationship between asthma and sinus disease?

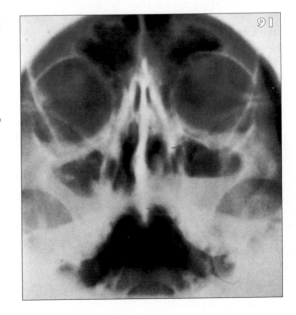

90 i. This BAL specimen contains predominantly alveolar macrophages and lymphocytes (the smaller cells).
ii. Lymphocytes are key cells in the cognate arm of the immune system, reacting to specific antigenic determinants rather than to generalized, non-specific stimuli. Most lymphocytes in the lung are T-cells which participate in the delayed type hypersensitivity and cytotoxic responses of cell-mediated immunity. The remainder are B-cells, responsible for antibody production in the humoral response, and other miscellaneous subsets. T-cells are central to host defence against viral and other intracellular pathogens and to the immune surveillance for malignancy. They augment macrophage antimicrobial and tumoricidal effects and directly lyse host cells bearing microbial or antigens. T-lymphocytes recognizing a persistent environmental antigen or self antigen can contribute to the lung injury characteristic of a myriad of immunologically mediated lung diseases including asthma and virtually all of the interstitial lung diseases. T-cell subpopulations in BAL fluid may be characterized as to their cell-surface marker phenotype. Cells expressing CD4 are called T-helper lymphocytes and cells expressing CD8 are called T-suppresser lymphocytes. Identification of the relative proportions of CD4- and CD8-positive cells in a lymphocytic alveolitis has been used to help distinguish among different types of interstitial lung disease. Sarcoidosis is typically associated with a high CD4/CD8 ratio whereas hypersensitivity pneumonitis usually results in a low ratio. There may be considerable overlap in these criteria, however, which may complicate using this ratio when evaluating an individual patient.

91 i. Paranasal sinusitis. There is bilateral mucosal thickening and air-fluid levels in the maxillary sinuses, worse on the left. Symptoms include headache, pain and tenderness over the affected sinuses, periorbital swelling in children, nasal congestion and obstruction, purulent nasal secretions, postnasal drainage, cough, sore throat and purulent sputum. CT scan of the paranasal sinuses is very sensitive and specific means of showing sinus disease.
ii. Predisposing factors include acute viral, bacterial, mycoplasma or other respiratory tract infections, foreign bodies, nasogastric or nasotracheal tubes, nasal packing, exposures to respiratory tract irritants, barotrauma associated with flying, swimming and diving. More long-standing risk factors include allergic rhinitis, nasal polyposis, immunoglobulin deficiencies, AIDS, anatomical disorders, cystic fibrosis or the ciliary dyskinesia syndrome.
iii. Sinusitis is a frequent finding in patients with asthma and can lead to a worsening of asthma. Sinusitis with nasal mucosal congestion and oedema results in decreased humidification and temperature rectification of inhaled air. Sinusitis is associated with postnasal drainage which can carry bacteria and/or inflammatory material to the lower respiratory tract. Asthma and sinusitis are also linked through a common allergic response pathway or a aspirin sensitivity.

92 These are the chest radiograph (**92a**) and bronchoscopic (**92b**) appearance of a 24-year-old girl in whom systemic lupus erythematosus had been diagnosed 6 months earlier. Her initial joint symptoms and rash had been successfully controlled on steroids but 4 weeks before admission to ICU she developed symptoms suggestive of cerebral involvement and the steroid dose was increased. She was admitted with respiratory distress, circulatory collapse and disseminated intravascular coagulation (DIC). Gram-negative sepsis was confirmed and she improved with antibiotic and standard supportive therapy. Pulsed cyclophosphamide was subsequently started for lupus cerebritis diagnosed at MRI scanning. Several weeks later she suffered a massive haemoptysis and the chest radiograph and bronchoscopy were performed at this time. Similar lesions to those pictured were present throughout the bronchial tree.

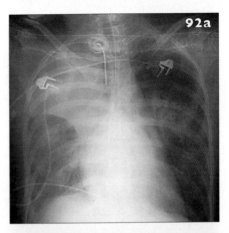

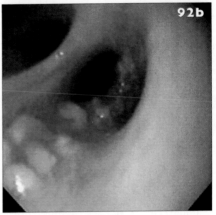

i. Describe the bronchoscopic appearances.
ii. Which organism is likely to be responsible for the respiratory problems?

93 This 45-year-old white woman (**93**) presented with bilateral hilar lymphadenopathy on chest radiograph and this painful rash.

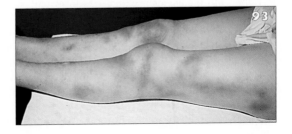

i. What is this syndrome called?
ii. What is her prognosis?
iii. What other cutaneous manifestations may occur in this disease?

92 i. The chest radiograph shows (92a) a densely consolidated right upper lobe with infiltrates in the middle and lower lobes. The bronchoscopy (92b) shows mucosal infiltration with white, nodular lesions, suggestive of a fungal infection.
ii. Histology of the bronchial biopsies showed extensive infiltration with fungal hyphae but minimal inflammatory infiltrate. *A. fumigatus* was subsequently isolated. The diagnosis is invasive aspergillosis, an important complication in immunocompromised patients. It usually presents as a necrotizing cavitating pneumonia unresponsive to standard antibiotics. The pulmonary features in this case are rare but a wide variety of presentations have been described. Diagnosis may be difficult with both sputum culture and serology frequently being negative. Biopsy specimens are usually required to make the diagnosis. Extrapulmonary dissemination to the liver, kidney, gastrointestinal tract and brain occurs in about 25% of cases.

Treatment was with intravenous liposomal and nebulized amphoteracin followed by oral itraconazole. The patient recovered, and a follow-up chest radiograph at 3 months was normal.

Aspergillus species can affect the lungs in several ways:
- Allergic bronchopulmonary aspergillosis in asthma (see 82).
- Aspergilloma – i.e. a fungus ball infects pre-existing cavities (see 78).
- Invasive aspergillosis, as in this case.
- Aspergillosis pneumonia.
- Tracheal infection.

The last three develop in immunocompromised hosts.

93 i. Lofgren's syndrome, after a Swedish physician who described this in 1946. It consists of bilateral hilar lymphadenopathy and the rash of erythema nodosum. Lymphoma and granulomatous infections should be considered. An elevated serum ACE may reduce the need for a biopsy confirmation in the absence of atypical features. The syndrome usually occurs in young women who often present with fever, malaise, arthralgias and painful lesions on their legs (probably due to circulating immune complexes). The condition occasionally relapses and is uncommon in men.
ii. This woman is in the best prognostic group in whites with a 90% chance of spontaneous remission or her sarcoidosis within 2 years without corticosteroids. The erythema nodosum should fade within weeks.
iii. Cutaneous involvement with sarcoidosis may occur on the anterior surface of the legs with erythema nodosum. The most common other skin manifestations are papulonodular lesions. Nodules are smooth reddish-brown, often solitary or in small groups whereas papules are often numerous and often on the face or neck. Lupus pernio occurs mainly in older women and more commonly in blacks and is associated with chronic fibrotic sarcoidosis. Although often across the nose and cheeks, these violaceous plaques may be found on the arms, buttocks and thighs. Nasal septal perforation may occur. It is treated with prednisolone and weekly methotrexate. Sarcoidosis also has a predilection for scars and tattoos and can cause subcutaneous nodules.

94 A man, aged 58, with a
4-week history of
dysphagia, presented with
a short history of vomiting
followed by dyspnoea and
chest pain. The chest
radiograph (**94**) was taken
before any intervention.
What does it show and
what is the likely cause?

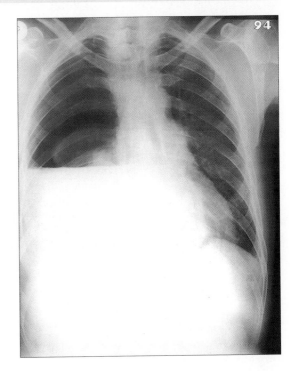

95 i. A 22-year-old girl sought
advice from her general practitioner
because her dormitory co-habitors
complained of her snoring.
i. What is shown in **95** and what is
the natural history of this condition?
ii. What is the diagnosis?
iii. How would you confirm the
diagnosis?
iv. How would you treat her
condition and what precaution
would you take?
v. What other physical abnormalities
may predispose to OSA?

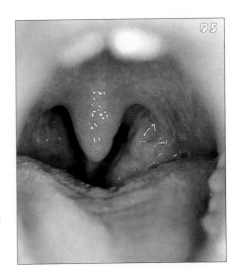

94 Hydropneumothorax. The presence of a large quantity of both air and fluid in the pleural cavity in a patient with these symptoms is strongly suggestive of rupture of the oesophagus. The fluid was turbid, but not purulent. The underlying cause was ulceration of the oesophagus by tuberculous mediastinal lymph nodes. Rupture of the oesophagus can occur in previously fit individuals, for example after violent vomiting or impaction of food bolus or foreign body, and is a medical emergency. It initially may cause retrosternal or pleural pain. It may be missed at oesophagoscopy if the tear is small, and is best diagnosed by a barium swallow. Immediate repair by a thoracic surgeon is the treatment of choice. Rupture can also occur as a result of an oesophageal tumour causing necrosis of the wall. This may also occur with tracheal tumour or metastatic subcarinal nodes. Ensleevement of the lesion with an oesophageal tube can give good palliation. Other possible causes of hydropneumothorax include rupture of a large lung abscess, empyema or rupture of a tuberculous cavity into the pleural space. Simple aspiration would be inadequate and drainage with a large-bore intercostal tube is mandatory, together with appropriate intravenous antibiotic therapy.

95 i. Enlarged tonsils. In adults, tonsils normally atrophy but some individuals with persistently enlarged tonsils can develop obstructive sleep apnoea.
ii. Obstructive sleep apnoea due to large tonsils.
iii. Sleep study. Polysomnography is considered the gold-standard for the diagnosis of OSA. Other limited or partial sleep studies which are also used include the following:
- Pulse oximetry alone to measure arterial oxygen desaturation (specificity 100%, sensitivity 31%).
- Pulse oximetry + measurement of respiratory effort + body position + snoring + measurement of sleep fragmentation.

Respiratory effort can be measured by a video-camera recording, assessing irregularities in the thoracoabdominal movement (phase-angle paradox) by inductance plethysmography or by measuring airflow limitation.
iv. Tonsillectomy. If the OSA is severe, the patient should be on nasal CPAP immediately after surgery because anaesthesia, opiates and pharyngeal oedema/haematoma may aggravate OSA postoperatively.
v. The physical signs to look out for are: those that can cause OSA such as obesity, nasal obstruction, significant overcrowding of teeth, micrognathia, retrognathia, a swollen and oedematous palate, oedematous and swollen pharynx with redundant folds, tonsils, large tongue, large neck circumference, inspiratory snore or snort even when awake, hypothyroid facies, acromegalic facies, spider naevi and alcoholic breath.

96 Shown (**96a**) is a high-power photomicrograph of a Gram stain of expectorated sputum produced by a 68-year-old man with steroid-dependent COPD. He had symptoms of fatigue, weight loss and pleuritic chest pain of 5 weeks' duration. A chest radiograph showed a cavitary left upper lobe infiltrate extending to the pleural surface.

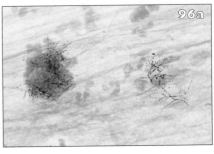

i. What is seen on the Gram stain (**96a**)?
ii. What is the differential diagnosis of the clinical and microbiological findings?
iii. What are the relevant diagnostic and therapeutic considerations?

97 The peak flow chart shown in **97** was recorded by a spray painter who worked from 9 am to 5 pm, Monday to Friday. His symptoms were often worse at night.
i. Is this consistent with occupational asthma?
ii. Why is there peak flow improvement during the first few hours at work?

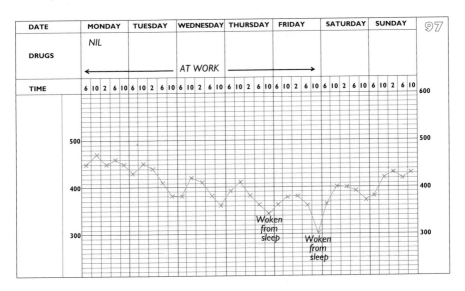

96 i. The Gram-stained specimen contains numerous polymorphonuclear leukocytes, strands of mucous, and clumps of beaded, branching Gram-positive rods.

ii. The Gram stain suggests either *Nocardia* or *Actinomyces* species.

iii. Either can produce an insidious or subacute pulmonary infection, mimicking fungal or mycobacterial infection, or malignancy. Actinomycosis occurs more often in men with periodontal or underlying lung disease, and may progress to chest wall invasion and sinus tract formation. Direct invasion of thoracic viscera and systemic dissemination are possible. Yellow 'sulphur granules' in the draining pus are virtually diagnostic of actinomycosis. However, isolation of *Actinomyces* from the respiratory tract is non-specific because the organism can exist as a commensal oropharyngeal colonizer. Definitive diagnosis requires isolation from a sterile site or histological demonstration of tissue invasion. Nocardiosis occurs more commonly in immunocompromised patients and has a greater propensity to disseminate, especially to the brain. Because *Nocardia* are rarely isolated in the absence of clinical disease, a positive culture is usually considered diagnostic. *Nocardia* are often weakly acid-fast when stained with the modified Ziehl–Neelsen method. Actinomycosis should be treated with a long course (e.g. 6 weeks) of penicillin G followed by up to 1 year of oral penicillin. Clindamycin, erythromycin, tetracycline, chloramphenicol, doxycycline, and cephalexin are suitable alternatives. Ceftriaxone has recently been shown to be useful in the initial phase of treatment. When pulmonary actinomycosis is treated with isoniazid and rifampicin, rapid clinical and radiological response may be observed, erroneously reinforcing the suspicion of TB.

High-dose intravenous trimethoprim/sulphamethoxazole is the treatment of choice. Resistant nocardiosis may be treated with a combination of sulphadiazine, ceftriaxone, and amikacin. Other alternatives include imipenem or meropenem, amoxicillin/clavulanate, and doxycycline.

97 i. There are many patterns of occupational asthma; this pattern is one of the more common and shows a decline in peak flows as the week progresses, with worsening at night after leaving work and variable improvement at the week-end. Isocyanate in the paint was the likely cause in this case as the reaction and drop in peak flow is often delayed. Other patterns of occupational asthma include development of symptoms within minutes of arriving at work or, more chronically, sometimes fixed airflow obstruction which gradually improves only after weeks away from work. Recovery from asthma due to isocyanate may be very slow, particularly in cases of chronic exposure. Patients may remain asthmatic after removal from the offending agent.

ii. In occupational asthma, as with other forms of the condition, peak flows are often at their lowest on waking so that by mid-morning there may be an apparent improvement despite the patient being at work. This phenomenon may also affect peak flow records performed at unusual hours of the day in shift workers.

98 A cytological specimen
(98) is taken from a lymph
node of a HIV-positive
homosexual Caucasian
patient who has a CD4
count of 0.02×10⁹/l,
complains of intermittent
fevers and weight loss, and
has developed anaemia and
lymphadenopathy.
i. What is the diagnosis?
ii. How may this condition
affect the lung?
iii. What are the treatment
options?

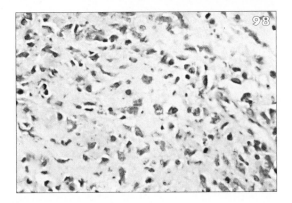

99 The hypnograms (99) reflect a computerized summary of the sleep stages
in an individual with obstructive sleep apnoea (OSA) before (top trace) and
immediately after (bottom trace) beginning therapy with nasal continuous
positive airway pressure (CPAP). REM sleep (highlighted in blue) and sleep
stages (1, 2, 3, 4) are shown.
i. The durations of which sleep stages are increased by initiation of CPAP?
ii. What are the potential consequences of this?
iii. What are the effects of benzodiazepines, tricyclic antidepressants and
alcohol on the hypnogram?

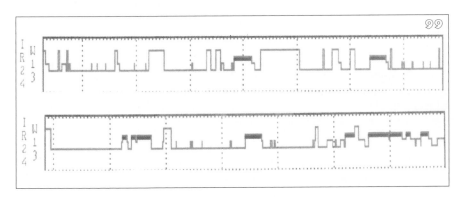

98 i. The slide shows mycobacteria (pink staining). In view of the history (very low CD4 count, typical clinical history and lack of risk factors for tuberculosis) this is most likely to be atypical mycobacteriosis – most usually organisms of the *Mycobacterium avium–intracellulare* complex (MAC). However, such a patient should be treated as tuberculosis until the bacterial cultures prove otherwise.
ii. Pulmonary involvement can occur during MAC infection although other atypical mycobacteria (e.g. *M. kansasii*) are more likely to be detected in primary lung disease. The presenting features of pulmonary disease due to atypical mycobacteria are similar to HIV-related tuberculosis, although as these organisms normally only cause disease at very low CD4 lymphocyte counts ($<0.1\times10^9/l$). Non-specific interstitial shadowing and hilar/mediastinal adenopathy are the most common features.
iii. *In vitro* antibiotic sensitivity patterns are less helpful for these organisms than for *M. tuberculosis* in that with MAC in particular, antibiotics to which the organism shows *in vitro* resistance often show clinical efficacy. Combinations of rifampicin or rifabutin and ethambutol with clarithromycin and clofazamine often bring about a short-term remission. If fever and other systemic features do not respond to antibiotics, oral steroids can bring about symptomatic relief in what is likely to be a patient with a poor prognosis.

99 i. Sleep apnoea syndromes may be associated with suppression of slow wave (Stages 3 and 4) and rapid eye movement (REM) sleep. REM suppression is more common in adults, in contrast to the predominance of slow wave suppression in children. On initiation of CPAP, there is a large rebound of slow wave and REM sleep which is most marked during the first night and which lasts about a week.
ii. There is a marked depression of arousability and unusually long and intense REM episodes occur. Sleep-disordered breathing tends to be more frequent and severe during REM sleep, and patients may become susceptible to hypoxaemia as a result of this. Patients with severe sleep apnoea who are treated with inadequate CPAP pressures may be especially at risk of severe hypoxaemia. For this reason, some experts recommend that such patients be treated for the first night under close supervision.
iii. Benzodiazepines tend to suppress slow wave sleep but do not affect REM sleep. Tricyclic antidepressants and alcohol tend to suppress REM sleep. Withdrawal from a drug which tends to suppress a stage of sleep is usually associated with a rebound of that stage. For example, as alcohol is metabolized there is often a rebound of REM sleep after an initial period of suppression.

100 This patient presented with breathlessness and reticulonodular shadowing on chest radiograph (**100**) suggestive of cryptogenic fibrosing alveolitis. A transbronchial biopsy was negative. List the arguments for and against open lung biopsy.

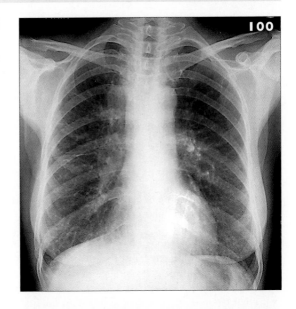

101 A 22-year-old man is resuscitated in the emergency department and treated for a presumed diagnosis of pulmonary oedema. Shortly after admission to ITU a pulmonary artery catheter was placed and the following haemodynamic data obtained 2 hours after his arrival in the emergency department (pressures in mmHg (kPa) measured from sternal angle with patient semi-recumbent): RAP, –1 (–0.1); mean PAP, +12 (1.6); PAOP, +8 (1.1); systemic arterial pressure, 105/75 (14/10); mean MAP, 83 (11.1); heart rate,100; cardiac output (Q), 4 l/min.

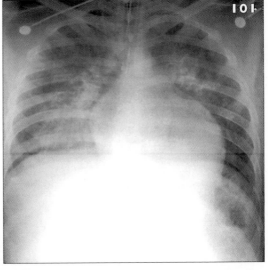

i. What does the chest radiograph (**101**) show and how do you interpret the PA catheter findings?
ii. What other investigations would be of relevance?

100 Arguments for:
- Open lung biopsy allows analysis of a greater quantity of alveolar tissue and strengthens the chance of detecting a range of fibrosis intensities. At least two biopsies should be taken from lung regions which appear different in terms of disease effect.
- In cases where transbronchial biopsy has not made an alternative diagnosis such as sarcoidosis or lymphangitis carcinomatosa, an open lung biopsy can rule these out with certainty.
- Histology which is predominantly cellular may persuade the physician to persist longer with anti-inflammatory therapy.
- It may allow for analysis of metals and silicates in cases where an occupational cause is suspected.

Arguments against:
- Most clinicians still give a trial of steroids regardless of whether the biopsy is predominantly cellular or fibrotic as response to therapy is not always predicted by the biopsy.
- OLB is often performed in patients who are severely compromised in terms of gas exchange. The added trauma of the procedure may result in the patient requiring prolonged positive-pressure ventilation. Complications include persistent air leak, empyema and haemorrhage. Mortality may be as high as 5%.
- High-resolution CT scans provide high-quality images which allow the diagnosis to be made with reasonable certainty.

101 i. The CXR shows a globular enlarged heart, diffuse pulmonary infiltrates, perihilar fullness suggesting pulmonary hypertension, and a right paratracheal density that is consistent with azygous vein enlargement. These findings would all be consistent with congestive heart failure from cardiomyopathy, aortic or mitral insufficiency. The findings from the PA catheter, however, suggest otherwise as the pulmonary arterial occlusion pressure of 8 mmHg (1.1 kPa) is too low for cardiogenic oedema, and the cardiac output of 4 l/min is too high. In addition, the pulmonary arterial pressure of 12 mmHg (1.6 kPa) excludes pulmonary hypertension.

CXRs obtained in the anterior–posterior plane on supine patients at varying degrees of lung inflation do not accurately distinguish between pulmonary oedema and diffuse lung injury. Similarly, the accuracy of the data obtained with the PA catheter may vary with positioning of the catheter, interpretation of the information relative to the intrathoracic pressure and, with regard to the cardiac output, the extent of tricuspid regurgitation.

ii. A mixed venous (or even a central venous) oxygen saturation may be extremely useful; it is <75% when the cardiac output is lower than needed to provide adequate oxygen delivery (e.g. in cardiogenic or hypovolemic shock) and is >80% when cardiac output is high (e.g. in sepsis) and oxygen delivery exceeds consumption. Calculation of the systemic vascular resistance (i.e. [mean arterial pressure – right atrial pressure]/cardiac output) may also be useful as it is low in sepsis and high in cardiogenic shock, volume depletion, cardiac tamponade and massive pulmonary embolism. Normal systemic vascular resistance = 21 Woods units, approximately 1500 dynes/sec/cm^{-5}.

102 A patient complained of coughing with drinking and had a past history of hiatus hernia repair in infancy with subsequent oesophageal stricture formation and multiple dilatations.

i. What examination (102) has been performed and what does it reveal?

ii. What is the likely mechanism for this process?

iii. What other more common condition can cause this problem and where would the lesion typically be located?

iv. What are the therapeutic options?

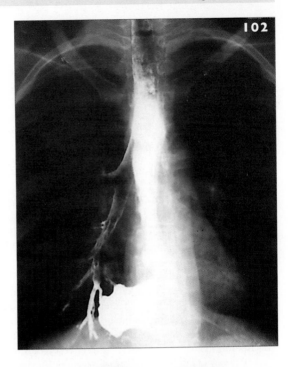

103 Shown (103) is the chest radiograph of a 44-year-old man with a non-productive cough for 3 months that resolved after treatment for post-nasal drip. Skin tests were negative for tuberculin and positive for histoplasmin. He recalled no childhood respiratory illnesses and had been raised on a farm in Illinois.

i. What are the radiographic findings?

ii. What is the differential diagnosis?

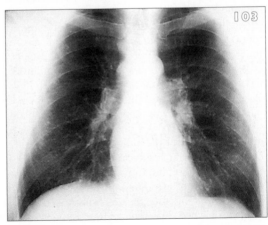

102 i. This is a barium swallow that shows an oesophagobronchial fistula. There is a distal oesophageal stricture with a right paraoesophageal abscess cavity communicating with the oesophagus and the lower right bronchial system.
ii. It is likely that the distal oesophagus was perforated at a dilatation attempt. This has resulted in the paraoesophageal abscess cavity which has eroded into the right bronchial tree.
iii. More commonly this problem results from an oesophageal carcinoma involving the trachea or proximal left main bronchus. This is particularly likely to result from radiotherapy for an advanced oesophageal tumour. Erosion of a proximal bronchogenic carcinoma into the oesophagus is also possible, but less frequent.
iv. In this case, an unusual situation, right thoracotomy to disconnect the lung from the paraoesophageal abscess cavity would be necessary. The oesophagus would have to be repaired and the stricture corrected. Chronic inflammatory changes can make surgery in this situation very difficult. For an oesophagotracheal fistula due to tumour, an endoprosthesis or sheathed stent offers the best prospect for both relieving obstruction (usually oesophageal) and occluding the fistula.

103 i. The chest radiograph (103) shows hilar and paratracheal adenopathy, and diffusely scattered, small, calcified, parenchymal lung nodules. This appearance suggests a remote, and now 'healed' disseminated infection.
ii. The differential diagnosis includes previous infections (e.g. Varicella or histoplasmosis) or, less likely, sarcoidosis. Miliary tuberculosis or disseminated coccidioidomycosis are unlikely to have resolved spontaneously, and transbronchial lung biopsies failed to demonstrate active peribronchial granulomatous inflammation. Thus, 'old' histoplasmosis is the most likely explanation for this patient's radiographic abnormalities. Histoplasmosis results from the inhalation of spores of the dimorphic soil fungus, *Histoplasma capsulatum*, which is endemic to the central river valleys of North America. Acute infection is often asymptomatic but occasionally can result in a pneumonia-like illness or even the acute respiratory distress syndrome. Parenchymal infiltrates and hilar adenopathy may be seen even in asymptomatic patients. Fibrosis and calcification often accompany resolution of these infections, and hepatosplenic calcification may also be present. Most patients recover without medical intervention. Some patients (generally those with underlying lung disease) fail to clear the initial infection and develop chronic pulmonary histoplasmosis which clinically and radiologically resembles tuberculosis. Progressive disseminated histoplasmosis can be life-threatening, especially in patients with defective cell-mediated immunity. This may occur during progressive primary infection but more often results from reactivation in previously infected patients. Both chronic and disseminated histoplasmosis should be treated with amphotericin B, although oral itraconazole may be used in milder cases. Immunocompromised patients require chronic suppressive itraconazole therapy.

104 A colleague asks for assistance interpreting the lung volumes measured in the patient with radiograph in **104**. The total lung capacity measured by helium dilution was 83% predicted and the residual volume was 95% predicted.

i. How can you explain the normal TLC and RV?

ii. What test would you recommend?

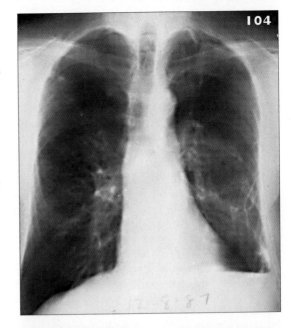

105 **i.** What process is being performed here (**105**)?

ii. What is the most common acute respiratory illness associated with this process?

iii. What are the causal agents and underlying pathophysiology?

104 i. The total lung capacity (TLC) and the residual volume appear falsely low because the radiograph shown suggests larger than normal lung volumes with flat diaphragms. This is a common problem when the helium dilution technique or any other inert gas technique is used to measure lung volumes in the presence of severe airflow obstruction or bullous lung disease. This is because the test does not allow sufficient re-breathing or washout time for the inert gas to enter the poorly ventilated areas of the lung. Thus, there is often a gross under-estimation of the true lung volume. Gas dilution techniques are, however, quite accurate when used in normal subjects or patients without airflow obstruction.

ii. Repeating the measurement of lung volumes using a body plethysmograph will provide much more accurate estimates in patients with airway problems and emphysema. The method has the advantage that it measures the total volume of gas in the lung, including any that is trapped behind closed airways which are not communicating easily with the mouth. Plethysmography is, therefore, the technique of choice in patients with airflow obstruction.

105 i. Electric arc welding using a manual system remains widespread, despite automation, and requires the worker to be close to the work piece and accompanying welding plume. Local exhaust ventilation (present in this instance) and the use of an appropriate mask respirator limit the worker's exposure to fumes.

ii. Metal fume fever. This self-limited illness resembling influenza afflicts most career welders at least once during their lifetime. A mild pharyngitis and cough may be present during the exposure. Constitutional symptoms are delayed 4–8 h after the initial exposure and consist of fevers to 41°C, myalgia, malaise, nausea, headache and cough. Complete resolution occurs within 24–48 h after exposure. Therapy is limited to antipyretics and mild analgesics.

iii. Zinc oxide fumes are the most common cause of metal fume fever. Fumes of copper, magnesium and, less commonly, aluminium, cadmium, chromium, nickel and tin are also associated with metal fume fever. Repeated exposure to fumes produces tolerance to the illness which is rapidly lost with time away from work. This phenomenon produces 'Monday morning fever', a well-recognized presentation among welders.

106 Shown (**106**) is a photomicrograph of PAS-stained lung tissue obtained at autopsy from a 41-year-old man with AIDS who presented initially with dyspnoea, cough, malaise and fever. An induced sputum specimen suggested the diagnosis of *P. carinii* pneumonia, but he deteriorated and died despite treatment.

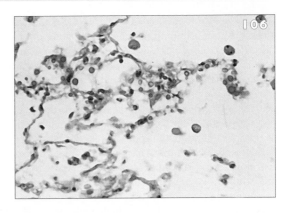

i. What diagnosis is suggested by the histological findings?
ii. How could this diagnosis be confirmed?
iii. What is the appropriate treatment?

107 These radiographs (**107a, 107b**) are from a patient who has undergone laser resection of a tumour occluding the left main bronchus.
i. What has happened?
ii. What predictive factors are there for this occurring?

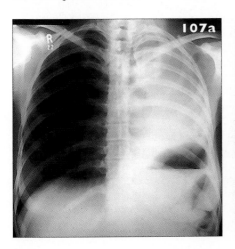

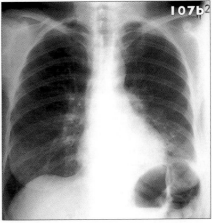

106 i. The histology shows alveolar tissue with minimal inflammatory changes but numerous, pink-staining yeast forms with varying degrees of encapsulation. A fungal culture of the lung tissue grew *C. neoformans*. Cryptococci are encapsulated yeasts with a worldwide distribution. As with the geographic fungi, it is a soil organism which flourishes in areas enriched by sources of organic nitrogen (e.g. bird droppings) and is acquired by inhalation. A thick capsule inhibits phagocytosis by neutrophils, although virulent acapsular strains exist. A cell-mediated immune response is necessary to contain cryptococcal infection. Asymptomatic pulmonary infection is common and spontaneous resolution is the rule in normal hosts. Patients with defects in cell-mediated immunity can develop progressive lung involvement. Extrapulmonary spread is common, especially to the meninges.

ii. The diagnosis of cryptococcosis is complicated by the fact that the organisms can colonize the upper airway and contaminate cultures of respiratory secretions. The chest radiograph may show a single mass, multiple nodules, or infiltrates with associated hilar adenopathy. Encapsulated yeasts invading the tissue are easily seen using routine histological stains. Finally, cryptococcal antigen can rapidly be identified in the blood of most patients with pneumonia and in the CSF of nearly all with meningitis.

iii. No treatment is necessary for cryptococcal pneumonia in an immunocompetent host without meningitis. The usual treatment of cryptococcal meningitis is with amphotericin B for 2 weeks followed by lifelong oral fluconazole in HIV-infected individuals. In case of resistant organisms or side-effects, itraconazole and voriconazole may prove useful. If there are serious toxicities with amphotericin B, liposomal preparations of this drug may be required.

107 i. There has been re-expansion of a totally collapsed lung due to removal of the endobronchial part of the tumour. Improved breathlessness and lung function occur and improved ventilation and perfusion of the previously collapsed lung can be demonstrated by radionuclide scans. It may also permit drainage of infected retained secretions.

ii. It is difficult to predict which patients will have such improvement. Where a tumour has progressed radiographically from the periphery towards the hilum the obstruction is unlikely to respond to removal of the proximal part of the tumour by laser. Shorter duration of collapse (up to 3 months) is more likely to respond to attempts at re-expansion. During the procedure it may be difficult to know how far distally an obstruction extends; a CT scan can sometimes help in this regard. An attempt should be made early in the procedure to pass through the obstruction and assess the patency of the distal airways. If these are occluded the likelihood of a favourable outcome is small.

108 The chest radiograph in 108 is from a 40-year-old patient.
i. What is the major abnormality that is seen?
ii. What is the differential diagnosis of this abnormality?

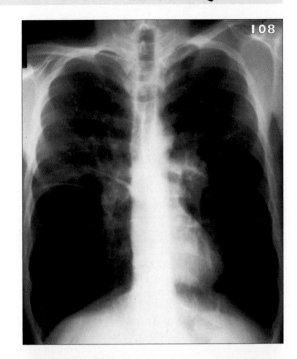

109 i. What operation has this patient undergone (109)?
ii. Why is there a scoliosis?

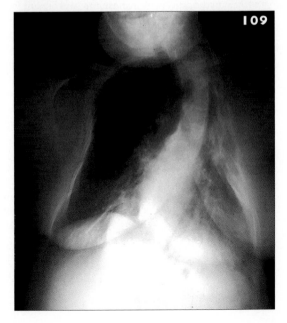

108 i. Emphysema, primarily affecting the lung bases bilaterally.
ii. Bibasilar emphysema in a relatively young patient most commonly results from α-antitrypsin deficiency. Recently, this pattern has also been described as a result of i.v. methylphenidate (Ritalin®) abuse. α-1-Antitrypsin deficiency is an inherited lack of this protease which can lead to panlobular emphysema in the third or fourth decade of life, particularly in those who smoke. Intravenous injection of Ritalin, an amphetamine-like substance, can produce panlobular emphysema indistinguishable from that caused by α-1-antitrypsin deficiency. Emphysema secondary to smoking is usually centrilobular, is more commonly apical than basilar, and typically does not cause severe airflow obstruction until patients are in their mid-60s.

The management of α-1-antitrypsin deficiency is: (a) smoking cessation; (b) attempts to optimize bronchial dilatation (usually ineffective); (c) aggressive treatment of respiratory tract infection; or (d) single lung transplantation. Replacement therapy is too expensive to be routinely available. Family members should be screened to identify heterozygotes. There is no evidence of deterioration in the lungs of heterozygotes even if they smoke.

109 i. Left thoracoplasty. The most common indication for this operation was tuberculosis in the pre-chemotherapy area to collapse the lung in the face of progressive or uncontrolled advance of the TB. Initially the patient would have been treated by an artificial prierothorax, often for up to 1 or 2 years – also reducing the aerobic environment the *M. tuberculosis* organism enjoys. It was performed in 1–3 stages developed to discern the extent of patient tolerance of the procedure.

Other methods used to achieve the same result were plombage (plastic spheres inserted extra-pleurally inside the chest) and oleothorax (installation of paraffin wax). Thoracoplasty may rarely be performed now in patients who have chronic lung cavities with ongoing systemic symptoms, usually due to infection by resistant organisms, or in patent pleural spaces with failure of the lung to expand and fill the space.
ii. Scoliosis can develop after thoracoplasty in pre-pubertal patients and its severity was related to the number of ribs removed. The scoliosis is convex to the side of the surgery. Spinal tuberculosis may also have been a concomitant feature in such patients.

Patients with this type of chest wall deformity are at risk of nocturnal hypoventilation, particularly when there is accompanying chronic obstructive airways disease (many of these patients continue to smoke!). Ultimately, hypercapnic respiratory failure (hypoxaemia with hypercapnia) and pulmonary hypertension develop requiring oxygen therapy at night and non-invasive ventilatory support – often just at night.

110 This patient has had a series of lower respiratory tract infections, sometimes associated with wheezy breathlessness, particularly at night. The cause is shown on the lateral chest radiograph (110a).
i. What is it?
ii. What other investigations can confirm the diagnosis?

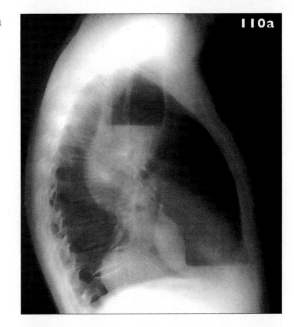

111 The pulmonary function tests (Table) were obtained on a 23-year-old, 225-kg male before a gastropexy planned for obesity.
i. What is the pulmonary function test abnormality?
ii. Does the patient have an intrapulmonary cause for a restrictive pulmonary disease (e.g. pulmonary fibrosis)?
iii. What pathophysiological processes contribute to the restrictive pattern seen?
iv. Will these tests improve with weight loss?

Function	Predicted	Best measured	% predicted
FVC (l)	6.05	3.72	61
FEV$_1$ (l)	4.80	3.05	64
FEV$_1$/FVC	0.79	0.82	104
PEFR (l/s)	–	6.10	–
FEF $_{25-75\%}$ (l/s)	4.51	3.45	76
FRC (l, BTPS)	4.15	1.42	34
RV (l, BTPS)	2.27	1.01	45
TLC (l, BTPS)	8.23	4.94	60
RV/TLC	0.27	0.20	75
DL$_{CO}$ (ml/m/mm Hg)	47.78	29.13	61
DL$_{CO}$/VA	5.27	4.95	94

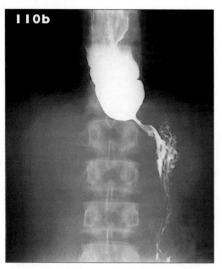

110b

110 i. The lateral chest radiograph shows a mega-oesophagus which is tortuous within the thorax and has a clearly shown fluid level at the level of the manubrium, which also illustrates the large size the oesophagus has attained. A PA chest film may show mediastinal widening and sometimes a fluid level. The abnormality is due to chronic contraction of the lower oesophageal sphincter. Occasionally, chronic obstruction by benign or malignant disease may lead to mega-oesophagus. Sometimes these patients are treated and diagnosed as asthma.
ii. A barium swallow will confirm the diagnosis and exclude other causes of obstruction (110b). The condition is usually treated by oesophagoscopy and dilatation of the sphincter, but sometimes a surgical myotomy is required. The respiratory tract infections and wheezing bouts are due to aspiration of oesophageal contents into the lung, particularly when the patient lies flat.

111 i. A restrictive pattern of disease.
ii. These tests are consistent with obesity, i.e. an extrathoracic cause. Without further clinical information, no other diagnosis, including that of pulmonary fibrosis need be sought. For obesity to cause a reduced TLC the weight (in kg)/height (in cm) ratio must generally exceed 1.0. Reductions in functional residual capacity (FRC), vital capacity (VC) and residual volume (RV) can occur with lesser degrees of obesity. The reduced gas transfer (DL_{CO}) corrects to normal when alveolar volume (K_{CO}) is incorporated. This implies normal pulmonary gas exchange and the low DL_{CO} is probably due to basal hypoventilation as a direct consequence of obesity.
iii. Obese individuals have increased chest wall mass, resulting in a reduction in net outward elastic recoil pressures. Lung and chest wall compliances fall as weight increases. The increased mass of the abdominal wall and abdominal contents reduces the FRC. Accordingly, these patients develop airway closure in dependent lung zones that become most pronounced when the patient lies supine. The changes in PaO_2 observed when these patients lie supine can be great.
iv. Pulmonary function tests improve toward normal as weight is lost.

112 This patient has limited disease small-cell lung cancer (**112**).
i. What is meant by 'limited disease' and how is it staged?
ii. What is the optimal treatment?
iii. What is the likely 2- and 5-year survival?

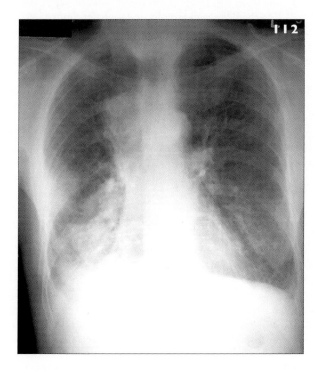

113 The data shown in the Table were obtained at maximal exercise testing in a 45-year-old man with breathlessness on exertion.
i. What does maximal oxygen uptake (VO_2max) measure and what parameters are needed to measure it?
ii. Would this patient be capable of performing a job involving packing shelves with light weight boxes?

Measurement	Observed maximum	Predicted maximum
Heart rate (beats/min)	162	160
Ventilation(l/min)	55	60
VO_2max (l/min)	1.9	–

112 i. Limited stage disease is confined to that hemithorax and the ipsilateral supraclavicular fossa. More detailed staging using the TNM system has little prognostic value, although is mandatory in the occasional SCLC that appears truly operable. The recommended staging tests for SCLC are a blood screen, a liver ultrasound and a bone scan. A CT thorax is usually unnecessary as the mediastinum often appears bulky on the plain radiography and adds little extra information.
ii. The optimal treatment is combination cytotoxic chemotherapy. Ideally, six courses should be given, one every 3 weeks. Radiotherapy to the mediastinum is recommended for patients who achieve a complete response. About 50% of patients presenting with limited disease should achieve a complete response on chest radiography and other staging tests. Radiotherapy confers a small but significant survival advantage at 2 years after the end of treatment and also reduces the incidence of relapse within the chest.
iii. The 2-year survival of limited disease of SCLC is 7%. For those patients with good prognostic variables (high performance status and normal biochemistry), then the 5-year survival is 15–20%. Of all patients alive at 2 years, 25% will still relapse with SCLC and another 20% will develop non-small-cell lung cancer within 5 years of starting treatment for SCLC.

113 i. VO_2 measures the amount of oxygen extracted by the tissues during exercise and is directly related to the amount of work performed. VO_2 = cardiac output (Q) × oxygen content difference of arterial and mixed venous blood $(CaO_2 - CvO_2)$, or $VO_2 = Q \times (SaO_2 - SvO_2) \times 1.34$.

SvO_2 (the saturation of mixed venous blood) reflects the ability of the exercising muscles to extract oxygen from the blood. VO_2max is defined as the plateau of oxygen uptake where attempting to go beyond that work capacity is associated with increasing ventilation but no increase in cardiac output. This is the point where the subject has reached maximal aerobic power. Many subjects do not reach this point as it requires considerable effort and determination with unpleasant sensations of breathlessness and muscle soreness. Therefore what is often reported is the maximum VO_2 achieved and not the true VO_2max. VO_2 can be obtained from work performed on a cycle ergometer, treadmill or even stepping exercise, provided that measures of minute ventilation and mixed expired O_2 and CO_2 tensions are available.
ii. To be able to perform heavy physical labour throughout an 8-hour shift, subjects should achieve a VO_2max of >25 ml/kg/min. Subjects whose VO_2max is <15 ml/kg/min would be unable to walk at more than a normal pace. Therefore, the result here suggests he should be able to perform his relatively light tasks.

114 Shown (114) is the response of heart rate and ventilation to increasing oxygen uptake during a progressive work rate test in a man with alveolar proteinosis. Exercise has stopped with a heart rate at the upper limit of normal and a ventilation that was higher than normal, and the patient complained of breathlessness. The subsequent exercise test followed a procedure that improved the patient's breathlessness.
i. Comment on the two exercise test results.
ii. What was the procedure that improved the patient?

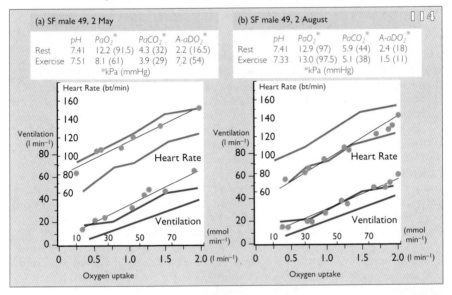

(a) SF male 49, 2 May

	pH	PaO_2^*	$PaCO_2^*$	$A\text{-}aDO_2^*$
Rest	7.41	12.2 (91.5)	4.3 (32)	2.2 (16.5)
Exercise	7.51	8.1 (61)	3.9 (29)	7.2 (54)

*kPa (mmHg)

(b) SF male 49, 2 August

	pH	PaO_2^*	$PaCO_2^*$	$A\text{-}aDO_2^*$
Rest	7.41	12.9 (97)	5.9 (44)	2.4 (18)
Exercise	7.33	13.0 (97.5)	5.1 (38)	1.5 (11)

*kPa (mmHg)

115 What surgical procedures might be of benefit to the patient with this CT (115)?

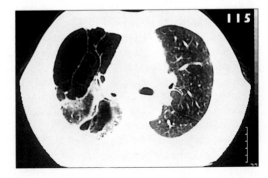

116 i. What are the usual bacterial pathogens in cystic fibrosis?
ii. How has the increase in *Burkholderia cepacia* affected clinical management?
iii. What are the clinical indications for intravenous antibiotics?

114 i. 114a shows excessively high ventilation from the beginning of exercise to the completion of the test. Arterial blood gases show hypoxaemia with increasing hypoxia at the end of exercise and a widened alveolar arterial oxygen gradient (A-aDO$_2$, 2.2 to 7.2 kPa).

The post-treatment exercise test (114b) shows a considerable improvement in resting heart rate and the heart rate response during exercise and the ventilatory response remained within the normal range. The arterial PO$_2$ and the alveolar arterial oxygen gradients were considerably improved.
ii. The procedure that improved the patient was a bronchoalveolar lavage of 10 l which is the treatment of choice in flushing out the abnormal protein from the alveolar spaces in these patients.

115 The patient has giant emphysematous bullae on the right with the left lung looking healthy. Removal of large bullae can result in reduction of dyspnoea and improved exercise tolerance. Two surgical techniques are available. Bullectomy is particularly indicated for the removal of a large single cyst. The operation was previously undertaken via a thoracotomy but excellent results are now being reported via the thoracoscope. The basis of the operation is to staple or suture the base of the cyst which is then excised and to fully expand the remaining lung. Nd YAG laser is also being used to perform 'lung reduction pneumoplasty'. The other option is a Monaldi-type decompression. The basis of this operation is to effect a pleurodesis so that the risk of pneumothorax is reduced and to drain individual bullae using large Foley catheters attached to underwater drainage systems. The Foley catheter balloon is inflated and the catheter is secured in the bullae by a purse string suture at the entry site. The bullae are then allowed to decompress slowly.

116 i. In an adult CF clinic the prevalence of common infecting bacterial pathogens is *P. aeruginosa* (80–90%), *Staph. aureus* (30–35%), *B. cepacia* (0–30%), *H. influenzae* (10–15%), *Str. pneumoniae* (1–3%) and *E. coli* (1%).
A. fumigatus colonizes 10–15% of patients. Its significance is uncertain.
ii. *B. cepacia* has increased in incidence and prevalence in large CF centres over the past decade. It is characterized by natural increased antibiotic resistance, greater cross-infectivity between patients, and accelerated lung disease in some patients.

Clinical management has been directed at patient segregation which has been shown to reduce the incidence and prevalence of *B. cepacia*.
iii. Intravenous antibiotics are indicated for all patients who have an infective exacerbation which is characterized by increased sputum volume, reduction in pulmonary function and weight loss.

How aggressively and frequently CF patients with relatively asymptomatic disease should be treated is uncertain. Persistently elevated serum inflammatory markers in asymptomatic patients suggests chronic progression of lung disease.

117 A patient with advanced intrathoracic squamous cell carcinoma has presented 3 weeks after completing palliative radiotherapy with confusion, vomiting and dehydration. Discuss the possible causes and management.

118 Shown are the chest radiograph (**118a**) and an abdominal CT scan (**118b**) performed 24 hours later on a 45-year-old diabetic man who had presented with abdominal pain and increasing respiratory distress.
i. What do the radiograph (**118a**) and CT scan (**118b**) show?
ii. What is the unifying diagnosis?

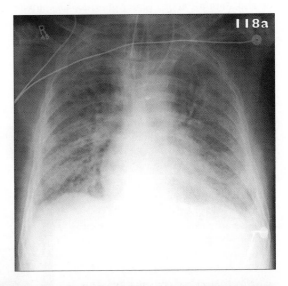

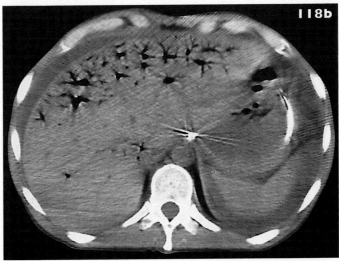

117 Possible causes include:

- Hypercalcaemia if thirst polyuria, dehydration, confusion, constipation and, ultimately, coma develop. If there is no evidence of bone pain, the likeliest cause is the primary tumour. Treatment is by rehydration, intravenous hydrocortisone and an infusion of a diphosphonate. The latter often produces dramatic effects and the benefit can last for 3–6 weeks, but may have to be repeated with either intravenous or oral diphosphonates.

- Cerebral metastasis. A CT brain scan (**117**), ideally with contrast enhancement, may show usually multiple lesions with ring enhancement from the contrast and often surrounding areas of cerebral oedema. Initial treatment is with intravenous or oral dexamethasone, 16 mg/day. If this achieves a major clinical improvement within 48 h, then whole-brain irradiation is recommended to maintain this

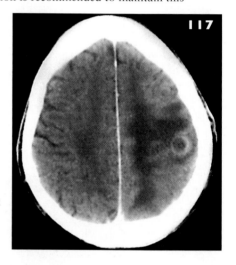

  improvement. The dexamethasone should then be rapidly reduced and stopped to reduce steroid myopathy. Should the patient not respond to 48 h of dexamethasone, then the steroids should be withdrawn and radiotherapy not offered.

- Poor attention to analgesic treatment. The opiates and, in particular, slow-release morphine preparations can cause drowsiness and rapid dehydration and constipation. This can cause vomiting and dehydration. Opiates should always be given with a strong laxative, i.e. lactulose 20–30 ml b.d. or co-danthramer, 10–20 ml daily.

118 i. The chest radiograph (**118a**) shows that the patient is intubated and a line in the left internal jugular vein. The lung fields show widespread diffuse alveolar shadowing that would be compatible with an atypical pneumonia, acute respiratory distress syndrome and possibly pulmonary oedema. The abdominal CT scan (**118b**) shows gas in the portal venous system.
ii. The unifying diagnosis is extensive bowel necrosis leading to bowel gas and contents entering the portal venous circulation producing a severe inflammatory response with pulmonary capillary endothelial damage leading to the development of adult respiratory distress syndrome (ARDS). This clinical picture of extensive gas in the portal venous system is diagnostic of extensive bowel necrosis and is uniformly fatal.

It is important to establish the underlying cause of ARDS. ARDS is only an intermediary mechanism of disease that could be compared with jaundice or a raised RAP: the appropriate management depends on discovering the primary pathology. Management of ARDS is supportive while the underlying problem is hopefully identified and successfully treated.

119 This patient (**119**) had a pleural effusion aspirated 2 months previously. What is shown, what is the likely diagnosis and how might this complication have been avoided?

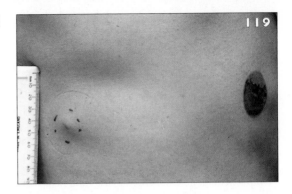

120 This 52-year-old man presented with this painless rash on his ankles (**120a**) and wrists (**120b**). The chest radiograph was abnormal.
i. Describe the rash.
ii. What pulmonary conditions are associated with this type of rash?

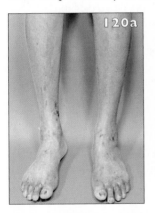
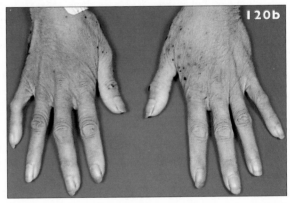

121 A 75-year-old male smoker requires surgery for bronchogenic carcinoma. His screening pulmonary function tests are: FEV_1 0.9 l (19% predicted); FVC 2.34 l (33% predicted); FEV_1/FVC 38%. His gas transfer factor (DL_{CO}) is 50% predicted.
i. Can this patient tolerate wedge resection, lobectomy or pneumonectomy?
ii. Which patients should have preoperative spirometry and other lung function tests before surgery?

119 Subcutaneous tumour nodule due to malignant pleural mesothelioma. Tumour seeding to the skin following aspiration, needle biopsy or surgical incision is a common complication of this condition and also of pleural adenocarcinoma, occurring in up to 50% of cases. The nodules may grow to a considerable size and cause discomfort and distress. This phenomenon can be prevented by prophylactic irradiation of needle biopsy and aspiration sites and it is therefore important to mark these sites indelibly in patients where mesothelioma is a possible diagnosis. 21 Gy, given in three fractions, is effective. Tumour seeding of this sort is much less common in malignant pleural effusion due to metastatic carcinoma or carcinoma of the bronchus.

120 i. The patient has a typical vasculitic rash with small haemorrhagic lesions on the forearms and shins.
ii. Vasculitis can affect the lungs as part of a systemic condition. The more common conditions include:
- Wegener's granulomatosis – see **152**.
- Allergic granulomatosis and angiitis (Churg–Strauss syndrome). This comprises asthma, hypereosinophilia with eosinophilic infiltrates, vasculitis and granulomata in various organs. It can be controlled by oral steroids, but the vasculitis can be life-threatening. The condition usually begins with asthma, at about 35 years of age, is of equal sex incidence, and vasculitis follows some years later. Upper airway lesions are common usually as allergic rhinitis. The ANCA test is positive in 50% of patients – predominantly p-ANCA.
- Polyarteritis nodosa (PAN) – affects medium-sized arteries, while Churg–Strauss affects small ones. There is usually no history of allergic illness in PAN and pulmonary involvement is not common. Pulmonary involvement includes asthma, pulmonary infiltrates, fibrosis and effusions. The c-ANCA test is negative.

121 i. The patient has severe airflow obstruction with an FEV_1 of <40% predicted. Lobectomy or pneumonectomy therefore carry too great a risk of post-operative ventilatory failure. A wedge resection is possible.
ii. In general, patients with an FEV_1 and DL_{CO} >80% normal will tolerate pneumonectomy. Those with both values <40% will not tolerate lobectomy or pneumonectomy. Those with intermediate values should undergo split lung function to estimate the predicted post-operative lung function, either by counting the segments to be removed or by using the percentage of perfused lung to be removed, calculated on a technetium perfusion scan, e.g. post-operative FEV_1 = pre-operative FEV_1 × (number of segments remaining/total number of segments).

If pre-operative lung function is borderline (FEV_1 and DL_{CO} between 40% and 80% normal), cardiopulmonary exercise testing is valuable. A maximal oxygen uptake (VO_2 max) of >20 ml/kg/min is safe; <10 ml/kg/min is a contraindication and values between constitute higher risk.

122 This patient with CF presented with haemoptysis of 300–400 ml/day. He was very breathless with this due to poor underlying lung function.
i. What procedure (122) is being performed?
ii. What are the causes of haemoptysis in CF?

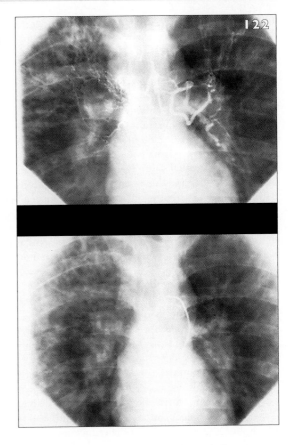

123 i. What is the device in 123?
ii. What are its advantages and indications for use?
iii. What are its complications?

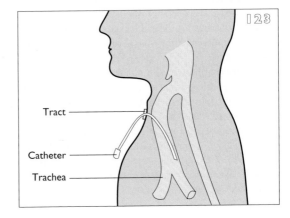

122 i. The procedure is bronchial artery angiography and embolization. The upper illustration shows a single common bronchial trunk and a flush of hypervascular vessels in the left upper lobe. There is bronchiectasis in the right upper lobe. The lower illustration shows the result following embolization of the left upper lobe vessels with PVA, a fine particulate material. The hypervascularity has been corrected, and there was complete cessation of haemoptysis. Other materials used include gel foam and small metal coils. The aim is to occlude small vessels, as occluding the larger aberrant trunk often results in opening of collateral channels. ii. Haemoptysis is common in CF, particularly in older patients and usually only requires reassurance. Small haemoptyses (10–20 ml) usually settle with a course of antibiotics. The usual cause is rupture of small mucosal vessels where the mucosa is ulcerated and fissured due to chronic infection. Repeated coughing will aggravate haemoptysis. Contributing factors include reduced platelet count (hypersplenism) and vitamin K deficiency (liver dysfunction). Large haemoptyses (>300 ml over 24 hours) may cause severe breathlessness and be life-threatening, although this is a very unusual scenario. Intravenous pitressin is a useful holding manoeuvre. Where a bleeding bronchial artery has been demonstrated the treatment of choice is bronchial artery embolization. Surgical resection may be required in extreme cases.

123 i. The device pictured is a transtracheal catheter for the delivery of oxygen. The catheter may be positioned to exit through the skin directly overlying the trachea or may be tunnelled under the skin of the anterior chest wall to exit over the abdomen. ii. The advantages of transtracheal oxygen delivery (compared with nasal cannulae and face masks) include:
- Improved comfort.
- Improved cosmetic appearance. An approximate 50% reduction in oxygen requirements which allows for extended delivery of oxygen from cylinders and liquid containers and increased patient mobility.
- Reduced dead space, thereby reducing ventilation and improving exercise tolerance.

Transtracheal oxygen therapy is indicated for individuals with stable chronic lung disease requiring prolonged oxygen therapy in the following situations:
- Reluctance to utilize nasal or mask oxygen therapy because of cosmetic concerns.
- Poor compliance with nasal or mask oxygen therapy because of discomfort.
- High O_2 flow rates are required to maintain adequate O_2 saturation such that routine delivery methods are not sufficient or produce excessive drying of the upper airways.

iii. Insertion of a transtracheal oxygen catheter requires local (for percutaneous catheters exiting in the neck) or general anaesthesia (for tunnelled catheters exiting elsewhere). The catheters must be removed or flushed twice daily to maintain patency. The most common complication is obstruction of the catheter by mucus plugs. On occasion these plugs can enlarge to obstruct the trachea itself.

124 Shown (124) is gallium-67 scan of a patient with sarcoidosis.
i. What features are physiological and pathological?
ii. What is the role of the gallium scan in sarcoidosis?
iii. Does it have prognostic value?

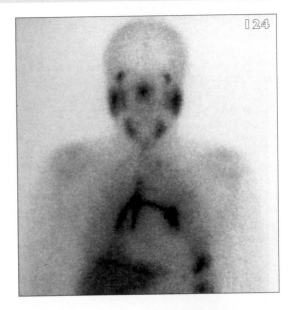

125 This collecting jar (125) is full of sputum. The patient, a 64-year-old man, filled it to 2 l in 2 days.
i. What is his phenomenon called?
ii. With what malignant lung disease is it associated?

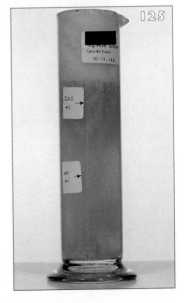

126 i. What are the main types of asbestos fibres?
ii. What are the risks to health from asbestos in homes and public buildings?

124 i. Physiological uptake occurs in the liver, bowel and breast with some uptake in the eyes and nose. It is taken up non-specifically in infections, inflammatory conditions and malignancy. Most scans are reported subjectively. In this patient there is increased uptake in the parotid and submandibular glands, lacrimal glands, hilar and mediastinal lymph nodes as well as the lungs. The parotid, lacrimal and hilar node uptake has been described as the 'panda–lambda' appearance, a phenomenon occurring in about 10% of sarcoid patients. This is highly specific and may obviate the need for histological confirmation in the presence of an elevated serum ACE in some patients. Pulmonary uptake can occur in most interstitial lung diseases. About 20% of patients with stage I disease have increased lung uptake despite clear lungfields on chest radiography.
ii. It cannot be recommended for routine use. It is useful for detecting sarcoidosis in selected patients such as a cardiomyopathy of unknown cause and to reassess patients with long-standing active disease.
iii. There are no studies that show conclusively that increased gallium uptake in the lungs correlates with prognosis.

125 i. The fluid is either saliva or sputum. The quantity is hugely excessive and sputum production at this rate is termed bronchorrhoea. Patients occasionally expectorate their saliva, complaining of excessive oral secretions, but sputum is more turbid and viscid and easy to distinguish from saliva.
ii. Alveolar cell carcinomas can cause bronchorrhoea due to the excessive mucous gland formation along the alveolar surfaces. It is untreatable with no response to cytotoxic chemotherapy, steroids or atropine. The chest radiograph will show a diffuse reticular distribution of disease, often extensive in one lung, and becoming bilateral quite commonly late in the disease.

126 i. The two main types are serpentine fibres such as chrysotile (White asbestos) and amphiboles (straight fibres) such as crocidolite (Blue asbestos)and amosite (Brown asbestos). Amphiboles are more capable of penetrating the lung periphery, whereas chrysotile fibres can be more readily removed from the lung by the mucociliary escalator. All fibre types are fibrogenic; however, amphiboles – particularly crocidolite – are more potent in terms of the development of mesothelioma. Most workers with asbestos have probably been exposed to a range of fibre types.
ii. Where asbestos has been used as an insulator around pipes and in walls and ceilings the greatest risk occurs when it is being removed, in which case workers must use respirators and protective clothing. At other times, where the surface of walls is not intact, there is a risk of asbestos dust being shed and subsequently inhaled. Where the surfaces are intact the risk of development of disease is thought to be negligible.

127 A patient with disseminated adenocarcinoma develops pain in the rib cage, left shoulder and right thigh. The pain is not controlled on eight paracetamol and codeine tablets a day. What steps would you take to control the pain and improve quality of life?

128 These bronchoscopic views (**128a, 128b**) are of the left main bronchus in a patient with inoperable lung cancer with recent increase in breathlessness.
i. What therapeutic strategy is appropriate?
ii. What has, in fact, been done?

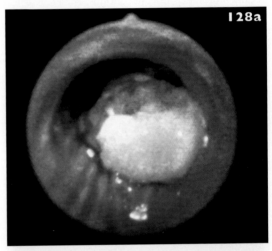

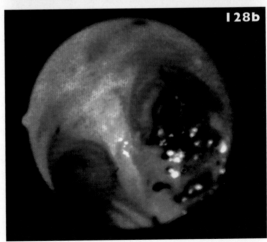

127 The pain is almost certainly due to bone metastases. If there is doubt, perform a bone scan (**127**). Bone pain is best initially treated with analgesics, such as paracetamol and codeine, together with a non-steroidal anti-inflammatory drug. The latter should be given as a slow-release preparation, i.e. b.d. or nocté.

If this is not adequate, short-term relief can be obtained by adding a corticosteroid. It is better to change the analgesics to a morphine preparation – ideally morphine sulphate continus (MST). The non-steroidal drug should be continued. Breakthrough pain should be controlled by rapid-acting morphine tablets, which should be taken whenever necessary. An anti-nausea preparation should be routinely prescribed with the introduction of morphine. Also, an aperient is essential, either lactulose or co-danthrusate. Aperients may also have to be increased. Fentanyl patches may be used for the management of chronic cancer pain once the required

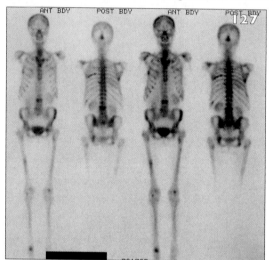

dose of morphine has been established. Further medication that may be helpful is a tricyclic anti-depressant such as amitriptyline given at night. Very occasionally, nerve blocks or selective cordotomy can be effective for resistant, locally produced pain, although this is an unusual requirement with modern analgesia.

128 i. The tumour is in an intramural location in a major airway and there is no extrinsic compression. Therefore YAG laser resection is appropriate. The procedure is performed under general anaesthesia using a rigid bronchoscope through which the patient is ventilated and instruments are passed. A flexible glass fibre coated with protective cladding delivers the laser beam onto the tumour surface. As shown, an aiming beam, itself a helium–neon laser with no thermal properties, is used to show the point where the invisible YAG laser beam is being directed. Laser therapy can produce excellent symptomatic and palliative improvement. This is best obtained for tumours in the large central airways. There are few controlled trials comparing laser treatment to other modalities such as cryotherapy, diathermy, and brachytherapy where indicated. The treatment is complicated and should be performed in specialist units.
ii. This patient has received laser therapy with refashioning of the patent airway, as in **128b** which shows the procedure in progress with the laser fibre visible in the foreground.

129 The patient whose hand radiographs are depicted in 129 suffers from difficulty swallowing, arthralgias and a waxy appearance of her skin on her face and distal extremities.
i. What disorder accounts for these abnormalities?
ii. What are the two general types of pulmonary disease associated with this disorder?

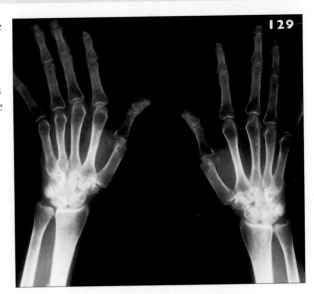

130 i. What procedure (130a, 130b) is this patient undergoing?
ii. What side effects may result from this treatment?

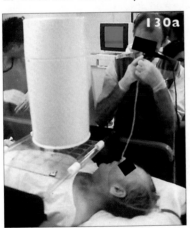 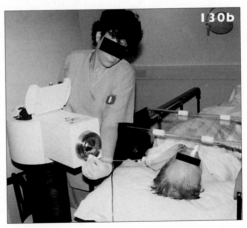

131 i. What are the most common infections following lung transplantation?
ii. What are the non-infective causes of lung damage following transplantation?

129 i. Progressive systemic sclerosis (or scleroderma) is a connective tissue disease in which progressive fibrosis and collagen replacement affects multiple organs, including the skin, oesophagus, joints and lung. The hand radiographs depict acro-osteolysis or erosion of the distal phalanges. Pulmonary symptoms include dyspnoea and cough.

ii. The most common pulmonary manifestation of systemic sclerosis is fibrosing alveolitis, the pattern of which is indistinguishable from idiopathic pulmonary fibrosis (CFA). A second, less common pulmonary manifestation is pulmonary hypertension. The severity of the pulmonary hypertension of progressive systemic sclerosis is not predicted by the degree of restrictive interstitial disease.

130 i. Endobronchial brachytherapy. Its role is primarily palliative for breathlessness but also for cough and haemoptysis. It is indicated for endobronchial tumour with a mural and or endobronchial component, preferably without extrinsic compression. Occasionally it may be used with curative intent in patients with small endobronchial tumours. It allows radiotherapy to be positioned and given directly to the tumour. Its effects take 10–14 days to become apparent and it is therefore of no use for acute relief of symptoms due to airway obstruction. However, it may be used as combined therapy with laser resection, stenting or external beam radiotherapy. The proximal and distal ends of the tumour are marked using the flexible bronchoscope and fluoroscopy. A catheter is then passed into the bronchus affected by tumour and the bronchoscope removed. Radioactive material, usually iridium (^{192}Ir) is then loaded into the distal end of a catheter using the Microselectron afterloading device as depicted. High-dose rate (HDR) brachytherapy is now the most common form of brachytherapy and 10–15 Gy is delivered over 10–20 min, with the maximum diameter of effect being 1 cm.

ii. The procedure is performed under local anaesthetic with intravenous sedation and is generally well tolerated.

131 i. The most common infections are:
- Bacterial: *P. aeruginosa*, *Str. pneumoniae*, *H. influenzae*, *Staph. aureus*, *B. cepacia*.
- Fungal: *A. fumigatus* and *C. albicans*.
- Viral: Cytomegalovirus.
- Other: *P. carinii*, *T. gondii*.

ii. The non-infective causes causing lung damage following transplantation are:
- Acute rejection, which occurs in nearly every patient in the first few months following transplantation.
- Obliterative bronchiolitis occurs in 40% of patients as a late complication of transplantation, probably due to previous lung injury which includes infection and rejection. It responds poorly to treatment and is the major cause of late mortality.
- Lymphoproliferative disorders due to T- or B-cell types. B-cells are usually associated with the Epstein–Barr virus.

132 This patient complained of dependent oedema, abdominal discomfort and chronic fatigue.
i. Describe the abnormality present in the radiograph (132).
ii. What is the likely aetiology?
iii. What are the pathological processes and what are the physiological consequences?
iv. What form of treatment is required?

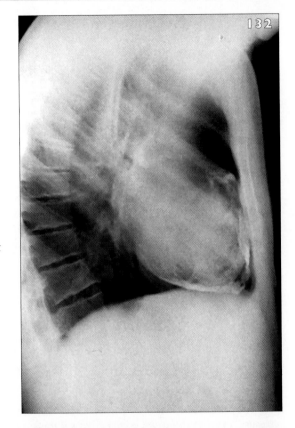

133 i. What is the mechanism of action of CPAP (133) in obstructive sleep apnoea?
ii. What are the potential side effects of nasal CPAP?
iii. How compliant are OSA patients who are prescribed CPAP?

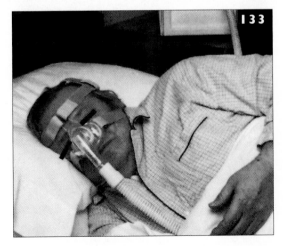

132 i. Pericardial calcification.

ii. Tuberculous pericarditis is the most likely aetiology, but calcification can occur following suppurative bacterial disease.

iii. The pericardial sac in this condition is obliterated by adhesions. The parietal pericardium is grossly thickened, fibrotic and calcified and the visceral pericardium is also rigid and fibrosed. There is consequently impaired diastolic filling as the heart cannot expand and venous inflow is further reduced by fibrous cuffing of the great veins as they enter the right atrium. Cardiac output is reduced and venous pressure chronically elevated causing hepatic engorgement, high jugular venous pressure and leg oedema. Residual foci of active TB are very rare.

iv. Pericardiectomy is required. This can be very difficult because of dense fibrosis and pericardial adhesions. It is usually necessary to either excise the visceral pericardium or to create multiple relieving incisions in order to adequately free the trapped myocardium and this increases the risk of haemorrhage or myocardial damage. Cardiac function can be very poor in the immediate postoperative period so that inotropic support is required and it may take many months to gain maximum benefit from the procedure. A pericardial specimen should be sent for culture and histology.

133 i. CPAP acts as a pneumatic splint. It increases the intraluminal pressure within the upper airway and thus counteracts transmural forces which favour airway closure. The typical site of obstruction in patients with OSA is between the nasopharynx and the larynx. This region is narrowed during sleep due to reduction in muscle tone, and OSA patients on average have a smaller diameter of pharyngeal lumen.

ii. Poorly fitting masks result in air leakage. This not only reduces the applied airway pressure, but also can cause conjunctivitis if the air leak is directed towards the eye. A poorly fitting mask can also bruise or cause ulceration of the bridge of the nose. These problems can be avoided by selecting and properly fitting the appropriate mask type and size. Most patients initially experience nasal congestion but this complaint frequently diminishes with continued use. Intranasal vasoconstrictors, anticholinergics or steroids have been used in this setting. Humidification of air within the CPAP system can also help if these measures are ineffective.

iii. Compliance rates vary from 45 to 80%. Many studies show average hours used to be less than 5 per night. There are no consistent clinical predictors of compliance, although one study suggested that patients who complain of side effects were those found to be less compliant. Follow-up and support by physicians and personalizing the type of CPAP device and mask may be important in improving patient compliance.

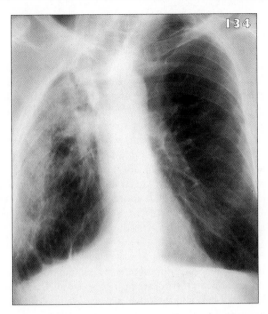

134 Shown is a chest radiograph (**134**) of a 70-year-old man with a 3-month history of cough, low-grade fever, weight loss and pulmonary infiltrates. As a young man, he had been successfully treated for pulmonary tuberculosis by thoracoplasty and right upper lobe resection. Multiple sputum specimens over the past 2 months were negative for tuberculosis by AFB stain. Mycobacterial, fungal and routine sputum cultures grew only mixed oral flora. Three 14-day courses of either erythromycin or ampicillin resulted in transient improvement that was followed by prompt recurrence of the symptoms. Bronchoalveolar lavage (BAL) cytology and transbronchial biopsies showed chronic inflammatory changes without evidence of neoplasm, granulomas or eosinophils. All BAL stains and cultures were negative, with the exception that quantitative bacterial cultures grew 500 cfu/ml of *Moraxella catarrhalis*. What is the most likely diagnosis and why?

135 i. How does a pulse oximeter work?
ii. The accuracy of most pulse oximeters decreases below what percent saturation?
iii. What factors affect the accuracy of pulse oximetry?

117

134 This patient has the chronic pneumonia syndrome, i.e. chronic symptoms of respiratory infection associated with radiographic abnormalities. The chronic and insidious nature of this syndrome suggests a variety of subacute, infectious processes including mycobacterial, fungal and parasitic diseases. Unusual bacterial infections (actinomycosis and nocardiosis) should also be considered, as should eosinophilic pneumonia (note the peripheral appearance of the infiltrate). Although less common, non-infectious lung diseases (e.g. neoplasms, connective tissue disease) can also present in this manner. Common bacterial respiratory pathogens rarely cause chronic pneumonia and usually do so only in patients with underlying diabetes, immunodeficiency or structural lung disease. Usual quantitative culture criteria for the diagnosis of bacterial pneumonia may not be applicable, and a prolonged course of antibiotic therapy appears necessary. Given the broad spectrum of potential causes for the chronic pneumonia syndrome, a comprehensive evaluation is warranted. In the absence of a relevant exposure history or systemic manifestations of an underlying disease, invasive diagnostic procedures may be necessary.

135 i. A pulse oximeter is a spectrophotometer which measures the absorption of light at two wavelengths; one in the infrared range at a wavelength of 940 nm (absorbed by oxyhaemoglobin) and the other at a wavelength of 660 nm (absorbed by reduced haemoglobin). The absorption at these two wavelengths is compared and the percentages of oxygenated and reduced haemoglobin calculated. The pulse oximeter compares absorption measured during systole and diastole and uses the difference to reflect only the absorption of arterial blood, thereby limiting errors induced by absorbance in venous blood and other tissues.
ii. The accuracy of most oximeters decreases below 75% saturation. Above this level, the accuracy is approximately 4%.
iii. Standard pulse oximeters are unable to distinguish dyshaemoglobins, most notably carboxyhaemoglobin and methaemoglobin, from oxyhaemoglobin. In smoke inhalation pulse oximetry reflects absorption by both oxyhaemoglobin and carboxyhaemoglobin, and thus may overestimate the true oxygenation status. Any factor which affects assessment of the arterial pulse (e.g., motion, low perfusion states) may distort the reading. Specific light sources, such as fluorescent or infrared lamps, can cause erroneous signals if the oximeter probe is not shielded. Dark skin pigmentation and darker coloured nail polishes can also interfere with light transmission, thereby lowering oximeter readings.

136 A 45-year-old female is admitted to the emergency department with a 3 hour history of severe anterior chest pain and breathlessness. She made a transatlantic flight 24 hours ago. Her pH is 7.47, PaO_2 8kPa (60 mmHg), and $PaCO_2$ 3.5 kPa (26.3 mmHg). She is tachypnoeic, her heart rate is 120 beats per minute in sinus rhythm, and the ECG shows no abnormality. Her CXR is shown (**136a**).

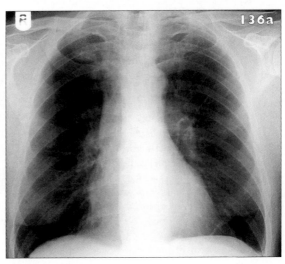

i. What is the likely diagnosis?
ii. What is the optimal way of making the diagnosis?

137 i. Describe the CT appearance (**137**).
ii. What clinical findings are expected in this patient?
iii. What treatment would be appropriate in this condition?
iv. According to the current classification, what condition is shown?

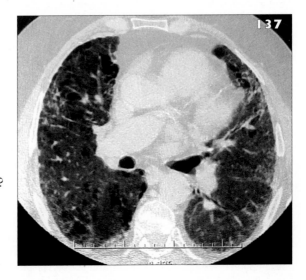

136 & 137: Answers

136 i. Pulmonary embolism.
ii. Normal CXR and ECG are common findings in pulmonary embolism. Examination of the calves is helpful for signs of a DVT. The investigation of choice is a computed tomography pulmonary angiogram (CTPA; 136b). This should be performed as soon as possible after admission and anticoagulation should be started as soon as the diagnosis is made. With rapid sequence multi-slice CT scanners, emboli can be identified as far peripherally as the lobar segments. In

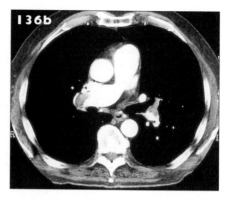

the case of strong clinical suspicion of pulmonary embolism and negative CTPA, the patient should have Doppler ultrasonography of the pelvis and lower limb veins.

137 i. Widespread ground-glass opacification is seen: patchy airspace opacities and a hazy increase in lung density (i.e. that does not obscure the underlying lung parenchyma). A reticular pattern is observed, consisting largely of thickened interlobular septa and intralobular lines. Honeycombing and sub-pleural fibrosis are apparent.
ii. Dyspnoea, cough, bilateral fine inspiratory crackles at the lung bases, and possibly clubbing may be present. Systemic features such as fever, myalgia, weight loss, fatigue, and arthralgia may be seen in up to 50% of individuals.
iii. Empirical treatment with corticosteroids is commonly used. Cytotoxics such as cyclophosphamide and azathioprine are the most commonly used second-line agents. It is believed that treatment is more likely to be successful in the earlier, more cellular stage of the disease before scarring predominates. If there is no objective evidence of early response, treatment is usually discontinued.
iv. Currently, the idiopathic interstitial pneumonias are classified into four major types: usual interstitial pneumonia (UIP), desquamative interstitial pneumonia (DIP), non-specific interstitial pneumonia (NSIP), and respiratory bronchiolitis-associated interstitial lung disease (RBILD). There are also other types such as chronic eosinophilic pneumonia, hypersensitivity pneumonitis, non-specific chronic bronchiolitis, and BOOP.
The typical HRCT appearances of UIP are of intralobular interstitial thickening, visible intralobular bronchioles, traction bronchiectasis and honeycombing. The pathological features are of patchy, dense, interstitial fibrosis with fibroblastic foci. DIP is characterized by ground-glass attenuation, predominantly in the middle or lower zones and sub-pleural in location. This most closely resembles the scan shown. Pathologically, there is cellular airspace involvement particularly with macrophages. This condition has a better response to treatment. NSIP is sub-divided into fibrotic (interstitial fibrosis without the temporal heterogeneity of UIP and usually showing a diffuse uniform involvement of lung tissue) and cellular (chronic interstitial inflammation without fibrosis) types. RBILD is histologically similar to DIP but is mainly confined to the peribronchiolar region and is strongly associated with smoking. This classification requires histological examination.

138 Shown is the chest radiograph (**138**) of a 56-year-old woman from south-east Asia with chronic cough, malaise and weight loss. Multiple sputum specimens submitted for mycobacterial and fungal culture have yielded negative results.

i. What are the radiographic findings?

ii. What is the most likely diagnosis and how can this be established?

iii. What is the appropriate treatment?

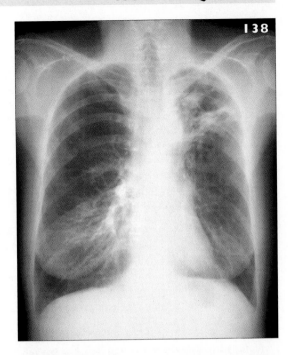

139 The chest radiograph in **139** is of a patient with cystic fibrosis (CF).

i. What does it show?

ii. What is the optimum medical management?

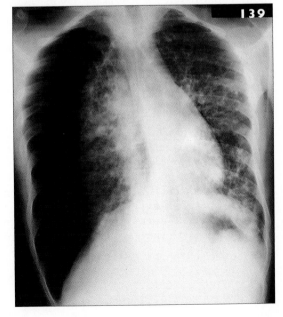

138 i. There is a cavitating infiltrate in the apical segment of the left upper lobe.
ii. Melioidosis is an important cause of respiratory infection in tropical regions, especially south-east Asia. It is caused by the Gram-negative bacterial pathogen, *P. pseudomallei*, yet it is acquired by cutaneous inoculation with haematogenous spread to the lungs. Melioidosis may present acutely, with evidence of cellulitis at the inoculation site, prominent systemic and respiratory symptoms, and diffuse pulmonary infiltrates. A more insidious or chronic form of the disease may develop long after an infected patient leaves the endemic area. The presentation of chronic melioidosis is characterized by indolent wasting symptoms, cough and apical infiltrates which may become fibrotic or cavitating – features indistinguishable from pulmonary tuberculosis. The diagnosis of melioidosis should be considered whenever a compatible syndrome develops in a patient who has been in an endemic area. The organism can readily be cultured from respiratory secretions or other sites, and infection can be confirmed by serologic testing.
iii. *P. pseudomallei* is sensitive to a variety of antimicrobial agents, but resistance is variable and antibiotic selection should be based on *in vitro* sensitivity testing. For acute disease, combination intravenous therapy including an aminoglycoside is recommended for 1 month followed by several months of oral treatment. For chronic disease, a 3- to 6-month course of an oral agent such as trimethoprim/sulphamethoxazole may be used.

139 i. A large right tension pneumothorax. The incidence of pneumothorax increases with disease severity and may be associated with a poor prognosis. It occurs due to rupture of subpleural blebs through the visceral pleura, usually in the upper lobes. The incidence of pneumothorax is higher in patients with widespread pre-existing lung disease.
ii. Pneumothorax in CF is different from that in other patients due to its association with large amounts of purulent secretions. This can make physiotherapy difficult and lung re-expansion very slow. In addition, CF patients who get pneumothoraces usually have severe disease and with a pneumothorax can become extremely sick.

Patients with pneumothoraces need prompt medical treatment. At the time of the pneumothorax they should be commenced on intravenous antibiotics. If large it should be drained immediately. If the patient is breathless a small pneumothorax requires intercostal drainage under radiological control. An intubated pneumothorax makes physiotherapy easier. A small pneumothorax in an asymptomatic patient may be aspirated or observed for 2–3 days.

If a pneumothorax fails to resolve with maximal medical management within a week then prompt surgical intervention should be considered. With the advent of organ transplantation extensive pleurodesis or pleurectomy are not appropriate. The best surgical option is video-assisted stapling of the apical subpleural bleb under direct vision.

140 **i.** What operation has this patient undergone (**140**)?
ii. How should the procedure be monitored postoperatively?

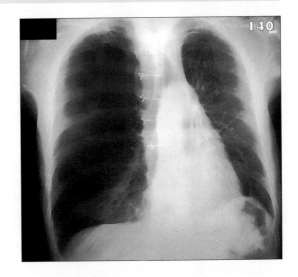

141 These high-resolution chest CTs (**141a, 141b**) are from a 37-year-old man who presented with a spontaneous pneumothorax.
i. What diagnosis does the CT suggest?
ii. What is the typical clinical presentation of this disease?
iii. What abnormalities are seen on histopathological examination?

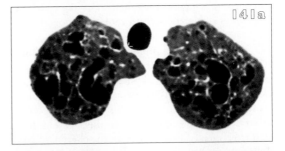

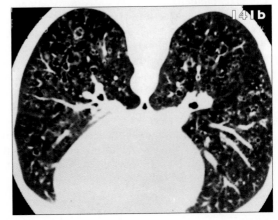

140 i. Left single lung transplant for COPD (still evident in the right lung).
ii. Patients perform a vital role in monitoring for the complications of lung transplantation which include infection related to immunposuppression, graft rejection and anastomotic complications. Cough, breathlessness, fever and falling peak flow measurements may herald any of these complications and should be investigated promptly. In addition, regular transbronchial lung biopsies are performed in some centres to monitor for the development of graft rejection. Chest radiographs may not show evidence of early graft rejection, particularly after 3 months. Rejection may be hyperacute, acute or chronic and results from host T-cell activation due to MHC molecule cell surface differences between host and donor. Acute rejection occurs up to 12 months and most patients have at least two episodes. Histology ranges from infrequent perivascular infiltrates of inflammatory cells to diffuse perivascular, interstitial and airspace infiltrates with an ARDS-like picture. Biopsies and lavage are also screened for infection which may coexist.
Chronic rejection usually arises at 8–12 months with variable symptoms and progressive airflow obstruction. It occurs in 40% of cases remains a significant cause of late mortality. Histologically it manifests as bronchiolitis obliterans.

Bronchoscopy is also useful for surveillance of the anastomosis site for complications such as bronchial strictures which may require stent placement or surgery, or dehiscence which requires reoperation.

141 i. Eosinophilic granuloma. The major findings on chest CT are irregular, cystic structures of variable size, most being 3–5 cm in diameter (**141a**), suggestive of eosinophilic granuloma. The chest radiograph in this disorder is characterized by diffusely increased interstitial markings. A nodular or reticular nodular infiltrate is present, sometimes accompanied by cystic lesions (**141b**). Most commonly the infiltrate is found in the lung periphery and in the upper lobes. Volume loss is characteristically absent on both the chest radiograph and the CT.
ii. Primary pulmonary histiocytosis X or eosinophilic granuloma of the lung can present at any age, but is most frequently seen in the third and fourth decades of life. Patients complain of cough and exertional dyspnoea, but may be asymptomatic. Spontaneous pneumothorax is a classical association. Progressive decline in lung function and the occurrence of multiple pneumothoraces implies a poor long-term prognosis. Pleurodesis may be of use in these patients. Immunosuppressive treatment is of unproven value. The eosinophilic granulomata can also occur in the pituitary gland causing diabetes insipidus and may cause asymptomatic bone cysts, detected on a radiological skeletal survey.
iii. The classical pathological findings are discrete parenchymal nodules composed of fibrous tissue, eosinophils and 'histiocytosis X' cells which resemble Langerhans cells of the skin. These histiocytosis cells are characterized by intracytoplasmic X bodies which may be visualized by electron microscopy.

142 This 45-year-old, non-smoking man produced the flow–volume curve in 142.
i. Is it of normal or abnormal shape?
ii. What is point A? How is it usually measured?
iii. Why does the expiratory curve decrease progressively in flow as the residual volume is approached?
iv. Why is the inspiratory curve semi-circular in shape and dissimilar to the expiratory curve?

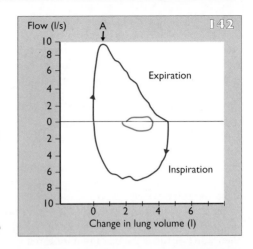

143 This patient (143) had polio 30 years ago and was clinically stable until recently when he developed fatigue, joint pains, muscle weakness, swallowing difficulties and dyspnoea.
i. What disorder does this patient have and what are the underlying factors responsible for his breathing abnormality?
ii. How is sleep affected in this disorder?
iii. How is this disorder managed?

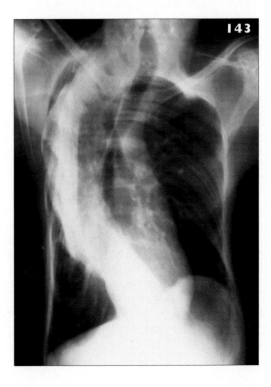

142 i. This is a normal-shaped curve.
ii. The expiratory limb is triangular in shape. Following a full inspiration, the lung's recoil pressure is maximal, as is pleural pressure, because the thoracic muscles are stretched to provide maximal expiratory force. The onset of expiratory flow is explosive and reaches its peak rate within 0.01 s, i.e. point A. This is the peak expiratory flow rate and is usually measured with a peak flow meter.
iii. The expiratory curve decreases its flow gradually as the lung volume drops from total lung capacity to residual volume. This graded decline reflects the gradual drop in the lung's elastic recoil as the lung gets smaller; also, muscular force on the lung (pleural pressure) slowly decreases as the thoracic cage changes position during expiration and the respiratory muscles shorten.
iv. Inspiration does not reach an instant maximal flow in contrast to expiration. As the respiratory muscles contract, the power increases progressively from the start of inspiration to achieve a maximal flow. This takes a relatively long time and maximal inspiratory flow is only achieved by the mid-point of the inspiratory vital capacity; it then slows again as the maximum inspired volume is reached (total lung capacity; TLC). This results in the semi-circular appearance of the inspiratory flow–volume curve.

143 i. This patient has the post-polio syndrome which usually occurs two to three decades after the acute infection and recovery. These patients usually have kyphoscoliosis which causes restriction and can blunt the hypercapnic drive because of mechanical impairment. In addition, they may also have decreased respiratory drive as a result of damage to their medullary neurones and may also have respiratory muscle weakness. Patients who did not have respiratory involvement with the initial infection are unlikely to develop such weakness or kyphoscoliosis.
ii. In the early stages, respiration during sleep is more likely to be affected. Initially, short central apnoeas occur and as the condition progresses these become longer and more frequent. Sleep abnormalities include decreased sleep efficiency and increased arousal frequency. Eventually, awake respiration can be affected.
iii. Patients with predominantly central sleep apnoea should be managed with bi-level positive airway pressure during sleep which is delivered via a nasal mask. A 20 cmH$_2$O inspiratory pressure support can be achieved with this, with expiratory support of 5 cm H$_2$O delivering a defined number of breaths. This must be timed support, per minute rather than triggered by the patient's breathing. Some patients who have more severe disease which includes irregularities in awake breathing, will require ventilatory support both during sleep and wakefulness. Early ventilation systems included negative-pressure tank apparatus. Nasal positive pressure ventilation is now more commonly used.

144 This woman developed a rash (**144**) 1 month after completing cytotoxic chemotherapy for small-cell lung cancer. What is the rash? Why did she develop it? How would you treat it?

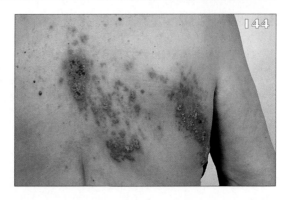

145 A 62-year-old woman is noted to have a low diffusing capacity during evaluation for dyspnoea.
i. What does the diffusing capacity measure?
ii. What physiological abnormalities result in a low diffusing capacity and what diagnoses might be associated with these abnormalities?
iii. What effect would anaemia have on the value?

146 This 68-year-old man had been unwell for 2 weeks, with a dry cough, dyspnoea and drenching sweats. What do the radiographs **146a** and **146b** show, what are the likely causes and how should the condition be managed?

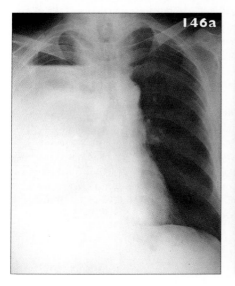

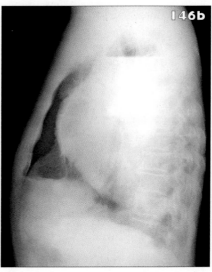

144 The rash is due to infection with herpes zoster, i.e. shingles. It occurs most commonly in immunosuppressed patients and is not uncommonly seen during or after a course of cytotoxic chemotherapy. The more widespread the underlying cancer, the greater the prospect of significant immunosuppression and hence the increased likelihood of developing shingles.

If the shingles is severe, and painful, treatment initially should be with i.v. acyclovir four to five times a day for 2 days and then orally for a further 3 days. Treatment is only likely to be effective if commenced within 48 h of symptoms commencing.

145 i. The diffusing capacity (DL_{CO}) measures the amount of carbon monoxide that transfers from a volume of inspired gas into the blood over a standard time – usually 10 s.
ii. The test is sensitive to reductions in diffusing surface (e.g. emphysema, lung resection, effusions, pneumothorax, atelectasis, bronchiolitis obliterans, fibrosis) and capillary blood volume (pulmonary emboli or other pulmonary vascular disease).
iii. A low haemoglobin may lead to an erroneous interpretation of the diffusing capacity as there is a reduced capacity of the blood in the alveolar capillaries to carry CO (and O_2) away. The correction of DL_{CO} for anaemia should be routine in all pulmonary function laboratories. The DL_{CO} falls by 7% for each 1 g/100 ml fall in haemoglobin.

146 Pleural empyema. This is usually a complication of an acute pneumonia – particularly pneumococcal – but may arise as a primary infection of the pleural space, in which case the organism is often an anaerobe producing 'stinking pus'. A tuberculous pleural effusion may also progress to an empyema, particularly if a cavity ruptures into the pleural space. A previous history of vomiting and aspiration is not uncommon and carcinoma of the bronchus is also a predisposing factor.

Empyemas tend to adhere to the chest wall, causing loculated collections of fluid. This differs from a simple pleural effusion and the lateral chest radiograph (**146b**) here confirms a large quantity of fluid adherent to the posterior aspect of the left thoracic cage.

There is accumulating evidence that video-assisted thoracoscopic surgery has higher success rates and can shorten length of hospital stay and requirement for analgesics in empyema compared to the traditional approach of intercostal chest drainage with instillation of intra-pleural streptokinase. In any event it is necessary to drain the pleural cavity as soon as possible and treatment with systemic antibiotics is required. In some cases, despite vigorous treatment, it may be necessary to perform a surgical decortication. This should be done, if possible, several weeks after antibiotic therapy is completed to remove a thick cortex of debris which has prevented adequate re-expansion of the lung.

147 The radiograph **147** is from a patient with CF.
i. What concomitant condition does it show?
ii. What is the optimum treatment?

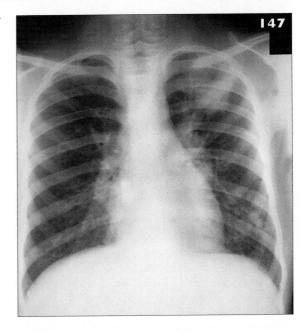

148 This nurse (**148**) is inserting a cleaning agent into an automated bronchoscope washer.
i. Which respiratory condition might she develop?
ii. Which other hospital professionals may develop this?
iii. Which infectious organisms may resist cleaning?

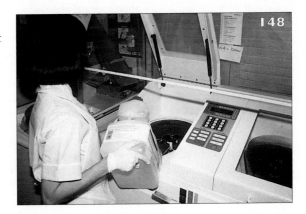

147 i. Allergic bronchopulmonary aspergillosis (ABPA). Changes due to CF are not particularly marked, but the rounded lesions and linear shadows in the left lower lobe are bronchiectatic airways. There is bronchial wall thickening in the upper lobe confluent with an area of consolidation. Although consolidation due to infection is possible, the airway damage and presence of CF make ABPA possible. Classically the shadowing in ABPA is particular and associated with proximal bronchiectasis. The role of *A. fumigatus* in the pathology of CF pulmonary disease is complex. The organism is commonly found in the sputum of 50% of patients and precipitins are associated with increased disease severity, but ABPA may not be present.
ii. The optimum treatment for a definite diagnosis of ABPA in CF is oral corticosteroids. These may need to be long term. A reduction in total IgE levels is the best monitor of a response to treatment.

Antifungal agents (itraconazole) have been used with some success but there are no published long-term controlled trials.

148 i. The cleaning agent is glutaraldehyde which can cause occupational asthma, hence the use of the fume cabinet and the enclosed washer. Glutaraldehyde is an airway sensitizer, and may also cause skin hypersensitivity and irritant effects on the eyes and throat. Onset of symptoms is usually after an interval of months to years from first exposure. Symptoms usually improve after returning home from work each day. If peak flow records are suggestive, specific bronchial provocation tests can be performed with glutaraldehyde to prove the diagnosis. In keeping with the airway-sensitizing effects, there may be a delayed reaction to the inhaled glutaraldehyde on bronchial provocation, although immediate reactions are also seen. Glutaraldehyde is also contained in radiographic film developer, and is used as a fixative in electron microscopy.
ii. Other hospital professionals who may come into contract with substances that cause occupational asthma include radiography technicians, mortuary workers and pathologists (formaldehyde), orthopaedic surgeons and nurses, and dentists (adhesives), those using and handling latex rubber gloves or chlorhexidine, and research workers exposed to laboratory animals.
iii. Glutaraldehyde is the most effective cold sterilizing agent for bronchoscopes. However, very occasional transmission of infection from bronchoscopes may occur with atypical mycobacteria, *Pseudomonas* spp., *Serratia marcescens* and *Bacillus* spp. A 10-min soak in glutaraldehyde should inactivate all viruses and bacteria, whereas 1 hour is recommended for mycobacteria.

149 Patient A has a large left pleural effusion and a single breath gas transfer factor (DL_{CO}) of 55% normal along with a transfer coefficient (K_{CO}) of 90% normal. Patient B with bullous emphysema has a DL_{CO} of 55%.
i. What is the K_{CO}? How is it measured?
ii. Why does the K_{CO} in Patient A correct to near normal?
iii. What is the K_{CO} likely to be in Patient B (i.e. high, normal or low) and why?

150 You are called to see an 81-year-old smoker who 24 hours after an elective cholecystectomy has developed respiratory distress, fever, a cough and a left lower lobe infiltrate on the chest radiograph.
i. What is the most likely causative organism?
He deteriorates and is admitted to intensive care for intubation and assisted ventilation. He responds well to initial treatment but 1 week later deteriorates and develops further bilateral shadowing while still on the ventilator.
ii. What is the most likely cause for this change?

151 These lung function tests (Table) are from a 42-year-old woman with progressive systemic sclerosis. Chest and cardiac examination were normal, as was the chest radiograph. What is the pathogenesis of the abnormality?

Test	Predicted	Range	Result	% predicted
FEV$_1$ (l)	2.10	1.79–2.42	2.10	100
FVC (l)	2.84	2.42–3.26	2.50	88
FEV$_1$ (%)	73	62–84	83	115
FRC (l)	3.00	2.55–3.45	2.42	81
TLC (l)	5.18	4.40–5.96	4.32	83
VC (l)	2.84	2.41–3.26	2.44	86
RV (l)	1.90	1.62–2.19	1.88	99
DL$_{CO}$ (mmol/min/kPa)*	7.23	6.15–8.31	3.48	48
VA(l)	–	–	3.73	–
K$_{CO}$ (mmol/min/kPa/l)**	1.65	1.40–1.90	0.93	56

*DL$_{CO}$ = transfer factor. **K$_{CO}$ = transfer coefficient in DL$_{CO}$/VA.

149 i. The K_{CO} is the single breath gas transfer factor (DL_{CO}) corrected by the alveolar volume (VA). The alveolar volume is measured by an inert gas technique – usually using helium – which is inspired together with the carbon monoxide. As the helium is inert, it will not escape from the lungs and the dilutional decrease measured on expiration will give the alveolar volume, that is, the volume of lung that saw the helium and, therefore, the carbon monoxide, i.e. it is the amount of volume that was available under the circumstances of this test for gas exchange. The DL_{CO} divided by the alveolar volume gives the transfer coefficient, which is the quality of gas exchange in those areas of the lungs that were available to the two gases.
ii. The K_{CO} in Patient A corrects to near normal as the alveolar volume will be essentially that of the non-affected lung, i.e. the right lung.
iii. Here, the K_{CO} is likely to be low. In a patient with emphysema, the DL_{CO} will be low because of poor ventilation and perfusion due to parenchymal damage. The lung volumes, however, will be normal or larger than normal and the alveolar volume will be normal or high. Correcting a low DL_{CO} by a normal or high alveolar volume will give a low K_{CO}. This low K_{CO} (often very low) is characteristic of emphysema.

150 i. Although this is a postoperative pneumonia the most likely causes are the bacteria which are normal commensals in the oropharynx, so *Strep. pneumoniae* and *H. influenzae* would be the most common causes of pneumonia occurring this soon after hospital admission. The antibiotic treatment therefore is as for any other community-acquired pneumonia. At his age, so-called atypical organisms such as mycoplasma, chlamydia, coxiella or legionella would be unlikely.
ii. This time, nosocomial (hospital-acquired) infection is the most likely cause of his lung shadowing although other non-infective causes of lung shadowing such as pulmonary oedema or pulmonary infarction would need to be considered. The most common cause of nosocomial pneumonias are Gram-negative enterobacteria, followed by staphylococci; in the intensive care setting, *P. aeruginosa* is perhaps the most common and most difficult to deal with. The treatment of choice would be with a combination of a third generation cephalosporin which has anti-pseudomonal cover, with or without an aminoglycoside.

151 Reduction of gas transfer is often the earliest abnormality seen on pulmonary function tests in these patients and may be due to pulmonary vascular disease or fibrosing alveolitis. The preservation of lung volumes here suggests pulmonary vascular disease. Small pulmonary arteries and arterioles become narrowed due to marked intimal thickening by myxomatous connective tissue. Sequelae are pulmonary hypertension, which may improve with nifedipine if detected early, and eventually cor pulmonale. Pulmonary vascular effects and fibrotic pulmonary disease can occur independently but often the two pathologies are combined.

152 This 72-year-old woman presented with a 3-month history of malaise, sweats, weight loss, cough and occasional haemoptysis. She developed a pneumonia which was treated with antibiotics but responded poorly and she remained unwell with a low-grade fever. She was mildly anaemic with an ESR of 120 mm in 1 hour and a C-reactive protein (CRP) of 92.

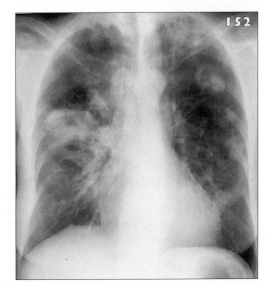

i. What does the radiograph (152) show and what is the differential diagnosis?
ii. How would you make the correct diagnosis?
iii. How would you treat the patient?

153 The peak flow chart shown in 102 was recorded by a patient with exertional breathlessness.
i. Is it consistent with asthma?
ii. How would you proceed?

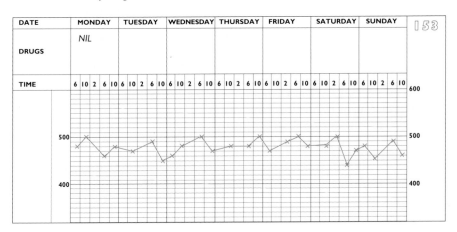

152 i. The chest radiograph shows multiple lesions of variable size throughout both lung fields and most have cavitated. The differential diagnosis includes staphylococcal pneumonia, lymphoma, TB, cavitating squamous cell carcinoma and a vasculitis – most likely Wegener's granulomatosis.

ii. This woman had Wegener's granulomatosis. The diagnosis was made by identifying c-ANCA (anti-cytoplasmic antibodies) in high titre in the peripheral blood. This is positive in more than 90% of cases and negative in classic polyarteritis nodosa and other vasculitidies. The titres of c-ANCA parallel disease activity and returned to normal when the disease is in remission. They can predict reactivation if a rise is detected in patients in remission.

iii. Untreated disease is fatal with a median survival of 5 months. The treatment of Wegener's granulomatosis, whether confined to the lung or more extensive with renal involvement, is with prednisolone and cyclophosphamide. In general, prednisolone is given at 1 mg/kg for 4 weeks and then slowly tailed down to a maintenance of 10 mg/day. Cyclophosphamide commences at 100–150 mg orally, and this is reduced by 25 mg every 2–3 months to 50 mg/day. Treatment is continued for 1 year after remission is achieved. Some 75% of patients achieve a complete remission and a further 15% a partial remission. Serial c-ANCA titres should be performed to predict relapse, which can occur in up to 50% of cases. The prognosis is better for Wegener's that is confined to the lungs.

153 i. No. The diagnosis of asthma is supported if peak flow variations of at least 20% occur between the highest and lowest readings, especially if the lowest readings occur repeatedly in the mornings. Although the chart shows variability it is within normal limits as peak flows in normal patients may vary up to 8%. This variability is due to circadian variation, with airway calibre being narrowest early in the mornings. The causes of this are thought to include diurnal rhythm of cortisol and catecholamine secretion and vagal tone, as well as reduced nocturnal mucociliary clearance.

ii. One non-supportive peak flow chart does not exclude asthma. The symptoms should be reviewed looking for cough, wheeze or breathlessness with diurnal variation. If still suspected, either repeating the PEFR record (stressing the need for measurements during symptomatic periods) or a 2-week trial of inhaled therapy may be performed. If the peak flow chart is undiagnostic a bronchial provocation test can be performed with increasing concentrations of inhaled methacoline. Bronchial hyperreactivity, if present, is strongly suggestive of asthma.

154 These chest radiographs (**154a**, **154b**) were obtained in an asymptomatic 65-year-old retired pipe fitter with a history of substantive exposure to asbestos.
i. What are the primary abnormalities on **154a** and **154b**?
ii. What is the differential diagnosis for these abnormalities?
iii. What is the significance of these findings?

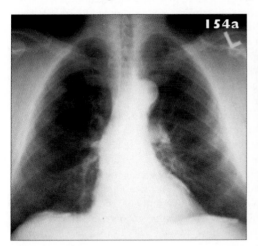
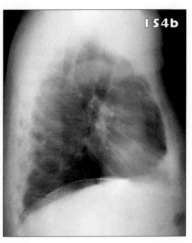

155 i. What is the impact of OSA on mortality?
ii. What is thought to be the risk factor associated with these nocturnal deaths?

156 Shown (**156**) is a swollen right ankle and diffuse macular rash in a young female with CF.
i. What is the diagnosis?
ii. What is the medical treatment and prognosis?

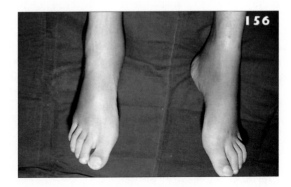

154 i. Bilateral calcified diaphragmatic plaques. Radiologically, uncalcified *en face* plaques appear as indistinct hazy opacities while plaques seen on edge appear as linear or oval pleural thickening. Calcified plaques can appear as irregular densities or dense linear opacifications along the diaphragm or chest wall.

ii. Extrapleural fat in more obese patients and serratus anterior shadows may be confused with uncalcified lateral chest wall plaques but are usually symmetrical bilaterally. A CT scan often resolves this uncertainty. Pleural calcification may develop following traumatic haemothorax, pleural tuberculosis and empyema, but is usually unilateral. Bilateral pleural calcification may occur in scleroderma and following exposure to mica and talc.

iii. Pleural plaques are the most common manifestation of asbestos exposure, eventually developing in 30–50% of exposed workers with a mean latency from first exposure to diagnosis of 20 years. In general, the extent of pleural involvement correlates with the intensity and duration of asbestos exposure. Plaques are bilateral, though not necessarily symmetric, and they are predominantly located on the mid-thoracic chest wall, adjacent to the ribs, in the paravertebral gutters, and over the central diaphragmatic tendon. Historically, pleural plaques have been considered to be a marker of asbestos exposure without any physiological effect. Recently, however, a statistically significant association between pleural plaques and reductions in forced vital capacity has been shown. The interpretation of these studies remains somewhat controversial, however, and isolated pleural plaques without coexistent parenchymal fibrosis likely have little, if any, clinically significant effects on lung function.

155 i. OSA has been demonstrated in several studies to be associated with a greater risk of cardiovascular morbidity and cerebrovascular disease. However, the effect of OSA on mortality has not been well measured. One study has demonstrated that conservatively treated patients, compared to those treated by tracheostomy, had nearly five times the risk of cardiovascular- or stroke-related death. However, other studies have not demonstrated any definite effects and further randomized studies are required to clarify the effects of treatment of OSA on mortality.

ii. The lack of autonomic nervous system control during rapid eye movement sleep may represent a risk period for health and may be a precipitating factor in nocturnal death.

156 i. This illustration shows a diffuse vasculitis involving the skin and synovium. Vasculitis of the skin may also be nodular or purpuric (without thrombocytopenia). It is associated with severe pulmonary disease and chronic *P. aeruginosa* infection. It has been attributed to the overspill into the systemic circulation of immune complexes resulting from the hyperimmune stimulation associated with chronic pulmonary disease.

ii. Medical treatment consists of short-term, high-dose oral steroids. This will usually produce complete resolution. Immunosuppressive agents have been used, but experience is limited.

157 An HIV-positive African patient has a CD4 count of 0.25×10^9/l and auramine-positive organisms in the bronchoscopic lavage fluid.
i. What does the chest radiograph (157) show and what is the likely diagnosis?
ii. How well does this condition respond to therapy?
iii. Can this disease be prevented?

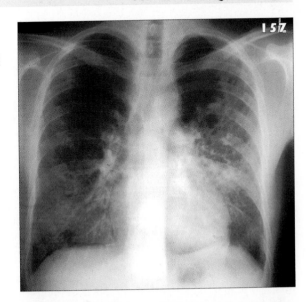

158 This optic fundus (158) of a 40-year-old woman who presented with bilateral facial palsy of sudden onset and also complained of headache and sore eyes.
i. Which multisystem disorder is the likely diagnosis?
ii. What other neurological manifestations occur in this disease?
iii. Comment on the sore eyes.

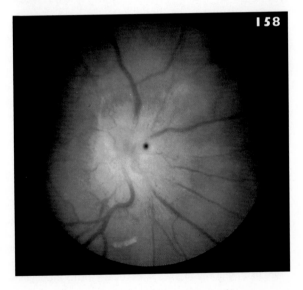

157 i. Patchy shadowing of the right lower zone and the left mid- and upper zones with large nodules on the left. Tuberculosis is the most likely cause given the patient's ethnic origin and the relatively high CD4 lymphocyte count.
ii. Tuberculosis in HIV-infected individuals should be with isoniazid, rifampicin, pyrazinamide, and ethambutol for an initial phase of 2 months followed by a second phase of isoniazid and rifampicin for 4 months. When anti-retroviral therapy with non-nucleoside reverse transcriptase inhibitors and anti-proteases is concurrently administered, rifampicin should be replaced by rifabutin and doses may need to be adjusted. If there is slow response to treatment, the second phase of treatment should be prolonged to 7 months. If drug resistance is demonstrated to first-line therapy, then second line agents such as cycloserine, ethionamide, levofloxacin, p-aminosalicylic acid, streptomycin, kanamycin/amikacin, moxifloxacin, or capreomycin may need to be considered for a 12 month period.
iii. Primary chemoprophylaxis with isoniazid given for 12 months will benefit certain HIV-positive patients namely: tuberculin-positive (>4 mm Mantoux reaction) individuals from countries or groups (e.g. intravenous drug users) with a prevalence of tuberculosis greater than 10%. Tuberculin-negative patients from these areas who show anergy on skin testing with other antigens will also benefit from primary isoniazid prophylaxis. Secondary prophylaxis (long-term therapy with isoniazid following successful treatment of tuberculosis) is recommended by the British and American Thoracic Societies.

158 i. This woman has raised intracranial pressure with papilloedema from neurosarcoidosis which has caused her facial palsies. She has meningeal involvement with increased CSF pressure, a mild lymphocytic pleocytosis and increased protein but without meningeal symptoms. Papilloedema can also be caused by direct involvement of the optic nerve as well as by space-occupying masses of sarcoid tissue. Facial paresis, either unilateral or bilateral is the most common CNS manifestation.
ii. Involvement of the occulomotor, trochlear and abducens nerves are rare. Trigeminal sensory loss, sensorineural hearing loss and vertigo are fairly common. The most common abnormality of the peripheral nerves is a symmetrical peripheral neuropathy, although scattered patchy sensory neuropathies are also common. Motor involvement is less common and should not be confused with chronic sarcoid myopathy.
iii. About 25% of patients have some form of eye involvement. Sarcoid involvement of the lacrimal and salivary glands is very common and causes a sicca syndrome with dry mouth and sore, gritty eyes which may mimic Sjögren's syndrome. Artificial tears and saliva are useful. Anterior uveitis is the most frequent ocular finding which occurs more in commonly in blacks, the acute form (iridocyclitis) causing a painful, red eye with photophobia and blurred vision. Posterior uveitis occurs more commonly in whites and can cause visual loss from neovascularization. Fluorescein angiography is useful for demonstrating sarcoid retinitis. A slit lamp examination should be done in all patients with sarcoidosis and a Schirmer's test to assess lacrimation.

159 i. Name the systemic disease that most likely accounts for the findings seen in **159a** and **159b**.
ii. Name six pleuropulmonary manifestations of this disease.
iii. Characterize the expecting findings from a thoracentesis of a pleural effusion that has occurred as a result of this disease.

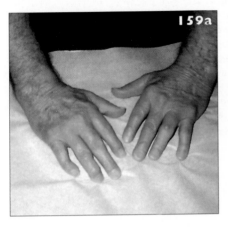

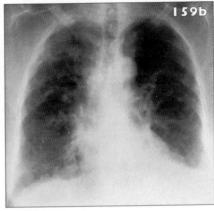

160 i. What is the differential diagnosis of daytime hypersomnolence?
ii. How would the history help in differentiating these diagnoses?

161 When this patient (**161**), who has a CD4 lymphocyte count of $0.15 \times 10^9/l$, became ill several weeks previously with malaise and subcutaneous swellings, lymphadenopathy was the primary finding. Investigations for mycobacteria were negative. He now complains of dyspnoea of 2 days' duration and is hypoxic at rest.
i. What is the probable cause of his respiratory symptoms?
ii. List the possible causes of the mediastinal widening. How may the cause be confirmed?

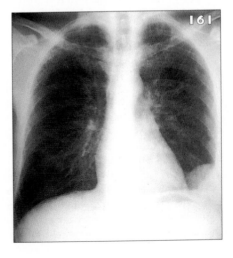

159 i. Rheumatoid arthritis is the most likely diagnosis. The hands (**159a**) depict ulnar deviation, characteristic in this disorder. The chest radiograph (**159b**) findings include the presence of pleural effusions and interstitial fibrosis. The basal and peripheral distribution of the shadowing is characteristic of fibrosing alveolitis; and the lung parenchymal pathology and management is identical to that for cryptogenic fibrosing alveolitis (CFA).

ii. The pleuropulmonary manifestations of rheumatoid arthritis include pleural effusions, diffuse interstitial pneumonitis and fibrosis, necrobiotic rheumatoid nodules, Caplan's syndrome (rheumatoid pneumoconiosis), obliterative bronchiolitis and pulmonary vasculitis. Pleural disease is the most common intrathoracic manifestation – vasculitis affecting the pulmonary vasculature is exceptionally rare.

iii. Pleural fluid of patients with rheumatoid arthritis is characteristically exudative (protein >30 g/l), and the cellular component is predominantly lymphocytic. The glucose content may be exceedingly low (e.g. <30 mg/dl) even in the absence of infection. Rheumatoid factor titres can be very high.

160 i. The differential diagnosis includes: intrinsic causes such as obstructive sleep apnoea, narcolepsy, idiopathic hypersomnia, post-traumatic hypersomnia, periodic movements of the legs/restless sleep and extrinsic causes such as poor 'sleep hygiene', insufficient sleep, hypnotic/sedative abuse and alcohol abuse.

ii. In obstructive sleep apnoea, there is a history of steady progression of symptoms, often over many years. Initially there is snoring which becomes more pronounced, turning into periods of apnoea and restlessness which becomes more numerous and prolonged. This is noted by the partner rather than the patient. It develops fully by middle age, is more common in men and is associated with weight gain, increased alcohol intake and night sedation. In classical narcolepsy there is a history of cataplexy and at least one of the other three symptoms: sleepiness, sleep paralysis and hypnagogic hallucinations. In periodic leg movement there is an irresistible urge to move the legs, causing insomnia and sleep disruption. In post-traumatic hypersomnia, there is a history of preceding head injury, stroke or brain surgery .

161 i. Any acute respiratory illness such as this should be considered to be PCP until proven otherwise. The differential diagnosis is bacterial pneumonia, tuberculosis, histoplasmosis (in endemic areas) and pulmonary oedema due to left ventricular failure. Infections with atypical mycobacteria, *C. neoformans* and cytomegalovirus are less likely given that the CD4 count is above 0.1×10^9/l. PCP does not explain the pleural shadow.

ii. Given his history of recent onset generalized lymphadenopathy, the pleural pathology is likely to be caused by the same pathology, and include mycobacterial infection, lymphoma, Kaposi's sarcoma and cryptococcal infection. The diagnosis in this patient (lymphoma) would be confirmed by lymph-node biopsy from one of the subcutaneous lesions. If there are no suitable subcutaneous nodes, the cause in this case may be found by biopsying the pleural mass. Lymphoma might also be found on bone marrow biopsy although the diagnostic yield of this procedure is low.

162 Shown in **162a** is the radiograph of a previously fit 42-year-old woman who was seen in the emergency department with a 36-hour history of a flu-like illness and increasing respiratory compromise. Her fingers and nailbeds shortly after admission to intensive care are shown in **162b**.
i. What would be the factors that you would take into consideration when deciding whether to admit this patient with pneumonia to the intensive therapy unit?
ii. Which complications are suggested by **162b**?

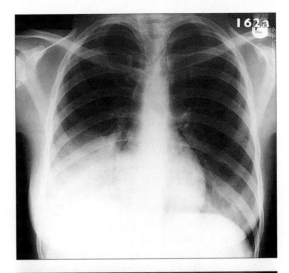

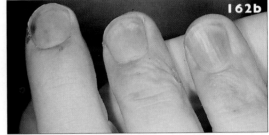

163 A previously healthy athletic 32-year-old male has worked in this environment (**163**) for 3 years. Over the past several months he has experienced worsening nocturnal chest tightness and wheezing.
i. What is the differential diagnosis?
ii. What are risk factors for occupational asthma?
iii. What is the likely antigen in this case?
iv. Should the patient be advised to seek other work? Why?

162 i. The chest radiograph shows a right lower lobe consolidation and in a previously fit 42-year-old, the most likely organism is a pneumococcus. The following factors have been shown to be independently associated with mortality: age >50 years, any of five coexisting illnesses (neoplastic disease; congestive heart failure; cerebrovascular disease; renal disease; liver disease) and any of five physical examination findings (altered mental status; pulse ≥125 beats per minute; respiratory rate ≥30 per minute; systolic blood pressure <90 mmHg [12 kPa]; and temperature <35°C [95°F] or ≥40°C [104°F]).

The following findings on investigation are also important in determining the severity: arterial pH <7.35; blood urea nitrogen ≥30 mg/dl (11 mmol/l); sodium <130 mmol/l (130 mEq/l); glucose ≥250 mg/dl (14 mmol/l); haematocrit <30%; PaO_2 <60 mmHg (8kPa); pleural effusion.

A prospective study analysing the ATS guidelines on community-acquired pneumonia (1993) revealed that the presence of two out of three baseline criteria (systolic BP <90mmHg [12 kPa]; multilobar involvement; PaO_2/F_1O_2 <250) and one out of two criteria assessed during the course of the illness (requirement for mechanical ventilation; requirement for vasopressors >4 h [septic shock]) were strong predictors for severe pneumonia and admission to the intensive care unit.

ii. The photograph of the fingers/nailbeds shows peripheral cyanosis and a distal vascular infarct. Although the limb peripheries may be cold and poorly perfused the global systemic vascular resistance is frequently low, emphasizing the marked variation in regional vascular tone that typifies sepsis. While it is important to ensure that the intravascular volume is adequate and some colloid infusion may be necessary, this should neither be excessive nor administered too rapidly if deterioration in pulmonary gas exchange and marked tissue oedema are to be avoided. The infarct may be a thrombotic manifestation of disseminated intravascular coagulation (DIC) a frequent complication of severe pneumococcal pneumonia.

163 i. Bronchial hyperreactivity and airflow limitation associated with occupational asthma, non-occupational asthma, gastro-oesophageal reflux, and posterior nasal drip may present with nocturnal chest tightness and wheezing. Acute extrinsic allergic alveolitis (or hypersensitivity pneumonitis) should be considered but usually presents with prominent constitutional symptoms of fever, chills and myalgias in addition to cough, dyspnoea and chest tightness.

ii. More than 200 agents have been implicated in occupational asthma. High-molecular weight sensitizers (i.e. >1000 kDa) such as proteins and polysaccharides typically produce an immediate asthmatic reaction through IgE-mediated mechanisms. Atopy and smoking are risk factors. Low-molecular weight compounds (<1000 kDa) are associated with an isolated late asthmatic response occurring 4 to 12 h after exposure. A biphasic response with early and late reductions in expiratory flow with intervening recovery or a prolonged early response may also occur. Non-atopic individuals are affected more commonly.

iii. Western red cedar (*Thuja plicata*) is widely used for shakes, shingles and lumber in North America. Plicatic acid (440 kDa) is the primary sensitizer in red cedar asthma. Nocturnal cough, wheeze and chest tightness are characteristic presenting features.

iv. Eliminating exposure to the antigen is the primary therapy for occupational asthma. Asthma persists in 60% of affected workers, even after leaving the industry.

164 i. What medications can be used to treat OSA?
ii. Patients with OSA should have what additional abnormality before being considered candidates for progestational agents?

165 This high-resolution CT scan (165) of a 30-year-old man with sarcoidosis showing a reticulonodular pattern.
i. What is the advantage of HRCT over conventional CT?
ii. Describe the HRCT findings in sarcoidosis.
iii. When would you do a HRCT?

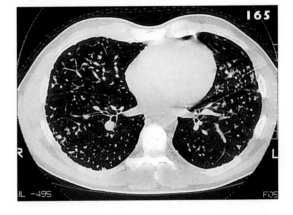

166 A 25-year-old Asian Indian man presents with fevers, cough and weight loss over 3 months; 166b was taken four months after 166a.
i. What is the likely diagnosis?
ii. Enumerate the abnormalities on the chest radiographs.
iii. How quickly and to what extent will these changes improve with treatment?

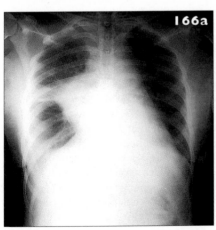

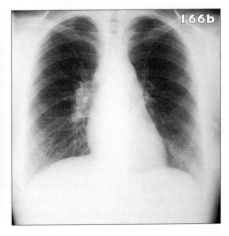

164–166: Answers

164 i. The role of drugs in the management of OSA is limited. Protriptyline, a tricyclic antidepressant, has been shown to reduce sleepiness, improve nocturnal oxygenation and decrease apnoea frequency in patients with OSA by reducing the proportion of total sleep time spent in REM. Since apnoeas tend to be more frequent and severe during REM sleep, this tends to improve oxygenation and the frequency of sleep-disordered breathing. It has also been proposed that protriptyline augments the activity of upper airway dilator muscles. The clinical utility of protriptyline remains small.
ii. Progestational agents have no role in the treatment of eucapnic patients with OSA. They may have a role in treating hypercapnic patients with sleep-disordered breathing, in particular those with obesity hypoventilation syndrome, though this may be due to its effects on alveolar hypoventilation rather than sleep-disordered breathing. A beneficial effect in reducing sleep-disordered breathing (either central or obstructive) in hypercapnic individuals has not been demonstrated specifically.

165 i. HRCT gives outstanding definition of the lung parenchyma by taking rapid thin slices (1–2 mm). Conventional CT takes 8–10-mm slices and is therefore less useful for small nodules and more subtle abnormalities.
ii. The characteristic parenchymal abnormalities of sarcoidosis are small nodular densities along the lymphatics, particularly the bronchovascular bundles and interlobular septae. Subpleural nodules are also very common. A hazy ground-glass appearance (alveolar filling), although uncommon, is usually associated with severe dyspnoea and hypoxia. Other features seen include linear opacities, end-stage fibrosis and cysts, traction bronchiectasis and honey-comb lung.
iii. Sometimes with more patchy and focal sarcoidosis HRCT can be useful to guide the bronchoscopist performing transbronchial biopsies. HRCT may show severe diffuse alveolar disease not obvious on chest radiography, but it has a limited role. It cannot be recommended as a routine screening tool or to assess response to treatment.

166 i. Tuberculosis is the likely diagnosis.
ii. The abnormalities include a large right hilar mass. There is opacification of the right upper lobe probably due to bronchial narrowing by the hilar nodal mass. There is also cardiomegaly, possibly due to pericardial effusion.
iii. The second radiograph (**166b**) was taken 2 months after starting standard four-drug anti-tuberculous chemotherapy and shows significant resolution with only residual right hilar shadowing. Improvement had started after 1 month. In monitoring for the effects of TB treatment lack of radiographic improvement by 2 months may mean either the changes are chronic or there is a problem with therapy, usually due to non-compliance. However, the changes seen on the chest radiograph are not a good predictor of response to treatment. Radiographic improvement is usually complete by 6 months, although some patients continue to improve for 12 months. However, the most important sign of improvement is sputum smears and culture becoming negative; failure here means the disease has not been eradicated.

144

167 An elderly woman complained of shortness of breath on exertion but was otherwise in good health.

i. What abnormalities are evident on the chest radiograph (**167a**) and CT film (**167b**) and what is the likely diagnosis?

ii. What further diagnostic tests are likely to be of value?

iii. What risks are associated with this condition?

iv. What management is advisable and what specific risks should be mentioned to the patient?

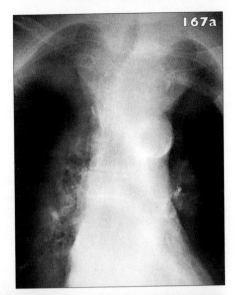

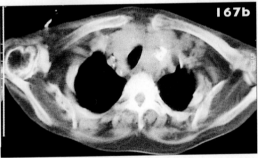

168 Describe the important aspects of good sleep hygiene.

169 A 60-year-old man complained of increasing back and left-sided chest pain for approximately 6 months. What does the scan (**169**) show and how would you confirm the diagnosis?

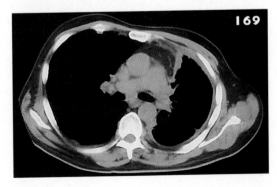

145

167 i. There is an upper mediastinal mass which exhibits areas of calcification (poorly seen on radiograph). The trachea is markedly deviated. The features are those of a retrosternal thyroid goitre.

ii. None. Radio-iodine scanning is frequently performed but is almost never of value as the goitre will not take up the iodine. Bronchoscopy is non-contributory. Needle biopsy might reveal a thyroid carcinoma but this would be unlikely to exhibit calcification and a negative core would not exclude this diagnosis.

iii. Any airway obstruction can worsen with deteriorating exercise tolerance. Haemorrhage can occur into the gland causing acute enlargement and an airway emergency. Malignant degeneration has been reported very rarely.

iv. Subtotal thyroidectomy is indicated to relieve airway compression. This is usually possible through a collar incision. The chief hazards are damage to the recurrent laryngeal nerves and transient postoperative hypocalcaemia from parathyroid injury. Very occasionally, tracheomalacia may exist which results in instability of the tracheal wall postoperatively and difficulty with respiration.

168 Diagnosing and treating sleep problems requires knowledge of good sleep hygiene. Recommendations can be divided into broad categories:

- Encouraging normal homeostatic and circadian rhythms. The patient should maintain regular bedtime and arising times. Naps should generally be avoided but if necessary be limited to 20 minutes . Daily exercise in the morning or afternoon is helpful. A warm bath 20–30 minutes before retiring can promote sleep.
- Maintaining a conducive sleep setting. The bedroom should be dark, quiet, well-ventilated and at a comfortable temperature. The mattress and pillows should be comfortable. The bedroom should be only used for sleep and sex, not for other activities which require prolonged arousal. Avoid heavy snacking or drinking just before bedtime.
- Avoiding drugs that interfere with sleep. Tobacco, caffeine, and alcohol should be avoided within several hours of sleep.

169 Malignant pleural mesothelioma without effusion. The scan (**169**) shows gross irregular pleural thickening, with characteristic constriction of that hemithorax. Approximately 30% of malignant pleural mesotheliomas present as either diffuse pleural thickening or as a localized pleural mass without significant effusion. Thoracoscopy is impossible in these cases as the pleural cavity is often obliterated. The diagnosis can usually be confirmed by CT-guided needle biopsy. Thoracotomy should be avoided. Pain is often severe and intractable and neurolytic procedures, such as cervical cordotomy, may be necessary for its control.

Most patients with mesothelioma recall significant exposure to asbestos. The greater the exposure the higher the chance of developing this complication. About 30% of cases have no history of any contact with asbestos, confirming that this tumour has other causes – as yet not known. Other inorganic fibres such as tremolite, which occurs naturally in the soil in some countries (for example Cyprus), can also cause mesothelioma.

170 Shown is a high-power photomicrograph (170) of the Gram stain of sputum expectorated by a 19-year-old man with symptoms of fever, rigors and a productive cough of 2 days' duration. He has experienced four episodes of radiographically documented pneumonia and numerous episodes of acute otitis media and sinusitis in the past.

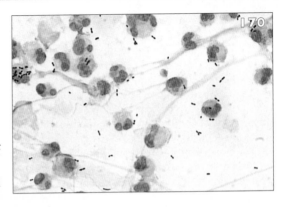

i. What does the Gram stain show?
ii. What is the most likely diagnosis?
iii. What additional the diagnostic considerations are raised by this clinical presentation?

171 A patient presents with a 2-week history of progressive weakness of the arms and shoulders, difficulty in swallowing and a dry mouth. The chest radiograph (171) shows a mass in the right paratracheal region.
i. What is the likely diagnosis of this presentation?
ii. How would you make the diagnosis?
iii. How would you treat the patient?

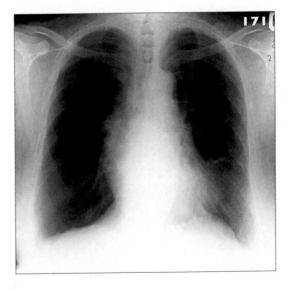

170 i. The sputum Gram stain (170) shows numerous polymorphonuclear leukocytes, strands of mucus, and many Gram-positive, lancet-shaped diplococci. Refractile capsules are evident on many of the bacteria.

ii. This young patient has an acute pneumococcal pneumonia and has suffered numerous recurrent respiratory infections.

iii. Most patients with recurrent respiratory infections have no identifiable host defect. However, recurrent pneumonias in the same lobe or segment should suggest an anatomical abnormality. When multiple sites have been involved, disorders of mucociliary clearance such as cystic fibrosis or the ciliary dyskinesia syndrome (Kartagener's syndrome) are important considerations. Recurrent infections with encapsulated organisms such as the pneumococcus are consistent with a defect in opsonization (e.g. complement, IgG or IgG subtype deficiencies). Deficiencies of complement components are rare and are best managed by immunization and by early treatment of infectious complications. Immunoglobulin deficiencies also can be primary (inherited), or acquired due to acquired B-cell disorders, medications or intercurrent illnesses. IgA is heavily concentrated in mucosal secretions where it inhibits bacterial adherence. Although selective IgA deficiency is common, it rarely results in serious respiratory infection unless other deficiencies coexist. IgG deficiency (either generalized or restricted to subclasses IgG1 and IgG3) predisposes to more frequent and to more severe respiratory infections. Intravenous immunoglobulin replacement may be helpful.

171 i. The chest radiograph (171) shows a perihilar mass likely due to a malignant tumour. The patient has a myopathy and the difficulty in swallowing and dry mouth is suggestive of the Lambert–Eaton syndrome (LEMS). The tendon reflexes will be absent, but will become present after repetitive forced contraction of the relevant muscle group. Repeated short-term use of muscle groups will also increase their strength temporarily. An EMG will show post-tetanic potentiation.

ii. LEMS is a para-malignant syndrome strongly associated with small-cell lung cancer. It may precede the clinical appearance of a tumour by many months. The diagnosis is made by the diagnosis of SCLC, the neurological physical signs and the response of the tendon jerks to muscle activity and the characteristic findings on EMG.

iii. Treatment is both specifically aimed at the LEMS and also, more generally, at the primary tumour.

Specific treatment for LEMS is high dose corticosteroids, e.g. prednisolone 60 mg daily, and 3–4 mg/day aminopyridine, which is an anti-cholinergic antagonist. Resolution of the tumour will provide the greatest symptomatic benefit and the best chance of remission. The syndrome can show considerable improvement with resolution of the primary tumour, but recurrence of the syndrome usually heralds relapse.

172 A patient presents with bilateral hilar lymphadenopathy and parenchymal infiltrates. A diagnosis of sarcoidosis is made. There is no other active organ involvement. What is the role if any of oral corticosteroids (OCS) in this case?

173 Fever, cough and dyspnoea were the presenting features of this man's illness (173a). His CD4+ lymphocyte count is 0.08×10^9/l.
i. Describe the cytological finding in the bronchoalveolar lavage (BAL) specimen (173b) and give the diagnosis of his condition.
ii. What is a more common presentation of disease caused by this agent?
iii. Discuss the management of this condition and any potential complications.

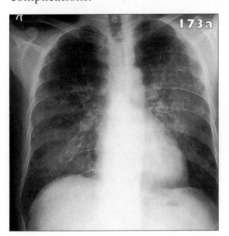

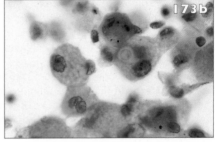

174 This patient whose upper trachea is shown (174) underwent tracheostomy for prolonged mechanical ventilation 6 months previously. Breathlessness is now occurring.
i. What has occurred?
ii. How is this managed?

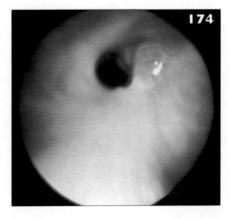

172 i. A recent study by the British Thoracic Society has helped to clarify the role of OCS in pulmonary involvement by sarcoidosis. If the symptoms and functional measurements are deteriorating, then OCS should be commenced at a dose of 40 mg per day for 1 month, then slowly reduced. The majority of such patients will improve on therapy, although relapse is common on reducing or stopping the steroids. If the condition remains stable when untreated, the addition of OCS for at least 18 months will produce small improvements in the radiographic and functional measurements compared with no treatment, but the advantage of treating stable disease is small and will inevitably be associated with some steroid-related side effects. It is still not clear whether OCS affect the long-term outcome in sarcoidosis but it seems reasonable to treat patients whose condition is deteriorating during the first 6 months of the clinical course.

173 i. This encapsulated intracellular yeast is typical of *Cryptococcus neoformans*. This can be confirmed by antigen testing of the blood and culture of blood and BAL fluid. Other yeasts that cause lung disease include *Candida* sp. and *Histoplasma capsulatum*, but these can be distinguished on morphology and culture.
ii. A sub-acute meningitis would be the most common presentation of illness caused by this organism in AIDS.
iii. Cryptococcal infection is treated with intravenous amphotericin B, sometimes with the addition of flucytosine, in more severe cases. Alternatively, fluconazole (orally or intravenously) is used for less severe cases. High-dose treatment is given for 4–6 weeks, followed by long-term secondary prophylaxis – usually with oral fluconazole. Treatment response is usually monitored by clinical parameters and falling cryptococcal antigen titres. Respiratory disease may lead to respiratory failure and meningitis can progress to widespread involvement of the brain (cryptococcomas) and hydrocephalus.

174 i. A post-tracheostomy tracheal stricture.
ii. Definitive management in symptomatic patients is surgical resection of the involved tracheal segment. The maximum length of trachea that can be resected is 50%, i.e. about 5–6 cm. In cases where there is acute breathlessness, temporizing measures include YAG laser resection to widen the orifice. Laser treatment may be particularly useful in preventing surgery if the patient is still recovering from their initial illness. Best results are obtained when the stricture is primarily mucosal and does not have extensive fibrosis of the tracheal wall. In the unusual case of a long segment of stenosis, tracheal stenting may be used. Non-metal stents are deployed so that they may be removed at a later date. Prolonged stenting occasionally causes a stricture usually more than a year after placement. With the increasing use of percutaneous tracheostomy performed in intensive care units this complication of tracheostomy may decline.

175 Pleural biopsies from two patients with large pleural effusions are shown in **175a** and **175b**. The reported differential diagnosis for both was adenocarcinoma and mesothelioma.
i. How can the two be differentiated?
ii. Why is it important to make this distinction?
iii. Should primary sites be looked for in cases of metastatic pleural adenocarcinoma?

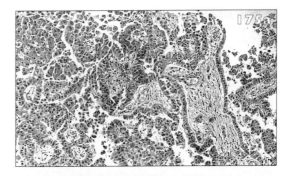

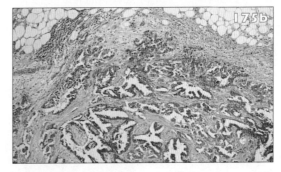

176 This is the chest radiograph (**176a**) of a 65-year-old man, a 40 pack year smoker.
i. What is the likely diagnosis?
ii. What investigations are necessary to stage the patient?
iii. What is the treatment of choice?

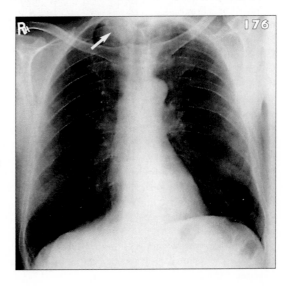

175 & 176: Answers

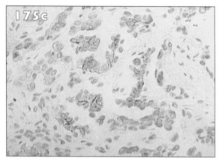

175 i. 175b shows papillary and glandular structures and 175a also shows glandular structures, making distinction between the two difficult. 175b was also stained for AUA 1 (175c) and was positive, which is specific for adenocarcinoma. Staining of the other biopsy (175a) was negative suggesting mesothelioma. Positive confirmation of mesothelioma is more difficult and requires the use of electron microscopy.

ii. Confirmation of a diagnosis of mesothelioma is very important for patients with documented asbestos exposure who wish to pursue compensation claims.

iii. No survival advantage has been shown in pursuing the primary site of adenocarcinomas in these patients. The most common site is the lung itself, followed by breast and gastrointestinal tumours.

176 i. The lesion in the right apex has a 95% chance of being a primary carcinoma of the bronchus in a man of this age and smoking history. The irregular margins seen first on CT (176b) make a malignant lesion probable. Benign lesions would be

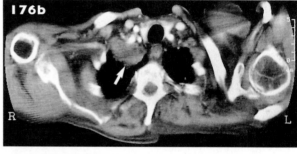

smoother as would a solitary metastasis.

ii. The lesion ideally should be removed. A fine-needle aspiration is not useful as it will either confirm what one suspects, and is unlikely to be diagnostic if the lesion is benign. A pneumothorax following a needle biopsy may 'soil' the pleura and increase the risk of postoperative infection. A CT scan of the thorax and upper abdomen is the investigation of choice. Nodal enlargement in the mediastinum needs to be excluded. If present, mediastinoscopy should be performed to confirm or exclude metastatic nodal spread. The CT will also confirm whether the lesion is solitary. There is no benefit in performing a fibre-optic bronchoscopy as it is unlikely to yield a diagnosis or any new information.

iii. The treatment of choice is a thoracotomy. A frozen section of the lesion is mandatory as benign disease requires no more than enucleation or a segmental resection. A primary tumour should be removed by lobectomy. If lung function is poor, then segmentectomy can be performed, but the 5-year survival is not as good as for lobectomy, which is in the region of 50–70% for a stage I lesion, i.e. solitary with no hilar or mediastinal nodal involvement.

177 A 34-year-old woman in otherwise excellent health presented with a non-specific cough. Chest film (**177a**) and CT scan (**177b**) demonstrated a cystic lesion in the mediastinum.

i. What is your differential diagnosis?

ii. What treatment is indicated and why?

iii. What specific difficulties may surgery present?

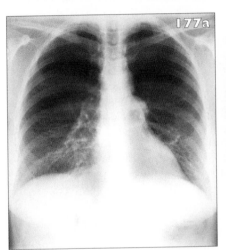

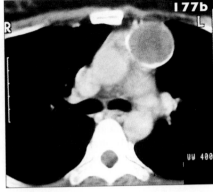

178 **i.** How does the small hole in the nebulizer base allow jet nebulizing to occur (**178a, 178b**)?

ii. What parameters of flow rate and nebulizer volume are most effective?

iii. What percentage of nebulized solution will be deposited in the lungs?

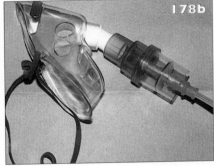

177 i. This lesion is located in the anterior compartment. It is fluid-filled and has a thick, calcified wall suggesting a benign origin. The most likely possibility is, therefore, a dermoid cyst. A thymic cyst would usually have a much thinner wall. In the relevant countries, echinococcus would have to be considered. Pleuropericardial cysts arise posterior to the anterior edge of the pericardium.

ii. The likely benign nature would suggest that a policy of observation would be satisfactory in the elderly or infirm. There exists, however, the concern that the true diagnosis is uncertain unless the lesion is excised. There are also reports of these medastinal cysts eroding into a great vessel or becoming infected and rupturing into the pericardium. In most cases it is usual to advise excision of the lesion.

Note : In this case the lesion is cystic and a benign germ cell cyst is suspected. Had the lesion been solid, a malignant germ cell lesion would have to be considered, particularly in young males. Alpha-fetoprotein and beta-HCG should be measured. Elevated levels are encountered in all non-seminomatous-type tumours and in about 10% of mediastinal seminomas. Excision or biopsy is undertaken in this situation depending upon resectability. Chemotherapy should be given and radiotherapy to the mediastinum is also indicated for seminomas.

iii. Adhesions can be dense around dermoid cysts and in extreme cases it may be necessary to excise a portion of the cyst and 'deroof' it rather than excise the whole lesion.

178 i. As the driving gas (either oxygen or compressed air) enters the hole a jet is created. Liquid contained in the base of the nebulizer is drawn upward in a funnel towards the jet and drawn into it by the Bernoulli effect. As the jet hits the baffles above it (**178b**), larger particles are removed, their size depending on the characteristics of the baffles. Deposition of particles >10 µm may occur in the oropharynx, those of 5–10 µm in the tracheobronchial tree, and those of 2–5 µm reach the alveoli. Factors other than particle size affect pattern of deposition, including the effect of airway humidity, evaporation, and particle agglomeration.

ii. Approximately 1 ml of solution is usually left on the baffles or in the well of the nebulizer at the end of a treatment. As solvent evaporates during nebulization there is a proportionately high amount of active drug in this residual fluid. Some 4 ml of solution is needed to counteract this problem, to allow the majority of the active drug to be nebulized. The recommended flow rate is 6–8 l/min, which allows high nebulizer output and generates suitably sized respirable particles.

iii. About 12% of the drug will reach the lung, making this mode of delivery no more efficient than metered dose-aerosols, spacers or powders.

179 A woman complained of mild back ache. Her radiographs (**179a, 179b**) and CT (**179c**) were as shown.
i. What abnormality is present and what is the differential diagnosis?
ii. What further investigation may be helpful?

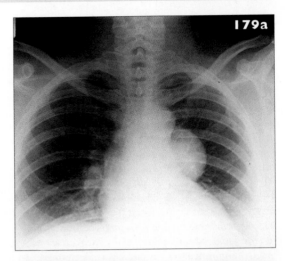

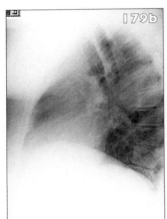

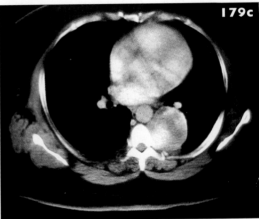

180 i. What are the presenting symptoms of narcolepsy?
ii. Which tests are useful in diagnosing narcolepsy?

179 i. A large mass is present in the left paravertebral sulcus adjacent to the vertebral column and rib heads. This position implies that the lesion is almost certainly a neurogenic tumour (**179a–c**). The differential most likely lies, therefore, between a neurilemmoma (schwannoma), neurofibroma or sarcoma (possibly in association with Von Recklinghausen's disease), ganglionoma and neuroblastoma. The simple neurilemmoma is much the most probable. Rarer possibilities in this site are: phaeochromocytoma, fibrosarcoma, lymphoma and mesenchymal tumours.
ii. It is important to establish whether a neural tumour extends into the vertebral canal and MRI may supplement CT scanning in determining this issue. An exterior mass can be excised at thoracotomy alone whereas a mass entering the vertebral foramen will require a combined approach with a neurosurgical team.

180 i. Unwanted episodes of sleep, daytime drowsiness, hypnagogic hallucinations, disturbed nocturnal sleep, cataplexy, and sleep paralysis are common symptoms of narcolepsy. Unwanted episodes of sleep can occur several times a day and in a variety of situations. Narcoleptics usually awaken refreshed from these episodes which can last from minutes to over one hour. Sleep onset can be accompanied by visual or auditory hypnagogic hallucinations. Cataplexy refers to an abrupt decrease in muscle tone which is often elicited by emotion. Cataplectic attacks can vary from a complete loss of muscle tone to a brief weakness of a particular muscle group. Sleep paralysis occurs at sleep onset or upon awakening. Patients find themselves unable to move, speak or open their eyes and often experience hallucinations. These episodes are usually less than 10 minutes in duration. Laser palatoplexy, which stiffens the uvula by inducing scar tissue, is probably as effective.
ii. HLA typing and Multiple Sleep Latency Testing (MSLT) are useful in the diagnosis of narcolepsy. An association between the major histocompatibility complex class II antigens DQw6 and Drw15 and narcolepsy has been established. DQw6 is the best current genetic marker and most, but not all, narcoleptics carry it. The MSLT consists of five or six scheduled naps during which the subject is monitored polygraphically in a dark, quiet bedroom. It is designed to measure physiological sleep tendencies in the absence of stimulating factors. Sleep latency and REM latency are measured. Mean sleep latencies less than 8 minutes are considered abnormal and consistent with excessive somnolence. REM sleep that occurs within 15 minutes of sleep onset is considered a sleep onset REM period. The presence of two or more sleep onset REM periods following a nocturnal polysomnogram which demonstrates normal sleep and the absence of other sleep disorders, supports the diagnosis of narcolepsy.

181 This chest radiograph (181) is from a 51-year-old man from south-east Asia with dyspnoea and leg swelling. He was jaundiced and had jugular venous distension and ascites on physical examination.
i. What are the radiographic findings?
ii. What infection could account for both the clinical and radiographic abnormalities?
iii. How can this diagnosis be established?
iv. How is it treated?

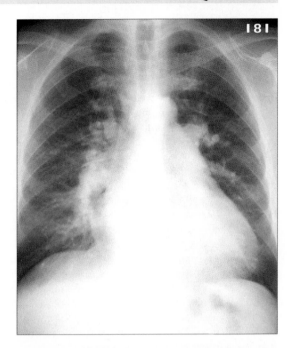

182 The chest radiograph (182) is from a 32-year-old female presenting with exertional dyspnoea.
i. What symptoms, physical findings and lung function abnormalities would you look for to confirm a diagnosis of idiopathic pulmonary fibrosis (IPF) associated with this disorder?
ii. Is there an association between this disorder and lung cancer?

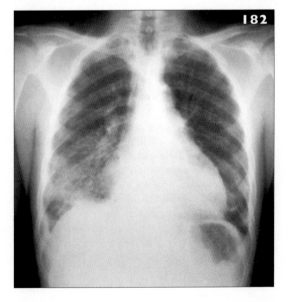

181 i. The chest radiograph (**181**) shows enlargement of the pulmonary arteries, suggesting pulmonary hypertension.

ii. The combination of pulmonary hypertension and hepatic failure should suggest the diagnosis of schistosomiasis when the patients originate from areas in which this infection occurs. Schistosomiasis is caused by one of the blood flukes, *Schistosoma mansoni, S. japonica* or *S. haematobia,* which are endemic to tropical areas with an appropriate intermediate host population of freshwater snails. Free-swimming cercariae penetrate human skin, then become schistosomulae which migrate through the lungs to mature in specific mesenteric venous plexuses. Pulmonary manifestations including cough, wheezing, and infiltrates can accompany the systemic symptoms of 'Katayama Fever' during the migration of schistosomulae through the lungs in acute schistosomiasis. Eggs produced by the mature flukes are carried downstream from the mesentery and lodge in the liver. A massive and inappropriate granulomatous inflammatory response to the schistosomal eggs then results in tissue injury and fibrosis. The liver eventually becomes cirrhotic and portosystemic collateral channels permit embolic eggs to reach the lungs where a similar inflammatory response ensues. The end result is pulmonary hypertension and cor pulmonale.

iii. The diagnosis of schistosomiasis is based on the identification of eggs in the stool or urine of patients having a compatible clinical presentation and a history of travel or residence in an endemic area (parts of South America, the Caribbean, Africa, and the Middle and Far East).

iv. Treatment with praziquantel is effective in preventing further egg production but may not improve established lesions.

182 i. Cough and dyspnoea on exertion are the most common presenting symptoms in patients with IPF. Up to one-half of patients have systemic complaints such as fever, fatigue, weight loss, myalgias or arthralgias. Fine 'Velcro' crackles may be heard late in inspiration, particularly at the bases. Early in the disease auscultation of the chest may be normal. Clubbing of the fingers and toes may occur. Cyanosis and signs of pulmonary hypertension, with or without cor pulmonale, are late findings.

Pulmonary function abnormalities include a reduction in lung volumes, often with the vital capacity being reduced out of proportion to the other volumes. Spirometry may be normal in the early stages. Single breath diffusing capacity for carbon monoxide (DL_{CO}) is reduced. In the later stages of the disease, arterial blood gas tension may show resting hypoxaemia. In a young female, an underlying connective tissue disease such as SLE or rheumatoid arthritis should be suspected.

ii. There is an increased incidence of lung cancer in patients with idiopathic pulmonary fibrosis. This increase in thought to result from the known association between scarring in the pulmonary parenchyma and the development of pulmonary neoplasm. All cell types of lung cancer can occur.

183 The chest radiographs **183a** and **183b** and barium swallow **183c** belong to 68-year-old female.
i. What lesion is demonstrated?
ii. Of which symptoms would the patient be likely to complain?
iii. Which form of management is likely to be advised and why would it be recommended?

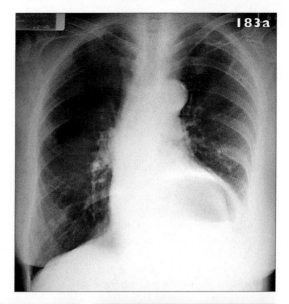

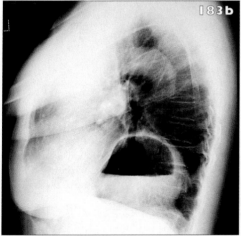

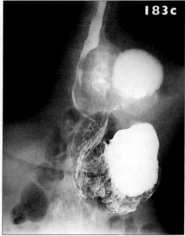

184 What are the therapeutic options for obstructive sleep apnoea (OSA)?

183 i. A 'rolling' hiatus hernia. In this condition the herniated stomach protrudes into the chest through the hiatus beside the lower oesophagus. The oesophagogastric junction is usually normally located.

ii. These patients may be remarkably symptom-free and the condition may be spotted as an incidental finding. Moderate dysphagia and fullness with meals are, however, common and may worsen as a meal progresses due to distension of the intrathoracic stomach. Acid reflux is not a feature because the oesophagogastric junction is usually competent and because the intrathoracic stomach further prevents reflux by pressing on the lower oesophagus.

iii. Surgical management is usually advised. This is the only effective way to manage dysphagia due to this condition and if the hernia is not reduced there is a risk of ulceration and perforation or even strangulation of the herniated stomach.

Reduction of the hernia may be accomplished via a low left lateral thoracotomy or a laparotomy. Advantages of a thoracic approach include better access to the oesophagogastric junction and hernia sac. An abdominal approach may be helpful in the event that concurrent abdominal surgery is required but offers poorer access to divide the adhesions, which are frequently present in the hernial sac.

184 Simple advice for patients with mild to moderate OSA includes sleeping on their side, no alcohol after 6:00 p.m., no sedatives, lose weight, stop smoking and keep the nose as clear as possible.

The medical treatment of choice is nasal continuous positive airway pressure (nasal CPAP) breathing. This is successful in patients with severe symptoms who gain considerable and rapid relief and improvement in well-being.

Surgical treatments include:
- Tonsillectomy and adenoidectomy, especially in children with enlarged tonsils and adenoids which can cause OSA.
- Uvulopalatopharyngoplasty – (see **88**).
- Nasal surgery – generally not useful except in a few who benefit from anterior nasal reconstruction, septal straightening and polyp removal.
- Maxilla and/or mandibular advancement, a major operation bringing forward the mandible and the maxilla to preserve teeth alignment. This is only appropriate if there is a considerable degree of retrognathia with a very narrow retroglossal space and if the patient is unable to tolerate nasal CPAP.
- Tracheostomy. This was used before the availability of nasal CPAP. The tracheostomy is kept closed during the day and open at night.
- Weight loss by gastric surgery – gastroplasty has become popular in some centres.

185 The building shown (185) is located at the home of a 52-year-old man who presents with recurrent episodes of dyspnoea and fever. His symptoms worsen after he works in this building, especially in early spring.
i. What is the most likely diagnosis that would account for this patient's complaints?
ii. List two other antigens which can produce syndromes similar to the one described.
iii. What are the characteristic radiological manifestations of this disorder?

186 Shown (186) are pneumococci growing on a blood agar plate with a zone of inhibition around an optochen disc. This came from a sputum sample from a patient with community-acquired pneumonia.
i. What is the treatment of choice?
ii. Why may this no longer be the treatment of choice in 10 years' time?

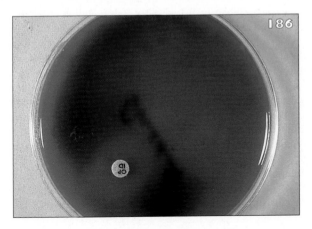

185 i. The presenting complaints are most consistent with farmer's lung, a specific syndrome which is a manifestation of hypersensitivity pneumonitis or extrinsic allergic alveolitis. The disease generally occurs after exposure to mouldy hay and is most frequently seen during the early spring or late winter months – the times of the year when previously harvested hay that has been left undisturbed for prolonged periods is used for feeding cattle. Farmer's lung results from sensitization to thermophilic bacteria, including *Thermoactinomyces volgaris* and *Micropolysporia faeni*.
ii. Other organic antigens known to cause extrinsic allergic alveolitis include avian proteins (e.g. bird fancier's lung, especially pigeons and budgerigars), rat urine (e.g. laboratory worker's lung), *Penicillum caseii* (e.g. cheese worker's lung) and *T. sacchari* (e.g. bagassosis in sugar cane workers).
iii. Early in the disease the chest radiograph may be normal. As the condition progresses findings may include ground glass opacities, reticulonodular infiltrates and diffuse interstitial fibrosis that may evolve into a honeycomb pattern with loss of lung volume. This would only occur in the setting of prolonged exposure; therefore, once the condition is diagnosed, removal of the subject from the offending allergen is the main objective. Face masks should also be worn at times when exposure to airborne fungal spores from mouldy crops may occur. Steroids may have a place in treatment; however, if the exposure has been very prolonged and insidious (e.g. with budgerigars) the disease may have caused extensive pulmonary damage. Steroids and removing the birds seem to produce scant improvement.

186 i. If the illness is not severe, oral amoxicillin is the treatment of choice with erythromycin or clarithromycin as alternatives in case of penicillin allergy. If intravenous treatment is required, ampicillin or benzylpenicillin should be used. In severe illness caused by penicillin resistant organisms, intravenous cefuroxime, cefotaxime, or ceftriaxone may be required. Treatment should be guided by local resistance patterns.
ii. Pneumococcal penicillin resistance was first reported in Australia in 1967 and is now documented to be a worldwide problem. The frequency of penicillin resistance in pneumococci varies geographically, being particularly common in South Africa, Spain and Eastern Europe and rare in the UK and Scandinavia. Up to 40% of pneumococci in the USA show *in vitro* resistance to penicillin (drug resistant *Streptococcus pneumoniae*; DRSP). There is also often *in vitro* resistance to cephalosporins, macrolides, doxycycline, and trimethoprim/sulfamethoxazole. However, it is felt that clinical failure with high-dose β-lactam therapy is currently unlikely in the absence of meningitis. In general, combinations of β-lactams such as high-dose ampicillin, ceftriaxone, or ceftazidime and a macrolide are recommended. If pneumococcal MIC values to penicillin are ≥ 4 mg/l, then a new anti-pneumococcal fluoroquinolone (e.g. levofloxacin) or clindamycin could be used as alternatives, but there have already been some reports of levofloxacin resistance. Vancomycin should be reserved for particularly resistant or meningeal disease. Owing to the rapid change in resistance patterns, a combination of a cephalosporin and an anti-pneumococcal fluoroquinolone or azithromycin may become the treatment of choice for CNS infections.

187 These two patients were referred for diagnostic mediastinal biopsy. Dyspnoea was a feature of patient A (187a, 187b), and hoarseness of patient B (187c, 187d).
i. What radiological features are present in these cases and why do they have the symptoms described?
ii. What method of access might be appropriate to obtain the diagnostic samples?

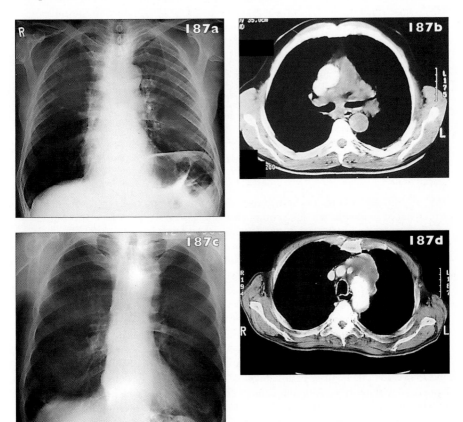

188 A patient with stage II sarcoidosis has moderate exertional dyspnoea, cough and lethargy.
i. What lung function tests would you order and what would you find?

187 i. Patient A (**187a, 187b**) has a large irregular mass in the visceral compartment extending from hilar level to the thoracic inlet. The left diaphragm is elevated due to phrenic nerve involvement. The mass is due to gross lymphadenopathy which is clearly visible on the CT cut in the subcarinal and subaortic areas. This patient clearly has either advanced lymphoma or disseminated bronchial carcinoma.

Patient B (**187c, 187d**) has a mass in the upper part of the visceral compartment which is associated with tracheal deviation to the right. The mass has caused only partial obliteration of the aortic knuckle, suggesting that it must lie quite anteriorly. This is confirmed on the CT cut where the mass can be seen applied to the anterior end of the aortic arch. Vascular involvement would preclude excision and the hoarseness of voice, due to involvement of the left recurrent laryngeal nerve, suggests significant disease in the subaortic and medial aortic areas.

ii. Patient A: trans-oesophageal ultrasound-guided fine needle aspiration, where available, is the ideal method for lymph node sampling where significant sub-carinal lymphadenopathy has been identified on CT scan. Mediastinoscopy would be necessary if this proved unsuccessful or technically impossible.

Patient B has disease which might be difficult to access at mediastinoscopy but which could be sampled via a left anterior mediastinotomy or by a video-assisted thorascopic surgery (VATS) approach. (Small-cell carcinoma was present in the para-aortic mass).

188 i. Although sarcoidosis characteristically causes a restrictive ventilatory defect with reduced lung volumes, lung compliance and gas exchange, it may also cause significant airflow obstruction both of small and large airways. Occasionally it causes upper airways obstruction and laryngeal involvement and rarely sleep apnoea. Flow volume loops, full lung volumes and diffusing capacity would help in assessment and follow-up. A mixed obstructive/restrictive ventilatory defect or even a purely obstructive defect may be found. Even in stage I disease significant lung function abnormalities including reduced diffusing capacity commonly occur. Although the respiratory muscles may be affected it rarely causes any functional problem. Exercise testing (cycle ergometry) may be useful in selected patients and can also detect hitherto unsuspected cardiac involvement. A fibreoptic bronchoscopy is advisable for suspected endobronchial sarcoid especially in the presence of obstructive spirometry, and to exclude other causes of cough. Stage III and IV disease is more likely to be associated with more severe reductions in diffusing capacity, which may also be due to damage to the pulmonary vasculature. Usually with corticosteroid treatment lung volumes improve sooner than carbon monoxide uptake.

189 i. How would you manage a young man presenting with this chest radiograph (189) for the first time?
ii. What is the risk of recurrence?
iii. How would you manage this?

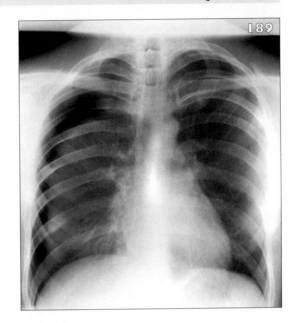

190 i. What abnormality is present on the flow–volume curve in **190**?
ii. Explain the pathophysiology.
iii. What are possible causes?

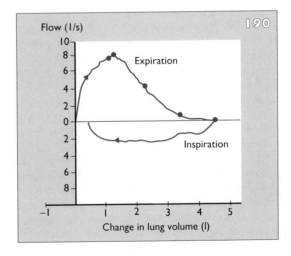

189 i. The majority of spontaneous pneumothoraces occur as a result of rupture of subpleural apical blebs in otherwise fit and healthy individuals. Rarely there is an underlying inflammatory or degenerative disease process such as TB, scleroderma or interstitial pulmonary fibrosis that requires attention. If the rupture of a small bleb results in a small pneumothorax (<20%) and the patient is asymptomatic then often nothing needs to be done other than advising the patient to reduce activities. In larger pneumothoraces where the patient is breathless, the pneumothorax should be aspirated via a small cannula attached to a 50 ml syringe via a 3-way tap, introduced into the second anterior intercostal space. A volume of air up to 2.5 l can be aspirated, but the procedure should be stopped earlier if lung is blocking the needle, or no more air is coming out with ease. A chest radiograph taken 1 h later will show if the procedure has been successful. If the lung has not re-expanded then intercostal tube drainage should be undertaken. Most patients will have their lung re-expanded rapidly and will leave hospital within 5 days. If there is a persistent air leak after this time surgery should be considered.

ii. The risk of recurrence after a first, conservatively treated pneumothorax is in the order of 30–40%.

iii. A second pneumothorax should lead to consideration of surgery. The operation of choice is a pleurectomy using video-assisted thoracic surgery (VATS). VATS may also be used to resect or staple sub-pleural bullae which may have been responsible for the pneumothorax. Mechanical pleurodesis by pleural abrasion may also be carried out.

190 i. The flow–volume loop demonstrates an extrathoracic obstruction, with greatly reduced inspiratory flow with preserved expiratory flow.

ii. As the expiratory flow curve is normal (i.e. airway calibre must be normal) and the inspiratory loop is grossly reduced (i.e. the airway must be narrowed), the airflow obstruction must be variable, and worse during inspiration. Normally, during inspiration, the intrathoracic negative pressure pulls the intrathoracic airways open – this is not happening here and clearly suggests that the obstruction causing airway narrowing is in the upper airways outside the thoracic cage, i.e. an extrathoracic variable upper airway obstruction.

Conversely, if the obstruction was in the thorax, expiration would be abnormal, but it is preserved in an extrathoracic obstruction as this does not affect expiratory flow as much as it affects inspiratory flows. In the case shown here during forced inhalation, the pressure inside the upper airway decreases below atmospheric pressure and, unless stability is maintained by the pharyngeal muscles and other supporting structures, the cross-sectional area of the upper airway will decrease, truncating the inspiratory curve.

iii. Variable extrathoracic upper airway obstruction can be caused by tumour, fat deposits, pharyngeal muscle weakness, vocal cord paralysis or enlarged lymph nodes.

191 These three radiographs
(191a–c) were all taken within 24
hours in a patient admitted to the
ITU and ventilated for an aspiration
pneumonia. He had made
reasonable progress over the
subsequent 5 days but then suddenly
deteriorated following
physiotherapy with oxygen
saturations falling to 70% on FiO_2:
0.65. A cuff leak was detected and
an emergency change of
endotracheal (ET) tube was
performed just before the first chest
radiograph was taken.
i. Describe the appearances on the
chest radiographs and explain the
sequence of events.
ii. What are the other common
causes of an acute fall in oxygen
saturation (SaO_2) in a ventilated
patient?

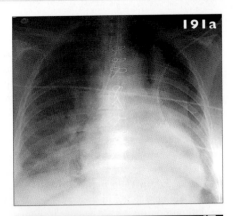

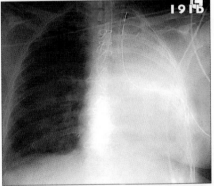

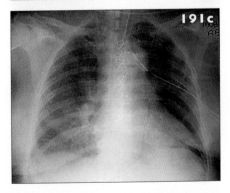

192 i. Would the management of asthma in a pregnant patient differ from
usual asthma treatment?
ii. How would pregnancy be affected by asthma?
iii. What is the effect of pregnancy on asthma?

191 The first chest radiograph (**191a**) shows a left pneumothorax and an ET tube that is too long and passed into the right main bronchus. The second radiograph (**191b**) shows the appearance after insertion of a chest drain and a complete 'whiteout' on the left side. The mediastinum is shifted to the left, indicating complete collapse of the left lung rather than a left haemothorax. The patient had been producing copious secretions and bronchoscopy revealed thick inspissated mucopurulent secretions occluding the left main bronchus and segmental bronchi. The third chest radiograph (**191c**) is taken after extensive bronchial toilet.

The sequence of events was almost certainly that physiotherapy with 'bagging' released some thick secretions that were not aspirated with routine suctioning and also led to the left pneumothorax. The emergency change of ET tube resulted in intubation of the right main bronchus.

Other causes of acute falls in oxygen saturation in ventilated patients include:

- Pulmonary oedema.
- Pulmonary embolus.
- Patient 'fighting' the ventilator – this may be due to discomfort and anxiety alone or may be precipitated by and exacerbate any of the other causes.
- Technical problems – accidental changes in ventilator settings, e.g. FiO_2, disconnection: accidental or suctioning, particularly in patients dependent on high levels of positive end-expiratory pressure (PEEP) and prolonged I:E ratios.
- Changes in posture.
- Increase in oxygen consumption: pain, anxiety, shivering/rigors, increased temperature, sepsis, drugs.

192 i. No, although there should be increased vigilance of asthma control particularly close to the time of delivery. Delivery is usually uncomplicated if the control is good. As with all asthmatics, inhaled therapy is preferred. No increased teratogenesis has been reported when mothers receive beta-agonists, inhaled steroids, sodium cromoglycate or theophylline. When systemic steroids are used neonatal hypoadrenalism is very rare.

ii. A prospective study of 504 pregnant asthmatic women showed that of 177 patients not initially treated with inhaled corticosteroids, 17% had an acute attack in contrast to 4% of the 257 patients who had been on inhaled anti-inflammatory treatment from the start of the pregnancy. No differences were observed between the two groups as to length of gestation, length of third stage of labour, or amount of haemorrhage after delivery. Neither were any differences observed between these groups with regard to relative birth weight, incidence of malformations, hypoglycaemia or need for phototherapy for jaundice in the neonatal period. In an earlier smaller prospective study of 198 pregnant women, there was a small increase in pre-eclampsia and a higher incidence of caesarean section in asthmatic patients compared with non-asthmatics.

iii. There is no specific effect. In about 40–50 % of women, asthma remains unchanged, in 25% it improves, and in another 25% it deteriorates.

193 This 22-year-old woman presented with non-specific malaise and an irritating cough for which her GP arranged a chest radiograph (193a, 193b), and a CT scan was then performed (193c).
i. What abnormalities are present?
ii. What diagnoses are possible?
iii. How might a diagnosis be achieved?

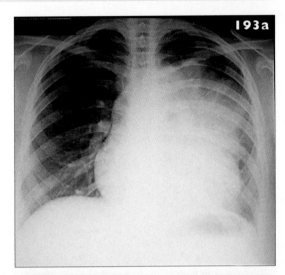

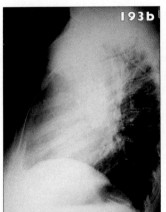

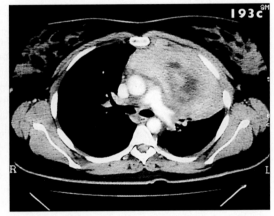

194 i. Explain the difference between occupational sensitizers and irritants as they relate to the development of asthma.
ii. Are there legal implications for the difference?

193 & 194: Answers

193 i. There is a huge smooth mediastinal mass located in the anterior compartment. Note that the trachea is not deviated laterally despite the left-sided preponderance of the mass suggesting an anterior origin from the plain chest film. On the CT (**193c**) there is marked posterior displacement of the visceral structures. Airway obstruction or even superior vena caval compression may occur.

ii. These appearances could be present with a variety of rapidly growing malignancies but in a female of this age group a lymphoma would be a high probability. Other possibilities would include a germ cell tumour (in a male), a thymic carcinoma, a primary sarcoma and metastatic chorioncarcinoma.

In 90% of adult cases of mediastinal lymphoma, nodular sclerosing Hodgkin's is diagnosed (as in this case); 75% of Hodgkin's patients have mediastinal involvement.

iii. Approximately half of the patients with a mediastinal lymphomatous mass have nodes palpable in the neck and excisional biopsy of one of these would be the least invasive method of getting a tissue sample. If cervical nodes are not present a CT-guided core biopsy can be performed. Anterior mediastinotomy offers a good way of obtaining a larger specimen. A right- or left-sided biopsy is performed depending upon the direction of enlargement of the mass. Mediastinoscopy would be quite impossible and dangerous in a case such as this, but can be helpful in providing a diagnosis in patients with modest mediastinal lymphadenopathy.

194 i. Sensitizer-induced occupational asthma has the features of an allergic response as there is a latency period between exposure and sensitization. Once the patient is sensitized symptoms of asthma may occur on exposure to lower levels of the substance. Symptoms initially occur only in response to that substance. Sensitization is unpredictable, occurring in 5–20% of exposed individuals. Sensitization is permanent and asthma may reappear upon re-exposure to the substance after years of non-exposure. There is specific and non-specific airway hyperresponsiveness. Patients with pre-existent asthma may become sensitized to an agent upon entering a new workplace.

Irritants produce asthma without a latent period and are associated with only non-specific airway hyperresponsiveness. Examples include diesel exhaust fumes and sulphur dioxide or perfumes. Irritants possibly contribute to the sensitization process by damaging airways and preventing adequate healing after initial early exposure to sensitizers.

ii. In the UK, to qualify for industrial injuries disablement benefit the worker must have asthma caused by an identified respiratory sensitizer, whereas for common law compensation the asthma may be of any type, either sensitizer- or irritant-induced. In this case however the individual must prove that the employer was negligent with work practices substantially worse than the norm for similar employers.

195 This HIV-positive man has a CD4+ lymphocyte count of 0.15×10⁹/l and presents with acute onset of fever cough and dyspnoea.
i. What are the likely causes of the chest radiograph (195a) abnormalities?
ii. What is the actual cause as revealed in the cytological specimen (195b)?
iii. How frequently would this condition present as the first AIDS-defining condition?
iv. Describe the management of this patient.

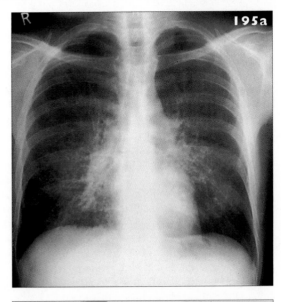

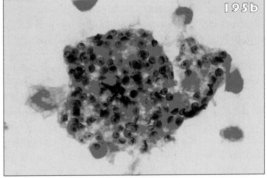

196 i. Approximately what percentage of chronic cigarette smokers develop airflow limitation?
ii. What are the benefits of smoking cessation in terms of pulmonary function?
iii. What strategies are available for aiding smoking cessation?

195 i. Bilateral interstitial shadows such as these (**195a**) are most likely to be due to *P. jiroveci* pneumonitis (PCP). Bacterial pneumonia, tuberculosis, histoplasmosis (in endemic areas) and pulmonary oedema due to left ventricular failure should also be considered. Infection with atypical mycobacteria, *C. neoformans* and cytomegalovirus are less likely given that the CD4 count is above $0.1 \times 10^9/l$.
ii. This bronchoalveolar lavage specimen (**195b**) has been stained with Grocott's methenamine silver and reveals numerous *P. jiroveci* cysts (staining black).
iii. At the start of the AIDS epidemic in the early and mid-1980s, PCP accounted for 50% of new cases of AIDS but with the more widespread use of primary prophylaxis with agents such as co-trimoxazole and nebulized pentamidine, PCP now constitutes approximately 30% of first AIDS-defining conditions.
iv. The diagnosis is usually confirmed by microscopy after silver or immunofluorescent staining of a bronchoscopic alveolar lavage specimen although a smaller proportion can be diagnosed by microscopy of sputum induced after nebulized saline. High-dose co-trimoxazole (120 mg/kg/day) is the drug of choice and is given orally or by intravenous infusion for 3 weeks. There is a high rate of reactions to this drug (rash, fever or hepatitis). Alternatives include intravenous pentamidine, clindamycin with primaquine, dapsone with trimethaprim or atovoquone. In moderate or severe cases (resting arterial PaO_2 <9.3 kPa on air) or those failing to respond quickly to antibiotics alone, a short course of high-dose glucocorticoids is beneficial. Supplemental oxygen is often required and severe cases may require ventilatory support, which is still compatible with recovery. Survivors should be given long-term prophylaxis as discussed above.

196 i. Only approximately 15% of smokers develop airflow limitation. Accordingly, other unknown factors must contribute to this problem (e.g. genetic susceptibility, other yet to be determined protease abnormalities).
ii. The rate of decline in FEV_1 in continuing smokers (~30–140 ml per year) is greater than that of ex-smokers and approaches that of non-smokers (30 ml per year). Thus, smoking cessation can reduce the rate of loss of lung function and thereby determine, to a large extent, the patient's subsequent clinical course. Clearly, much depends on the habitual activity of the subject as to when he or she presents. A manual worker may notice dyspnoea before a sedentary person. Unfortunately dyspnoea occurs with gross deterioration in lung function having already occurred in the majority of susceptible smokers.
iii. Smoking cessation clinics and hypnotherapy has been generally unsuccessful. Transdermal nicotine patches, and to a lesser extent nicotine gum seem valuable. The nicotine dose (5, 10 or 20 mg per patch) can be titrated to the patient's level of addiction. The patches should not be worn overnight. Just advising the patient not to smoke should always be offered.

197 i. What is this syndrome (197) most likely to be caused by?
ii. How would you make the diagnosis?
iii. How would you treat the patient?

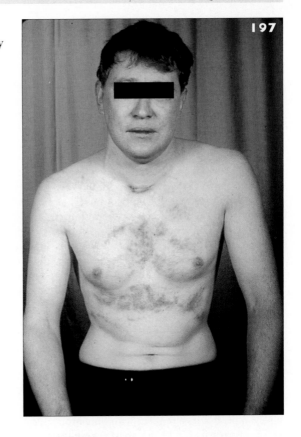

198 i. What is shown (198) in this asthmatic patient?
ii. What is the cause of it?
iii. Name two other local side effects of this therapy.
iv. How would you prevent this problem?

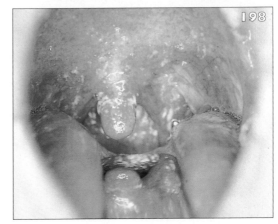

197 i. In an adult over 40 years of age, lung cancer is the most common cause of superior vena caval obstruction (SVCO) and small-cell the likeliest cell type. In a younger patient, lymphoma is the usual cause. Rarely, fibrosing conditions can affect the mediastinum and produce SVCO.

ii. In lung cancer, the diagnosis is often possible by fibre-optic bronchoscopy. A visible lesion should be brushed before biopsy to assess the likelihood of troublesome bleeding. If bronchoscopy is unhelpful, then the diagnosis will be made by mediastinoscopy, which is not a hazardous procedure as abnormal tissue will extend high into the thoracic inlet and be accessible to the surgeon. A diagnosis should always be made. There might be other sites to biopsy apart from within the chest, e.g. a supraclavicular lymph node or skin metastasis.

iii. If lymphoma, then the patient should be referred to a specialist unit for combination cytotoxic chemotherapy. If lung cancer, the differentiation from SCLC and non-small-cell lung cancer is important. If SCLC, treatment should be by combination chemotherapy and, if a complete response is obtained, then this should be consolidated by radiotherapy to the mediastinum and, if possible, the primary site.

Non-small cell lung cancer should be treated by radiotherapy. The dose will depend whether palliation or radical treatment is the intention. Cover with dexamethasone is recommended during radiotherapy.

Should the SVCO be a result of relapsed disease and it is not possible to give further radiotherapy, and the patient's general condition is reasonable, then stenting of the SVCO by a wall stent inserted via the femoral vein can provide rapid and excellent palliation.

198 i. Oral monilial infection (thrush).

ii. Inhaled corticosteroids (ICS). Oral moniliasis is the commonest side effect of this application of steroid medication. It is as common with beclomethasone and budesonide, but less frequent with fluticasone. Oropharyngeal candidiasis may occur in 5% of patients.

iii. The next most common problem is dysphonia, which may occur in up to 40% of patients and is particularly noted by teachers and singers. Laryngeal deposition of the inhaled corticosteroid causes vocal cord myopathy. It usually resolves upon cessation of inhaled steroids or changing the type of steroid. Patients with persistent dysphonia should have indirect laryngoscopy to exclude other causes.

iv. Use a spacer with metered-dose inhalers and rinse mouth after the inhaled therapy. The doses of ICS should be taken in two divided doses daily as the incidence of oral moniliasis increases with more frequent application. A course of antifungal lozenges may be necessary. Any dentures should also be treated overnight with an anti-fungal solution. This problem also occurs with dry-powder inhalers and is helped by rinsing and anti-fungal lozenges.

199 This 58-year-old man presented for a chest radiograph with an 18-month history of pain in the left upper arm and shoulder. An orthopaedic opinion a year previously advised physiotherapy. The pains continued and he developed numbness of the finger tips and difficulty performing fine movements of the hands.
i. What is the radiographic abnormality (**199a**) and what is the condition?
ii. Comment on treatment and prognosis.

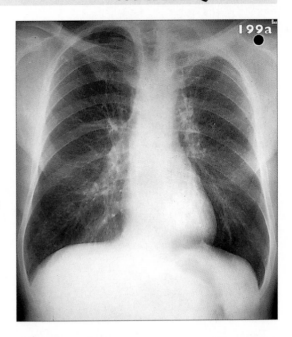

200 A confused woman of 82 years is brought to the emergency department, distressed, severely dyspnoeic and complaining of pain in the chest. A radiograph was taken (**200**). What is the diagnosis and how should the condition be managed?

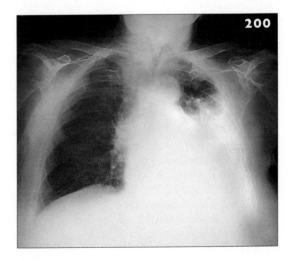

199 i. The radiograph (199a) shows opacification of the left apex with erosion of the posterior third of the first and second ribs. The patient has an apical, superior sulcus, tumour (Pancoast syndrome), usually an adeno or squamous cell lung cancer which grows into the brachial plexus, causing symptoms related to the T1 and C8 nerve roots. The pains are often not recognized as a brachial plexus lesion for months, often not until weakness develops in the small muscles of the hand, together with parasthesia. A CT of the tumour commonly shows extensive medial spread into a vertebral body (199b) as well as posterior extension through the ribs into the underlying muscle planes. This is well illustrated on the CT scan in this particular patient.

ii. The tumour is resectable if only the ribs are involved. Once it has penetrated

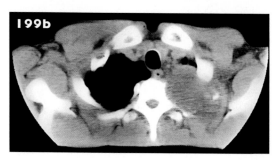

through to the muscle layers or encroached onto a vertebral body it is no longer resectable. If unresectable, radical radiotherapy should be given. As these tumours often do not metastasize widely, pain control together with progressive loss of use of a limb is a very major problem.

200 Traumatic haemothorax. Careful examination of the radiograph (200) reveals the presence of rib fractures on the left side. Thorough drainage through a wide-bore intercostal drain is essential to prevent an organizing intrapleural haematoma. Blood transfusion may be necessary and pain control may present difficulties. Intercostal nerve blocks can be effective if up to four ribs are fractured. Patients who hypoventilate in this situation are at risk of stasis pneumonia. If there is a flail segment of chest wall due to rib fractures in two places, severe respiratory insufficiency may result and a period of intubation and positive-pressure ventilation may be necessary until the fractures heal and the chest wall stabilizes. Care must be taken to exclude more serious complications of chest trauma such as:
- Ruptured bronchus suggested by massive air leak from an intercostal drain and confirmed at bronchoscopy.
- Ruptured aorta causing hypotension. A CT scan or oesophageal echocardiogram will make the diagnosis here.
- Haemopericardium which causes hypotension in the setting of a raised JVP, and requires diagnostic echocardiograph.
- Ruptured oesophagus (see 94).

201 A 52-year-old man is admitted semi-conscious with a 1-week history of dry cough, fever and headache. Two of his workmates have apparently been in hospital with pneumonia in the last month. He has signs of consolidation at the right lung base confirmed on chest radiograph and admission blood gases show a PaO_2 of 53 mmHg (7 kPa), $PaCO_2$ of 46 mmHg (6.1 kPa), pH 7.32, bicarbonate 15, base excess −2 breathing 60% oxygen.
i. What is wrong with this man?
ii. What is the relevance of the occupational history?
iii. How would you manage him?

202 This 70-year-old patient has had haemoptysis with recurrent episodes of pneumonia in the left lower lobe for 15 years. A mass (**202a, 202b**) was seen at bronchoscopy to be partially occluding the left lower lobe and was removed by laser resection. What is the likely diagnosis?

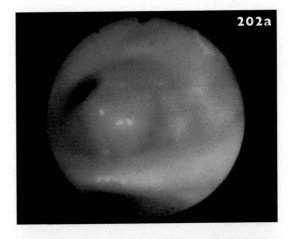

202a

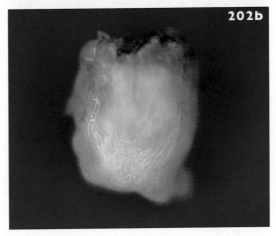

202b

201 i. He has features of a severe community-acquired pneumonia, the presence of mental confusion, hypoxia and hypercapnia indicating that he is severely ill despite the confinement of the consolidation to his right lung.

ii. The occurrence of pneumonia in three people working in the same place suggests that they may be part of some form of outbreak. Outbreaks of pneumonia have been described with *Str. pneumoniae*, *C. psittaci*, *C. burnetti* and legionella species, the latter perhaps being top of the list unless his job involves work with animals (Q fever) or birds (psittacosis).

iii. Immediate management requires improvement in his gas exchange, fluid balance and institution of appropriate antibiotic treatment. Persisting hypoxia despite high inspired oxygen suggests that he needs additional therapy. As a first step, continuous positive airways pressure (CPAP) may be effective without running the risks of endotracheal intubation. However, this may be required together with assisted ventilation. Appropriate antibiotics would best be a combination of a second- or third-generation cephalosporin together with a macrolide to cover all of the likely common pathogens causing severe community-acquired pneumonia, mainly *Str. pneumoniae*, *H. influenzae*, *Myc. pneumoniae*, *L. pneumophila* and *Staph. aureus*. The two approaches to rapid confirmation of a diagnosis of legionnaires' disease are to examine his urine for the presence of legionella antigen and to examine a sample of a lower respiratory tract secretion, either sputum or direct lower respiratory tract aspirate, by direct fluorescent antibody staining for legionella organisms. With confirmation of a diagnosis of legionnaires' disease a macrolide remains the treatment of choice with the addition of either rifampicin or a quinolone for those who are severely ill.

202 Given the long history, this polypoid mass is likely to be a benign endobronchial tumour. The majority of these are carcinoid tumours although they can be locally invasive and metastases to hilar lymph nodes may be seen at resection. These tumours show neuroendocrine differentiation but the carcinoid syndrome is rare in bronchial carcinoids. Other benign bronchial tumours are of mesenchymal origin and include lipomas, leiomyomas and fibromas. This tumour was a mixed fibrolipoma and the laser resection line can be seen at the base of the polyp. Rigid bronchoscopy and laser were used because significant haemorrhage may occur with removal of these tumours, particularly carcinoid tumours.

Endobronchial obstruction should be suspected in cases of recurrent pneumonia, particularly when associated with haemoptysis. Inhaled foreign bodies may cause the same syndrome. Foreign bodies may not be visible on chest radiographs. Other non-malignant causes of endobronchial obstruction include amyloidosis and tracheopathia osteoplastica, a cartilaginous proliferation in the major airways. The latter may be a long-term sequel of amyloidosis. Both of these conditions may be resected using laser if the obstruction is symptomatic.

203 Shown (**203**) is the chest radiograph of a 39-year-old man with the acquired immunodeficiency syndrome who had no prior respiratory complications. He presented with symptoms of fever, headache, stiff neck and cough. The patient was born and raised in Arizona but had lived for 12 years in the Pacific Northwest.
i. What are the radiographic findings?
ii. What diseases could account for the clinical and radiological abnormalities?

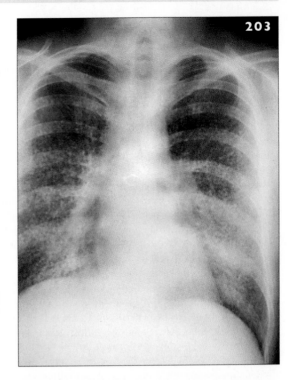

204 A previously healthy 28-year-old male complains of wheezing and dyspnoea which worsens over the working week and improves at weekends. He has been employed in a car body repair shop (**204**) for 5 years and routinely performs work shown in the accompanying figure but occasionally forgets to use his respirator. Spirometry performed at the end of a working week demonstrates reversible airflow limitation. His chest radiograph is normal.

i. What is the most likely diagnosis?
ii. What is the likely offending agent?

203 i. The chest radiograph (203) shows diffuse nodular infiltrates and hilar and mediastinal adenopathy.
ii. Disseminated (miliary) tuberculosis or disseminated fungal infections could explain both the radiographic appearance and the meningeal symptoms. *P. carinii* rarely causes adenopathy. The geographic or endemic fungi, *Histoplasma capsulatum*, *Blastomyces dermatitidis*, *Paracoccidioides braziliensis* and *Coccidioides immitis* as well as the ubiquitous *C. neoformans* could all cause this presentation. *C. immitis* was especially likely based on the history of residence in an endemic area. Coccidioidomycosis is acquired by inhalation of arthrospores in the endemic area (the south-western United States and Northern Mexico). Most infected persons remain asymptomatic although they usually develop skin test reactivity. Some experience a self-limited but sometimes severe syndrome termed 'valley fever' which includes cough, fever, pleuritic chest pain, headache and arthralgias, often accompanied by a skin rash. The radiographic findings of primary coccidioidomycosis include localized infiltrates and hilar adenopathy. Healing with calcification or thin-walled cavity formation is common. Persistent primary coccidioidomycosis is the term used to continued symptoms and radiographic progression after 6 weeks. Dissemination can occur, more commonly in immunocompromised patients, pregnant women, and in dark-skinned races. The skin, bones and joints, and meninges are most commonly involved. A definitive diagnosis is made by the isolation of *C. immitis* or by the identification of characteristic spherules containing endospores in sputum or histological specimens. Serial serological testing can be useful for following disease activity. Primary pulmonary coccidioidomycosis usually requires no treatment. Persistent or disseminated infection should be treated with systemic antifungal therapy. Amphotericin B, fluconazole and itraconazole all have activity against but most clinicians favour amphotericin B as initial therapy. Immunocompromised patients require chronic suppressive itraconazole therapy.

204 i. Occupational asthma. Wheezing, dyspnoea, reversible airflow limitation and the normal chest radiograph secure the diagnosis of asthma. Worsening symptoms during the working week with recovery over the weekend, or while on vacation, in a patient with known or suspected workplace exposure to a sensitizing compound strongly suggest occupational asthma.
ii. Diisocyanates are potent, low-molecular weight sensitizers that are widely used in polyurethane. Toluene diisocyanate (TDI), diphenyl methane diisocyanate (MDI), and hexamethylene diisocyanate (HDI) are the most commonly encountered and have all been linked to occupational asthma. HDI is a component of urethane paints used in automotive body repair and is the most likely cause of occupational asthma in this case.

Serial self-measurement of peak expiratory flow rates (PEFR) performed over 2 weeks at work and 2 weeks at home is often helpful with making the diagnosis. A 20% decrement in PEFR during or after work with recovery away from the workplace is diagnostic. Occasionally, specific bronchoprovocation testing with the suspected allergen or a workplace challenge may be required.

205 A 72-year-old man presented to his general practitioner with a history of hoarseness. Other than moderate hypertension, he had no other past history of note. A radiograph (205a) and CT (205b) were done.
i. What abnormality is present and what is the likely aetiology?
ii. What classification system can be applied to this abnormality?
iii. Why is the patient hoarse?
iv. How would this condition be managed and what risks should be discussed with the patient?

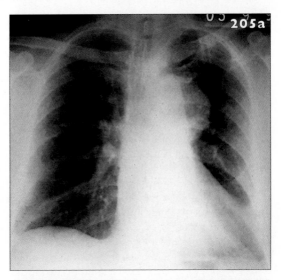

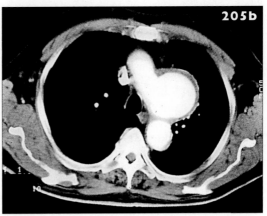

206 A CF patient may wait a year following listing for organ transplantation. Which are the clinical areas that most need close medical attention to ensure fitness for eventual transplantation?

205 i. This patient has a large aneurysm of the aortic arch. The most likely aetiology is hypertension, but syphilis serological testing would be appropriate. If it had been located at the junction of the arch and descending aorta a post-traumatic origin would have been a possibility.

ii. Aortic aneurysms may be classified in several ways. A 'true' aneurysm is contained within all the layers of the aortic wall, although these may be greatly thinned and it is common for the aneurysm to be lined with old and new thrombus. Depending on the appearance of the aneurysm, it may be described as 'saccular', as in this case, or 'fusiform' if the dilatation is more cylindrical.

If the aneurysm is formed from a localized hole in the aortic wall connecting with a cavity lined only by thrombus, it is described as a 'false' aneurysm.

An aortic dissection is often labelled as a 'dissecting aneurysm'. This condition is characterized by the entry of blood into the layers of the aortic wall through a split in the intima with prograde and/or retrograde extension of this process along a variable length of the aorta.

iii. The left recurrent laryngeal nerve has been stretched by the aneurysm.

iv. Hypertension should be controlled and the aneurysm size monitored. If it is static a conservative approach may be appropriate in someone of moderate general health or advanced age in view of the operative risk. Expansion would dictate surgical excision, probably with replacement of the aortic arch under hypothermic circulatory arrest. The patient should be warned of the magnitude of operative risk (>10% mortality) and advised specifically of the additional risk of perioperative cerebral damage.

206 Clinical areas include:

- Pulmonary sepsis must be controlled. Intensive treatment may require continuous antibiotics. Physiotherapy may need to be increased. New treatments such as DNase, which decrease sputum viscosity, may help some potential transplant recipients by improving physiotherapy and decreasing breathlessness.
- Nutrition and body weight must be maintained. Patients awaiting transplantation are hypercatabolic and have a poor appetite. Body weight can be maintained either with nasogastric feeding or gastrosotomy feeding. A gastrosotomy is the best-tolerated option. This can be used to provide overnight feeding and may also be used following transplantation.
- Respiratory failure with carbon dioxide retention can be treated with nocturnal nasal ventilation. This allows provision of safe nocturnal oxygen supplementation, rests respiratory muscles and allows mobility during the day.
- Mobility must be maintained. This can be achieved with gentle exercise. If the patient is very breathless, supplemental oxygen can be used.

All CF patients listed for transplantation should receive their continuing care in an **accredited CF centre** due to the requirement for multidisciplinary care.

207 The drug sensitivities of *Mycobacterium tuberculosis* isolated from sputum in a 45-year-old TB patient are shown in the Table.
i. What are the predisposing factors to this situation?

Drug	Sensitivity
Isoniazid (H)	Resistant
Rifampicin (R)	Resistant
Ethambutol (E)	Sensitive
Pyrazinamide (Z)	Sensitive
Streptomycin (S)	Sensitive

208 The tracing in **208** is from a young woman who complains of excessive daytime somnolence. Her bed partner also notes that she snores.
i. What is the name of her breathing-related sleep disturbance and what are the clinical and polysomnographic features of this disorder?
ii. How is this diagnosis confirmed?
iii. What is the treatment of this disorder?

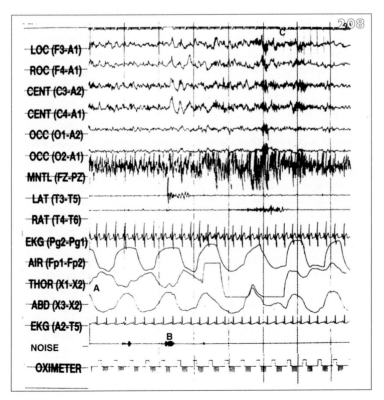

207 i. Drug-resistant TB is usually seen in patients who have had prior treatment for TB which was not completed or included inappropriate drug doses or combinations. Poor compliance is the major factor particularly in the inner cities, and is common in the vagrants, alcoholics and underprivileged subjects who contract the disease. The normal length of treatment of tuberculosis is 6 months and multiple drugs are used because *M. tuberculosis* infections normally include a small percentage of resistant bacteria which may be 'selected' if single drugs are used. Also, different drugs affect organisms at different sites where they may be growing (intracellular or extracellular). The most active anti-tuberculous drugs are isoniazid and rifampicin, as both are bactericidal and in combination prevent the development of bacterial resistance. Primary resistance (in patients not previously treated) also occurs and is most common in patients from areas where drug-resistant TB is most common (Africa, Asia, Latin America),

ii. These patients need close supervision and directly observed therapy. Where H resistance alone occurs, R, S, P and E should be given for 2 months followed by 7 months of ER. Where there is resistance to both H and R, as in this case, the regimen should include at least three drugs to which there is known sensitivity, and preferably drugs the patient has not received previously. Treatment should continue for 9 months to 2 years after sputum cultures are negative. To prevent the further development of resistance, new drugs should be added in combinations of two or three. Therefore, second line drugs are needed and include ethionamide, cycloserine, PAS, amikacin, ciprofloxacin and clofazimine. However, all of these drugs are associated with a higher incidence of side effects and are less effective than the first-line agents.

208 i. This patient has upper airway resistance syndrome. These patients present with excessive daytime somnolence. In the majority a history of snoring can be elicited. They are generally non-obese and have characteristic anatomical features including: a triangular face, a steep mandibular plane, a highly arched palate, and a class II malocclusion or a retroposition of the mandible. Standard polysomnograms show repetitive, transient alpha EEG arousals following increases in snoring. No significant change in oxygen saturation is seen and the respiratory disturbance index is low (<5). On this tracing paradoxical thoracic and abdominal movements (A) and snoring (B) are seen during the event, which is terminated by an arousal (C).

ii. Oesophageal pressure monitoring during polygraphic monitoring is helpful in demonstrating increases in respiratory effort that occur with each breath before a transient decrease in airflow which triggers arousal.

iii. A therapeutic trial of nasal CPAP. The patient should demonstrate subjective and objective evidence of improvement in daytime somnolence within 1 month.

209 Shown are the chest radiograph (**209a**) and CT scan (**209b**) of a 14-year-old boy from Alaska whose only complaint is a non-productive cough.
i. What are the radiographic abnormalities?
ii. What is the most likely diagnosis?
iii. How can this diagnosis be established?

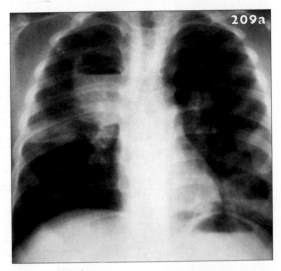

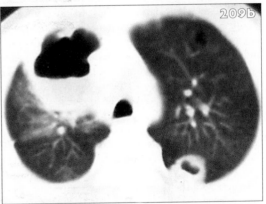

210 A pleural effusion in a 45-year-old woman was milky white. Investigations confirmed a high level of triglycerides but no cholesterol crystals. What does this imply and what are the possible causes?

211 What is the ILO classification for pneumoconiosis?

209 i. There are multiple, spherical lesions with smooth margins. The chest CT shows that most of these are moderately thin-walled cysts, many of which contain air-fluid levels.

ii. Cystic abnormalities of this size are most likely the result of Echinococcal infection. Pulmonary sequestrations may occasionally manifest in this fashion as may infected bullae or bronchogenic cysts. Sequestrations are almost always in the lower lobes and usually the left.

iii. Echinococcosis results from the ingestion of eggs of the ubiquitous carnivore tapeworms *Echinococcus granulosa* or *E. multilocularis*, prevalent in areas where dogs coexist with the natural intermediate hosts (i.e. sheep and cattle). Oncospheres released in the gut enter the portal circulation and larvae then develop in the liver, lungs or, less commonly other systemic sites. *E. granulosa* larvae form encapsulated cysts (cystic hydatid disease) which grow slowly and cause symptoms only if they rupture, become secondarily infected, or reach sufficient size to compress adjacent structures. The chest radiograph typically shows one or more homogenous masses with sharply defined margins. The 'lily pad' sign may be present if air enters the cyst. This results from collapsed cyst walls and debris floating on the surface of the fluid. Eosinophilia may be present and serological tests are usually positive. CT, and particularly MRI scanning, can reveal the cystic nature of these lesions and can identify coexistent hepatic cysts. Needle biopsy of suspected hydatid cysts should be *avoided* and treatment by intact surgical excision is desirable because spillage of cyst contents can cause anaphylaxis and may lead to larval dissemination. *E. multilocularis* cysts fail to mature and the invading scolices cause continued inflammation and tissue destruction (alveolar hydatid disease). Pulmonary involvement is focal or diffuse and treatment with systemic antihelminthic drugs is recommended (e.g. praziquantel or mebendazole).

210 Chylothorax. The presence of multiple small fat globules in the pleural fluid produces a milky white appearance. The most likely cause is accumulation of lymph due to obstruction of, or damage to, the lymphatic duct. This may be due to chest trauma or surgery of the aorta or oesophagus. Chylothorax may also be due to obstruction of the thoracic duct by lymphoma (as in this case) or other mediastinal tumours.

The onset is often acute with dyspnoea. The patient can become malnourished and immunocompromised although the effusion itself remains sterile. It has to be distinguished from an empyema, and from a chyliform or pseudochylous effusion that is often chronic and occurs in long-standing tuberculosis or rheumatoid disease. They contain high levels of lecithin or globulin complexes or cholesterol crystals.

Treatment is that of the underlying cause, though repeated aspiration may be necessary. Ligation of the thoracic duct may occasionally be necessary. Feeding with medium-chain triglyceride diets or total parenteral nutrition decreases thoracic duct flow and maintains the nutritional status. Most cases of traumatic rupture of the thoracic duct resolve in 2 weeks.

211 It is a method of grading the size of opacities on chest radiography due to pneumoconiosis, primarily for epidemiological reporting. The number of opacities correlates with the quantity of dust in the lungs. The opacities may be the dust itself or the consequent fibrosis. There is a broad division between opacities up to 1 cm (simple pneumoconiosis), and those >1 cm diameter (complicated pneumoconiosis, or progressive massive fibrosis, PMF). PMF arises on a background of simple pneumoconiosis. Profusion gives an estimate of the density of the nodules, and is determined by comparison with a set of standardized radiographs (Tables).

Each profusion category can be subdivided into three, to give a 12-point scale.

p nodules are mostly seen in coal workers' pneumoconiosis (CWP) whereas r nodules are associated with silicosis.

Lung function changes with simple CWP are usually minimal and often overshadowed by the effects of cigarette smoking, although coal dust does contribute to the development of emphysema. Radiographic changes do not progress after the miner leaves the coal face with simple CWP but they can occur with PMF. However, with silica exposure simple changes may progress despite removal from the offending agent. Those developing PMF have usually been exposed to a high dust burden. Progressive hypoxaemia usually occurs. It is important to exclude other causes of large irregular opacities such as tumours and infection.

Simple			
Nodule size	**Rounded nodules**	**Irregular nodules**	**Profusion of nodules**
<1.5 mm	p	s	0, 1, 2 or 3
1.5–3 mm	q	t	0, 1, 2 or 3
3–10 mm	r	u	0, 1, 2 or 3

Complicated	
Nodule size	**Category**
1–5 cm, or several with combined diameter up to 5 cm	A
Between A and B	B
One or more with combined area >1/3 of lung field	C

Index

Numbers refer to questions and answers, not pages.

Index

Index